Deception in the Rainshadows

Lieutenant Brian Kierzek made his way to the core of the riverpark where he saw the heavy activity taking place inside a large rectangular area cordoned off by bright yellow police-line barrier tape. The atmosphere was hushed as everyone moved around warily, speaking in lowered voices—strange, but typical behavior whenever a corpse lay in their midst. *The death scene*, he thought. Slowly approaching the site, he inhaled deeply when he saw the still bulge lying near the edge of the riverwalk, covered with a black body tarp.

Officer Ed Cuyler kept his distance as Kierzek ducked his gangly body underneath the tape. He knew not to crowd the vigilant detective at this moment. He'd learned to leave his boss alone while he adjusted to the realism of the grim discovery. All the activity in the immediate area slowly ceased. Everyone who didn't already know Kierzek's style in treating death had been briefed before he'd arrived. The casual veil of "just another stiff" had to be lifted. Moreover, any gallows humor, a common undercurrent at most crime scenes, would be dealt with harshly if Kierzek got wind of it.

Kierzek steadily pulled the body tarp back, gently laying it on the woman's waist. He turned back and looked into her face, seeing her motionless but distinct features projecting through the gray-white pallor of death. Even now, in the primary stages of rigor mortis, she appeared beautiful and cultured, although void of *being*. He instinctively ran his index finger down her stiffening cheek and onto her neck, noticing that she still had some warmth in her body. He looked at his watch, shaking his head as he thought how violently she must have fought for the body to cool this gradually…

Deception in the Rainshadows

BY
RILEY ST. JAMES

SHADOWCREST
PUBLICATIONS

If you purchase this book without a cover you should be aware that this book is stolen property. It was reported as "unsold and destroyed" to the publisher, and neither the author nor the publisher has received any payment for the "stripped book."

This is a work of fiction. The characters and events described here are imaginary. And any similarity to actual persons living or dead ... is purely coincidental.

DECEPTION IN THE RAINSHADOWS
A ShadowCrest Publications Paperback
Post Office Box 1069
Tustin, CA 92781-1069 U.S.A.
Fax: 714-730-4008

www.shadowcrestpub.com

First Edition
June 1999

Copyright © 1999 by ShadowCrest

ISBN: 0-9662612-2-4

Library of Congress Catalog Card Number: 99-90206

All Rights Reserved. No part of this book may be reproduced or used in any means without written permission except in the case of brief quotations embodied in critical articles or reviews. For information address: ShadowCrest Publications.

Cover design by Lynn Phillips, Ocean Avenue Design

Page composition by
New Image Graphics, Inc. • Ashland, OH 44805

Printed in the United States of America by
Malloy Lithographing • Ann Arbor, MI 48103

ACKNOWLEDGEMENTS

At the roots of any successful book are the people who offer their ongoing support and confidence as it takes shape. While it would be impractical to recognize everyone here, a few do deserve special tribute.

My utmost appreciation goes to *Teri Rhea* and *Jan Morrison*. Without their insistence and inspiration, this endeavor might never have progressed past a plot synopsis. Thank you, you *convinced* me of what my vision could *be*. And you were right.

Of course, nothing would be worthy of readership without the stamina of test readers who offer critical insight, alternative perspectives and overall guidance as the plot and characters develop into a life of their own. Therefore, I offer my sincere gratefulness to *Norris Doty, Sallie Adams, Tom & Mary Riley*, and *Karen Wilkins*. A special reflection goes to my dear friend from London, *Debi Turner*, who carefully read it not only for sense of story, but also for United Kingdom colloquial compatibility.

Finally, it would be a gross oversight not to salute two of the talented people who were instrumental in bringing this story to *visual* life: ShadowCrest's delightful and gifted design artist, *Lynn Phillips*. And *Robert Juran*, the vigilant editor from Portland, who provided flawless copy editing.

With your help, penning this novel has been an exciting and rewarding experience for me. My heartfelt appreciation to you *All*.

For you, Gretchen. As promised. Thank you.

We are never deceived; we deceive ourselves

— Goethe

Chapter One

A rainy September night, Portland, Oregon

A slight drizzle from the lingering storm trickled down the hotel windowpane, mocking the tears of the dispirited woman peering through her reflection into the soggy night. As she tightly clutched a heart-shaped pendant, she wiped her moist cheeks with the back of her trembling hand and turned away from the window. In the faint illumination from the downtown streetlights, she focused on the man who lay still on the bed in the darkened far corner. Lowering her head, she whispered, "I'm so sorry." She straightened, stuffed the pendant into her hip pocket, and fastened her jeans.

Mustering all her strength, she buttoned her blouse and quickly shuffled into her shoes. She grabbed her jacket from the chair and hurried to the door. She opened it, allowing the hallway light to cast a brassy glare throughout the room. Looking back at the bed, she stopped when she saw his eyes flickering toward her. Covered only by a rumpled sheet, he remained still and silent as she slowly turned and walked out, closing the door on the man she loved.

Slipping on her jacket, Laura Jansen-Bearnes dashed down the empty corridor, her eyes still tearing. Reaching the elevators, she channeled her remaining courage through a shaky forefinger and pressed the down button. When the elevator arrived, she quickly entered the vacant cubicle. She leaned against the back wall, closed her eyes and gripped the handrail. The doors closed and she began to descend, but her heart had been left above. *I can't go back. It's taken too much to come this far,* she thought as the elevator came to an abrupt stop.

She stepped into the lobby and made her way to the bank of pay phones. Ducking into the phone nook, she lifted the receiver and punched in the number. Anxiously tapping on the coin-return cover, Laura wondered why her good friend hadn't answered as she listened to the staid greeting on the other end: "Hello, this is Rebecca. I'm unable to take your call right now. Please leave a message and I'll get back to you as soon as I can. Thank you."

Why isn't she worried about me? Laura wondered. *She must be sleeping.* She drew a nervous breath and spoke into the phone. "Hi, I've done it. I'm still at the Riverpark Towers and Jonathan is up in his room. I'm sorry I didn't get over there for dinner like we planned, but things didn't go well. Anyway, I hope you covered for me with Monte if anything came up, and…" She hesitated, suddenly startled by the powerful boom of walloping thunder. Gathering her wits, she continued, "Um, I'll come over and see you before I go home this afternoon. But don't worry if I'm late. I'm going to hang around the hotel, at least until the storm breaks, then maybe grab some tea somewhere. I just need to be alone for a while. Oh, if you do get this message and want to try and reach me, leave word at the front desk. I'll check with them on my way out. Thanks, Rebecca, see you soon. Love ya. Bye." Laura hastily stuffed the receiver into its cradle and paused, planning her next move.

On the other end of the line, Rebecca Jane Newell rested against her kitchen wall with her arms crossed and stared at the answering machine, listening very closely to the last of Laura's words. She sighed, and reached over to the machine. Rewinding the tape, she listened again to the tense message. She shook her head and turned for the bedroom. But she then paused and reached down for the telephone receiver. Picking it up she began dialing.

Laura stepped into the middle of the lobby, seeing the windswept downpour pounding harshly against the front windows. Spikes of barbed lightning repeatedly lit up the inky horizon with a shuddering crack.

Damn this storm! Can't go out in that. Nor could she go to Rebecca's apartment yet either. Her friend would ask too many questions that Laura wasn't ready to answer. She glanced at her watch: two-thirty in the morning. She looked around and frowned.

Nothing would be open at this hour, not even in the hotel. She paused and patted her coat pockets, realizing she'd left her new umbrella in the hotel room. Still frowning, she decided she couldn't go back up for it. She'd have to make up something to tell Monte when he discovered she didn't have the present he'd given her only last week. It wouldn't take long in rainy Oregon for him to discover it was missing.

She looked down the hallway into the spacious front vestibule, seeing only a lone bell captain quietly reading at his station and the front desk clerk shuffling papers.

Her thoughts turned to Jonathan. He was surely still in his drunken stupor. She knew he wasn't used to drinking heavily and would probably be out for the rest of the night. She doubted that he'd really known she'd left, even though he appeared to be somewhat conscious. *He'd have said something*, she thought.

Up in his hotel room, Jonathan Philip Timmers began to stir restlessly under the rumpled bed sheet. He cracked his bleary eyes to scan the room as the storm crashed outside his window. Disoriented, he reached over for Laura, finding only an empty pillow and the fading scent of her perfume. His mind fought desperately to sort out the vague events that had taken place earlier, but he failed.

Laura turned and wearily made her way down the hallway, deciding to seek refuge in the hotel for the time being. She stopped at the high-arched entrance of the expansive lobby bar and peered inside the empty room. Leaning against the doorway, she looked over at the massive red-brick fireplace, embers of the dying fire still glistening behind the golden screen. Taking a deep breath, she turned her stare to the deep cushioned sofa where earlier that evening she and Jonathan had sat, the spot where she'd told him that she couldn't go on leading a double life, and that they must end their affair.

Jonathan abruptly sat up in bed and called out weakly for Laura. Hearing nothing, he fell back against the pillow, his eyes slamming shut as he attempted to fend off the searing pain that thrashed inside his head.

Laura slowly walked over to the fireplace and tossed a couple of logs onto the starving fire. After stoking the smolder into a modest blaze, she sat on the sofa, gradually sinking into the soft satiny cushions. She drew her legs up onto the couch as the persistent storm pelted the broad skylight high above her.

Pulling the heart pendant out of her pocket, she reclined and laid her head against the side cushion as the heat from the crackling flames began to warm her. Closing her eyes, she lightly brushed the pendant against her lips, reliving the torturous scene that had taken place earlier that night.

The elegant lobby bar had emptied early, the sparse weeknight crowd thinned even more by the storm. The adjoining restaurant had already closed, leaving one couple seated at the vacated piano bar finishing their after-dinner liqueur. Laura and Jonathan, sitting at the end of the main bar, were the only other patrons.

Jonathan was discussing last weekend's football game with the bartender while Laura leaned forward on the leather-tufted bar edge, nervously fingering the stem of her wine glass. *How am I going to tell him it's over?* she lamented inwardly. Why couldn't she go through with it at dinner? Why hadn't she somehow prepared him before they'd met today? Why couldn't she deny him this afternoon, instead of collapsing in bed the minute they embraced?

Suddenly her troubled thoughts were interrupted by Jonathan's nudge.

"Hey," he said, flashing a wide smile. "Where'd you go?"

She looked up, seeing both the bartender and Jonathan staring at her.

"Oh, sorry," she replied, managing a slight grin. "I guess I spaced for a minute while you two were talking football."

Jonathan chuckled. "The bar is closing down. Need more wine?"

She glanced down at the slight residue of Merlot in her glass. "No, I don't think so. I'm okay, thanks."

Jonathan lifted his snifter and swirled the swallow of brandy left in it. He finished it and pushed the glass toward the bartender. "How about a bottle of champagne, and the bill, please."

Laura looked away and grimaced. She didn't want him creating any more diversion from what had to be done. She needed him to be clear-headed when she told him. But she said nothing.

The bartender reached into the cooler. Pulling out a bottle of brut, he held it up for Jonathan to examine.

"Ah, vintage, excellent," Jonathan said as he pushed his stool backward and motioned toward the fireplace. "How about over there by the fire?"

Carrying the flowery embossed flutes, Laura walked with him to the couch, while the bartender followed them. After filling the glasses that Laura held out, the bartender placed the bottle into the icy chilling urn that he had set on the small cocktail table in front of the couch.

As Jonathan turned to hand the bartender his credit card, Laura settled herself and quickly scanned the room, noting that the other couple had left. *It'll have to be now*, she decided. *As soon as we're alone.*

Jonathan turned to her and reached for his champagne, gesturing a toast. Laura emitted a forced smile and slightly tinkled his glass before they each sipped on the sparkling wine.

Jonathan set his glass down and reached for her hand. "Thank you for everything, sweetheart," he said softly, looking at her with longing eyes. She remained mute as he continued, "You know what? On the plane up here today I suddenly realized how alone I've really been all these years."

Laura's eyes moistened. She was filling with guilt over what she was about to tell him, knowing how much she was going to hurt him. Yet she had to wait until they were completely alone. She squeezed his hand and smiled, managing to hide her growing stress.

The immediate pressure decreased as the bartender walked up with the bill. Jonathan pocketed his card and jotted a notation on the receipt. The bartender smiled when he saw the sizable tip. "Thank you very much, sir." Turning to leave the room, he added, "If you need anything else, you can get it from room service until midnight."

Alone at last, Laura thought. She cast her eyes downward, saddened over what she was about to do. She began gently. "Jonathan, I need to talk to you…"

"Wait," he interrupted excitedly. "I have something for you."

Surprised, she watched him reach into his coat pocket and pull out a small oblong jewelry case. He held it toward her, slowly lifting the cover.

Laura's eyes widened as she saw the heart-shaped pendant, adorned with a golden chain, tucked in a bed of plush red velvet. A glossy black pearl was attached to the stem of the diamond-crusted pendant with a silver filigreed clasp.

Speechless, she set her champagne on the table and reached over, carefully removing the necklace from its case. She loosely wrapped the chain around her palm, leaving the pendant to dangle from her hand. She turned toward the fire and raised her arm. Using the shimmering flames as a backdrop, she inched her eyes over the glittering pendant.

Jonathan smiled proudly, seeing that she was in awe over the pendant's beauty.

Laura dropped her arm to her lap, turning away. Tears streamed down her saddened face.

Jonathan quickly realized something was seriously wrong. "What is it, sweetheart?" he asked, tensing up.

"Oh, Jonathan," she murmured, reaching for his hand. She slowly looked up at him. "I have something very bad to tell you."

Laura twisted her head on the cushion and looked up at the skylight, seeing that the storm had weakened, yet still hovered threateningly. *Not yet*, she thought, checking her watch: two fifty-five. She repositioned her head on the cushion and closed her eyes, recalling how the mood between her and Jonathan had become strained after he'd given her the pendant. How anguishing the moment had been when she'd told him they must end their affair…

Jonathan sat frozen with a stunned look as he absorbed Laura's words, realizing that her sole reason for bringing him to Portland was to leave him. "I don't believe you're doing this to me, and under these circumstances," he said in a raspy voice as he anxiously finished his champagne and refilled the glass.

"I'm sorry," she said, carefully placing the pendant she'd been holding back in the case and laying it in her lap. "I don't know how else to do this. I couldn't do it over the phone. I needed to face you when I told you."

"But why, for Chrissake? You know we've been through the worst of it," he mumbled, looking down as he fidgeted with the rim of his glass. "Why all of a sudden?"

"It hasn't been all of a sudden," she answered. "Cheating on Monte constantly gnaws at me. I can't go on living a lie and hurting him the way I have. He's a good man, devoted and…"

"Do you think he knows what's going on?" Jonathan interrupted, looking up abruptly, his voice sharp. "Is that what brought all this shit on?"

"No, I don't think he knows, but I want to end this before he does find out."

"Dammit, leave him for me. We'll get married," he blurted, his words beginning to slur, his eyes beady. "Dammit, I can make you as happy as he can!"

She paused, looking around nervously. His last statement and his sudden combative attitude surprised her. He'd never before indicated that he felt he was competing with Monte. That wasn't an issue. She realized he was hurt and confused and was drinking too much—totally out of character for him. However, she'd continue. She had to. She looked up, animatedly searching for words that would tell him how determined she was to end this tonight.

He knew by now that she was holding strong in her resolve to leave him as he drank his champagne and focused on her, bracing himself.

"But there's one person you can't compete with," she said. "Tamra."

Jonathan sat perplexed and silent, his head bobbing as he looked vacantly at the fire and reached over for Laura's champagne, gulping it down.

She continued, explaining how much Tamra adored her dad, and how it would devastate her world if Laura ended the marriage, breaking up their family. She pleaded for him to understand that her daughter's happiness wasn't a price she was prepared to pay for them to carry on their affair. And, finally, it was Tamra's welfare that Jonathan couldn't "compete" with—not Monte's love. It was over. It had to be. He would have to move on with his life without her.

Laura sat back and grimaced when he said nothing. He blankly checked over the empty champagne bottle with an unsteady hand, then hastily rose from the couch and walked to the front desk to order a bottle of bourbon from room service.

She wanted to leave for Rebecca's apartment, but reluctantly waited for him to return, knowing he was too crushed to be left alone at this point. Yet she became further disturbed when he got back, realizing that he had only listened, but had not accepted what she had told him. He swilled the bourbon, his mood wavering. He appealed sorrowfully with incoherent begging for her to reconsider. When she remained steadfast in her decision, he demanded loudly and angrily that she leave her husband and marry him, and kept repeating it, until the hotel manager stepped into the bar to see if everything was all right. When Laura assured the manager it was only a harmless lover's quarrel, Jonathan calmed down, looking downward as the manager left.

Laura wiped her tired eyes and gripped the pendant tighter as she remembered his dejected expression when he had urged her to keep the pendant. Concerned about his state of drunkenness, she'd agreed that their farewell would be as painless as possible, promising she'd stay with him this last night—anything to get him out of the hotel bar and stop his drinking.

She closed her moistened eyes and began to drift off, remembering how her well-intentioned plan hadn't worked. He didn't stop drinking when they got to the room, and she couldn't brave the persistent agony of their inevitable separation. As she began to lose consciousness, she remembered breaking free from his feeble embrace and leaving him as he passed out drunk on the bed.

Laura shook her head to rid herself of the drowsiness of her brief nap and looked up at the skylight. The fast-moving storm had dwindled to an intermittent sprinkle. She glanced at her watch: three-forty. She felt stronger, relieved that the toughest part of her night was over. Now she needed to escape completely. She rose from the couch and headed toward the front entrance of the hotel, stopping at the front desk.

The surprised clerk glanced at his watch and then at her, inquiring, "Yes?"

"My name is Laura Bearnes," she said. "Were there any phone messages for me within the last couple of hours?"

"Let me check," he said, walking to the back to check with the operator.

Laura waited patiently, knowing that if Rebecca had gotten her message she'd surely call. She'd certainly be worried about her.

The clerk briskly returned through the doors, shaking his head. "Nope," he said crisply. "The operator said there haven't been any guest messages since about one a.m."

"You're sure?" Laura asked.

"Yes," he confirmed. "We've both been here since midnight, along with Larry." He pointed toward the bellman, who had heard their exchange and was joining them at the desk.

Laura looked at the bellman, who was shaking his head and shrugging. "Nope, me either. I didn't take any messages."

"Okay, thanks," she said, bolting past the bellman. But she paused at the front doorway when he asked her if she needed an escort to her car, or maybe a cab.

"No, thank you, not just yet," she answered. "Maybe a cab later."

Turning, she stepped through the sliding glass doors into the pre-dawn darkness to begin the rest of her life.

She zipped up her jacket snugly, pulling the collar out to ward off the saturated chill. Plucking her red silk scarf from her coat pocket, she stuffed her mussed hair back over her ears and wrapped the scarf around her head. She pulled the ends taut, knotting it tightly, again feeling disappointed that she had forgotten her umbrella.

Looking upward through the mist, she saw that the clouds had begun to break up. She leveled her gaze across the street, seeing the pale beam of the exposed half-moon pitching thick rainshadows onto the spacious wooded park that bordered the Willamette River. With an odd serenity overcoming her, she felt a sense of peace and relief from her earlier distress. Spotting a bench on the perimeter of the park, she made her way across the street and sat down, facing the shoreline.

Although she was close to the streetlight, she gradually became wary of her risky location and buttoned the jacket flap-pocket containing her wallet. She cautiously scanned the area for any suspicious movement, but seeing nothing, she reassured herself there was rarely any trouble in this area.

Regardless, she planned a quick retreat to the hotel in case of trouble as she settled back on the bench and peered at the light fog wafting across the rippling surface of the wide river.

Back at the hotel, Jonathan crawled off the bed and stumbled to the desk to pour the last of the bourbon into a tall glass, mixing it with the remaining Coke. Befuddled, he downed the drink and clumsily put the glass on the desk, knocking the bourbon bottle onto its side. Stumbling to the closet nook, he fumbled in his carryall for his clothes. He managed to get dressed, then sat back down on the bed, growing more confused as the new tumbler of booze quickly began to take effect on his already alcohol-soaked body. Groggy, he sat motionless, staring toward the door.

Laura sat comfortably on the bench, enveloped in thought. She reflected on the time when her life had been less complicated. Just before that sunny weekend last spring in Laguna Beach, California. That fateful weekend at the gallery when she'd met the man who would totally upend her charmed and untroubled life.

Chapter Two

The connection, early last spring, Southern California

The late morning sea breeze streamed gently through the open bay windows of the modest beachfront gallery: an intimate yet chic showroom, nestled among other distinguished shops in downtown Laguna Beach. Inside, people strolled around leisurely, consumed by the extensive exhibit of dazzling artwork. Stylish abstract and figurative oil paintings, along with unusual aquatint etchings, were hung busily but neatly on all the walls. Decorative ceramics, lustrous wood sculptures and small bronze figurines were grouped strategically on numerous tables and white display columns, placed in all available space. Freshly cut greenery bouquets, sprinkled throughout the main rooms, gave off a sweet fragrance, permeating the salty ocean air.

In the far corner of the main room, two attentive women mingled kindly with a few patrons huddled around a slender oak bar in the tea nook. They made small talk and offered tepid cups of herbal tea and warmed scones to any requesting guest. One of them turned and noticed a refined-looking man transfixed before one of her paintings near the front entrance.

She turned back to the group of patrons, but felt drawn to the man in front of the painting. She again looked his way, immediately sensing that his demeanor was smooth and professional. He was attired appropriately in Laguna fashion, a trendy cardigan sweater, slacks and sandals. The tinge of swirling gray at his temples complemented his wavy sun-streaked hair and bronzed skin.

Unable to curb her interest in him, she politely excused herself from the group and walked over, stopping directly behind him as he continued to look at the painting. She felt a stirring inside her body that was unusual, momentarily confusing her, but she shook it off.

"Do you like it?" she asked cordially, pleased by his intense interest.

"Oh, yes," he answered instantly, not taking his eyes off the colorful rectangular cityscape. "It's New Orleans, one of my favorite cities."

"Yes," she confirmed. "I captured the setting while on a Mississippi riverboat one gray morning. So I improvised the sunrise."

"I'm captivated by the composition," he interrupted enthusiastically. "The background colors extend so deeply." He pointed to the center of the painting. "They're perfectly blended with the silhouette of each building against the skyline. The focal points of the French Quarter are so stark, as though they demand to be noticed." He stepped back, sweeping his hand downward, continuing his aesthetic plaudits, "The mid-ground light source fuses so evenly with the foreground. Almost like the painting itself was illuminated. It does look like a natural sunrise."

"Very impressive," she said. "You must be a connoisseur of fine art."

"No, not really," he answered. "I'm only a dabbler. I attended some night classes at a local college." He lowered his eyes, locating the signature, adding, "I'm not that much of a critic, but I'm sure the artist must have worked diligently on this."

"Why don't you ask her?" she replied, beaming over his sincere flattery.

He turned around, blinking while weaving his penetrating gaze into hers. He was instantly taken with her. Her auburn-red hair glittered radiantly in the sunlight, encasing her vivid, near-perfect features. Her skin, fair and smooth, balanced flawlessly with her dazzling white smile and ice-blue eyes.

Although stunned by her beauty, he again diverted his eyes to the signature at the base of the painting. "Is this really your work…Ms. Jansen?"

"Yes, it's my work," she answered proudly. "Thank you for the lovely praise."

"You must specialize in realism," he said, inspired. "This looks almost like a photograph."

"Thank you again," she replied appreciatively. "I like to think my portfolio is considered versatile. However, I admit abstract isn't really my forte. And I suppose I'm most comfortable with paint."

"You've got my vote, Ms. Jansen," he said, holding out his hand. "I'm very excited about meeting you."

She extended her hand, still surprised over her immediate attraction to him, charmed by the boyish shyness that accompanied his genuine respect.

They joined hands, both realizing that their touch was stimulating.

"Jonathan Timmers," he offered, before gently withdrawing his clasp. "I live in Newport Beach. I decided to take in some artwork on this beautiful day."

She turned and glanced toward the sun-drenched window that overlooked the life-size sculpture garden bordering the front perimeter of the building. "Oh, yes, springtime by the ocean is enchanting. It's like nature's yearly wake-up call."

He followed her glance, then turned back toward her, asking, "Ms. Jansen, do you live in Laguna Beach?"

"No, Eugene, Oregon," she answered, turning back to him. "I rent space from the gallery owner, Marilyn, and come here monthly to show my work. Incidentally, Mr. Timmers, I prefer Laura."

He nodded. "Okay, sure, Laura, if you call me Jonathan."

She returned the nod, asking, "Jonathan, are you an aspiring artist? Your description of my work was remarkably astute."

He smiled, pleased over her returned flattery. "No, I'm a novelist. Believe me, that's enough of a creative challenge."

She seemed at a loss, searching her mind. "Umm…I'm sorry, your name doesn't ring a bell," she confessed, blushing. "I'm afraid I'm not much of a fiction reader…oh, an occasional romance novel on the plane now and then…"

He gestured okay with a wave of his hand. "No offense taken, I understand," he replied. "I write a mystery series. My main character is Jason Thornhill, an insurance investigator."

"And he always cracks the so-called perfect crime?" she interjected with a grin.

"Yeah, that's right," he answered, smiling more broadly. "Although one day I'll come up with the perfect crime he can't crack, and then we'll both have to retire."

"I see," she replied with a chuckle. "What'll you do then?"

"Oh, I'll try my hand at travel booklets or something." His laugh faded as he looked into her eyes. A new wave of adoration swept through him. It had been a long time since he'd been struck by something other than beauty—maybe never like this. She emitted a natural splendor from every pore of her body.

She swallowed nervously, sensing his stronger attraction to her. Moreover, she was growing more concerned over her increasing fascination with him. She was intrigued by his aura of confidence. The way he spoke; his manly charisma. Regardless of her uneasiness, she knew they both needed to know more about each other.

He turned back to the painting, saying, "Anyway, I do appreciate successful artwork when I see it." He fingered the price tag, reading the hefty price. "Impressive," he said, adding a soft whistle. "And you must be very successful."

"I have my days," she quipped, exposing traces of humility. "However, I boast that this is one of my best oil pieces." She hesitated. "Tell you what. Since you admire the painting so much, I'll let it go for…oh…say $7,500."

He grinned, cocking his head. "Hmm, not exactly pocket cash for me. I'm afraid none of my novels has made the best-seller list…and no movies yet."

"I see," Laura answered, inwardly disappointed over his balk. She wasn't sure whether it really had anything to do with making the sale or whether it was simply wanting him to own one of her paintings. "Then tell me what you think you could afford."

"Well, um, I…" he muttered, before pausing and losing all awareness as they again made intense eye contact.

Speechless, she now perceived a closeness that could turn risky. It was unmistakable.

He lowered his eyes to the large diamond wedding band on her left hand, unable to mask his disappointment.

She noticed. "Laura Jansen-Bearnes is my married name. My husband is a professor at the University of Oregon." She paused, then added in a hushed tone, breaking the spell, "I also have a nine-year-old daughter, Tamra."

"That's a beautiful name," he remarked.

"I try to make everything beautiful," she said, glancing at his bare left hand.

"I'm not married," he responded quickly. "I live alone."

Out of nowhere a female voice shattered their intense exchange, "Excuse me, Laura, there's someone I want you to meet in the tea nook."

Laura pivoted toward the approaching woman, relieved that she had interrupted the arousing connection that was moving much too fast. "Oh, Rebecca, sure," she agreed, emerging from her daze. Stepping backwards, she gestured for introductions. "But first I'd like you to meet Jonathan Timmers." Laura turned toward him. "Mr. Timmers, this is my good friend and assistant, Rebecca Newell from Portland. She travels with me regularly."

Jonathan extended his hand, and orally completed the obligatory greetings.

Laura looked into Jonathan's eyes, saying quietly, "It was a pleasure to meet you, Jonathan. Please let me know if you're still interested in the painting." She pulled a small business card from her pocket, handing it to him.

"Sure, Laura," he responded, accepting the card. "Thank you."

As the women walked away, Jonathan turned and scanned Laura's painting as he gradually exited through the front door. He concealed his annoyance over Rebecca's unexpected intrusion.

Laura peripherally watched him leave, surprisingly disappointed at the thought of maybe not seeing him again. She wondered if he was as disappointed. *Hold it!* she abruptly scolded herself. *It doesn't matter, the attraction to him was all wrong. It was good that he left. It's over.*

She was barely able to forget him by absorbing herself with the gallery guests before heading off to lunch with Rebecca.

Saturday afternoon travel was horrendous at best on Pacific Coast Highway. Bumper-to-bumper traffic crept through downtown Laguna Beach. Finding a parking spot was almost impossible. The sunny seashore was packed with bathers and Frisbee-chasing dogs, frolicking in the white glistening sand and heaving surf. Hordes of casual shoppers visiting the quaint boutiques and restaurants lined the sidewalk, taking in the brilliant day.

Laura and Rebecca chatted idly as they sat under the awning of the veranda table, finishing their late lunch of shrimp salad and chilled California Chardonnay.

When Rebecca turned away to deal with the check, Laura suddenly faded into deep thought. After tallying up the bill, Rebecca noticed Laura's distant mood as she laid cash on the tab-tray.

Reaching over, she touched Laura's arm. "Hey, what's up? I don't think you've really heard a word I've said all afternoon. You're distracted. C'mon, what is it?"

Laura looked at her, answering slowly, "Do you remember that man I introduced you to this morning, Jonathan Timmers?"

"Sure," Rebecca answered questioningly, "the good-looking one who liked your painting so much. Why?"

"Well, I can't forget him," Laura admitted. "The minute I met him I felt irresistibly attracted to him."

"Do you mean romantically?" Rebecca asked, surprised.

"I dunno," Laura replied. "But it was a scary closeness...like forbidden."

Rebecca sat back, astounded, exclaiming, "I've never known you to act like this! You're a happily married woman. And a rational one."

"I know it sounds crazy," Laura responded, confused. "I don't understand it either. I just felt so drawn to him."

"But you don't play that game," Rebecca insisted. "It's not in your make up."

"Not intentionally," Laura agreed. "But now I believe allurement has something to do with chemicals in the brain. It has to. There's no other explanation. Damn, I was attracted to him before I even looked into his eyes...some type of affinity."

Rebecca's brow furrowed. "I don't believe this, Laura. Is this happening because Monte is so busy at the university lately? I know you're upset that he won't ever come with you to Laguna anymore like he used to."

"That might have something to do with it," Laura admitted, looking puzzled. "Maybe I'm needy and don't really realize it. Monte is spending more and more time away from Tamra and me." She paused as she thought it through further, then said, "However, I can't really use that as an excuse. Handsome men are always approaching me. But this one is different." She looked at Rebecca, adding slowly, "And the truth is, I was the one who approached him."

Rebecca shook her head. "You're really screwed up over this guy."

Laura suddenly became agitated over her situation. "I know it's confusing. I admit it. And it bothers me to think I might not see him again." Now frustrated, she abruptly pushed her chair back and stood. "Let's go."

Rebecca rose, silently following Laura, who had accelerated her gait up the hill toward the gallery, brusquely sidestepping the sauntering crowd.

Laura mindlessly swiped at the paintings with a fluffy feather duster, oblivious to the few Sunday evening stragglers milling around inside the gallery. She was thinking more about Jonathan Timmers and how he'd remained on her mind most of last night until she managed a few hours of sleep. She was mildly upset that he hadn't called her back, not even to discuss the painting.

She moved to the next painting, recalling how strange it had been when she was in church this morning looking for guidance to get past this volatile predicament. Instead of getting any celestial support to forget Jonathan, it had occurred to her that she could easily contact him if she really wanted to. She could find out who his publisher was through a bookstore and then get a message to him through them or his agent. She could use the painting he admired as the reason to contact him. He'd surely remember the painting. He'd surely remember *her*. Then he'd surely call her back.

She lowered the duster, pausing to think again how very strange it was that instead of receiving any righteous guidance against further contact with him, she was helped by those thoughts on how to reach him. *How odd, indeed,* she thought.

She resumed brushing off the paintings while scolding herself. *Dammit! This is crazy. I'm a married woman, with a young daughter and an upstanding husband in the educational community. Even if he was becoming a bit neglectful lately.*

She quickly decided to block this weekend out of her mind. It would be easy. She would avoid coming back to Laguna next month; maybe even pass on the whole summer. She could then spend more time with Tamra before returning in the fall. *Gotta get out of here, now.* She frowned. *Why didn't I just fly back this afternoon with Rebecca when I had the chance? Maybe I could still get a flight out tonight yet. Sure! I'll call the airline.* And if she couldn't get out, she'd isolate herself in her hotel room and fly back early in the morning as scheduled, she decided. She'd call the airline and find out—*right now.*

She laid the duster down and turned for the phone, but stopped when she saw Jonathan enter through the front door.

He smiled nervously. "Hello again, Laura," he said awkwardly at the sight of her. He glanced over at the painting he'd favored yesterday. "Good, I see it's still for sale." He faced her. "Perhaps we could haggle over the price?"

Her eyes widened, conspicuous of her gratification at seeing him. It was useless to attempt any false guise. She was enamored by his innocent uncertainty.

"Sure…umm, yes, of course," she answered, fidgety, turning toward a small round table where her valise sat. "Would you like to sit down?"

He shook his head, now feeling more confident by her cordial reception. He'd seen it in her eyes. He stepped farther along, suggesting, "I was hoping we could do it over dinner tonight. Maybe someplace along the beachfront."

She hesitated, but knew she couldn't deny the invitation despite how improper it appeared. She smiled, answering, "Why not, Jonathan? I'm not scheduled to leave Laguna until tomorrow anyway. And I have no plans for this evening."

Laura felt the slight raindrops falling against her face, bursting her thoughts of that special day in Laguna Beach. She glanced across the river seeing some heavy clouds rolling in. She looked back at the hotel and the wide, covered entrance, deciding she could get there quickly for shelter, if necessary. She'd sit here a while longer.

Up in his hotel room, Jonathan managed to get up off the bed and look around, again trying to gather his wits. He called out for Laura—but heard nothing. With an unsteady gait, he left the room and made his way down the hallway and entered the elevator.

Descending to the ground floor, he tottered into the main lobby and plopped down on the reception couch. With the bell captain watching him curiously, Jonathan worked to focus his piercing stare through the large plate window into the dark.

Still seated on the bench, Laura tightened her scarf a bit more snugly. She crossed her arms and sat back, recalling how she and Jonathan had left the gallery that special night and went to dinner at the Laguna beachfront restaurant. The night everything really all started. And how after she had left for Oregon they had both tried to squelch the bonding that had taken place.

CHAPTER THREE

The bonding, Laguna Beach

Drifting behind a passing cloud, the pale quarter moon barely cast a glimmer on the calm ocean breakers lapping gently against the yachts moored just outside the restaurant window. Jonathan signed the dinner tab and handed it to the server. Laura watched him through the rim of the water goblet as she nervously took a swallow. She was still uneasy over her growing attraction to his every move, regardless of how trivial. However, she had maintained her composure well as they discussed the painting and its price during dinner. She was inwardly pleased that he had finally agreed to the purchase, bonding them closer.

Jonathan looked over at her, asking, "Wine and cheesecake to finish off that fantastic dinner? I know a great little dessert shop just a short way up the beach. After all, we should make this celebration complete for our deal on the painting."

She wanted to go, but knew she needed to decline and escape from his emotional grasp. "Sounds delicious," she replied. "Unfortunately, I really must be going. I have a long day tomorrow. I fly out of Orange County in the morning and then have to teach a class at Portland State University tomorrow night."

"Oh," he responded, looking puzzled. "Didn't you say you lived in Eugene? That's quite a distance from Portland, isn't it?"

"Correct," she answered, "about a hundred miles. But PSU has one of the finest Master of Fine Arts program in Oregon. That's where I earned my degree. Anyway, I couldn't pass up their offer."

"I see," he interjected. "Sounds like a good position. But isn't the commute a bit difficult?"

"Not really too bad," she answered. "I fly up once a week and stay with my friend Rebecca. It also gives me an opportunity to visit my acquaintances at the Portland art galleries before I return home the next afternoon."

"I'll bet you have a lot of friends there," he flattered, suddenly realizing how special she really was with her artistic talent—even though she was so modest.

"Yes, I know a lot of people there," she replied. "That's my home town."

He sat back, saying, "Then you must really miss the Portland scene."

"Oh, I do. But it was important that we move to Eugene so Monte could be close to his work. It's much easier for me to maneuver my schedule to handle the distance. So I get up there as much as I can."

"You sound like a very busy lady…and managing a family yet."

"Quite busy, I guess," she agreed. "Yet I have to do it now while I'm young. We all should have goals in life, shouldn't we?"

He nodded, speechless in his increasing awe of her.

She brightened, adding, "My main goal is to one day win the governor's lifetime achievement award for the arts. It's an annual event. I am also fortunate enough to have some of my work displayed in Portland's art museum."

He smiled, and reached over to touch her hand. "I'm really proud to be getting to know you," he said admiringly.

Her eyes slowly lowered toward their joined hands. She looked back up at him. "Thank you," she answered nervously.

Sensing her uneasiness over their touch, he gently withdrew his hand to lighten the tense moment. "Tell me, doesn't your husband mind you being gone those days?"

She shrugged. "No, not at all. He's very busy with his work at the university. Besides, my absence provides him time to be alone with our daughter. It gives them a chance to get to know each other better." She paused. "Hey," she said abruptly, "Enough about me. What about you?"

He sat back to gather his thoughts. "Oh, I dunno," he answered nonchalantly. "There's nothing really very exciting about me, I guess."

"You call being a published author non-exciting?" she responded, cocking her head questioningly.

"Well, I suppose I'm quite fortunate to be successful at something I love to do," he answered. "Even though I'm not really obsessed with my craft."

"What drives you, then?"

"I strive not to view my writing as labor," he replied. "I want to enjoy my story and characters, especially Jason Thornhill. I want to have fun creating and challenging their lives." He paused, looking deeper into her eyes. "I also want to enjoy the real world around me," he added. "I try to mix both of those worlds."

She listened intently, yearning to know him—growing closer to him. "May I ask you something personal?" she asked.

"Sure."

"Were you ever married?"

He nodded. "Yeah, once. I married my college sweetheart from UCLA." Knowing she wanted to hear more, he continued, "She died about five years ago of leukemia. She was very young."

"Oh, I'm so sorry," Laura said, lowering her eyes.

"It's okay," he replied, turning to peer out the window at the ocean to relieve the uncomfortable moment. "Life's tough. We all experience severe pain sooner or later. I was just dealt mine sooner, that's all."

She looked up, watching him scan the ocean's horizon. She now knew that he was a good man. And probably very lonely. She also now fully realized that even though she was wrongly attracted to him, she couldn't walk away. Not now. For she knew from the depths of her heart that he needed something from her.

She reached over to touch his hand. "You know what?" she said softly as he turned toward her. "I think that wine and cheesecake sounds pretty good after all."

"Great!" he exclaimed, as they rose from the table and headed for the door.

Laura blankly stared out the porthole window at the aircraft tugs hustling baggage around the airport apron as the airliner slowly taxied up to the passenger ramp-bridge and docked. She remained seated, oblivious to the planeload of passengers springing up to haul out their baggage from the overhead compartments and anxiously cram the aisles to make their way to the front exit. She was drained from the grueling weekend trip, and dispirited over parting from Jonathan in California earlier that morning. She was also very confused over what had happened to her in the last twenty-four hours.

Sudden sprinkles from the overcast skies began to trickle against the thick pane of glass, reminding her she was back in Portland. She grabbed her purse and scooted into the aisle, filing behind the remaining passengers exiting the plane.

Looking straight ahead, she ambled up the ramp and out the gate, entering the main concourse. She hastened her pace toward the baggage area, but stopped and pivoted when she heard a voice calling out her name from behind her.

Rebecca made her way through the crowd and caught up with her. "Laura, wait, slow down," she said, moderately agitated.

"Oh, hi, Rebecca. I wasn't sure if you were going to pick me up."

"But you didn't even look around for me," Rebecca replied, realizing that Laura sounded strange.

"Sorry," Laura apologized. "I'm just tired and a little anxious about tonight's class at the college, I suppose."

"Sure, I understand," Rebecca said, sensing that weariness and nervousness wasn't Laura's problem. She grasped Laura's forearm. "C'mon, we'll grab a cup of tea after we fetch your baggage."

Laura nodded, following her through the busy terminal toward the baggage carousels.

Laura toyed with her empty teacup as Rebecca eased back in her chair at the small lounge table, asking, "So, what happened after you two had dinner?"

"We left the restaurant and strolled up the boardwalk to a little dessert shop and had a glass of wine and strawberry cheesecake."

"Is that all that happened?"

"Basically, yes," Laura answered. "Neither one of us was tired, so afterward we sat on the pier, chatting about our hopes and goals. It's been a long time since someone listened to me the way he did. It was special." She paused. "After that I went back to my hotel and got a couple hours of sleep before I headed for the airport."

"Laura, how'd you leave it? Are you going to see him again?"

Laura appeared indifferent. "I'm not sure. Later this week he's going to mail me a check for the painting. Then I'll clear it with the gallery to release it to him. After that I suppose he'll pick up the painting, and that's it."

Rebecca looked straight at her. "Laura, please quit stalling," she pressed. "Remember, I'm your best friend. How much trouble are you in? Did you have any physical contact with him, like…"

"No," Laura interrupted adamantly, "nothing like that!" She hesitated. "But I assume we're going to be good friends."

Rebecca remained silent, knowing that Laura needed to open up, and would. She knew Laura had no one else to talk to. She didn't have to wait long.

Laura abruptly turned away. "All right, Rebecca," she said guiltily, "I wanted to. I wanted to make love to him right there on the pier. I didn't even care who was around or watching." Rebecca sat attentively as Laura took a deep breath and continued, "I can't believe my feelings. God! What has happened to me?" She shook her head.

"Why are you so attracted to this guy?" Rebecca asked, baffled. "I realize he's good-looking and charming, but he's probably just some slick womanizer."

Laura looked up at her. "I wish that's all there was to it," she replied soberly. "I wish it were only animal instinct. Then I would have just gone to bed with him and walked away. I could get over that guilt. No, I'm afraid it's more than that." She paused. "To make matters even worse, he's a lonely man, a widower…I know intuitively that he needs me."

Rebecca nodded understandingly, knowing her friend was deeply disturbed. She bent forward and reached for Laura's shaky hand, saying affectionately, "I understand, sweet friend." Rebecca sighed, then asked carefully, "Okay, what happens after the painting business? You need to talk about this."

"I don't know," Laura quickly replied, gripping Rebecca's hand. "I just don't know. I need more time to figure things out."

Rebecca slowly withdrew her hand and sat back, saying, "Just please keep in mind how important you are in this community. You're well known and becoming more so every day. A messy entanglement could really set your life back. It could ruin your family and everything you've worked so hard for."

Laura nodded, looking down. "I know," she agreed. "I know that well. I'm very worried about Monte and Tamra more than my work." She thought a minute, then suddenly appeared buoyant with revelation. "Damn, this is crazy, Rebecca. I can walk away from this. It'll be easy once the painting transaction is finished and I get back to my normal routine. This is crazy," she repeated, pushing her chair back. "Let's go. I have a class to prepare for."

As they both broke into a large smile, they stood and made their way toward the terminal exit as Laura told Rebecca she was sure Jonathan felt the same way about forgetting this whole event as she did. Because he'd certainly realize there was no future in any intimate relationship with a married woman of her position.

That night Jonathan Timmers walked out onto his patio and sat down on the chaise lounge, reclining the seatback halfway. Settling himself, he peered out at the western skyline of the Newport Beach harbor and the faint silhouette of the flaming red sun that was sinking majestically behind the ocean's horizon.

Closing his eyes, he tried to focus on the outline of his next novel, but couldn't get past the real-life events that had happened yesterday. His thoughts were focused only on Laura Jansen-Bearnes. The first woman he'd felt really close to since his wife. He already realized she was someone he could care about and be with comfortably—maybe even love. The talk they had had on the beach last night after dinner was incredible. He had thoroughly enjoyed her company, with her beauty and intelligence so complementing to her artistic talents. No woman since his wife had so quickly affected him like that.

But he grimaced, knowing she was beyond his reach. She was prominent and very married. He'd have to forget about her before it got out of hand. Moreover, if he wanted to stay productive in his writing he must remain free of unnecessary emotional pressure. He needed to stay focused on his work.

He opened his eyes as twilight was fading to dark. The decision was made. He'd simply send her the check and pick up the painting from the gallery. Indeed, the decision was firm. *He would have to get along in life without Laura Jansen-Bearnes, as before.*

◆◆◆

Laura looked up at the beginning signs of dawn breaking over the hushed city of Portland. With the visibility improving, she again scanned the area. Although the river park still appeared deserted, she noticed a couple of rumpled sleeping bags under the bridge. She then caught a glimpse of a male figure slipping into the shadows of the bridge shoreline piling and crouching down underneath the rear overhang. She lost sight of him, but felt secure, assuming they were all probably only sleepy homeless people who didn't usually bother anyone.

Turning back toward the river, she decided to wait a little longer for more light before heading for the coffee shop. She laid her head back and closed her eyes, recalling her life after that weekend; her life that was intended to go forward without Jonathan Timmers. That is, until that late June afternoon in Laguna Beach when he had showed up unexpectedly. Why hadn't she listened to Rebecca that day?

CHAPTER FOUR

The visit, Laguna Beach, California

The summer solstice drenched the beach-lined Pacific Coast Highway with brilliant sunshine as Laura sped toward the Orange County airport. With a rigid grasp on the wheel, she was inwardly flustered but continued to conceal it. Rebecca sat silently in the passenger seat, staring out the windshield with a concerned look.

Laura glanced over, saying, "You seem worried. I'm sure we'll be there in plenty of time."

"That's not what's wrong, and you know it," Rebecca replied solemnly. "I still think you should fly back with me tonight."

Laura grimaced. "Rebecca, please," she responded tensely. "We've been through this a hundred times this weekend. I always have to stay to help close up the gallery. I'll fly in tomorrow as usual. I'll be all right."

"And when Jonathan comes? Will you be all right then?"

"Yes!" Laura responded, rolling her eyes. "Yes, yes, yes!"

Rebecca sighed. "Okay," she said, conceding the point. "I'm sorry I'm interfering."

"Oh, Rebecca, you're not interfering," Laura answered apologetically, pulling the car into the airport parking lot. "I know how much you care about me," she added, angling the car into an empty space. "But please don't worry, I'll be fine."

"But you haven't seen him since that weekend in April," Rebecca pressed. How do you know how you're going to react?"

"I just know," Laura replied, letting the car idle. "It's not like we haven't communicated or anything. We talked on the phone once or twice. There wasn't any problem." She paused. "Hey, tonight's visit isn't meant to be clandestine."

"Okay," Rebecca replied, reaching for her purse to look over her tickets. She glanced at her watch. "But I still don't know why he didn't come around sometime when we were all there."

Laura didn't respond, because she lacked a valid explanation. She shut the engine off and reached for the latch, opening the door. "I'll come in and sit with you for a while."

Rebecca reached over and patted her arm. "No, I'll just pester you," she admitted. "And I know you're nervous. Just go on back to the gallery and prepare yourself. You had to face this meeting sooner or later."

Laura nodded and closed her door as Rebecca turned and stepped out. She reached into the back seat to grab her suitcase, saying, "I'll plan on picking you up at the airport tomorrow. If something goes wrong with your flight, call me at home. I'll be there about one-thirty. If I don't hear from you, I'll head for the airport around two-thirty to pick you up."

"Sounds good," Laura replied. "Don't worry, I'll be there. We'll grab a light dinner before my class."

Rebecca shut the door. "Okay, bye."

Laura smiled. "Have a good day at work tomorrow. Bye."

Rebecca turned and paced down the wide sidewalk toward the terminal entrance as Laura pulled her car out of the lot and headed for the south I-405 freeway entrance. She decided to shun the scenic coast highway so she could make it back to the gallery sooner. She wanted to make sure she was finished with her chores before Jonathan arrived. That way she'd be clear-headed.

As she made her way through the light Sunday afternoon traffic, she noticed that her grip on the wheel was moist and strained. She was growing apprehensive over meeting with Jonathan. Maybe Rebecca was right. Maybe she wouldn't be able to handle seeing him again. Yet they had done well over the last two months, with only a couple of token phone messages concerning the painting transaction. The exchanges had never indicated anything other than that they were only acquaintances. *Two people who simply enjoyed each other's company*, she reasoned.

So it wasn't odd for him to call and say he was going to stop by tonight on his way home from San Diego and say hello. After all, she had been here last month and he had never even called. And she was sure he knew she was in Laguna. *Didn't he?* Regardless, she could handle tonight's visit. And just like the last thing Rebecca had told her: *She had to face this meeting sooner or later.*

She'd serve tea and cookies and cut things off early. Tomorrow would be a long-drawn-out day, especially with her night class in Portland. She had to administer the first major exam and deal with all the advanced curriculum activities to get through the Fourth of July holiday. She'd need her rest. Jonathan would understand.

Beginning to relax, she turned onto the short highway that would take her west to the Laguna Beach gallery and her answers concerning Jonathan Timmers.

Laura sat at the bar in the tea nook, sipping on a cup of steaming herbal oolong looking over the gallery, tidied and secured for the evening. The owner, Marilyn, had gone, leaving Laura to close up. Laura looked down and swirled the tea around in her cup, cooling it. She felt confident and ready for Jonathan. He wouldn't stay long. They'd simply have tea together at the gallery and then she'd drive to her hotel; no dinner, wine or any more beach walks. And if he resisted or made a covert advance, she'd just tell him the truth. If they were to remain friends, their relationship would have to be aboveboard and completely platonic. *They could be friends without passion*, she decided. He'd understand. He'd have to. And so would she.

She looked up, smiling brightly when she saw Jonathan enter through the front door and eagerly look around the gallery to locate her.

"Hello," she greeted warmly, catching his attention.

He returned the smile as he walked toward her. "Well, hello," he responded, masking his extreme delight at seeing her.

She inhaled as he came into full view, the soft glow from the ceiling track lighting illuminating his full body. He looked fresh and rested, tanned from the summer sunshine. He wore a soft white mock-turtleneck T-shirt and faded baby-blue jeans.

She stood and met him at the entrance of the tea nook, shaking his hand. Their grasp was firm and steady. Both were obviously mentally prepared for his visit.

She released his hand and walked over to the front door, locking it. "We're actually closed," she said, walking back to him. "I was just waiting for you."

After they sat down, Laura poured him a cup of tea and they gracefully made small talk about how much he enjoyed her painting that he had purchased in the spring. They obligingly apologized to each other for failing to stay in closer contact. They both lied, using their busyness as the excuse.

Slowly their intense attraction for each other grew, weakening their façade. She was silent as her desire for him welled up inside her while he chatted excitedly about his new novel. Yet she caught herself, deciding she had to tell him the truth and then part. She was inwardly dismayed, because she now knew they couldn't ever be merely friends. Unfortunately, their friendship would have to be terminated tonight, before anything really started up. She began to conjure up the words in her mind to tell him. It would be awkward, but she'd find the courage. She'd just wait for the right moment to interrupt him.

However, she could save her dialogue. For Jonathan knew what she was thinking. He could see it in her eyes and her jittery motions. He always sensed what she felt and thought. They had connected mentally from the first moment they'd met.

He slowed his chat, looking toward her left hand and the wedding band to signal that he understood. He realized he needed to leave, for both their sakes.

He slowly pushed his teacup away and rose to leave. "I'd better go," he said with a faint smile. "It's getting late. And I don't think we have to explain anything more to each other."

She looked down. "I'm sorry, Jonathan. I...I...did want to be friends. I guess we just can't."

"Whoa," he said. "You've done nothing wrong. I've enjoyed knowing you, Laura. It made me realize there is something special out there again. Anyway, if I stay any longer it will only prolong the inevitable...goodnight."

She nodded as he quickly turned and headed for the front door. He twisted the deadbolt and opened the door, but stopped and turned around when he heard the words he needed to hear so desperately: "Jonathan, please wait." Laura looked up at him with a piercing emptiness sweeping through her heart. "Please don't go," she appealed softly.

He remained frozen in the doorway, the cascading moonlight encasing his silhouette as she walked toward him. Reaching up, she embraced him, burying her head into his shoulder. "Oh, God,

Jonathan. Please don't leave. I can't explain anything right now. I've never felt like this."

He put his arms around her and they tightened their embrace. "Oh, Laura," he whispered impatiently. "My life has been meaningless without you. I thought I'd go crazy last month, knowing you were here. It's been sheer hell trying to avoid you. I can't do it anymore…I can't."

She looked up as they locked longingly onto each other's stares, then kissed passionately, feverishly expressing their need for each other.

Laura slowly withdrew, gently pushing him backward. Mute, he stared at her, lost in her splendor. She reached up and delicately touched his face, running her forefinger up and down his cheek, her darting eyes undressing his total being, inside and out.

He whispered, "I need you so much, Laura."

Tears began to trickle down her cheeks. "I know," she said in a hushed tone. "Don't worry, sweetheart, I know."

Laura jerked backward on the bench, startled, as the clicking of the bike chain suddenly buzzed loudly behind her. She turned, catching the back of the early morning cyclist speeding down the wet riverwalk getting his morning exercise. A prickly mist from the racing tires splattered against her cheek and neck, sending a biting chill throughout her body. She wiped off the droplets and settled back against the bench, glancing at her watch: four fifty-two. It wouldn't be long before she could leave for the coffee shop. However, it was still too early.

Her thoughts returned to that night in the gallery when Jonathan had visited and they helplessly succumbed to their mutual need for each other. And how difficult it was when she had to call Monte the next morning, telling him she was staying in Laguna Beach another day to meet with the officials at the Laguna Art Muscum. How she had to discuss the plans for some informal lectures to be held there in the near future. He'd never check on that story. He'd never question her judgment about delaying her agenda to discuss something as important as her work.

It had hurt her badly to lie to Monte for the first time in their marriage. Yet she had to stay and deal with her obsession for Jonathan.

She had to try to understand what was happening and where her life would go from that point on. She couldn't just fly home the next day and carry on with her life as though nothing had happened.

She felt a twinge of guilt, recalling how she also had to call Rebecca that same day to tell her she wouldn't be flying into Portland, as though compelled to confess as to what was going on with Jonathan. She had to tell Rebecca. Not only might she need a cover with Monte, but she also had to confide in someone. Why not her best friend, who would surely understand? Yet she remembered how difficult it was to make that phone call, too…

Rebecca bolted through the front door, flinging it closed behind her. Rushing to the small wooden stand in the dining room, she answered the ringing phone. "Hello?" she rasped, winded, trying to catch her breath. "Oh, hi, Laura," she said. "You have? I'm sorry you haven't been able to catch me," she apologized, looking up at the kitchen wall clock, seeing one forty-five.

Rebecca continued, "I had to call on a couple of galleries this morning, and I discovered my answering-machine tape was bad when I got home last night. In fact, that's why I'm running behind. I had to stop and get a new one." Having caught her breath, she pulled the chair out to sit down. But she hesitated, suddenly realizing that Laura was unusually quiet. She was quickly suspicious of Laura's subdued behavior, asking, "What's up, Laura? Is your flight delayed or something?" She sat down, frowning over Laura's answer. "Why are you staying?" Rebecca listened closely, then responded, "All right, I see…Yes, I understand…No, there's no problem. I'd set up a coffee gathering for us tomorrow morning at the guild with some of our gallery friends like you asked, but I'll cancel us out," she replied, disappointed over her friend's unusual behavior. "What about Monte? Does he know you're staying in Laguna tonight?"

Rebecca listened intently, realizing that Laura was very confused. "Okay," she replied to Laura's explanation. "I can cover for you if I have to, but I'm sure he won't question what you've told him. Oh, what about your class tonight?…Uh-huh, oh, that was good of Dean Billings to fill in for you on such short notice."

Rebecca shook her head, wondering if she should offer any advice, but decided against it for now. She wouldn't preach to her today. "What?...All right, I won't plan on seeing you in Portland at all if you're connecting through San Francisco. Call me when you get home tomorrow night." She paused. "Laura, please be careful. Call me if you need me for anything. Bye."

Rebecca slowly hung up the phone and leaned her head back against the wall. She now realized that Laura was deeply distressed by becoming romantically involved with another man. She had already changed—so uncharacteristically. Yet she also knew that if Laura was able to halt this illicit slide before it was too late, she would manage to. However, could she do it alone? Would she ask for help?

Rebecca rose and went into the kitchen, shaking her head. Reaching into the refrigerator, she pulled out the carafe of Chablis. She retrieved a clean goblet from the cupboard and filled it to the brim. Sitting down, she began to sip on the chilled wine, mulling over the "Laguna Art Museum" story that Laura had cleverly woven for Monte. She'd have to be prepared in case he called. But she doubted he would. Professor Monte Bearnes would never suspect his loving, dutiful wife, Laura, would ever cheat on him, or, for that matter, even lie to him.

But what if he did suspect something was coming on differently with Laura? She couldn't take that chance. She had to be ready for him. But if he did call, maybe she should tell him the truth, if only for her friend's sake. Perhaps if Monte knew what was going on, he would understand, and stop her from straying any further. Then afterward maybe he would be more caring and attentive...perhaps.

No, she couldn't be the one to tell him. Anyway, things hadn't gone too far yet with Jonathan and Laura...*had they*? she wondered as she lifted the goblet and emptied it. She reached for the carafe and refilled her glass. As she sat back and fingered the stem, she glanced over at the phone.

Laura turned back toward the hotel at the sound of the shuttle pulling up to the front entrance. The sleepy chauffeur crawled out from behind the driver's side, gripping a bright red thermos cup of steaming coffee in one hand, a clipboard in the other. He lumbered through the front door to check with the front desk about the anticipated airport traffic.

Laura sat back, wondering whether after that first deceitful episode she'd contrived in Laguna Beach, Rebecca had really understood what a mounting battle she was facing with Jonathan entering her life. She sighed and looked at her watch: five-fourteen. About forty-five minutes until it was fully light, she calculated.

She probably could leave very soon now, stop dwelling over Jonathan and move on with her life. He'd go on his New York trip and forget things for a while. After all, that's what she had planned, wasn't it? Bring him up here before his trip to give him time away afterward to think about things and begin getting over her. She switched thoughts, concentrating on going home to Eugene today. *What would Monte's mood be tonight? Could she get away cleanly with last night's break from Jonathan?* It was strange how Monte had acted yesterday morning—as though he might even know about Jonathan. *No, he couldn't have known.* He was just more involved in his work because of the fall semester beginning at the university, and needed her at home. *That's all,* she told herself. But she lifted her head in thought as her mind wandered back to early yesterday morning in Eugene…

Professor Montgomery Andrew "Monte" Bearnes gently lifted the covers to look over Laura's nude body as he lightly ran his toes up the back of her calf, pausing at the bottom of her buttock, gently probing her thigh. Facing away from him, her eyes instantly opened. Full of stress over tonight's meeting with Jonathan, Laura cringed inwardly as she lay still, eyeing the morning gray sifting through the bedroom window blinds. She had slept only lightly at best, waking repeatedly to mull over the decision she had made about breaking off the affair with Jonathan.

She stirred slightly, faking slumber while thinking how odd it was that he was this interested in her again this morning. It would seem that after the marathon lovemaking session he had put her through last night, he wouldn't be so frisky. And why hadn't he risen immediately after waking as usual, especially when he had so much to do at the university?

He brushed her hair away from her ear, whispering in a feverish tone, "Good morning, beautiful."

She swallowed nervously as she slowly turned over. She didn't want to be this close to him, worried that she wouldn't be able to hide her anxiety over tonight's meeting with Jonathan. She could usually hide her anxiety when she headed to Portland for her clandestine rendezvous, but not under today's conditions. With a languid façade, she nuzzled close to his tall, lean frame, feeling the response of his eager manliness against her genital area as she laid her cheek on his, facing past his shoulder. She kept her eyes closed and offered no resistance as he pulled her closer and began to caress her back and softly kiss her neck with heated breath.

Laura sat at the breakfast nook, finishing her tea in tense silence. She set her cup down and pulled her bathrobe ties tighter to ward off the chill seeping through the slightly cracked window.

She looked up as Monte entered the room and sat down next to her. He sported an enthusiastic disposition, and was freshly showered and dressed in slacks and a sport coat. A faint scent of his cologne followed him. His ear-length, grayish blond hair was neatly groomed, polishing off his professional demeanor.

He reached over and gave her a quick kiss. "Thanks for this morning," he said with a roguish grin. "I don't know what got into me."

She smiled. "You're welcome," she replied, forcing a wink. "I didn't exactly suffer through it, you know."

He laughed and reached for the coffee pot. "Is Tamra gone already?" he asked, filling his cup halfway.

"Yes, she's as excited as you are about the new school year."

"That's true," he agreed, before emptying the cup. "I always love to meet the new students and set the tempo for a productive year."

She nodded as she stood up and went to the sink to close the window. She turned, noticing his strange stare toward her; a questioning stare.

She sat down. "What is it?"

"Is it really necessary for you to stay in Portland tonight?" he asked.

She furrowed her brow, surprised at his question. It was the second time he had brought it up. "Umm…yeah, it would be easier for me, like always," she answered. "We talked about this briefly yesterday. You didn't seem to mind then."

His serious look lingered. "I know," he said. "But it's such a busy time for me, and I dislike having to leave Tamra with Amy and Bill all night again. That's twice this month we've had to do this because of your unexpected meetings at the college."

Laura shrugged. "Amy and Bill don't mind," she replied, concealing her growing surprise at his unusual concern over her being gone overnight again. "They love Tamra. And Tamra loves them. They all get along beautifully." She paused. "Besides, maybe you can manage to get your work done early today and stay home tonight. Then you and Tamra can go out for dinner or something."

He shook his head. "No," he said. "I'll have to be there most all night. In fact, I'm having dinner with my friend Professor Filson, the new clinical psychologist. We're going to compare our fall curriculums. Sorry…."

"It's okay, I know how busy you are," she said, nodding, as she rose from the chair, hopeful that the conversation was finished. She laid the teacup in the sink, then hesitated when she heard from behind her, "Are you staying with Rebecca tonight?"

She turned toward him with a puzzled look. "Yes, of course," she answered quickly. "You know I always stay with her when I travel to Portland. Why would you ask that?"

He cracked a smile. "Oh, I dunno. I guess I just miss you, that's all," he said as he stood up. "We haven't spent much time together lately. Like I said, you seem to be gone a lot."

She smiled as she walked over and embraced him. "I know. I guess we're both just very busy," she said, reaching up to kiss him. "But we'll all get a chance to be together during the holidays."

"Right," he replied softly, looking into her eyes. "Hey, maybe we should get up to Mount Hood for another Thanksgiving skiing trip like last year."

She smiled wider. "Oh, I'd like that. But do you think we can get into the lodge? It's pretty late. I mean even with your pull with the Timberline staff…"

"Already talked to Harley Ferguson in Reservations," he said with a shrug. "They're holding our favorite room if we want it.

They're just waiting for you to call and finalize the plans." He matched her smile. "Of course, my donating one of your paintings for their ballroom kinda helped. I hope you don't mind the bribe."

Her eyes beamed. "Oh, honey, great!" she said, embracing him tighter. "Of course I'm pleased. I'd be honored to have one of my paintings hanging in the lodge ballroom."

"Okay, good," he said. "Anyway, I haven't solidified my holiday schedule yet but it certainly won't hurt to make the reservations."

"Oh, Tamra will be so happy," she responded. "She just loves to ski with you. She learned the basics so quickly last year."

"I know, dear," he replied, turning serious. "I want to advance her to the more difficult runs this year. She's going to be good." He gently pulled away from her and walked to the front door. He reached into the hall closet for his trench coat. As he put it on, he turned to her, saying slowly, "Goodbye, beautiful. I'll see you tomorrow." He turned and headed out the front door.

She walked to the open door, saying, "Have a good day, darling. I'll see you tomorrow evening. And I'll call Harley and arrange the skiing trip as soon as I get home tomorrow."

"Good," she heard from him as he got into his car. "Really good," he mouthed through the windshield before slowly backing out of the driveway.

She shut the door and leaned back against it, sighing. She was glad he'd brought up the skiing trip. She doubted he would have brought it up if he was secretly challenging her about meeting with Jonathan tonight. She was sure he still didn't know about the affair. It had to be just a coincidence that he had seemed suspicious earlier. *Probably caused by his lusty mood*, she decided, chuckling as she headed for the stairway. Her own mood turned somber again, thinking that even if he had known, he would have had to let her get through one more deceitful night. He didn't know that this time her overnight absence was absolutely necessary for his sake—and Tamra's. The final meeting so she could come back and be only his again—once more a faithful wife and mother. *One more night*, she thought as she headed upstairs for the bathroom and a long, steaming shower. *One more night.*

◆◆◆

Laura looked up at the breaking sky, turning a wistful look as she wondered if the skiing trip she and Monte had talked about yesterday morning would really happen over Thanksgiving. She turned eastward, fixing her gaze high above the tall office buildings to the faint outline of the lofty mountain range and the peak of Mount Hood, visualizing where the majestic Timberline Lodge was located. She recalled when she and Monte used to ski up there regularly during the winters until their careers and parenthood seemed to devour all of their time. She knew Monte missed the mountain trips, having been born and raised in that Oregon alpine wonderland.

He was such a marvelous skier, spending many years during his youth as a ski-school employee at the lodge. She was always so proud while they were in college and the Timberline management asked him to fill in as the master ski instructor during the peak seasonal holidays. She remembered how she would stand at the base of the slopes with the other students, watching him in awe as he gracefully glided down the most difficult runs, cutting a striking figure against the sunlit mountainside in his colorful skiing attire. And how many a night she'd be so worried when after skiing was shut down, he'd steal up to beyond the boundaries of the most difficult runs and race down the jagged mountain terrain with only his superior skill and the light of the moon as his protective guides. How afterward at the bottom, while holding her hand, he'd look up the mountainside and sneer at the ominous risk he'd taken, telling her that this part of the wilderness was as natural to him as any other part of the world, and always would be.

Laura missed those days and the frequent but glorious ski trips when she and Monte were newly in love. She was disappointed that now they'd managed to make it only an annual event for the last three or four years. And perhaps again this year. *But would it be the same?*

She sighed, wondering if Monte was able to pull himself away from his work this year, and she was able to get through this hardship with Jonathan, would the Timberline trip be as happy for all of them as the years past. And what about the precious moments she had been able to spend with Tamra on those past trips? How the two of them would talk, escaping from the pressures of everyday life and getting to know each other more, becoming better friends. Would those special moments be the same as last year? And would they really be as close this year?

Or had she unknowingly breached her daughter's closeness and love while being preoccupied with her affair? She fretted as she positioned her body on the bench to comfortably remain focused on the mountaintop, recalling last year's Thanksgiving trip and those cherished moments on the lodge veranda…

CHAPTER FIVE

The previous Thanksgiving, Timberline Lodge, Mount Hood, Oregon

The late-afternoon sun shone brilliantly through the clear crisp air that enveloped the snowcapped peaks of the mighty Cascade range, creating a magnificent backdrop. The grandiose Timberline Lodge, perched six thousand feet up the towering eminence of Oregon, Mount Hood, completed the natural splendor with its acres of snow-laden ski slopes and a thick boundary of dark green firs that reached as far as one could imagine.

Dressed warmly in their fashionable new ski outfits, Laura and Tamra sat silently on the lodge veranda, drinking hot chocolate, mesmerized by the breathtaking view. They were taking a break after having enjoyed a few runs on the intermediate hill. Occasionally they'd divert their eyes to the sparkling white ski runs that were already peppered with exuberant skiers of all ages who had eagerly begun the festive holiday. The lodge was filling up quickly. It would be jammed by nightfall, as it always was on the major holidays.

The Bearneses had arrived just after noon, having left Eugene early that morning to miss the laborious traffic that was common on Thanksgiving Eve. No sooner had they settled themselves in their room at the lodge than Monte had to apologize for his selfishness, asking if he could leave to get out on the slopes before she and Tamra were ready. Laura understood, knowing he had desperately missed his favorite pastime, and she smiled as she watched him slip into the ski lift and disappear up the steep mountain to begin his annual alpine adventure. She knew he wouldn't forget them for long and would be back soon. Like the past trips, it would only be a matter of time before he'd swoop up to them, creating a spiked wake from his slashing side-step stop. He'd then gently take Tamra by the hand, guiding her to one of the more difficult slopes to patiently instruct her. And her devoted, bright blue eyes would obediently follow his methodic lead before she would quickly master the advanced phase he was demonstrating—clearly confirming that she had inherited his natural skills. But for now, until he showed up, she and Tamra would enjoy their moments together.

Tamra looked over at her mother. "Mommy, when do you think Daddy will be back?" she asked, her breath steaming from the icy air.

Laura pulled off her mitten and reached over, gently pushing Tamra's straight blonde bangs back away from her stocking cap. "I don't know, honey. He's probably skiing where he did when he was a little boy, about your age," she answered, smiling. "But I'm sure he'll be back soon. I know he wants to ski with you today."

"I can't wait," Tamra replied with a widening grin. "I love to ski. Will I be as good as Daddy? Will I, Mommy?"

"Yes, sweetheart," Laura said. "I know you'll be as good as your daddy."

"This is so much fun with you and Daddy," Tamra chattered. "Are we going to stay all weekend like last year?"

"Yes, and we're going to have the big turkey feast in the ballroom tomorrow." Laura said. "And we'll sing. And we'll spend the whole weekend together…just the three of us. We'll ski and have fun. Just like last year."

"Yes, Mommy," Tamra said. " I like it when we're all together."

Laura turned toward the base of the slope. "Look, honey, here comes Daddy," she said, smiling, motioning at the man who was smoothly descending the hill toward them.

"Hi, Daddy!" Tamra exclaimed excitedly, jumping up at the railing and waving wildly. "Hi, Daddy! We're over here, Daddy!"

Laura turned back toward the river, again asking herself if moments like those on the lodge veranda would happen again this year. Would the trip be as cheerful and carefree? *No, of course not*, she admitted, but she'd work to make the best of it. She would try hard and be there only for Monte and Tamra. Be there again for them to love and cherish.

Her thoughts turned to those glorious sunrises that mesmerized her and Monte when they'd peer out over Mount Hood from their favorite room, cozily enjoying their Continental breakfasts. And how at night after Tamra was warmly tucked in bed, the feral lovemaking she and Monte would enjoy. How soon they were entangled in uninhibited frenzy in front of the blazing fireplace, with the glittering snowfall drifting under the icy window.

She grimaced, very aware that sex with Monte would probably never be like that again. Could she forever hide her deception from him during the deepest throes of their passionate episodes? It took everything inside for her to do that now. If he hadn't already realized her ongoing deceit, he surely would eventually. She closed her eyes, admitting to herself that the pleasure and closeness with Monte would never again reach the heights of those with Jonathan. And would it really be Monte *inside* her at the time, or would it forever be Jonathan she was fiercely grasping in the dark?

She dropped her head into her hands, suddenly confused again over her love for Jonathan. Knowing she had to get farther away from him, she planned her exit. This was one time she'd wished she'd bothered with renting a car. But then it would have just been another thing to deal with during this already difficult trip.

She thought about returning to the hotel to get a cab…*Aw, the hell with it*, she decided, shrugging. She'd make the walk to the coffee shop at the far end of the park grounds just like she always did after spending a night here with Jonathan. It would give her more time to be alone to think things through before returning to Eugene. After a cup of strong black tea, maybe she'd go ahead and grab a cab to Rebecca's. Perhaps then she'd be at work when Laura got there, giving her more solitary time to meditate. She tried to recollect Rebecca's weekly schedule at the art-supply store where she framed paintings and sold craft materials, but gave up after muddling through the numbers.

She furrowed her brow as she again thought about the phone call she had made to Rebecca after leaving Jonathan, and how Rebecca hadn't answered the phone. *She must've turned the volume down.* However, she was fully aware that Laura was going through this ordeal tonight. Wouldn't she be concerned about her best friend? Wouldn't Rebecca be worried that she didn't show up for dinner like they'd planned? Laura thought back to yesterday afternoon at Rebecca's apartment, the last time they had talked...

Laura and Rebecca embraced tightly in the open doorway of the downtown apartment. As they separated, Rebecca took hold of her friend's trembling hand, saying, "Are you strong enough to go through with this today?"

"Yes, I think so," Laura answered, lowering her head.

"Are you sure you can just walk away from everything that's happened between you two?"

"I have to," Laura replied, "for Monte and Tamra's sake."

"Damn, you really have it bad for this guy," Rebecca said with anger in her voice, displaying irritation over Laura's dilemma.

Laura looked up at her, appealing. "Please don't blame Jonathan. It's not all his fault. There were two of us who walked into this mess."

"But you're my best friend," Rebecca countered. "And he knew you were married when he first went after you. The bastard could have let it go."

"I know, I know...but..." Frustrated, Laura let her words trail off. She withdrew her hand, checking her watch. "Oh damn, I have to go and get this over with. I'm sure he's arrived at the hotel by now. I'm meeting him about three."

"Does he know you're going to break the affair off?"

"No, I'm sure he has no idea," Laura answered, shaking her head. "I only made the decision on Saturday. I called and told him I was teaching a special class at the college to get him here to Portland. I just couldn't wait until our next meeting in Laguna."

"How will he react? Is there a chance he could turn violent?"

"Oh, no," Laura answered quickly. "I'm sure he'll be deeply heartbroken, but he'd never physically hurt me. He wouldn't even know how."

"Okay, then I won't worry. But I'll be around if you need me."

"Good," Laura replied, "I may need some support. And just cover for me this last time with Monte if I need it."

Nodding, Rebecca stepped back with a smile as Laura turned and hurried out the door, bounding down the porch steps onto the walk. Laura turned. "Hey, I should be back by dinnertime. We'll go out for sushi," she yelled back before disappearing into the graying afternoon.

Rebecca returned the wave, answering softly into the breeze, "Yeah, sure."

Laura again dismissed Rebecca's telephone snub. *She must've been sleeping soundly*, she reasoned, finally pardoning her friend. Because if she had gotten the call, she would have contacted the hotel desk and left a message. Anyway, whether Rebecca was at home or not, she could rest up before heading back to Eugene this afternoon to begin the task of trying to revive the happy home life she'd once known. She'd immediately begin preparing for the holidays with Monte and Tamra. She'd definitely persuade him to take time off from the university for the holidays like he had implied yesterday. They would spend a pleasant Thanksgiving and Christmas together—just the three of them. And they would enjoy skiing at Timberline on Thanksgiving weekend again. And she would make it a happy time, just like last year. Yes, she'd make reservations at the lodge the minute she arrived home today. And it would be extra exciting this year, because Monte had arranged for her to donate one of her paintings to the lodge. Perhaps they'll hang it in their famous ballroom, complementing the hand-woven draperies and fixtures the lodge was famous for. Maybe she'd choose her favorite seascape to donate: the one of Puget Sound she'd captured while visiting her mother in Washington, right after Dad died. She recalled how her mood was sullen that early foggy morning, capturing the solitary fisherman against the deserted hazy shoreline, analogizing that scene with her being an only child, never having a sister or brother to share her grief and happiness throughout her lifetime. *Yes, that one,* she decided. The scene was again fitting at this time of her life. No blood relation to share her current anguish. She certainly couldn't talk to her mother, who wouldn't understand. *A staunch Christian, she would never accept cheating—especially not her daughter's infidelity.*

She needed to get going, she decided as she rose from the bench and robustly inhaled the fresh chilly air to energize herself.

The man leaning against the concrete piling raised his head slightly, watching the woman start down the shadowy riverwalk. With a scowl, he crept away from the piling, staying on the river perimeter of the park.

Laura began a rapid gait along the shrub-lined walk that edged the extensive wooded grounds. She looked up, seeing fresh rumbling thunderclouds beginning to cluster, darkening the horizon. She stopped and turned, seeing that the hotel was now far away, realizing it was not an easy haven any longer. She was nearly at the point of no return. The coffee shop was almost as close. She'd have to turn back now if she wanted to make the hotel her destination again. She instinctively looked toward the bridge, seeing the silhouettes of the sleeping bags, but not the man who had been sitting against the abutment. Yet, even though he was gone, she didn't notice anything else suspicious. She decided to continue on to the coffee shop—taking a chance on beating the rain. Turning, she again began making her way down the asphalt track, keeping a keen eye on her surroundings. But she wasn't really concerned. After all, she had made this trip plenty of times before, albeit it had been light then. *It would be light soon.*

Easing her pace, Laura turned her thoughts back to Jonathan. *Was he awake?* Was he lying there in pain from her walking out on him? Would he be able to forget her and move on with his life? Her eyes moistened as she attempted to force these tormenting images from her mind. Instead, she preferred to recall the times that she and Jonathan had met secretly in his Newport Beach apartment after that blissful summer night when they had acknowledged their attraction for each other at the gallery. How swiftly their love for each other had burst in full bloom. How she managed to increase her clandestine visits to Laguna Beach during the following months, using the "Laguna Art Museum lectures" as the excuse for Monte, while Rebecca would find ways to pad the lie if necessary. And how Jonathan would slip into Portland between her Laguna visits, giving them brief but cherished times together at their favorite hotel overlooking the flowing river.

Laura slowed her pace even more when she remembered the magical moment he had declared his deepest love for her on that lustrous summer weekend they sailed to Catalina Island. How they lay on the beach basking in the radiant sunshine while snuggled in each other's arms. How special she felt realizing he'd never really known love like this in his lifetime. Even though Laura knew he'd truly loved and served his wife well till the tragic end of her life, he'd admitted that his love for Laura was different and far stronger. She also knew he was unbearably alone without her.

She treasured that enchanting night in the cliffside cabin high above the rocky coves where he held her so tightly, pledging unending devotion until she breathlessly surrendered her complete love to him. And how afterward the guilt of her adultery only briefly haunted her. She knew then that guilt would be a useless deterrent to her infidelity. She'd never be able to resist his torrid advances. *Never. Not even on the night she would leave him.* She remembered when she got to the hotel yesterday how she couldn't help submitting to him—once more to become one being with him. *One more time before she had to leave him...*

A nearly empty Chardonnay bottle packed in an ice bucket and partially filled wineglasses sat on the floor next to the bed. Lipstick traces smeared one rim. The wind outside the hotel-room window was beginning to whirl as dusk faded through the heavy rain clouds forming from the northwest. Sprinkles ricocheted off the heavy glass pane. The room was shadowy, with only a small wall lamp casting a slight glow off the far wall. A vase of long-stemmed red roses sat on the nightstand, giving off a sweet bouquet. Shoes were scattered just inside the doorway. The rest of their clothes were draped carelessly over the side chair next to the window.

The entwined couple lay silent on the bed, looking into each other's eyes. Only their fervent breathing broke the fragile silence. Her breasts perked as he slowly ran his finger down the middle of her bare chest, coming to rest on her stomach. Yielding to his burning desire, her body began to tremble as he lightly fondled the elastic band of her panties. He gradually slid them down her legs and off.

Jonathan bent down and kissed her. Laura's mouth responded excitedly as she began to writhe passionately. He withdrew, gently brushing her cheek with his lips, moving down to her neck, whispering into her ear, "I adore every fiber of your body. I can't live without you any more."

"Yes, love," she purred, "Yes." She closed her eyes. A sudden twinge of guilt swept through her heart when she realized what she would have to tell him tonight. But now she couldn't resist him. *She'd break it to him at dinner,* she decided. Losing all reasoning, she wrapped her legs around him, drawing his naked body flush with hers. Her ardent breathing and erotic writhing increased as his passionate kisses moved slowly toward her breast.

Laura stopped on the riverwalk as the ache and pangs of that lovemaking memory began to overtake and weaken her. The farther she wandered from the hotel and Jonathan, the emptier she felt. Her head began to throb from her growing agony and feelings of hopelessness. Could she face life without Jonathan? And if so, could she ever tell Monte what had happened? If so, would he forgive her? *Could he forgive her?* Would the joyful life she'd once relished be forgivingly returned to her? Or would she lose Monte too, ending up truly alone?

Laura looked up at the coal-black horizon as she felt the heavy rain begin to fall against her face. *Damn!* she thought. *How had she dashed off and forgotten her umbrella?* She turned, seeing that the hotel was out of viable reach and the coffee shop was still too far away. She'd find shelter until the storm subsided.

Quickly stepping off the sidewalk, she hurried across the grass and brushed through a heavy thicket to seek refuge under a tall Douglas fir.

Laura ducked her head and crouched under the canopy of leafy branches dangling just above the ground. It was dark and dank in the small gnarled cover, but somewhat dry. Feeling fairly protected, she decided she'd wait until the rain stopped before she continued on her way. She felt around at the base of the tree, finding a dry bed of yellowing, dead needles. She turned, leaning her back against the trunk. Sitting down, she wrapped her arms around her knees and pulled her legs up against her chest.

She reached up and pulled a handful of long dark-green needles from a drooping branch. She pinched them between her forefinger and thumb, inhaling the tart, spicy aroma. It reminded her of Christmas as she pressed them against her cheek and set them in a bunch at the base of the tree. She continued to snatch more needles, adding them to the cluster on the ground until she had formed a small celestial star similar to the one that ornamented the peak of the annual Christmas tree that decorated their living room. She stared at it, smiling as she again thought about how she would show Tamra and Monte a joyous holiday season. Tamra loved Christmas. She was now old enough to fully enjoy it. They'd have a delightful time this year.

The rain fell harder. A heavy drizzle began sifting through the branches onto her damp scarf, wetting her hair. Although she was growing uncomfortable, her harsh physical position mattered little. Her real suffering continued to center around her internal grief. Was her marriage still sacred? *No*, she conceded. Yet it could be rebuilt. *Why not? She must love Monte...she must!* She had married him.

She laid her head back, remembering how thrilled she was on the day they first met as college juniors at Oregon State. How she had secretly adored the popular football player through those first collegiate years, but was always shy about trying to meet him until she felt secure with her own maturity and scholarly achievements. She knew the athletically gifted, good-looking and suave quarterback was very much a ladies-man and wouldn't easily commit to anything serious. And she was determined to have him in no other way but *committed*. To this day she was inwardly proud to have attracted him with her irresistible charm and budding self-confidence through her own social achievements—and they soon became inseparable.

After they graduated, they decided to separate as he gave up his eluding football aspirations to tend only to achieving his doctorate of psychology in behavior therapy, while she returned home to Portland to concentrate on honing her artistic skills through various graduate studies at the local university. But then how he suffered being apart from her and persuaded her to marry him and move back to Eugene. How they happily nurtured their togetherness, and within a year, culminating that union with their healthy, blonde-haired daughter, Tamra.

And how they were happy through the years as they prospered in their respective careers, she gaining fame in Portland artistic circles and he in his private psychiatry practice in Eugene until he swiftly gained the respect of peers and superiors alike, earning a professorship at his alma mater.

Yes, she decided, wiping the mist from her eyes. She'd put the pieces of her once charmed life back together with Monte. They couldn't let all those memorable years go to waste. She'd even tell him the truth about Jonathan. She was sure he'd respond positively when he found out why she'd drifted. After all, part of the problem might stem from his heavy workload and his growing neglect, wasn't it? Regardless, things between them could be patched up. Without Jonathan it could be done. *It had to be done!*

But her righteous justification abruptly failed her. Her longing for Jonathan lingered too strongly. She was rapidly becoming more dazed as she thought about Jonathan alone and abandoned. *Alone, without her.* Her eyes welled up as the aching in her head increased. Unable to think, she leaned her head against the tree and closed her eyes. The rain spattered off her soaked hair and down her face. *"Oh God, help me through this,"* Laura mumbled. *"Please help me through this."*

Drained from the pressure of distress and lack of sleep, she dropped her head forward, cradling it in her hands as she wept uncontrollably. The wind began to whistle in a ghostly fashion through the barren treetops as the atmosphere darkened.

She suddenly froze, cocking her head as she thought she heard a rustling noise behind her. Lifting her head, she pondered her remote position. She glanced around, seeing only spongy leaves and sodden thickets. She failed to make out the walkway from where she was situated. She was too far away. She wiped the drizzle off her watch: six-ten.

Exhausted, she leaned back against the tree and closed her eyes, trying to think out her next move. She'd rest a few more minutes before continuing on to the coffee shop.

It would have to get lighter soon, and the rain would surely slacken, she thought as she began to drift. Suddenly she heard more strange noises. Petrified, her eyes flashed opened when she sensed it was not the wind. Something or someone was there. Her head bobbed anxiously as her eyes darted futilely around the desolate greenery. She turned to look behind her, but saw only a thick canopy of shrubs. *There must be someone or something in there!* she feared. *A vagrant? A rapist? Maybe a mad dog. Yet maybe it was just her nerves.*

Regardless, she was now intensely concerned over her obscure location. She crooked her head around the tree. "Hello, is there someone there?" she called nervously. "Hello?"

Hearing only more noises closer to her, she pulled out the precious diamond pendant Jonathan had given her and gripped it tightly. She realized that even if she wasn't in danger, she'd been very foolish to take a chance in this area at this time of day. She crawled forward from under the branches, deciding to get out of there the quickest way possible. Yet she hesitated and looked down, realizing how tightly she was clutching the pendant, thinking only of Jonathan, *not Monte*. She needed to be with him now, warm and safely wrapped in his loving arms. *Not Monte's arms. She now knew she loved him like she'd never loved anyone else before.*

Her inner revelation stunned her. *My God, I am being told. It's a sign! It's Jonathan who is my life now, not Monte.* Why sacrifice both their lives when the only thing that mattered was that they were together. Thoughts raced through her mind. She now fully realized that she'd never been loved or needed the way Jonathan loved her; nor had she ever loved that way in return. *I have to go back to him! I love him! We can't part. I'll leave Monte. Tamra will soon understand. She'll have to.*

Scrambling free of the branch cover, she stood, but got no farther.

The vise-like grip around her neck silenced her, pulling her backward against the attacker's body.

Struggling fiercely, they bounced against the branches, falling to the ground.

She was no match for him as he pinned her between his legs, her neck being crushed in the crook of his arm. Her knotted, drenched scarf was being pulled down over her face and around her neck with his other hand.

Her eyes bulged in shock, as she realized she was being strangled! *Murdered!*

The pressure on her neck increased as the rope-like scarf replaced the forearm. It tightened against her throat!

Unable to utter a sound, she grabbed frantically for the tight silky weapon, but only managed to wrench her head around. She feebly reached up and pawed at his wrists, facing the man's murderous glower. Her surprised eyes begged him to stop! To listen to her plea! Begging him for mercy!

He only returned a loathing glare.

Weakening, she now lay supine under the branches. She gasped, her terror-filled eyes began to blur as her grasp on the unyielding scarf fell away.

With gritting teeth, he tightened his weapon to snuff out the last of her life.

As the moments passed, her internal cries ceased and the greenery of the trees faded from her opened eyes. As her body slackened in finality, she reached over to where the elegant heart pendant had slipped from her grasp. With her last ounce of strength, she pushed the pendant next to the soppy mound of pine needles that had been carefully crafted into the shape of a star at the base of the tree.

Chapter Six

The detective, early morning, Hillsboro, Oregon

Chief detective, First Lieutenant Brian Gregory Kierzek of Portland Homicide put his hand against the wall to steady himself as he dipped his foot into the freshly drawn bath water. Finding the temperature agreeable, he turned and slipped off his robe, hanging it on the door hook. Carefully stepping into the bathtub, he lowered his tired bones into a sitting position. He reached over and turned the "H" faucet on full, filling the tub to the overflow drain. He leaned back, sliding down the rear of the tub to maneuver his lanky body into a coiled position until the steamy water covered his chest. Soaking restfully, he closed his eyes, emitting a faint sigh of comfort.

He opened his eyes at the soft knock on the door, hearing, "It's me, love. Just brought you some coffee."

He looked up at the cheerful face of his wife, who was holding a cup of fresh brew. "Thanks," he said, returning a smile as he pushed himself upward to take the cup.

She stepped back. "You look quite mellow this morning," she said. "Enjoying your day off?"

"Sure am. I haven't soaked in a bath since last year," he answered, sipping on his coffee. "Sounded good when I was lying there not able to sleep in." He looked up and grinned. "And I was right. It feels great."

"I heard you come in last night," she said, matching his grin. "How was the poker game?"

"It was okay," he answered nonchalantly. "Won a few bucks. Drank a few beers." He laid his head back again. "But that goddamn smoke really gets to me now, though I admit I kinda miss my pipe."

"It's the best thing you ever did for yourself," she said, "quitting that nasty habit."

"Only because my heart wasn't into smoking any more," he cracked.

"That's not funny, love," she replied in a serious tone. "And will you please get some exercise today and make your doctor's appointment for your checkup. It's past due."

"Yes, dear, you're right," he said resignedly. "I suppose it is time for the yearly back-end ram test."

"Those organs aren't the ones I'm worried about, and you know it."

"Why do you always preach at me when I'm relaxing and don't want to move?" he muttered.

"Because you're looking tired and rundown again lately," she replied. "I'm worried about you."

"I'm just getting too old, I guess," he said with a chuckle.

"No, you're not," she replied. "Forty-nine is hardly too old. You just need to take care of yourself more, that's all."

"Yes, dear," he replied, reaching over to set the cup on the edge of the tub. He leaned backward and closed his eyes again, deadpanning, "You know what? I figured out yesterday I can retire early—in about ten years, if we hold our spending down."

She laughed. "Okay, I'll begin cutting back on the groceries."

"Thanks," he said, winking. "By the way, is Rob off to school?"

"Yes," she replied. "His girlfriend, Valerie, picked him up. He's pretty excited about being a college freshman this year."

"Yeah, I figured he would be," he answered. "It won't be long and he'll be gone." He began to drift, adding rhetorically, "Where in hell does the time go?"

"Oh, that reminds me," she said softly so as not to interrupt his increasing serenity. "You'll have the whole day to yourself. I'm meeting Carolyn for lunch, then we're going to hang out downtown and look for a winter coat. I'll be home in plenty of time for dinner."

"Okay, dear," he answered lethargically, "have a good time."

"Now, love, please, call the clinic and make your checkup appoint…" She turned at the sudden ringing of the phone.

His eyes flickered annoyingly at the ringing, but he disregarded the blunt interruption when his wife mentioned it must be Carolyn as she left the bathroom to answer the phone.

Minutes later he heard the knock on the door again. He looked up at his wife. Her look wasn't as cheerful. "Bad news," she said.

"Huh?" he replied, raising his head. "What?"

"It's Captain Ruskin. He needs to talk to you."

"What the hell does he want?" he grumbled, frowning. "It's my first day off in months."

"He knows that, but he's still insistent. He says it's really important."

Kierzek sighed in frustration. "That man is going to drive me crazy," he complained, then asked, "What time is it anyway?"

"About eight-ten."

"Aw, shit," he mumbled, angling himself upward to grab the towel from the rack. "Tell him to hang on, I'll be right there."

"Okay," she agreed, leaving the doorway.

He stepped from the tub, dried himself off and grabbed his robe from the door hook. He walked to the bedroom phone, muttering a couple of obscenities.

Sallie Jean Kierzek turned and wrinkled her face when she saw her husband coming down the stairs dressed in his usual workday attire: slacks, button-down-collar dress shirt, sans a tie. His ID badge was clipped to the breast pocket of his black blazer.

He stopped on the bottom stoop to adjust the high-ride hip holster that retained his Smith & Wesson .40-caliber pistol. He'd never really liked the new holster, bulging and grating against his side. He preferred his more comfortable original-issue shoulder setup. However, he was obligated to set the example for the rookies with the new easy-to-draw-and-aim arrangement. Whenever the issue arose at headquarters, he'd never openly protest but would quip inwardly, "There's hardly a need for quick-draw gunslingers in Portland."

"So much for your day off," she said as he stepped off the stoop and entered the kitchen. "What's so important that you have to go in for, anyway?"

"Not sure yet," he answered, reaching into the refrigerator for some orange juice. He filled a small glass and gulped it down. She waited patiently until he put the glass in the sink and turned toward her. "They found some woman in the riverpark this morning," he said. "She'd been murdered...strangled."

She grimaced. "That's awful, but can't they take care of things until tomorrow?"

He shook his head. "Ruskin says it doesn't look like a run-of-the-mill snuff. I understand she was pretty important in the social arena around here," he replied. "She's from Eugene, but was always up here mingling with the artistic crowds...whatever that means."

"So what," she replied, irritated, following behind him as he walked to the front entrance. "Can't they wait until tomorrow for you to begin your investigation? The coroner will have plenty to do today."

He remained silent, dipping his head to look out the side window, seeing the cloudy weather.

She pressed further, asking, "Why can't that rookie detective, Todd Jameson, handle the preliminaries? I think Ruskin does this just to upset you," she continued, yet she knew her appeal was a waste of breath. He was loyal to the core, setting out to do what was expected of him.

Kierzek straightened, grabbing his coat from the top metal claw of the coat rack and turning toward her. Draping the coat over his forearm, he answered, "Well, you're aware of the police chief's policy of wanting to be notified immediately of any murder, aren't you?"

She nodded.

He continued, "I guess when he got wind of who the victim was, he ordered Ruskin to put the senior people on it from the beginning. So I have to go and meet Officer Cuyler at the crime scene."

She shook her head in disgust over her husband's day off being ruined as she watched him grab his plain wool business hat from the rack. He aligned the small decorative feather in the hatband, and put it on. *A man deserves a little vanity,* he mused to himself as he gripped the top and snugly pulled the brim down over his balding crown. Reaching down, he plucked the small umbrella from the stand, stuffing it into the hip pocket of the coat.

She opened the front door for him. "You sure you don't want some breakfast before you go?"

"Nah," he said. "I'm sure Cuyler will have some coffee and doughnuts there."

She reached up and gave him a goodbye kiss before he turned and made his way into the dark gray morning, saying, "Have a nice time with Carolyn today, dear. I hope to see you at dinner."

"Okay," she answered weakly from the doorway, rubbing her forehead, deeply lined from being a cop's wife for so many years. *Fat chance,* she thought

CHAPTER SEVEN

Early morning, Riverpark Towers Hotel

Jonathan rolled over onto his side, feeling the stinging wet clothes twisting tightly on his body. He gradually cracked open his eyes. Disoriented and uncomfortable, he ran his hand across his wet shirt and pants. He looked down at his spongy, smudged socks. Raising his head, he managed to scan the empty hotel room, slowly realizing where he was. Muddling through last night's breakup with Laura, he remembered he was alone. Yet why was he soaking wet? He tried to piece the puzzle together, but failed. His head splitting from an excruciating hangover, he vigorously stroked his stressed temples while glancing out the window. The morning layer of steel-gray air swelling up outside only surpassed the ashen pall enveloping the stillness in the room. *More rain!* he thought, disgusted. *All it does is fucking rain up here!*

He glanced at the clock on the bedside table: 9:05. He hoisted himself up and swung his feet around, gathering his balance before standing. He took off his shirt and threw it in the corner next to his garment bag. Grabbing a clean bath towel from the bathroom, he draped it around his shoulders and walked to the phone.

"Mornin'," he mumbled groggily into the receiver, "Timmers, in 814. Please send up a pot of strong black coffee...really strong. Thanks."

He hung up and fumbled for the airline ticket sitting next to his wallet on the desk. *Need to get out of here today*, he thought. *Staying here will only prolong the agony.* He'd call after his head cleared, he decided as he looked over at the bourbon bottle tipped askew in a slight pool of the stale remains at the end of the desk. He then looked back over his shoulder at the slushy ice-bucket, containing an empty bobbing wine bottle and two used wine glasses, sitting on the floor at the foot of the bed. *Damn! Only more grim reminders of last night's break with Laura.*

Turning back, his wearied eyes moistened as he angrily brushed the bourbon bottle into the wastebasket. *Why!?* he lamented, hanging his head. *Why did she have to do this? They could've worked things out if only she'd given it more time.*

He walked to the window and leaned his palms on the sill, peering into the diminishing rush hour. Last-minute stragglers angled their cars from the street into the office-building parking lots. White-collars, trying to avoid the final bell, scurried around the rippling puddles left over from the passing rainstorms.

Feeling painfully alone, he wondered where Laura was. Where had she gone after she'd walked out on him? Again, he tried to sort out all of last night's events, but failed to get past the part where he thought he saw her heading into the darkness toward the park. *Or did he? Goddam booze,* he cursed inwardly as he struggled to recall what had happened after that. Was she now with Rebecca? Was she back in Eugene? He frowned. *Maybe she was already lying in Monte's arms confessing all, begging his forgiveness. Vowing never to stray again.*

Frustrated, he pounded his fist on the windowsill, wondering why she had done it this way. Bringing him up here to leave him. Why not a letter or a phone call? Why not wait until she was in Laguna next month to tell him? Why did she have to do it before his long trip to the East Coast? *Oh, yeah,* now he remembered her saying that telling him before his trip would allow them a few weeks to get over their split while he wasn't close by. *Yeah, right!* he thought, *how convenient.*

He recalled how only three days ago he was basking in the sunshine in front of his seaside condo thinking about his upcoming trip to the East Coast to meet with his agent to sign a lucrative new publishing contract. And how they would follow that up with a fun-filled week of deep-sea fishing. But then that unexpected phone call came in from Laura on that carefree Saturday morning, only three days ago...

◆◆◆

The California sun was high and brilliant, burning away the last of the coastal marine cloud layer and bringing on the beginning weekend crowd to fully populate the beach. Bathers were gingerly frolicking in the cooling surf, as others began to prepare their picnic lunches farther back from the shoreline.

Jonathan cautiously stepped down the steep wooden cliff-stairs with a small cooler in one hand and a canvas chaise lounge tucked under the crook of his other arm. A large beach towel was slung over his shoulder.

Striding off the bottom landing into the pebbled sand, he turned and made his way down the beach to find a secluded spot next to a shallow rocky cove. He plopped the cooler and chair into the damp sandbank, before spreading out the towel. Slipping off his terrycloth bathing shirt, he dropped it on the towel. He straightened out the chair and secured the reclining seatback in the quarter position. Shuffling out of his sandals, he sat down on the front rail. He reached over and retrieved a bottle of chilled tonic water from the cooler before leaning back in the chair, sporting a languid smile.

He sipped on his refreshing drink as the warmth from the blazing sun immediately began to soak into his skin. Resting the icy bottle against his chest, he closed his eyes as he listened to the heavy breakers crashing against the gigantic boulders and jagged outcroppings that extended far out into the whitecaps. The seagulls flew closely overhead, screeching excitedly as they scavenged the area for scraps of food being generously flung about the beach by the picnickers.

Jonathan soon lapsed into deep tranquil thought about where his life was heading. He was healthy, trim and felt good. His professional life was equally as prosperous, as he had just agreed to author two more books for his publisher, acquiring a sizable advance in return. It would be fun traveling to New York to meet with David and sign the contract before they'd head to the Florida Keys for some deep-sea fishing. He hadn't been to Florida since he'd been stationed in the Navy at Mayport, right after college. Maybe he'd even stop in Jacksonville for a little reminiscing at some of his old haunts. Yes, the upcoming month promised to be very exciting, and loads of fun.

However, his mood suddenly dimmed as he thought about Laura and how he'd miss her. His love and dependency on her companionship had grown considerably over the last few weeks. And he was feeling lonelier without her as the days wore on. It was agonizing when, on their rendezvous in Laguna Beach last week, they had had to part so soon because her husband had called unexpectedly. Monte had wanted her to come home early because he yearned for her. And then how guilty she'd felt for leaving him while she packed and left for home. He realized that her being lovingly attentive to two men and a daughter was taking its toll on her.

Moreover, their twice-weekly phone calls just weren't cutting it any longer. He couldn't go on being away from her. And he knew she felt as miserable as he did about their separation. She'd have to leave Monte. It would be a painful process for all concerned, but there was no other way. He'd talk to her right after he returned from Florida, while she was in Laguna for her monthly art showing.

Feeling comfortable, he began to fade as he finished his water and dropped the empty bottle onto the towel. He turned his head to one side and began to doze.

The pulsating ring jolted Jonathan forward in the lounge chair. Gathering his wits, he reached across the cooler to retrieve his small cellular phone from his shirt breast pocket. Pulling down the receiver flap, he punched the "on" button and said groggily, "Hello?...Oh, hi, sweetheart! What a surprise!"

Immediately roused by Laura's voice, he sat upright...."Yes, I was napping on the beach. And I want you to know you were the last thing on my mind before I fell asleep," he said through a widening smile...."Yes, I'm alert. ...Portland, Monday, so soon? Umm, sure, why not. I don't really have anything planned until after next week when I go to New York to meet with my publisher. I know my travel agent isn't reachable today, but I'll go up and make the arrangements myself. I'm sure I can get in there somehow....Okay, call me later if you get a chance or I'll see you on Monday....Bye, I love you, too."

Jonathan shook off his remaining drowsiness and rose from the chair. Slipping on his shirt and sandals, he began plodding through the sand toward the cliff stairs—dashing home to make the impromptu flight and hotel arrangements for Portland. He didn't know why Laura was going to be there on Monday, but he'd find out when he saw her. He was sure she'd thought of something so she could spend some time with him before he went on his long New York trip.

As he bounded up the stairs, his mixed emotions were increasing. As always, he was elated about seeing her so soon, yet he was becoming frayed from the roller-coaster consequences of the affair—both physically and mentally. The unknowable day-to-day situations that arose were wearing on his nerves. Worse, it was now affecting his writing. The emotional strain was constantly present. Somehow he'd have to be more stable in his lifestyle when he began his next book. Or his creativity would suffer greatly. *Yes, something had to change.*

Scurrying through the door of his condo, he decided that while he was in Portland he would ask her to brave the divorce with Monte. They could get through it together. After all, she'd always hated the thought of cheating on Monte, and they both knew that she now loved Jonathan more. Yes, he'd visit the jeweler on the way to the airport and buy her a present. He'd give her the token of his love on Monday night in their favorite spot, the hotel lobby bar, after dinner when they were both relaxed. He'd ask her then to leave Monte. She'd surely agree. She was ready. *He knew it.*

Feeling secure with his decision, he sat down at his desk and pulled out the phone directory to make the arrangements for his sudden trip to Portland.

The loud knocking brought Jonathan back to his senses. "Room service," he heard bellowing through the door as he turned from the window. He grabbed a couple of singles from the desk and walked to the door, opening it.

Noticing Jonathan's wet pants and socks, the room service attendant seemed perplexed when he walked in to put the coffee tray on the sink countertop; however, he said nothing as Jonathan signed the bill. He knew Jonathan was haggard for some reason and in no mood to talk. The attendant quickly left after Jonathan handed him the gratuity.

Jonathan promptly poured a cup of the hot coffee and took a few swallows. The caffeine immediately began to stimulate his mind. He refilled the cup and leaned up against the countertop, gathering his wits.

His thoughts again turned to Laura, realizing she had had to bring him up here to break off the affair. She couldn't have done it over the phone or definitely not in California. It was obvious she needed to be able to easily escape afterward.

Anyway, he knew there was no reason to hang out any longer in Portland. Even if she were to change her mind and decide to see him again, he was sure it wouldn't be soon. If she had changed her mind, she'd already have been back with him.

His ache from the loss of her was growing as he walked to the phone. He set his coffee on the desk and pulled out the chair. Seeing Laura's umbrella lying in the seat startled him. He winced as he remembered how last night she had told him it was a recent present from Monte. He thought about how he would get it back to her without causing a row. He knew she'd be worried about it. He picked it up and laid it on the desktop.

Sitting down, he looked at his airline ticket packet and dialed the 800 phone number listed on the envelope. Reaching an agent, he directly requested the flight change. He listened as she gave him the options, then responded impassively, "I don't care about the extra cost. Please book me on the 4:30 flight." He noted the flight information on the ticket, thanked the agent and depressed the cradle plunger, then released it. He called the front desk, easily acquiring a late checkout.

Beginning to feel better, he finished his coffee and walked to the bathroom, discarding the rest of his wet clothes on the way.

After a long soapy shower, he lay down on the bed and set the alarm for one forty-five. He'd then freshen up, pack his bag and decide on what to do about a late lunch before his flight left.

Laying his head back on the pillow, he turned toward the window to see the clouds beginning to break after only a slight sprinkle. Staring outward, he thought how difficult it would be going on with his life without Laura. How laborious his writing career might become. How could he be creative with her loss constantly on his mind? He knew the memories of her wouldn't fade quickly—if at all. She had been with him to every one of his favorite places in

Southern California, including his bed. He turned over and closed his eyes in mental pain.

As he began to drop off, he decided he'd just have to deal with the loneliness if she didn't come back to him. He'd handled loneliness before. He could do it again. But then what would happen when she came to Laguna next month for her weekend gallery visit? *Could they resist each other*? he wondered. She would certainly come. She wouldn't forsake her Southern California cultural connections. *Would she?* No, maybe she'd postpone her visit for a few months, but eventually she'd have to come back. *Wouldn't she?* Maybe she'd even come back to *him. Maybe. Wouldn't she?* He fell off to sleep.

CHAPTER EIGHT

The death scene

The boxy blue sedan cautiously made its way through the buzzing crowd that had quickly gathered along the street in front of the Riverpark Towers hotel. Seeing his way clear, Detective Kierzek pulled up behind the two squad cars that were parked across the walk to signify a blocking of the park entrance. He noticed that the rotating beacons atop the cruisers were off, signaling that the area was secured. Cutting the engine, he paused, amazed at the numerous Portland and Oregon state police officers scattered along the riverwalk and into the park area. He tried to remember a crime that had drawn this much force. Rigid and watchful, the officers eliminated any bystander intrusion or interference from the throng of reporters trying to get an early scoop from the death scene. Looking into his rear-view mirror, Kierzek saw a couple of TV station news vans parked under the hotel entrance apron.

They've moved in quickly, he thought as he exited the car, glimpsing up at the hint of sunlight breaking through the mid-morning clouds. Deciding that the storms were moving out of the region, he shed his trench coat and laid it over the passenger seat-back before closing and locking the door.

Recognizing Kierzek, a veteran TV reporter and his accompanying cameraman quickly emerged from the crowd, hollering out, "Detective Kierzek, can you tell us anything yet? Who was the victim? We hear it was a prominent high society woman! What can you tell us? Detective Kierzek…?"

Kierzek shook his head animatedly. "Nothing yet. I just got here," he answered loudly in no particular direction. "I won't have any comments until after I talk to the officer in charge." He chuckled to himself when he heard the cameraman say to the reporter, "Forget it, Harv—you know he ain't gonna say anything yet."

Kierzek bounded over the curb and walked up to the lead officer, who was standing behind a metal sawhorse serving as a police barricade. "Morning," he said. "I guess this is the hot spot of the city, huh?"

"Right, lieutenant," the officer replied with a slight smile, looking over Kierzek's ID badge. "It is if you're a cop on duty or a news reporter, anyway. I thought it was a policeman's convention when I got here," he quipped.

"Yeah," Kierzek agreed with a chuckle. "Sergeant Cuyler around?"

"Affirmative, sir," the officer answered crisply, stepping back to point down the walk. "He's down at the crime scene. Captain Ruskin made him the blue in charge until you got here."

"Thanks," Kierzek replied, looking past the officer toward the heart of the wooded park.

"It's quite a ways to the scene, sir," the officer advised. "I'm sure you could get your car down there. The medical examiner got his van through okay."

"Nah," Kierzek said, beginning to make his way down the winding walkway, his words trailing behind him. "I need the exercise."

Yet even though he knew he needed the exercise, that wasn't the main reason he wanted to walk. He wanted the extra time to gear up his professional façade. To don his cool calculating just-a-job demeanor for what he was about to encounter. He detested this part of his duties: investigating the initial homicide. He'd never really become used to looking over the corpse, regardless of its condition. He had trouble detaching himself emotionally from death. He appreciated life and the simple blessed things that it offered—probably too much for this profession. Why did a life have to end in this fashion? *Such a waste,* he would always say.

Regardless, he was seasoned and dedicated, knowing he was best suited for this police work. And the rest of his responsibilities surrounding the crime were always rewarding and interesting, although he wished they weren't ever necessary. He realized that the municipal force needed him with his uncanny, intuitive gift for solving crimes; always gleaning only the most important details from the big picture, and always knowing which fruitless details to swiftly disregard.

Moreover, he was proud of his ten-year homicide resolution rate of nearly ninety percent. Especially when the department's rate as a whole measured only about sixty. He always kept the other ten percent of his unsolved cases in a flexible folder on the floor next to his desk. Even though Captain Ruskin continually nagged at him to store them in the "unsolved" file and get on with things, he kept them near, hopeful that one day they would also somehow be successfully closed.

Indeed, he knew he was in the right profession. At times like this he'd frequently recall what his peers had told him many times: *Kierzek, you didn't pick this profession; it picked you.*

Anyway, even though Portland had a rampant heroin problem and the gang activity was increasing, the city didn't experience much fatal violence compared to other large cities its size. He'd often say that he'd never be able to handle working in large urban areas like Los Angeles, with its turbulent crime rate.

Nevertheless, rightly suited or not, he'd made a decision to request a transfer to the burglary division after the first of the year. He'd discuss the move with Ruskin in October. Although he knew the transfer might cost him a few grades and a little take-home pay, the peace of mind would be worth it. He wanted to finish out his career in a more moderate position—albeit it was still crime.

He felt that he'd earned the break. And the move was fairer to his family, especially after his heart attack last year had put them all on a constant health alert. This was regardless of the fact that the attack was mild and had been directly related to his being overweight and to his heavy smoking—harmful conditions that he'd managed to correct with the continual guidance of his wife.

Besides, even if he did transfer, he'd still be around for consultation if requested by the homicide division. Who knows, maybe this would be his last murder case. *Right,* he thought sarcastically. Ruskin probably wouldn't allow that even after his transfer was approved. *Who would the man have to pester any more?* Kierzek chuckled.

But the future mattered little at the moment. For now he was preparing to face a young woman who had been savagely murdered alongside a grassy riverwalk. And from what he was told, it had been a distinguished life that had been snuffed out. Although that part made no difference to him. All life was important in some way to someone. To him all victims were ranked the same: at the top of the scale. All that mattered was that it appeared she'd had her life taken away unmercifully. He shook his head as he hurried his pace down the walk.

As he turned the bend and headed for the core of the riverpark, he saw the heavy activity taking place inside a large rectangular area cordoned off by bright yellow police-line barrier tape. Wooden stakes had been pounded into the ground, strategically arranged to serve as temporary cornerstones. The atmosphere was hushed as everyone moved around slowly and spoke in lowered voices— strange, but typical behavior whenever a corpse lay in their midst. *The death scene*, he thought. He shook his head, again amazed at the number of police personnel.

Several officers stood guard on either end of the sector. Two others were positioned in the field across the riverwalk to ensure that the vagrants, curious on-lookers and a few rookie reporters with their notebooks in hand kept their distance. Three more state police officers were deployed on the river's edge, soundly protecting that flank.

Across the walk, adjacent to the scene, three squad cars and the medical examiner's van were parked single file on the grass. A black camper-van was parked a short distance down from the others, with the back doors open. The lettering on the side read: **Portland Crime Scene Search Unit** in large white letters.

He squinted to focus when he saw a dark blue minivan in front of the investigation vehicle, containing two men dressed in lab garb. He could barely make out the lettering **OSP** on the side of the van as it pulled away, but he immediately realized they were from the Oregon State Investigation Squad. *Interesting,* he thought, *everybody seems to be involved. Even the elite state boys.*

He returned his focus to inside the yellow boundaries, where a team of crime-scene investigators were meticulously picking at potential evidence around the site. They collected small samples of the upturned soil, grasping for anything that might look unnatural. One technician was on the ground carefully pulling apart the bushes that led into the heavy shrubbery surrounding the tall Douglas firs.

A police photographer was finishing the last of the shots, while his partner silently noted the technical characteristics of each exposure, ensuring that they had covered the complete scene, including the immediate outside parameters.

In the far corner of the sector, a wide aluminum folding table was set up with a tall pleated umbrella leaning against it, ready to be erected against the elements if needed. On the table sat a box of latex gloves, empty garbage bags and glass vials. A black case lay open, containing tweezers, scissors and a sharp paring knife. Notebooks, containing a few crime lab notes, and small gray adhesive labels sat next to the vials. On the ground, oversize tongs, grass clippers and a pointed turning spade lay spread out for easy access if necessary to dig or clear away obstructions that might conceal any possible evidence.

Kierzek diverted his gaze to the opposite corner. Standing rigid, he inhaled deeply when he saw the still bulge lying near the edge of the sidewalk, covered with a black body tarp.

Meanwhile, the Portland blue in charge, Edward Boyd Cuyler, a muscle-sculptured ex-Marine, had been standing next to the medical examiner's van when he spotted Kierzek approaching. The officer quickly headed up the walk as Kierzek resumed his pace. They met and stopped about forty-five yards from the scene.

"Morning, Ed," Kierzek said, giving his trusted street partner a hearty handshake before slowly turning toward the scene. "This one looks major."

"It sure is, Brian," Cuyler agreed, following Kierzek's gaze toward the activity. "I understand the lady ranked quite highly on the Portland social scale. Even the police chief knew of her."

"I heard," Kierzek said nonchalantly as he looked over at another state police car slowly pulling up behind the medical examiner's van. "Christ, I'm surprised I don't see a bunch from the FBI." He pushed his hat back. "Well, like the wife said, so much for my day off," he added sarcastically.

"Yeah, the captain told me he had to call you in."

"He was here?"

"Uh huh, to look things over," Cuyler answered. "He left about twenty minutes ago."

Kierzek raised his eyebrows and pursed his lips. "He must be nervous," he cracked as he glanced at his watch, growing serious. "Did you get all the pertinent initial information recorded?"

"Yes," Cuyler said, pulling out a small notebook from his back pocket.

"Who were the first blues here besides you?"

"Kelting and Bressler from the first shift," Cuyler answered.

"When was the body discovered?"

"About 6:30," Cuyler replied, looking down at his small notepad. "A vagrant found her and alerted the hotel bellhop, who was just coming on duty. The bellhop called us."

"Where's the vagrant?"

"Dunno," Cuyler answered. "I guess he was pretty well spooked over the whole thing and lit out fast. But the bellhop says he's seen him around the park before. So Bressler's out looking for him."

Kierzek shook his head. "Shit," he cursed, "we need to find him." He paused, then asked, "Are you sure nobody else had been here before you guys?"

"No, I'm sure it was only us," Cuyler replied. "Ruskin called me at home and told me to officially secure the area. I got here about 7:30, and Kelting and Bressler were already here. The three of us never took our eyes off the spot until the medical examiner and the lab techies arrived."

"Any reason to think the body was disturbed before they got here?"

"No," Cuyler answered. "Bressler said it didn't look like it."

Kierzek furrowed his brow as he looked toward the body. "You mean it looks like she was killed right there, out in the open?"

"Can't tell for sure yet," Cuyler said. "But it would be pretty hard for someone to cart the body into the park and dump it without being seen. And the preliminary indications are that she was dead only a short time before the vagrant spotted her."

"Okay," Kierzek said, keeping his eyes on the scene. "I'd better get down there." He paused, turning back to Cuyler. "Oh, were there any mistakes made that you know of? Anything that might corrupt the chain of evidence?"

Cuyler raised his head to think. "No, Brian, I don't believe so," he answered confidently. "I knew by the way Ruskin was acting that we'd better treat this one extremely carefully."

"Good," Kierzek answered, starting to make his way to the scene. "Let's go."

Cuyler put a hand on Kierzek's arm. "I think I should prepare you," he said, "Dr. Richardson is really stressed this morning. He's all finished with the body here. And it didn't lighten his day any when he had to wait for you."

Kierzek shrugged. "Thanks, I'll keep that in mind." Continuing his stride, unconcerned, he added, "But that crotchety old bone-buzzard had better understand it was my day off. And he'd better be in a good mood when I meet him at the morgue this afternoon."

Cuyler smiled as he matched Kierzek's stride down the walkway, pleased that his boss was now in charge.

"Hello, guys," Kierzek said calmly as one of the officers lifted the yellow tape, allowing him to duck his gangly body underneath.

Walking to the table, Kierzek noticed the brown bag of personal effects. The attached label read: "Victim: Laura Bearnes." Looking over at Cuyler curiously, the officer mouthed quietly, "Ruskin did it. There's only the wallet. It's already been dusted for prints. He left her jewelry for Richardson to handle."

Nodding, Kierzek slipped on a pair of latex gloves. Sighing, he stepped over to the bulging tarp in the corner and knelt down.

Cuyler kept his distance, knowing not to crowd the observant detective at this moment. He'd learned to leave his boss alone while he adjusted to the realism of the grim discovery. All the activity in the immediate area slowly ceased. Everyone who didn't already know Kierzek's style in treating death had been briefed before he'd arrived. The casual veil of "just another corpse" had to be lifted. Moreover, any gallows humor, a prevalent undercurrent at all crime scenes, would be dealt with harshly if Kierzek got wind of it.

Cuyler flinched when he looked across the walk and saw the gray-haired man step from the driver's side of the medical examiner's van and slam the door. He quickly walked toward Kierzek, wearing a scowl. Cuyler knew the timing was all wrong for the doctor to approach Kierzek, but he wasn't in a favorable position to warn him.

Kierzek was oblivious to everything around him as he steadily pulled the body tarp back. His eyes followed the unfolding slack as he gently laid it on the woman's waist. He turned back and looked into her face, cringing when he saw her motionless but distinct features projecting through the gray-white pallor of death. Even now, in the primary stages of rigor mortis, she appeared beautiful and cultured, although void of *being*. He instinctively ran his index finger down her stiffening cheek and onto her neck, noticing that she still had some warmth in her body. He looked at his watch, shaking his head as he thought how violently she must have fought for the body to cool this gradually.

"What a waste," Kierzek mumbled as he looked down at her hands, enclosed in small plastic bags that were rubber-banded at the wrists. He looked at her freshly manicured nails and saw how they complemented the large diamond ring on her left hand. Moving back, he murmured again, "What a waste."

Portland's chief medical examiner, Dr. Carl James Richardson, stood behind the detective. "She's dead, all right," he said gruffly. "It's about time you got here."

Kierzek managed to ignore the growl as he cautiously pushed Laura's reddish hair back, seeing the knotty scarf still tightly twisted like a rope around her bruise-creased neck. He froze, realizing the horror she must have gone through during the brutal attack. He momentarily saw his wife lying there, or a daughter that he'd always wanted but never had.

The silence grew brittle as everyone except Dr. Richardson sensed Kierzek's deepening empathy for the woman. Cuyler knew this was Kierzek's toughest moment. He just cared too much—an unfortunate trait for a homicide detective. A trait that all detectives are supposed to "leave at home."

"How long you gonna be, Kierzek?" the doctor asked impatiently. "I need to get this body to the morgue."

Kierzek, usually slow to rage, couldn't control himself. He sprang up, looking down at the crusty medical examiner. "You insensitive ass," he seethed through a clenched whisper close to his face. "Don't you ever see one of your own lying dead? Or is it just another slab of meat to you?"

Richardson appeared stunned over Kierzek's furious outburst as he glanced around at the silent scene, then down at the still woman. Kierzek calmed himself and turned away when Richardson looked back up at him apologetically. "I'm sorry, you're right."

Kierzek bent down and re-covered the body with the tarp as two of the morgue assistants, who had stayed by the van with the collapsible gurney due to Cuyler's timely hand signal, began to move slowly across the walk.

Kierzek rose and stepped backward. "Okay, I'm finished."

Richardson motioned for the assistants to pick up the body, saying, "Easy, guys." He walked over to Kierzek. "I just want you to know your words will stay with me from now on," he said softly.

"Okay, thanks. Sorry I lost it," Kierzek said. "I'll meet you at the morgue for the autopsy this afternoon. Go ahead and do what you have to until I get there."

Richardson nodded, turned and walked away, following behind his assistants.

The detective remained mute as he watched the collapsible gurney being slid into the back of the van. The assistants climbed in and settled themselves, pulling the rear doors shut. Richardson entered the driver's side and a police officer got in the passenger side to accompany the body to the morgue and claim the clothes. As the van snaked carefully up the riverwalk, a couple of police cars followed.

Kierzek walked over to the table where Cuyler was standing as the activity inside the sector began to subside. Only a few lab technicians and police security personnel remained.

Cuyler looked at him questioningly. "Brian..."

"What?" Kierzek responded.

"I saw the terror in her eyes before Richardson closed them," Cuyler replied sensitively.

"I'm sure," Kierzek responded, rubbing the back of his neck to relieve his stress. "I'm sure," he repeated.

"I'd like to work very closely with you on this one, if I may," Cuyler said.

"You bet, Ed," Kierzek replied. "As closely as you like." He looked over at the batch of insignificant evidence setting on the table. He added discouragingly, "But it looks as though we don't have much to go on right now." He read a couple of the scant lab notes on the pad. "Maybe something forensic will turn up during the autopsy."

"I agree, there's not much at all to go on," Cuyler said, shaking his head. "No eyewitnesses that we know of. And everything's pretty clean around here. One guy from the lab team said he'd never seen a death scene like this. Nothing telltale or crucial...not even any incriminating footprints."

"And, unfortunately," Kierzek interrupted, "with no eyewitnesses, the only thing we have going for us is the scene."

"I'll keep it tightly secured until you give the word," Cuyler said.

"Yes, please do," Kierzek answered as he reached into the paper bag containing Laura's wallet. "It may take a few days," he added as he lifted it out and thumbed through the cash, which was still intact. "Doesn't seem to be any clear motive yet," Kierzek commented, setting the wallet on the table. "No robbery, and since she was fully dressed it doesn't appear to be a sex crime."

"Right, no apparent motive yet," Cuyler interjected. "Other than somebody wanted her gone."

"Yeah," Kierzek responded slowly, still somewhat disturbed. "How long do they think she's been dead?"

"About four or five hours. Richardson figures she was killed just before dawn."

Kierzek instinctively glanced at his watch, asking, "What the hell was she doing out here at that time?"

"Don't know yet," Cuyler answered. "But she must have been killed in the darkness. Someone would have probably seen it if not."

Kierzek nodded as he scanned the area. "Probably, but she could have been moved," he said, pointing to the heavy foliage leading into the string of Douglas firs. "Maybe from in there."

Cuyler followed his point, answering, "The team did find signs that someone had been traipsing around in there. I guess some of the branches had been broken off the trees, too."

"Really," Kierzek said as he walked over to the foliage.

Cuyler followed behind him, saying, "The techies looked it over, but couldn't find anything substantial. They figure it was possible she'd been murdered back there. But then again, some vagrants may also have been using it for shelter or something." He paused. "Anyway, who'd want to kill her there and then move her body out in the open?"

"Who knows," Kierzek answered, looking back over to where the body had been lying. "But it doesn't look as though there was any struggle over there. And it appears she'd put up a helluva fight. The neck bruises and the body temperature suggest that." He looked up at the brightening sky and thought a moment. "Hey, get on the radio to the station dispatcher. See if she can locate somebody who works with plants and trees." He paused while trying to think of the proper name.

"I think they call them botanists," Cuyler said.

"Right—botanist, thanks," Kierzek replied. "Maybe there's somebody at one of the colleges. Or maybe someone at that big nursery downtown could look over the branches and give us an expert estimate of when they were broken. I know it's a shot in the dark, but we don't have much to go on anyway."

"Okay, sure," Cuyler agreed, turning toward his patrol car. He nodded when he heard Kierzek add, "We need the botanist here as quickly as possible."

Kierzek turned back to the table and picked up Laura's wallet again. He opened it, looking at the ID window to read the driver's license, absolutely confirming the picture with the face he'd seen under the tarp. He pulled out the laminated photo packet, and was momentarily taken aback when he saw the picture of Laura posing with a professionally dressed man and a little girl. Laura's bright blue eyes were glittering and full of life. He knew it must be her husband and daughter posing with her in the picture.

Folding the packet closed, he wondered if Ruskin had contacted her husband in Eugene to come up and identify the body. And of course, being the husband, he'd be an immediate suspect and would have to be questioned. Regardless, he wondered if he'd have to be the one to tell Bearnes his wife was gone—brutally murdered. It wasn't always a required part of his duty to notify the next of kin, but it seemed to always fall on his shoulders; the one man the department felt could do it best, with his sensitive demeanor. Perhaps this time he'd been spared this part of the dirty work. Nevertheless, the family would have to know soon. This woman's gruesome fate could not be kept quiet much longer. He'd check in with Ruskin when Cuyler got back.

Kierzek looked into the top credit-card slot, and pulled out a tiny booklet. He thumbed through it before keying on a page. He had begun reading it when Cuyler approached the table.

"The dispatcher is pretty sure she'll find a botanist somewhere in the city," Cuyler reported. "She's working on it right now. And I just asked one of the lab boys to wait and coordinate the search activity. He told me he would."

"Good job," Kierzek said, appearing preoccupied as he reread the page. "Incidentally, do you know if they've reached the husband yet?"

"I'm not sure," Cuyler answered. "I know they weren't able to reach him earlier. Ruskin said he'd keep trying. We definitely have to question him."

"Right," Kierzek confirmed.

Cuyler watched him curiously. "Can I ask what you found?"

"Sure," Kierzek answered, holding up the booklet. "It's a wallet-size day calendar. Yesterday's entry reads: special class at PSU."

"That's gotta be Portland State," Cuyler interjected. "Ruskin mentioned that she taught college somewhere in the area."

Kierzek nodded. "It also has a woman's name and a local phone number." He looked at the page, adding, "Her name is Rebecca Newell."

"Maybe she's somebody Bearnes worked with yesterday," Cuyler said. "Maybe it's a lead."

"Could be," Kierzek replied, sliding the booklet into his pocket. "I'll keep it and call her later. Possibly she can at least tell us what Bearnes was doing in the park at that time of night, if nothing else."

"Maybe," Cuyler replied, looking around the area.

Kierzek put the wallet back in the bag and glanced up at the sky. "By the way, didn't it rain most of last night?"

"Yup," Cuyler answered. "In fact, it was still raining when we got here."

Kierzek shot him a questioning glance. "If she was out here on her own accord, then why in hell was she out here without any protection? No umbrella, nothing..." He threw his arms up in wonder and looked around. "In the middle of the park. When it was most likely raining..."

Cuyler shook his head and shrugged.

Kierzek turned back to the table with a puzzling look. "Make sure the lab boys search for an umbrella or something like it. It could be small and lying around the area. Hell, maybe she fought off her attacker with it and the killer tried to ditch it or something."

Cuyler nodded and quickly walked over to one of the technicians, relaying Kierzek's request. When he returned to the table he saw Kierzek staring at him, smiling.

"What?" Cuyler asked, seeing his boss's rare widening grin.

"Evidence and umbrellas aren't the only things missing around here," Kierzek responded buoyantly. "Where the hell are the doughnuts and coffee? I'm kinda hungry. You're not living up to your cop's reputation."

"Shit," Cuyler answered, mocking abuse through a smile. "Ruskin didn't give me time for anything. He told me to get my ass over here as soon as I could if I wanted to maintain my promotional mobility. Whatever the hell that means."

Kierzek laughed along with him, then slowly sobered. "C'mon, take me to my car," he said. "There's not much more you and I can do around here right now. I need to give the reporters a brief statement, and then we'll get something to eat."

"Right," Cuyler agreed. "I'll tell them to keep the area tightly secured."

"Good," Kierzek replied as they ducked under the yellow tape and began walking toward Cuyler's cruiser. "I'll come back here tomorrow morning and have another look after it dries out. Then we can probably clear the area."

"Okay," Cuyler said, as he fished for his keys before entering the driver's side.

As Kierzek entered the passenger side and closed the door, he said, "I'll check in with Ruskin on the way to find out if he's somehow reached the woman's husband in Eugene. Then we'll call Rebecca Newell from the restaurant and find out what she knows."

Chapter Nine

The suspect, mid-afternoon, Riverpark Towers

Jonathan tossed the garment bag flat onto the bed, clumsily cramming the plastic sack of sodden clothes into the bottom pouch. He zippered the bag closed, folded it over and securely snapped the restraining hooks. Turning toward the desk, he picked up the airline ticket and slipped it into the breast pocket of his sport coat, draped over the chair back. Glancing at his watch, he saw that he had a couple of hours before the plane departed. He decided to head for the airport and get lunch there. Not wanting to deal with hauling his bag this morning, and wanting more coffee, he picked up the phone, dialing the front desk.

"This is Timmers, 814," he said. "Please send someone up for my bag in about twenty minutes, I'm checking out. I want to make the airport shuttle. And please have the bellboy grab a cup of coffee for me too, will ya?...Okay, thanks."

He paused and stretched languidly, feeling restful after grabbing a nap, which had allowed his system to regenerate somewhat. And the initial shock of Laura's abruptly walking out on him was beginning to wear off. He knew he'd be able to deal with the situation logically and prudently when he got back home. After all, she couldn't really have left him forever. Life just didn't happen that way. Two people couldn't love each other as much as they did and then just separate as if the whole thing was a fleeting emotion to just turn off at will. They'd communicate somehow. Regardless, if things didn't turn out, he vowed he would never get involved with a committed woman again—no matter how attracted he was to her, or how lonely he might be.

He glanced at Laura's umbrella, sitting on the desk next to his wallet. He'd simply leave it at the front desk and get word to her somehow so she could pick it up there, he decided as he looked out at the brightening afternoon. He was pleased that the sky was clearing. Yet warm and sunny Southern California would be a welcome relief from this saturated area. He wanted to go home. He'd hang out on the beach for a day or two and dry out. Maybe he'd even spend a week in balmy Palm Springs, where he always went when he needed time to rest and gather his creative juices. He'd call David and truthfully tell him that he'd been through a traumatic experience and needed the time away. David would understand the delay in getting to New York to sign the new book contract. *Agents always understood*, he thought. *Especially when he's a good friend, too.*

Feeling revived, he turned from the window, deciding to make a final room check to ensure he hadn't left anything lying around. After looking over the bathroom, he walked back into the main room. He then froze, suddenly remembering the diamond pendant he had given Laura the night before. *Where is it?* he wondered. He realized he hadn't seen it when he was packing. He turned and reached into the hip pocket of his blazer and pulled out the jewelry case, relieved when he saw it was empty. He scanned all furniture surfaces in the room, not finding the pendant. He quickly dropped to his knees, looking around the floor, under the bed, and around the desk and chair. *It can't be in the room.* She must have taken it with her, he decided, calming. He remembered pleading with her to keep it for a remembrance of their love. *She must have.*

But what if it was lost or stolen? He rose and pulled the bankcard receipt from his wallet and put it inside the case. After stuffing it into his toilet kit for safekeeping, he re-zippered his bag shut and sat down. He was pleased that she had taken the precious keepsake with her, yet it was still only minor comfort. He leaned back in the chair and rubbed his forehead, thinking how things had changed so drastically, so quickly. He remembered yesterday afternoon when he'd arrived at the hotel, happy and content. That part of the day remained crystal clear…

◆◆◆

Jonathan cheerfully dashed through the sliding glass doors of the hotel entrance with his bag slung over his shoulder. Whistling softly through a spirited smile, he approached the front desk, dropping his bag to the floor.

The petite desk clerk looked up and returned his smile. "Hello, Mr. Timmers," she greeted pleasantly. "Welcome to the Riverpark Towers again. It's good to see you back so soon."

"Yes, more urgent business, Keri," he lied as he handed her his credit card.

"I'm sorry we couldn't give you your favorite room overlooking the river," she said, taking an imprint of the card before handing it back to him. "But we received your reservation on such short notice. And you know how booked up we are on Mondays."

"That's quite all right," he replied crisply, "I understand. Incidentally, are there any messages for me?"

"Let me check." She turned to scan the room-key box. "Yes, you have one," she said, retrieving the note and handing it to him before stepping over to the computer keyboard.

He unfolded the note, immediately delighted over the message.

Jonathan,

See you about three in the lobby,

Laura

The clerk began entering the registration information, saying, "I have you staying two days. Is that correct, Mr. Timmers?"

He looked up from the note. "What? Oh, yes. Till the fourteenth," he confirmed, stuffing the note into his pocket.

Finishing the registration process, the clerk slid an oblong cardkey into a paper packet, along with a lounge coupon. Handing the packet to him, she said, "Your key for room 814 and a chit for free cocktails and hors d'oeuvres served in the lobby bar after 2 p.m. The treat is on us today."

"Thanks," he said, reaching down to pick up his bag. "I appreciate that."

"You're welcome," she replied courteously. "Why go out? It looks as though it's going to storm."

They both looked toward the entranceway, seeing the heavy gray air.

"Yeah, as usual," he quipped through a chuckle, putting the packet into the hip pocket of his sport coat. The lounge token would be appropriate, he thought. It would provide him and Laura with a pleasant beginning to their next few days of happiness together. *Maybe the beginning of a brand-new life together*, he thought.

"See ya later, Keri," he said, turning toward the elevators.

Jonathan approached Laura slowly as he made his way down the corridor toward the front lobby. He was in awe, as he always was when he first spotted her. She was sitting on the entryway fringe, quickly flipping through a news magazine. She looked radiant, even in her casual attire of a simple white blouse and blue jeans. Her face was only slightly made up, to enhance her natural beauty. Her khaki rain jacket was lying across her knees, a crimson silk scarf hanging from the pocket. A new folding umbrella with her initials carved in the mahogany handle dangled from her wrist by a soft leather strap.

He caught his breath as he reached her chair, deciding he already needed to be alone with her. He'd never been so attracted to a woman.

"Hi, baby," he said softly, looking down at her.

She looked up smiling. "Hi, back, sweetheart," she responded as she stood, laying her coat and umbrella on the chair.

They embraced, the warmth and rapture spreading through them electrically.

"I'm glad you wanted to see me again so soon," he said. "I was really surprised when you called and told me you were going to be here."

"It was unexpected," she lied. "I had to hold a special class at the college."

His eyes slowly began to glint from wanting her. "I've missed you, baby," he whispered hungrily. "Can we please go up and be alone…"

"Oh, I've missed you too," she interrupted softly. She gently pushed him backward, looking into his eyes. "Please, let's wait. You know how nervous I always am until we talk for a while." She looked down to avoid revealing how pensive she really was because of what she had planned. "I love you," she continued warmly, picking up her belongings from the chair. "You know that I can't help being with you. But my cheating on Monte really hurts me. Please understand."

He reached for her hand. "Of course," he said apologetically. "How thoughtless of me. C'mon, let's go to the lobby bar for some drinks and hors d'oeuvres."

They turned and walked down the corridor toward the center of the hotel.

A loud knock on his hotel room door shattered Jonathan's happy thoughts of yesterday afternoon when he'd first arrived. He turned toward the entrance. *Bellboy,* he thought as he quickly rose, walked over and opened the door, eager to be on his way home to Newport Beach.

His eyes widened in surprise as he faced two stone-jawed men, one dressed in police blues, the other in street clothes. Immediately perplexed, Jonathan's eyes darted to the laminated police identification tag hanging off the breast pocket of the taller man's blazer, then to the shining silver and bronze badge on the chest of the officer.

"Mr. Jonathan Timmers?" Kierzek asked in a calm tone.

"Yes, I'm Jonathan Timmers," he answered, puzzled. He immediately knew by the looks on their faces that they weren't here by mistake. *They want me*, he thought, growing alarmed.

"I'm Lieutenant Brian Kierzek from Portland homicide," he said pointing to his ID. "This is my partner, Sergeant Ed Cuyler. May we come in, please?"

Numbed and apprehensive, like one of the suspects in his novels, Jonathan slowly backed up, opening the door wide for the men to enter. Kierzek walked into the main room. Jonathan was holding open the door for Cuyler when the officer balked.

"Sir, please walk ahead of me," the officer said grimly as he stood still, his eyes squarely on Jonathan.

Jonathan furrowed his brow and nodded, turning to walk behind Kierzek. He knew this meant they considered him dangerous. He'd researched enough police procedures for his novels to understand this "sandwich" procedure. *What is going on?* he wondered as he heard Cuyler shut the door behind him.

The detective slowly surveyed the room, pausing to look closer at the umbrella sitting on the desk. Noticing LJB etched in the handle, Kierzek turned to Jonathan, who was standing rigidly behind him. "Mr. Timmers, do you know a woman named Mrs. Laura Bearnes?"

"Yes," Jonathan answered nervously, now knowing something was very wrong. He realized that Kierzek had recognized Laura's umbrella.

"Was she here with you last night?"

"Yes," Jonathan admitted quickly. Even without the incriminating umbrella, he knew this was no time to lie, regardless of the clandestine implications that might be exposed between him and Laura.

The detective looked down at the garment bag lying on the bed, then to the airline ticket protruding from Jonathan's coat pocket. "I assume you were planning on leaving?"

"Yes, lieutenant," Jonathan answered, shaking off some of his puzzlement. "I have no good reason to lie to you. And I won't. I was in Portland to visit Mrs. Bearnes. We had a big argument last night and she walked out on me. So I was heading back to my home in Newport Beach, California."

"I see," Kierzek replied calmly, inwardly sizing up Jonathan. "Mr. Timmers, were you aware of all the commotion that went on outside the hotel this morning?"

"No," Jonathan answered, gathering his thoughts. "To be very frank with you, I was extremely hung over today." He paused. "I guess I looked out the window this morning about nine or so, but everything looked normal to me. Then I took a shower and slept soundly until about one-thirty."

Kierzek walked over to the window and looked out, noting that the room was on the opposite side from the riverpark. He stood in thought, determining when to inform Jonathan of his Miranda rights. His timing was always accurate, especially when the respondent appeared cooperative. Kierzek was an expert at gaining critical information voluntarily before the suspect was formally advised to remain silent.

The atmosphere in the room grew tense as Jonathan looked anxiously over at Cuyler, who stood there with a steely stare fixed on him.

Kierzek turned away from the window, facing Jonathan. Deciding that he would still delay the Miranda maneuver, he asked, "Would you please tell me what your relationship was with Mrs. Bearnes?"

"We're friends. Very good friends…and…" Jonathan's eyes widened when he realized that Kierzek had used the word *was*. "Why?" he quickly asked. "What's wrong? Please tell me, lieutenant. We were more than friends, we were lovers."

The detective hesitated, choosing his words cautiously to fish for additional reaction from Jonathan. "I'm afraid I have to inform you that Mrs. Bearnes is dead…murdered."

Blanching, Jonathan collapsed backwards into the chair. He dropped his head into his hands; blinding pain seared throughout his body. "My God!" he uttered, his voice choking. "Oh, no, my God!"

Kierzek looked on intently, carefully observing Jonathan's every movement while he asked, "Mr. Timmers, can you tell me where you were late last night and early this morning, around dawn?"

"Here," Jonathan answered nervously with animated hand motions. "Right here at the hotel."

"Can anyone verify that?"

Jonathan shook his head. "No. I was alone when Laura wasn't with me."

Kierzek decided that he'd pushed the questioning far enough without having read Jonathan his rights. "Mr. Timmers, I'm afraid you'll have to come with us," he said. "And before you say anything further I would like you to please listen to Sergeant Cuyler very carefully."

Jonathan flinched as he felt the firm grip on his shoulder. "Please stand up, sir," Cuyler ordered.

Jonathan's jaw dropped as he looked up, seeing the officer removing the silvery handcuffs from his wide black utility belt. He knew that the next step was to have his rights read to him, meaning he was now officially arrested—*suspected of murder*. Weak with trauma, he slowly stood as the officer turned him and drew his arms around to his back, securing the handcuffs on his wrists.

Stunned, Jonathan stood frozen, listening tensely to the officer recite: "Mr. Timmers, you have the right to remain silent. If you decide to give up that right, anything you say…"

Chapter Ten

The interrogation, late-afternoon, Portland Justice Center

The fading sunlight was clouded, barely seeping through the tightly covered window on the far side of the barren yet non-threatening interview room in the Justice Center. Although lacking of any furniture or fixtures that might conceal or divert Jonathan's body movement when he answered Kierzek's questions, the room had a comfortable feel, with a couple of modest paintings on the wall and a new pale-yellow paint job. The fluorescent lights, directly overhead, illuminated the heavy air that surrounded the two men who sat on plastic molded chairs, closely facing each other. Kierzek, still impartial, held a notebook and pencil in his lap and had decided not to use a tape recorder, to make Jonathan feel more comfortable, hoping to draw more out of him. So far Kierzek had been firm but non-judgmental during the questioning. He was determined to remain this way regardless of the incriminating circumstances Jonathan seemed to be swallowed up in.

Jonathan leaned back in his chair and pulled a tissue from the small cellophane pack in his lap. He wiped away the salty perspiration that dripped from his forehead into his teary, bloodshot eyes, and dropped the soiled wad onto the small pile accumulating next to his feet. He shook his head, stroking his throbbing temples. "I couldn't have done it," he rasped, his voice racked with anxiety. "I just know I couldn't have killed her, even during a blackout. I loved her too much."

Rising from his chair, the rangy detective silently set his notepad on the seat and walked to the window. Pulling on the lift cord, he rolled the blinds up halfway. He twisted the window thumb lock and yanked upward on the bottom rail, allowing a stiff damp breeze to stream through the gap. He lowered the blinds, but separated the slats to maintain the fresh flow. He slowly walked over and picked up his notepad. Sitting down, Kierzek said solemnly, "But you keep telling me you can't remember much after you two fought in the bar last night."

Jonathan looked up, exasperated. "Can I please walk over to the window to get some air?"

Kierzek nodded, knowing he could still keep a keen eye on any telltale movements Jonathan might reveal while talking.

Jonathan jerked upward and paced over to the window, saying stressfully, "I've told you over and over again, I'd had too much to drink." He paused, looking out onto the police parking lot. "And dammit, we weren't fighting in the lobby bar. I keep telling you that, too."

"The hotel manager told us differently," Kierzek said pointedly, moving forward in his chair. "He heard you arguing with her."

"Okay, so I was probably very upset, and it may have sounded like fighting," Jonathan countered, growing more frustrated. "She was leaving me. I loved her more than anything in this world. You must believe me! My hostile reaction was only natural, but not violent." He turned and looked out the window.

Kierzek sat back in his chair, setting the notepad in his lap. He remained silent as he watched Jonathan stare out the window. He had wanted to wrap this case up quickly. It had all the earmarks of a crime of passion. And he surely wanted to be looking at the guilty one: a forsaken lover who'd flipped out, viciously ridding himself of the object of his rage—the woman. This man had both the motive and the opportunity to commit the crime. Wouldn't it only be a matter of time before he confessed? Or before some element of positive proof emerged, condemning him decisively? For sure, a clear-cut package all wrapped up in a neat little bow. Then it would only be a matter of carrying out a string of common judiciary procedures for conviction, punishment and final vindication for his victim's loved ones.

But he was still somehow unsure of this man's seemingly obvious guilt as he lightly tapped his pencil on his notepad. Why had it continued to gnaw at him from the moment he saw Jonathan's reaction to the news of Laura's death? Moreover, his eye and body movements during the questioning appeared typical of an innocent man. Or was it all an act? Had Kierzek met his match—a clever author who had planned this plot? And even if Jonathan was guilty, was he really a cold-blooded killer with malice aforethought? Was it premeditated murder in the first degree? Perhaps he did kill her, but during a blacked-out state of drunkenness. Therefore, guilty, but a murderer with no clear intent—only voluntary manslaughter. But, then again, she appeared to have been stalked in the riverpark. *Why wouldn't he have killed her in the hotel if it was because of a sudden quarrel? And when he wasn't in his right mind? Had he really been blacked out?*

Whatever the situation, Kierzek knew that this time he had an unusual homicide on his hands. *And it was far from a clear-cut package.* He needed to be careful and get to the truth. *However, regardless of his concern for justice, he'd have to remain neutral, emotionally uninvolved in this man's plight.*

Kierzek's thoughts waned as Jonathan abruptly looked over at him, appealing, "Look, lieutenant, do you think she'd have gone back to the room with me if she was afraid? She knew I was confused and hurt, but hardly dangerous."

"Okay, let's take it from that point again," Kierzek responded, picking up his notepad. "Come back over and tell me what happened next."

Jonathan walked over and sat down, facing Kierzek. "I vaguely remember us going up to my room," he answered. He sighed. "We decided to say goodbye by making love for the last time." He paused, then blurted, "Does that sound like a woman who felt she was in danger?"

"Nobody said you were a danger to her then," Kierzek replied quickly, diverting his eyes to his pad. "So, did you have sex, or argue some more? That point could prove important to your overall mood at the time she left."

"I don't remember," Jonathan answered, strained. "Like I told you before, it's very sketchy. I'd ordered a bottle of bourbon from room service and began to drink it as soon as we got to the room. I don't remember much after that. I had been drinking since that afternoon. I just don't remember if we made love or not, but I'm sure we were in bed together. The scent of her perfume was on my pillow. I remember she hadn't been wearing any during the afternoon."

Kierzek looked up from his notepad. "What about the wet clothes we found in your bag? And what about the bell captain's statement saying he saw you in the lobby around dawn? He also saw you go out the front door into the rain." Kierzek was growing uncharacteristically impatient with his indecisive suspect. "Goddammit, man!" he exclaimed. "You've got to be clearer than that if you want me to believe your story!"

"I never denied any of that," Jonathan responded quickly. "I'm sure the bell captain isn't lying." He shook his head. "And I'm sure I did go out looking for Laura. That must be the reason for the wet clothes. But the only thing I remember is waking up in the hotel room with those wet clothes on. You've gotta believe me, lieutenant! You know I've cooperated from the beginning." He paused, then asked tensely, "What about the vagrant? The witness you mentioned? The one that found her. Maybe he saw something. Maybe he even saw *me*. Why can't you find him, for God's sake?"

"We're trying to find him. We're trying to," Kierzek repeated.

Jonathan dropped his head into his hands, frustrated.

Kierzek looked up. "I'd like to believe you, Timmers, I really would. You don't come across like a killer. And you have no criminal background. Nevertheless, you don't give me much to go on for your innocence..." His words faded as he heard a sharp rap on the door. "Hold on," he said, rising and walking over to open the door. Kierzek stood in the threshold talking in an undertone to his visitor, who had remained in the hallway, out of Jonathan's sight.

Jonathan sat still, waiting nervously for Kierzek to finish his conversation.

Kierzek shut the door and sat down in his chair. "That was Officer Cuyler. I understand Mrs. Bearnes' friend, Rebecca Newell, was able to help the Eugene police locate Mr. Bearnes at the university where he teaches."

Jonathan slowly turned away, murmuring, "I suppose Bearnes knows pretty much everything by now, right?"

"I would think so," Kierzek said. "Cuyler said that when he was at Newell's apartment to get her statement, Mr. Bearnes had called and talked to her."

"Damn," Jonathan rasped, "what a mess."

"And soon all of Portland will know," Kierzek quickly added.

"What's that mean?"

Kierzek continued, opening up a little more to try to read Jonathan's reactions. "Bearnes gave his permission for Ms. Newell to confirm that it was his wife until he can meet me at the morgue tonight and officially identify the body."

Jonathan looked at him quizzically. "And what does that mean?"

"Unfortunately, a murder victim has no privacy, especially a woman of her stature," Kierzek answered. "Therefore, Mr. Bearnes realizes there's no way we can keep this quiet, so he reluctantly gave his okay to release preliminary news to the media after Ms. Newell looked over the body. It's unusual; however, the police chief approved it because of the extraordinary interest surrounding this case."

"And..." Jonathan prodded.

"Captain Ruskin is going to hold a press conference in about thirty minutes."

Jonathan asked haltingly, "Is Ruskin also going to announce that you have a suspect in custody?"

"I'm sure he will," Kierzek replied. "The reporters know about you anyway. A couple of them saw us escort you from the hotel this afternoon. And they talked to the bell captain. We've been getting constant phone calls about it ever since."

"Oh, shit," Jonathan mumbled. "I just can't believe this is happening."

"This shouldn't be a surprise to you," Kierzek said. "You told me you're a mystery writer. You must have written about police procedures like this somewhere along the line."

Jonathan looked up, surprised at the irony. "Yeah," he said. "I guess it just hasn't sunk in that it's really me who's criminally involved."

"Oh, by the way," Kierzek interrupted, again watching Jonathan closely, "Cuyler told me that Newell has given us a statement that implicates you further."

Jonathan shot him a worried look. "I'm not surprised. I know I wasn't one of her favorite people." He looked down, rubbing his tired eyes. "She always blamed me for all of Laura's problems in this affair."

Kierzek continued, "Anyway, she claims that Mrs. Bearnes left a message on her answering machine from the hotel after she left you. The message implied that Mrs. Bearnes was very fearful of you for what you might do to her physically."

"What!?" Jonathan exclaimed. "Oh, no! That can't be true."

Kierzek noted the outburst. "Mr. Timmers, I know you said you didn't need an attorney while you talked with us, but now I strongly urge you to arrange for one."

Jonathan swallowed hard, his face twisting in fear. He asked slowly, "Are you actually going to charge me with her killing?"

"Suspicion of," Kierzek replied. "It's based on enough circumstantial evidence and probable cause to warrant holding you."

"Where am I headed?"

"County jail," Kierzek answered. "It's here in the center."

"Any chance for bail?" Jonathan asked, his face filling with dread.

"I don't think so, but I assure you I'll try to move things along quickly."

Jonathan nodded weakly, then glanced at Kierzek. "I assume they've thoroughly searched the hotel room by now."

"Yes," Kierzek said. "Cuyler just told me the lab group released it back to the hotel. Why?"

"I just wondered if they'd found the diamond pendant I gave Laura last night," Jonathan replied. "It's very expensive...worth thousands. It was my opening gesture to ask Laura to leave Bearnes and marry me."

"I don't know anything about it," Kierzek answered, appearing interested. "I understand they only found her umbrella in the room. I can check again, though."

"Nah," Jonathan said, looking down. "She probably had it with her. It doesn't matter any more. I have no use for it. Anyway, if you want to check it out, the receipt is in the jewelry case in my luggage toilet kit."

Kierzek looked up, recollecting that he hadn't seen anything like that at the death scene. He would have remembered it while contemplating a robbery motive for her murder. He made a note to check with Dr. Richardson to see if he had found it at the morgue during the autopsy, but spared Jonathan that thought.

"Do you need a public defender?" Kierzek asked, changing the subject.

"Not yet," Jonathan answered. "I'll talk to my friend and agent, David Lowell, in New York. He's also my literary attorney. He might be able to arrange something legally for me out here. If he can't, then maybe I'll need some help."

"Okay," Kierzek said, glancing at his watch. "Do you want to try to reach him now?"

"Yeah," Jonathan mumbled. "I know his home number."

"Okay, let's go into my office," Kierzek said, rising. "You can use my phone while I prepare an official statement for you to sign. Okay?"

Jonathan nodded as he slowly stood and proceeded toward the door.

Kierzek followed closely behind, more confused than ever about the question of Jonathan's guilt. His lengthy and emotional interrogation had not cleared things up; they had only become more muddied. And now there might be a missing diamond pendant. *Maybe she had lost it in the park*, he thought. *Maybe she discarded it out of feeling guilty...maybe the vagrant got it. They needed to find the vagrant,* he decided.

CHAPTER ELEVEN

The autopsy, Multnomah County Morgue, Portland

Portland was calming as a final smattering of rush-hour traffic gradually exited the cloudy city. Leaving his car on the leafy boulevard, Detective Kierzek hurried up the shrub-lined walk toward the unpretentious white-brick colonial office building. *A fitting conversion*, Kierzek always thought whenever he stepped onto the small porch of the forensic facility that had once been a private funeral home. He pulled on the doorknob, opening the clear glass door, which had symmetrically arranged lettering printed in the center:

Multnomah County Medical Examiner
Offices and Morgue

Entering the dim reception area, he began making his way down the vacant hallway when he noticed the public telephone nook and thought he should have called his wife to tell her he'd be late for dinner. However, she'd surely have realized that by now, he decided as he passed by the darkened autopsy lab and stopped in front of the lighted office next door.

Looking in, he saw the profile of Dr. Richardson sitting at his desk poring over some paperwork. Kierzek noticed the bloodstains on the sleeves of his bright blue scrub suit, a harsh emblem of Richardson's daily labor. His cotton surgical cap was pushed back on his head, revealing a few strands of gray that sprouted from his balding crown. His face mask hung loosely around his chubby neck.

Kierzek knocked lightly on the door jamb, causing Richardson to turn and look up. "Oh, hello, lieutenant," he said pleasantly, as though there had been no friction between them at the death scene earlier that morning.

"Good evening, doctor," Kierzek replied amicably.

"I've been expecting you," Richardson said, gesturing toward the chair in front of the desk. "And just in time. I was just preparing the death certificate for the Bearnes woman. Have a seat."

"Thanks, I will," Kierzek said. "It's been a long day."

"I know, and it's going to get longer," Richardson replied, sounding spent. "Do you know when her husband, Monte, is coming in to identify the body?"

"Not exactly," Kierzek answered, glancing at his watch. "He said he'd meet Cuyler at the station about seven-thirty if he doesn't get caught up in traffic."

"Yeah, it's a good two-hour drive from Eugene even without any problems," Richardson said. He then sighed and murmured, "Oh, well…"

"Can't you wait until tomorrow to finish up with all this?" Kierzek asked.

"Nope," Richardson replied curtly, appearing perturbed. He sat back in his chair, hoisting his feet to the top of the desk. "Ruskin wants it completed tonight. Although I may be able to get away with a limited exam and skip the extensive inside stuff. It seems quite obvious how she was killed."

"The cause of death looked pretty clear to me, too," Kierzek agreed while grimacing over the thought of the beautiful woman he saw this morning requiring a major disfiguring autopsy.

"Right, very clear," Richardson confirmed, shrugging. "Anyway, I'm waiting for Ruskin to call back. I think he's going to decide how far we have to go, depending on some basic toxicology results. Although I didn't detect any skin discoloration, rashes or signs of unusual bodily-waste functions that would imply poisoning."

Kierzek wondered how Richardson managed to maintain his staid demeanor throughout this whole process, but disregarded his curiosity as he pulled out his notepad, asking, "Have you learned anything more about the circumstances preceding the murder?"

"Only a little more than we already knew," Richardson answered, moving forward in his chair as he lowered his feet to the floor. "I performed a few external tests besides the weighing, fingerprinting and the usual preliminaries. I took photos of everything. Anyway, I hope you don't mind that I didn't wait for you."

"Nah, why don't you just update me."

"Sure, I just finished with the tests," Richardson said. "She's in the lab. Wanna view the body while we talk?"

"Yeah, why not?" Kierzek replied blandly, pushing his chair back. "It might trigger some further questions."

Richardson swung around and stood, while Kierzek followed suit.

"Incidentally, how's it going with the suspect?" Richardson asked as they walked out of his office toward the autopsy lab. "What's his name—Timmers?"

"Correct, Jonathan Timmers," Kierzek confirmed. "He's being processed in the county lockup."

Richardson shook his head with a whistle, then commented, "I heard about some of the detail. This guy has a rugged road ahead of him—guilty or innocent."

"You're right on that account, doctor," Kierzek said, "so very right."

Jonathan wearily plunked himself down on the solid granite wall-seat as the steel-barred door clanked shut and locked behind him. Gripping a handful of paper toweling, he sat dazed in the desolate holding cell of Portland's Multnomah County jail, waiting to be taken through his next step in the excruciating booking procedure. He began to anxiously wipe away the remaining traces of fingerprint ink from his hands, while thinking how appropriate it was that they never allow an inmate to smile when they snap the mug shot. It produced a result that made him look as bad as he felt.

He grimaced as he remembered the humility he'd felt when he had to strip naked and his entire body was blatantly photographed. How the guard smirked when Jonathan was compelled to confess that the scratches on his back were a painful remembrance of yesterday's lovemaking. *"Passionate mementos," as he and Laura had playfully dubbed them while they were enjoying cocktails afterward.* Now it was a hardened police fact. Perhaps even evidence in open court. But like Kierzek had told him in the interrogation room: *A murder victim has no privacy.*

Looking down, he scowled at the bluish smudges on his yellow pullover sport shirt. However, his ink-stained shirt and wrinkled pants were of little consequence, as he was told his next stop in the process was to be issued a standard bright orange jumpsuit. He feared he might be wearing this garish garb for a long time to come if things didn't straighten out soon. It didn't take Kierzek to tell him he wouldn't be granted bail; not for a crime with this much notoriety. And certainly not for a suspect who lived out of state.

Feeling his stomach gurgle, he thought back to last night's dinner with Laura, the last time he'd eaten. He wondered if they'd feed him anything tonight. Regardless, the food would most likely be cold and unpalatable anyway. *It really doesn't matter*, he lamented inwardly. His uncomfortable pangs of hunger were a pale contrast to the severe mental anguish he was suffering because of the desperate situation he was caught up in. His precious Laura had been murdered, and he was the prime suspect: officially under suspicion of killing a human being whom he'd loved so much. *Oh, damn, what a disaster,* he thought, closing his eyes as he lay his head back against the abrasive concrete-block wall.

Lieutenant Kierzek felt uncomfortable as he always did when he had to attend the autopsies of his homicide cases. This was another part of his job he barely managed to tolerate. He stood silently next to Richardson, who was switching on the bright overhead lights of the cold autopsy lab. However, it wasn't the low temperature or the darkness that chilled Kierzek. It was the grim environment of the white-walled surgical room with the tiled floor. In the center, two stainless-steel tables were placed over a massive drainage system, close to an oversized sink. A long, heavy-duty water hose lay coiled up in the corner. On a wide counter, a few feet away from the tables, lay a saw, a scale, a drill, and various cutting and measuring tools. A double row of man-sized refrigerated cabinets with heavy steel doors were built into the far wall, and they were usually fully occupied with cadavers waiting to be released to the local funeral parlors or donated to the area's universities for research purposes.

Kierzek slowly followed Richardson toward the far corner of the room and the metal-tubed gurney that supported the woman's body, covered with a heavy white plastic sheet. He looked at the small plain label hanging off her blanched big toe with string, labeled "L. Bearnes."

Richardson plucked a pair of latex gloves from his smock pocket as he stood over the gurney. Reaching down, he pulled the sheet back to reveal only the neck and head of the woman, layering the sheet slack on her upper chest.

Kierzek winced as he focused on the expressionless face and the parted lips, formless and pale. Catching himself, he opened his notebook and pulled his pencil from his coat pocket.

Richardson pointed to her neck, saying, "Like I said, I'm quite positive her death was from strangulation only. Besides the obvious neck abrasion, her hyoid bone was broken. And she had traces of petechiae on her face and eyes."

"What about the hands?"

"Nothing telltale on the skin surface, no wounds," Richardson answered, "but we scraped a lot of grime and material from under her nails. I'm having Harold analyze it at the other lab. Maybe something tangible will turn up—like skin or hair. Prime fodder for DNA testing."

"Uh-huh," Kierzek replied, jotting down his notes. "What about the time of death?"

Richardson looked up and rubbed his chin, signaling an imprecise answer. "I'd say about when we first figured, somewhere around dawn. Her state of rigor mortis is an iffy barometer, as usual. However, that and her rectal temperature indicated we're probably as accurate as can be." He paused, then added, "Of course, you know I'm taking it into account that she died violently, and calculated her body temperature a few degrees higher then I would if she'd died normally."

Kierzek nodded while busily taking notes, then asked, "Can you tell if she'd been raped? I know the way she was dressed didn't suggest it, but..."

"No, it doesn't appear that she was," Richardson interrupted, abruptly drawing the sheet back to her knees. "She was wearing underwear. I didn't notice any unusual stains, and there didn't appear to be any type of injury to her pubic area."

Kierzek glanced over and quickly gestured that he'd seen enough with a wave of his hand as he looked back down at his notepad.

Richardson re-covered the body, saying, "Although..."

Kierzek looked up at him.

Pulling off his gloves, Richardson pitched them into the plastic-lined wastebasket, continuing, "After a closer examination I was able to determine that she'd had sex within the last twenty-four hours of her life. I found traces of semen, which I captured for DNA testing if necessary."

"Can you be more accurate on the time of the intercourse?"

"No, not really," Richardson replied. "Yet, like I said, I'm quite sure she wasn't violated at the death scene. Whenever and whomever she had the sex with is probably unimportant; it was most likely consensual." He shook his head. "I doubt there's any rape notion here."

Kierzek felt relieved that the murder charge wouldn't be compounded with sexual assault. This case was confusing enough. "It could've been her husband," Kierzek commented, inwardly pardoning Laura's infidelity out of compassion, as it made no difference now. "I understand she left Eugene about 10 a.m. yesterday."

Richardson shrugged. "Whatever. I'm only the doctor. You're the detective."

"Right," Kierzek replied with a slight frown. "Got anything more?"

"No, that's about it. Of course, I don't know if she was on drugs until we get the complete toxicology tests back from the blood samples we took."

Kierzek closed his notepad. "Well," he said, checking his watch, "let's go back to your office and wait for Cuyler and Bearnes to get here. I'm sure they'll be here any time."

"Okay," Richardson replied, looking toward the refrigerated lockers. "I think I'll leave her out until after the husband identifies her. It's a little more personal that way. She'll be all right for a while. It's cool enough in here."

"Right," Kierzek said as they headed for the door. "Oh," he said, pausing. "Do you still have her personal effects?"

"No," Richardson answered. "Officer Bressler left with everything a little while ago. I imagine they're checked in at the Justice Center by now. Why?"

"I was wondering if you found an expensive diamond pendant in her possession," Kierzek said. "Perhaps it had been in one of her pockets?"

"Nope, I made out the inventory list," Richardson replied firmly. "The only jewelry was her wedding ring and watch...not even earrings. I know because I personally checked through everything. Is one missing?"

"I dunno yet," Kierzek said, appearing puzzled. "But it's significant. I saw the receipt...big bucks," he added as they continued for the door.

"You know what, lieutenant?" Richardson said, turning off the lights.

"What?"

Richardson wrinkled his face. "The next-of-kin-identification process is the worst part of this job for me," he answered. "That lady, Rebecca Newell, was here this afternoon. She really fell apart when she saw her best friend lying there."

"Oh, really?" Kierzek said as they left the autopsy lab and entered Richardson's office.

"For sure," Richardson replied, sitting down at his desk. "She really took it hard. Cuyler even had to hold her up once when she almost collapsed." He sighed, adding, "And I still have to get through the husband part tonight."

"Maybe I can help with that," Kierzek said as he settled across from the doctor.

Jonathan dropped the wad of frayed toweling on the seat as he spread his arms out and laid his palms flat on the long cold slab. Stretching his legs forward, he arched his body to relieve the tightening cramps of anxiety. Jarred back to reality, he peered through the steel bars at the group of officers gathering around the desk at the end of the stark passageway. He grimaced, knowing that one would be coming for him soon.

His thoughts turned to Rebecca Newell and how Kierzek said she had told the police that Laura had left a message on her answering machine that insinuated she was afraid of him. *It couldn't be true, could it?*

He was well aware that he and Rebecca had had their differences; she always felt he was the villain, causing Laura's heartache because of the affair. Yet why would she so quickly incriminate him so decisively and vindictively? He'd never given her or Laura any reason to think he was dangerous. *Or had he?* He realized he'd been extremely out of character last night, but surely he wasn't a violent threat to the one he loved so much. She couldn't have been afraid of him. *But was she?*

Again he tried desperately to clearly recall the details surrounding the incident in the lobby bar. He remembered that things had turned ugly, and that he was upset and combative. But he had been deeply hurt and confused over the shocking turn of events. How he was going to ask her to leave Monte and marry him, and then she turned the tables on him before he could ask her. He remembered being very upset when he accused her of heartlessly drawing him to Portland only to tell him she was leaving him. Luring him here not because she missed him so much, but to properly wash her hands of him. Yes, it was a traumatic turn of events that he experienced, but not enough to transform him into a killer. *Or was it?*

His head was starting to pound as he looked around the bleak 12- by 14-foot concrete-walled cube. Now he knew what it actually felt like when the walls seemed to be closing in. Just like the scene he had fictionalized in his last book for one of his criminally convicted characters.

Bewildered, he picked up his feet and twisted his body to lie supinely on the bench as he fell deeper into dreaded thought. He couldn't have killed Laura, not even while entrenched in a drunken stupor. *Or could he have?* Was it possible that he was capable of doing something that heinous during an alcoholic blackout? No, Kierzek had said she was savagely strangled. He'd certainly have remembered a brutal encounter like that. *Definitely he'd have remembered that. Wouldn't he?*

Regardless, now he could only fully cooperate with Kierzek and wait until his agent got back to him. He was sure David might be able to arrange for someone capable to represent him. He said he would do his best to get someone there quickly. *Someone who would surely prove he was innocent.*

He cringed as he heard the clanking of the cell door opening. He closed his eyes in distress as he heard, "Timmers, come on, let's go."

Lieutenant Kierzek sat patiently while Richardson finished his phone conversation and hung up the receiver. He looked at Kierzek with a smile of relief, saying, "Ruskin said he's pretty sure I can bypass the full autopsy. He'll finalize it with the chief tomorrow. So I guess I can get outta here right after the body is officially identified and I get the final ID information from Bearnes."

"Sounds good," Kierzek said, looking down at his watch. "I'm sure Cuyler and Bearnes will be here any time. They're only a few minutes late."

"No problem," Richardson said nonchalantly. "It's all part of the job."

Kierzek shot him a curious look. "How do you do it, doctor? I mean, death, how do you just let it go?"

Richardson paused, thinking about how to answer that delicate question without offending the tough but death-sensitive detective. "It isn't easy, lieutenant," he answered slowly. "I suppose when I entered forensic pathology I trained myself to detach from the reality of it all. Perhaps I..." He hesitated, his words and train of thought interrupted by Sergeant Cuyler approaching the office door.

Following Richardson's glance of relief, Kierzek turned toward the doorway. He looked past Cuyler and into the hallway.

"Bearnes is sitting in the front reception area," Cuyler said to Kierzek. "I figured I'd better check with you before I brought him back here."

Kierzek rose. "Good move, but I think we're ready if he is."

Cuyler wagged his hand. "He's pretty shaky," he replied, "but I know he wants to get it over with."

"I'm sure he does," Kierzek said, "just like the rest of us." He paused. "By the way, did he say anything significant on the way over?"

Cuyler wearily massaged the back of his head while he thought. "No," he answered. "Like I mentioned, he seems really overwrought...numbed, I guess."

"All right, why don't you just go on home," Kierzek said. "I'll get Bearnes back to where he wants to go after we're finished here."

"Thanks," Cuyler said, as he turned to leave. "He's staying at the downtown Marriott tonight and heading back to Eugene tomorrow. We dropped his car off there. He didn't want to drive any more tonight after he went through this."

"Okay," Kierzek said as Cuyler left the office. "I'll see you tomorrow."

Kierzek turned toward Richardson. "How about if you let me do the dirty work this time?" he asked. "I'd like to conduct the identification process with Bearnes alone."

Richardson thought a moment. "Sure," he agreed. "I guess there's no problem with that. Although I'll need the info from him afterward to complete the death certificate. And I'll also need to know what he wants to do with the body, so I can complete the certificate of body disposition."

"I know," Kierzek replied, walking out of the office. "I know," he repeated, uneasy over his next duty. "Christ, we'll get to all that."

As he slowly headed down the hallway, he thought about Richardson's abbreviated answer concerning his detaching himself from the cold touch of death. Maybe someday he would learn how to do the same thing. *No, he'd surely be retired before that.*

Reaching the front reception area, Kierzek saw a lean, long-legged man sitting in a chair. Wearing jeans, a V-neck sweater over a colored T-shirt, and running shoes, he was bent forward, cupping his face with his hands.

He approached the chair, saying sensitively, "Mr. Monte Bearnes?"

The man sluggishly lifted his head. Appearing strained, he brushed a long shock of blonde hair away from his deeply lined forehead. "Yes," the man mumbled, looking up as he sat back.

He looked into Bearnes' reddened eyes while holding out his hand. "I'm Detective Brian Kierzek from Portland homicide."

Bearnes lifted his arm and weakly shook his hand, saying hoarsely. "Officer Cuyler told me I'd be talking to you...."

Kierzek nodded, seeing the anguish in Bearnes' handsome, chisel-featured face behind his day-old stubble. He thought how tough it was going to be when he would have to question this man about the crime; another one of his unpleasant duties whenever someone's spouse is murdered. However, that would come later, probably tomorrow, before Bearnes left town. But there was still the first chore to get through. "Mr. Bearnes," he said gently, but firmly. "I'm sorry, but I'm afraid it's necessary to take you through this. We should go."

Bearnes stood, saying in a quivering voice, "I understand. Let's just do it."

With Bearnes following Kierzek apprehensively, they made their way down the hallway and stopped in front of the autopsy lab entrance. Kierzek led the way inside and turned on the lights. Bearnes immediately focused on the white-sheeted bulge lying on the steel gurney in the corner. He flinched and took a deep breath. Swallowing hard, he followed Kierzek, who was walking to the gurney. The detective decided to bypass the latex-glove routine to eliminate the cold, clinical manner and get this difficult task over with faster. He turned toward Bearnes, who was standing next to the gurney, staring at the floor.

"Are you all right, Mr. Bearnes?" Kierzek asked gently.

Bearnes nodded vacantly, then lowered his head again.

Kierzek reached down and cautiously pulled the sheet back to the edge of Laura's chin, careful not to expose her neck. Bearnes slowly lifted his head and looked at her ashen features. His eyes opened wide and quickly closed as he clutched his contorted face with both hands and leaned against the gurney. "Oh, no," he murmured through a moan, "no...no...no..."

Chapter Twelve

The attorney, Wednesday, Beaverton, Oregon

Lacey Anne Rosetto, associate criminal attorney for the Hansen, Jacob & Malcolm law firm, stood in the office library facing the line of bookshelves, sipping on a cup of lukewarm coffee. Setting the cup down, she stretched upward to retrieve the Oregon penal code from the top shelf, but was unable to quite reach it. She scowled as she raised her eyes, thinking, *Lord, you've been good to me, but another inch or two would have been nice.* Breaking into a smile over her quip, she pulled the stepstool over and used it to retrieve the thick blue volume. She stepped down and flipped through it until she found her targeted section. Uttering a soft "Aha," she set the book down on the table and jotted a couple of notes onto her small notebook. She then replaced the book, picked up her cup and left the room.

Perky as always, she breezed through the large office, wearing a friendly expression as she passed the two receptionists settling in for their day's work. They smiled obligingly in return, but knew the enthusiastic attorney was already mentally engrossed in whatever assignment she was tackling today.

Ducking into the small utility nook, she rinsed her cup and set it on the small counter next to the coffee maker. Turning, she left the cranny and approached the desk of Audrey, the senior secretary.

Looking up from her computer monitor, the older woman lowered her reading glasses. "Good morning, Lacey. I've noticed you already scurrying around. How are you?"

"Fine, thank you," Lacey answered quickly. "I came in early to tune up my oral argument for George Cooper's court appearance this afternoon. I want to be prepared if the judge decides to give him jail time."

Audrey frowned. "I understand it's the third offense for that old geezer," she said through a slight chuckle. "That man is too old to be driving, much less drinking when he does."

"I know," Lacey replied, pursing her lips in disgust. "And this time he sideswiped a parked car and left the scene." Lacey threw her hands up, adding, "Then he just drove home like there was nothing wrong..."

Audrey interrupted, "Wow, I didn't hear that part. Anyone get hurt?"

"Fortunately, no. The people had just parked their car and were walking up the sidewalk. They saw it all and got his license number."

"No wonder he got caught," Audrey commented in surprise.

"Of course," Lacey responded. "Jeez, the police were waiting for him in his driveway when he got home. I was so angry with him I didn't even want to talk to him when he called me."

"But you did," Audrey said, smiling. "And if I remember correctly, you told him after his last conviction that you wouldn't represent him again."

Lacey cocked her head, answering defensively, "Yes, but it's only because he has agreed to plead guilty, give up his license for life and go to AA meetings at least twice a week. So I'm working to keep him from doing any hard time."

Audrey nodded mockingly and asked cynically, "And that's the only reason you're representing him?"

"Well," Lacey confessed softly, "that, and he keeps hugging me and telling me he wishes I was his daughter."

They both laughed loudly and shook their heads.

Lacey slowly turned serious, saying, "Anyway, I stopped to tell you that after I finish with my court appearance today I'm hoping to take a long weekend to go home and see my parents. Jack said he'd cover for me if anything came up."

"Oh, good, Lacey," Audrey replied, well aware of the weariness and distress that the young lawyer concealed so successfully behind those bright brown spitfire eyes. "You deserve it. San Jose should be pleasant this weekend."

"Yes, it'll be nice to get away," Lacey agreed. "But I haven't talked to Mr. Hansen about it yet. He's been on the phone since I got in."

Audrey glanced down at the phone and noted that Hansen's extension light was still lit up. "Oh, yes, I understand he's been chatting with the Portland police and some attorney from New York all morning. I'm not sure what it's all about, though."

Lacey shrugged and turned toward her office, saying, "I don't either, but it must be important. So if I miss him, would you please mention my weekend plans to him? I was going to clean up things around here tomorrow morning and then take the afternoon and Friday off."

"Of course. Don't worry about it," Audrey said. "Mr. Hansen knows you need some time off. Heck, you were in here all Labor Day weekend preparing for the Shawn Griffith trial. Remember, I took care of the twins."

"Yes, I know," Lacey said, "But, still, if he has a problem with my leaving, I haven't made any flight arrangements yet. I was going to do all that when I got back in the office this afternoon."

"Sure, I'll tell him," Audrey replied. "But like I said, don't worry about it. And I'm sure Jack can handle anything that might come up on your agenda while you're gone."

"Thank you, I appreciate it," Lacey responded, turning toward her office.

Audrey reached over and took hold of her forearm, gently turning her around. "Lacey, I'd be glad to take the twins while you're gone," she said thoughtfully. "Wouldn't you like to have some time alone?"

Lacey thought for a moment. "No, Audrey. It's good of you to offer, though. But my mom would never forgive me if I didn't bring them with me." She laughed. "Besides, they're growing more spunky every day. I wouldn't want to burden you any more than I already have to."

"Okay," Audrey replied, releasing her arm. "But if you decide differently, I'm always available."

"I'll keep that in mind if I ever get angry with you," Lacey joked, again turning toward her office. "Incidentally, when Jack comes in, please tell him I'd like to go over my court argument with him as usual."

The secretary nodded as she watched Lacey dart into her office and shut the door. *If the twins end up with her spunk*, she thought, *they will be hard to handle.* Smiling, she slipped on her reading glasses and turned back to her computer.

Lacey sat down at her desk and set her notebook in front of her. Reaching into her bottom file drawer, she retrieved the folder containing her argument for the Cooper case and opened it up. She pulled off the top sheet and lined out a couple of words, replacing them with the ones from her notes. Leaning back in her chair, she began reciting aloud.

But she wasn't really concentrating on the professional side of her life. She knew the argument was ready and probably wouldn't be necessary anyway. The old man wouldn't go to jail. The prosecutor had almost guaranteed that at the arraignment if Cooper would fully cooperate when he appeared today. The judge would certainly go along with the DA's recommendation. Therefore, the whole issue was fast losing top priority with her by the minute.

Besides, she couldn't help changing her train of thought from professional to personal. The intent of Audrey's last exchange was too potent. In a way she was glad she couldn't completely hide her personal stress, even if it was diminishing as the days slipped by. Why should she always be the perfect little woman and carry on her life as though nothing was ever off kilter? After all, she had a right to languish in life's setbacks just like everyone else. And maybe Audrey was right about her needing a break.

She slowly sat upright in her chair and set the argument down. Bending forward, she opened the side drawer of her desk and pulled out the eight-by-ten framed photo of her kids and ex-husband, Allen: a photo taken during happier times on a Northern California beach. She tenderly traced her forefinger across his smiling face, sending a wave of anguish through her heart. *Why had he abandoned her?* she asked herself, as she had done a thousand times before. *Why had he given up?* Why couldn't she make him understand that his failing as a medical intern didn't matter? They could have gotten through that hurdle of him washing out as a doctor. If only he'd been stronger. However, as the marriage counselor had adamantly said during her brief therapy sessions, Allen had obviously felt belittled and a failure by her ongoing success and abundance of natural courage. Yet she was disappointed that her words and actions had never seemed to dismiss those feelings of inadequacy he suffered. She had tried over and over.

She looked down at her left hand and the fading ring line on her bare third finger. She felt satisfied that she had tried desperately to keep things together as long as she could; everything that was expected of a caring wife. *Nevertheless, he left me and the marriage is over*, she told herself. She had taken her birth name back, and life would now go forward for both of them, as though their life together had never existed. As though Allen Nichols had never entered her life. Although, surprisingly, she secretly hoped that Allen's new life was better now, even though his new life was with another woman. She only wished that he had stayed on the West Coast so that he could see the kids more. Why New York? *Did he have to abandon them also?* she wondered, sighing.

She replaced the photograph in the drawer and pushed it shut. Sitting back, she looked out the window at the morning sunshine. She thought of how pleasant it would be to get back home again to California. She loved the Bay Area at this time of year, with the beautiful fall days and crisp nights. Maybe she *should* let Audrey watch the twins this weekend. Indeed, she might need a break, she told herself again. The stress of managing her professional life and a house with two four-year-olds was beginning to show. The absence of an adult to communicate with when she needed to vent or discuss trivial nothings was trying. And the lonely nights when she would actually lie there and ache without the male companionship she longed for were becoming more frequent.

What if on my trip I were to find a man just for physical purposes? she wondered. Perhaps if for only a carefree emotional release. Maybe one night she'd find that handsome stranger, enjoy a great dinner, a few cocktails and an evening filled with careless conversation and seductive laughter—a fitting prelude to making passionate love with him. Perhaps she'd drive them both crazy with pleasure and then just leave without any strings attached. *How wild*, she thought.

She broke into a grin, thinking sarcastically, *Yeah, sure.* She probably wouldn't even know how to pull that trick off in a month, much less a long weekend. Besides, she knew she really needed the *caring* conversation and to be held with affection and tenderness to achieve that total carnal release. *And the chance of finding that special someone during a fleeting weekend was unrealistic.*

Her mood turned somber as she looked over at her attorney credentials and university diplomas hanging on the wall, and thought about her recent decision to leave the firm. Even though she was proud to be associated with such a well-established law partnership, she needed more of a challenge. William Hansen's posture of tailoring the firm toward mundane sleepy-eyed civil cases was his prerogative and his just reward after spending years as a tough, renowned trial lawyer in Denver. Yet *she* needed more. She couldn't help it. She was bored, and craved new stimulation of growth if she was to reach the goals she'd set for herself early in her career.

Beaverton was pleasant, and her lifestyle was acceptable when her husband was assigned to St. Vincent's Hospital and they were a family. But now that part of her life was over. She could relocate to San Francisco, where she really always wanted to be. Moreover, the kids could see their grandparents and she'd be close to Stanford University, her alma mater, where she'd like to teach someday.

She grimaced, thinking how difficult it would be telling Mr. Hansen she was leaving. He had been good to her. Giving her the opportunity to join the firm so soon out of college was gratifying—especially when he took her under his esteemed individual guidance. And his kind understanding during the trying times of her personal anxiety was always so significant. Regardless, she'd have to tell him soon. It was bothering her greatly to harbor her feelings, and she knew she couldn't conceal them much longer. She'd discuss the move with her parents during the weekend visit, and tell Mr. Hansen as soon as she got back in the office on Monday. Then she'd finish up the caseload on her docket and…

Her train of thought was broken by a soft knocking on her door. Feeling somewhat guilty over her daydreaming, she quickly turned toward her desk, shuffled the court argument in front of her and picked up her pencil.

"Come in," she said sharply.

The door opened and Jack Malcolm, the junior partner of the firm, wandered in with a cup of coffee, appearing tired. He was dressed in slacks and a cotton pullover sports shirt. "Morning," he greeted, sitting his burly frame down at the small conference table in the middle of the room.

She smiled as she rose from her desk chair and sat down at the table across from him. "Good morning," she said, handing him a copy of her court argument. "How are you, Jack? You look weary. Umm, bowling league last night?"

"Yeah," he answered before draining his coffee cup with a long swig. "Went to that new sports bar, Rocky's, afterward. Got a little buzzed playing pool. But I'm sure I'll live." He chuckled as he set the cup down and began looking over her statement.

She remained silent, as she always did when he was kind enough to review her work, especially when he had one of his "bowling league" hangovers. She respected his proven track record at getting to the heart of any court matter quickly and effectively—even though his personal drive to be a courtroom dynamo left much to be desired. She chuckled inwardly.

He shrugged, setting the argument down. "This is fine," he said nonchalantly. "The case is pretty well a lock anyway. I can't believe the old fart will do any time. His plea bargain was soundly accepted, wasn't it?"

"Correct," she replied. "The DA quickly agreed on a stiff fine and no jail time if he agrees to give up his license and go to AA. They don't want the old man in jail—just off the road. However, I need to be prepared in case the judge disagrees."

"Don't worry, that won't happen," Malcolm said through a wide yawn as he pushed his chair back. "Damn," he added, standing. "I need to wake up. I have to speak at the Rotary Club luncheon today."

She grinned. "Yes, wake up, or your speech might put *you* to sleep rather than your audience."

"Thanks a lot," he said, matching her grin as he walked toward the door.

"I do appreciate your time this morning, Jack," she said as he left.

"Any time," he answered back through the doorway.

She stood and picked up her paperwork from the table. Glancing at her watch, she thought she might get in to see Millie to have her hair trimmed before her court appearance. Then she wouldn't have to worry about it tomorrow while she ran the rest of her errands and got herself and the kids ready for the trip.

"Oh, by the way," she heard a voice call behind her. Turning, she saw Jack in the doorway. "You never did get back to me the other day," he said. "Do you want to take the Billy Thiebout case I talked to you about? His arraignment is scheduled for next Wednesday."

She thought a moment, then couldn't help animatedly wrinkling her face. "You mean the seventeen-year-old punk who robbed the Hillsboro gas station and beat up the owner's wife?" she asked sarcastically. "No, thanks."

"Okay," he answered, puzzled over her behavior. "But why the face?"

She was a little embarrassed over the impetuous ridicule that had just slipped out. She knew now was the right time to break the news to the firm. "I'm sorry, that was inappropriate," she apologized, turning away. She looked back up at him. "Do you have a minute, Jack? I'd really like to talk to you."

He looked at his watch. "Yeah, sure," he answered, seeing she was troubled. "My speech can wait." He walked in and shut the door, meeting her at the table.

Realizing her nervousness, he asked gently as they sat, "What's the matter?"

She locked her eyes on his as she blurted, "Jack, I need to deal with more than 502's, petty burglaries and maladjusted juvenile delinquents."

It took him a minute to comprehend what she was saying, and then he nodded. "I see, Lacey," he replied calmly. "But you know that anything other than those types of cases is going to be hard to get at this firm. Probably damn near impossible."

"Yes," she answered, "I'm well aware of Mr. Hansen's clientele preferences."

"You know the old man wants to bow out mildly," Malcolm said. "He's handled some big ones in his time. He's had his share of the hard-core stuff, and now he'd just as soon leave those cases for one of those other big groups downtown."

"I know," she answered, letting him talk before she'd tell him she was leaving.

"And they're not only Hansen's preferences," he continued, "but Jacob's and mine also. You know me; my personal life is just as important as my professional career. And Jacob..." He hesitated, chuckling. "Well, as long as he can handle the business end of the partnership, take on a little petty white-collar crime once in a while and chase the senior widows around before he retires, he's happy."

She smiled at hearing Malcolm's description of Corey Jacob's professional agenda. But then she appeared saddened as she said, "I don't resent the firm for its modest posture. But I've decided I need to leave." She quickly looked up. "However, it's also because I want to return to California…"

"Whoa," he interrupted. "Do you think we didn't know you'd be leaving for more opportunity? Especially after your divorce was final. We all knew it was only a matter of time. We just didn't think it would be this soon. Anyway, you're ready, lady. Go for it. We'll help you all we can."

She shot him a look of relief, demonstrating that she'd finally let go of what she'd been holding inside for so long.

He lifted his forefinger, signaling a halt to her relief. "Just a minute," he cautioned, smiling. "You're not going to get off that easily. You're going to have to be the one who tells William."

She swallowed, her eyes widening.

He continued, "You know he thinks the world of you. He deserves to hear this from you." He paused, then added, "Rest assured, I am not breathing a word of this to anyone. Sorry." He smiled.

She nodded. "Yes, of course," she replied, fidgeting with her pencil. "I'll talk to Mr. Hansen after I get back from San Jose. I need to discuss this with my parents first anyway. They may need to help me out with the initial relocation—definitely the timing details."

"Fine," he said in a comforting tone. "Although I wouldn't worry too much. Like I said, I think he's expecting this would eventually happen."

"Okay, thank you for listening," she said softly.

"Sure, you're welcome." He glanced at his watch. "Wow, I gotta get going," he said, getting up. "My speech needs more polishing."

She rose with him, looking exuberant. "Me too. I want to see if I can get in to my hairdresser for a trim," she said, fingering the brownish tresses that swept back over her ears.

"Good luck with the Cooper case today," he said, walking toward the door. "Oh," he added, turning, "I'll slip the maladjusted-juvenile-delinquent-Thiebout matter onto my docket."

"I'm really going to miss all of you," she said with a vigorous laugh.

"You'd better," he replied with a grin as he walked out the door. "We're a pretty damn good bunch, even if we are a little boring."

She nodded and wiped her moistened eyes, then turned and walked to her desk, flipping through the Rolodex to find her hairdresser's number.

Chapter Thirteen

The witness, Justice Center, Portland

Rebecca Newell, looking saddened and exhausted, entered Lieutenant Kierzek's office, escorted by Sergeant Cuyler. Settling herself in the faded green office chair in front of his desk, she looked up and thanked the accommodating officer as he left, pulling the door closed behind him. She silently peered across at Kierzek, who was facing away from her, fishing through his files for her statement while he took the last bite from an apple. Twisting her shapely body, she tugged on her long black hair as her eyes tensely swept over the bustling police activity outside his windowed office. She turned back toward him when he readjusted himself in his chair and dropped the apple core into the small bag that contained his used sandwich wrapper and empty Styrofoam coffee cup.

After crumpling the bag, he pitched the brown lump into the wastebasket and looked over and smiled. "Good afternoon, Ms. Newell. Sorry, but, I knew I wouldn't be getting much of a break today, so I had to squeeze lunch in when I could."

She managed a slight smile. "It's all right, lieutenant. Your eating doesn't bother me. I assume you're a very busy man."

"Sometimes," he said, sitting back in his chair, appearing relaxed. "Ms. Newell," he continued, "We appreciate your prompt cooperation during this trying time. It's very important that we get critical witness information as quickly and as thoroughly as we can in cases like this."

"It's no problem," she replied, appearing attentive, sitting motionless in the chair. "I understand."

"Ms. Newell," he said slowly, "some of the material we have to cover might be sensitive to you. If you would be more comfortable interviewing with Sergeant Loraine Marzell, I'm sure she'd be more than willing to come and…"

"No, that's okay," she interrupted. "Thank you for the considerate offer, but if you're the one in charge of this case I'd rather go over it with you first-hand. That way things will move faster, won't they?"

"Yes, umm…probably," he answered, a bit surprised by her directness. He pointed to the tape recorder. "We're short a stenographer today. Do you mind if I use the recorder during our interview?"

"Not at all," she said, her eyes darting to the recorder and back to him.

"Good," he said, "let's get started, then." He picked up a document and put on his reading glasses. "I have your initial statement that you gave Officer Cuyler yesterday." He quickly scanned it before looking up at her. "I see it contains most of the facts pertaining to the case as we know it. However, I need a little more information to fill in some gaps."

"No problem," she said, smiling nervously. "Officer Cuyler mentioned that was your usual procedure with key witnesses."

He nodded, reached over and depressed the "record" button, then turned back to her. "First, please tell me how long you've been friends with Mrs. Bearnes and her husband, Monte."

She thought a moment, looking pained. "Years," she answered slowly. "Laura and I were like sisters…" She hesitated, reached down and pulled a Kleenex from her purse. Kierzek waited patiently while she dabbed her eyes, took a deep breath and said, "You'll have to pardon me. I guess this has been harder on me than I realize."

"I know," he said consolingly. "Again, I'm sorry to have to drag you through this today, but I don't have any choice. I'll make it as brief as I can."

"It's okay," she replied tightly, grimacing, now appearing angry. "I'll do anything I can to help bring an end to this God-awful tragedy."

"Yes, of course," Kierzek said, looking back down at his pad. "How well do you know Mr. Bearnes?"

"Quite well as far as his life with Laura was concerned," she replied. "I don't know much about his professional life. No one really does. He's a very busy man."

"Can you tell me more about your relationship with them as a couple?" Kierzek asked. "How you met them, and when? Just tell me as much as you know."

"Sure," she answered, rubbing her strained forehead as she continued, "I met Laura and Monte years ago…"

Kierzek leaned back in his chair and tapped his pencil eraser against his lower lip as he listened intently to Rebecca while discreetly evaluating her attitude. This was a critical task that was required whenever he interviewed principal witnesses who held key pieces to the crime—witnesses who could make or break a case. He had to be more cautious with Rebecca, realizing that she appeared to be grudge-bearing, yet not necessarily lying. And her statement was absolutely necessary, because she was supposedly the last person to have any contact with Laura Bearnes before she was murdered. *Other than her killer, that is,* he thought. At any rate, he would strive to carefully dissect Rebecca's account into actual facts from what might be vindictive illusion. Or her testimony could be thrown out. He knew he had his hands full.

She explained how, soon after her husband was tragically killed in an automobile accident, she'd met Monte and Laura at the Portland art museum while they were all attending an art show about three years ago. How she and Laura had quickly become friends while discovering they shared a similar appreciation of art. Also, both of them knew most of the same gallery owners in the area: Laura through her frequent exhibits, and she through her work at the art supply store.

She told how their friendship was further solidified during Rebecca's new role of lonely widowhood when she began travelling with Laura to California on her monthly art excursions. And how they all became closer by Rebecca's spending numerous weekends at the Bearnes house in Eugene, and in return their daughter, Tamra, would visit her in Portland for extended stays.

Rebecca paused and wiped her watery eyes. "Sorry again," she said.

Kierzek reached over and shut off the recorder, asking, "Can I get you some coffee or something?"

"No, thank you," she declined, looking down. "I'd just as soon keep going."

"Sure," he said, switching the recorder back on and sitting back. "Tell me, how did the Bearneses get along lately? Is there any reason to think they were quarreling or fighting unusually?"

Rebecca looked up, frowning. "Lieutenant," she said pointedly, "I don't understand that question. What would that have to do with Timmers killing Laura? I mean, isn't this an intrusion on their private lives?"

"Ms. Newell," he answered politely, quickly shutting off the recorder again, "it's important that we get all of the aspects of the case nailed down, especially the conduct of the key individuals. If the case does go to trial, and the defense…"

"*If* it goes to trial!?" she interrupted indignantly, crossing her arms across her chest, shooting Kierzek an icy stare. "What do you mean *if*? My statement alone should convict that son of a bitch! What more do you need, for God's sake?"

"That didn't mean how it sounded," he replied patiently, quickly realizing that he had to be more delicate with his questioning, so as not to shut down her cooperation. "I'm sure it'll go to trial. It's just that we need to research every area that affects the case. I'm sure the defense will raise questions surrounding the husband's actions. It's pretty much standard procedure."

"Okay," she said quietly, uncrossing her arms and gesturing toward the recorder as she eased up. "I guess I understand."

"Thank you," he said as he turned the recorder back on and sat back. "Let me rephrase the question. In your estimation, what was Laura's view of her marriage?"

Rebecca readily explained that despite Laura's involvement with Jonathan, she had recently told her that Monte had been her lifeblood since the first day they'd met at college. How she was still committed to their loving relationship that had lasted more than fifteen years. How Laura was still proud that Monte kept himself trim and handsome through vigorous evening workouts at the gym. And even though he had been working much more than usual lately, neglecting her somewhat, she still loved him dearly. And it was ironic that only last week, when they were all sitting around chatting at dinner, Monte mentioned that their healthy and wealthy family life together with Tamra was like a fairy tale. It was almost as though Monte knew about Jonathan and was "asking" her to come back. And Rebecca was sure that was why Laura had decided to break off her affair and repair her "broken life."

Rebecca's eyes narrowed, adding bitterly, "That is, until Timmers came along and wouldn't allow it."

"So the Berneses weren't fighting?" he asked, disregarding her last comment.

"No, they weren't," she answered. "I'd just say they weren't as close as they once were, mainly because of his demanding workload."

Kierzek finished jotting that note and looked up. "Tell me, Ms. Newell, were you always fully aware of the affair between her and Timmers?"

She moved forward in her chair. "Oh, yes," she answered sharply, her dark violet eyes narrowing. "I knew what was going on from the beginning."

"Where'd they meet?" he asked, wanting to corroborate her account with Jonathan's version that he'd gotten yesterday.

"He approached her while she was working in the Laguna Beach gallery last spring," she answered. "He even bought one of her finest paintings to stay close to her—a very expensive painting."

"So the affair started last spring in Laguna Beach?"

"Not exactly," she said. "That's when they met, but the affair actually started a few months later when she was unable to discourage his persistent advances any further. He was constantly after her."

"Then I take it she wasn't the type of woman to…um…"

"Play around?" Rebecca interrupted, helping Kierzek with his uncomfortable question about her good friend. "No, not at all. She was upstanding and completely faithful to her husband. I'm sure of that. I watched her turn many charming men down flat when they made improper moves toward her."

Kierzek appeared puzzled. "What do you think was different about Timmers?"

"His timing."

"His timing?"

She nodded, looking at him directly. "I think she was lonely and didn't really know it," she replied. "Like I said earlier, her husband was totally wrapped up in his work and was paying less attention to her. And she'd never been neglected like that before in her life." She paused. "I don't think she understood her own vulnerability, or she probably would have discussed it with Monte before it was too late."

Kierzek looked up from his notes, saying, "So you believe Timmers was the first one to come along who made a difference?"

"Yes," she answered firmly. "That's the way I saw it. He's very attractive and charismatic, and wouldn't leave her alone until she finally caved in to his pursuit."

"Uh-huh, I see," he said as he glanced back through his notes, flipping a former page to the front. *Timmers' account of his pursuit was less than persistent*, he thought, but he concealed that point. Looking up, he asked, "Can you go into a little more detail about what transpired between you and Mrs. Bearnes on the afternoon before she went to meet with Timmers?"

"Umm, sure, I think so." Rebecca squinted upward to gather her thoughts. "Let's see," she said slowly. "I picked Laura up at the Amtrak station about noon..."

"Oh," Kierzek interrupted, "that reminds me. Do you know why she didn't drive up from Eugene?"

"She rarely drove when she came up to meet with Timmers," Rebecca answered. "She didn't want to take the chance her car might be spotted in the wrong place at the wrong time. Once in a while she'd rent a car here..." She frowned, then looked down, lamenting, "God, if only she had rented one this time...and not walked through the park."

Kierzek remained still as she shook off her stab of sadness and continued, "Anyway, we had a light lunch somewhere near the station and then went back to my apartment to drop off her overnight bag."

Kierzek asked, "What was her mood at this point? Did she seem apprehensive or fearful about her upcoming meeting with Timmers?"

"Yes," she answered quickly, glancing at the recorder's flashing indicator light. She turned toward Kierzek. "As a matter of fact, the last conversation we had centered around that very thing. I remember it vividly..."

Kierzek listened closely as Rebecca began to clearly recount the last conversation she'd had with Laura in the doorway of her apartment, just before Laura left to meet Jonathan at the hotel...

◆◆◆

Laura and Rebecca embraced tightly in the open doorway of the downtown apartment. As they separated, Rebecca took hold of her friend's trembling hand, saying tenderly, "You seem frightened. Are you worried about how Jonathan is going to react?"

"Somewhat," Laura answered, lowering her head. "He sounded upset when I talked to him yesterday. As though he knew I was going to break off our affair."

"Maybe you shouldn't do this alone," Rebecca said worriedly. "Would you like me to come along with you?"

"No," Laura replied, "I have to do this by myself."

"But he's got it really bad for you," Rebecca said with anger in her voice, displaying irritation over Laura's dilemma. "Isn't there a chance he could turn violent?"

Laura looked up at her, appealing, "Please don't worry about me. I'm sure he'll be deeply heartbroken, but I don't think he'd ever physically hurt me."

"I do worry. You're my best friend," Rebecca countered. "You don't know for sure how he'll react. You even told me once you thought he might have a dark side."

"I know, I know...but..." Laura's words trailed off. Frustrated, she stepped back and withdrew her hand. "Please, Rebecca," she appealed again. "Let's not confuse this situation any more than it is."

"Okay, I'll try not to worry," Rebecca replied, a lingering concern evident in her voice.

Laura glanced at her watch, mumbling, "Oh, hell, I have to go and get this over with. I'm sure he's arrived at the hotel by now. I'm meeting him about three."

"Just remember," Rebecca said, "I'll be around if you need me."

"Good," Laura replied. "I may need some moral support later. And please be available to cover for me this last time in case Monte calls, okay?"

Rebecca nodded with a warm smile. She watched Laura turn and step through the doorway.

Bounding down the porch steps onto the walk, Laura suddenly turned and yelled back to her friend, "I'm sure it'll be a very late night for me. I won't be able to tell Jonathan right away. Although I will be coming back to stay with you tonight."

Rebecca returned the wave. "Yes, sure, I'll plan on it."

Rebecca turned away from Kierzek and pulled out another Kleenex. "That's the last time I had any direct contact with her," she said, dabbing her eyes.

Kierzek asked, "What do you think 'a very late night' meant to her?"

Rebecca shrugged. "I thought I'd hear from her by eleven or so. I worried about her all evening, but I didn't dare interfere. I thought surely she'd stay in the hotel or take a cab to my place."

"But you fell asleep waiting for her?" Kierzek asked curiously, looking down at the statement Cuyler had taken at Rebecca's apartment.

"Yes," she replied timidly. "I finally took some Dalmane to relieve my nervousness and fell asleep about midnight. I awoke around five and found her message on my answering machine..."

Kierzek interrupted, "You mean the message Laura left you from the hotel after she'd left Jonathan?"

"Yes," she answered, looking away.

"And you hadn't heard the phone ringing?"

"No," she answered. "Because I'd also had a couple of glasses of wine and I was pretty much out of it and..."

Kierzek shot her a concerned look, interrupting her train of thought.

"Yes, you're right, lieutenant," she said, addressing his silent concern. "Alcohol isn't something that should be mixed with sleeping drugs to potentiate the effectiveness. However, I've been taking Dalmane ever since my husband died, to relieve many restless nights. So I've not only built up a tolerance, but I've learned what my body can and can't handle."

Kierzek looked back down at his notes.

"Anyway, I realize now that taking that sleeping pill was a big mistake," she continued. "I just didn't think a thing like this could happen. I just didn't..."

"I understand," Kierzek said, looking over at the recorder, seeing it was just about out of tape. Giving her time to compose herself, he ejected the cassette, flipped it over to the other side and restarted the recorder. "Okay, would you please go through the details of the phone message again?"

"I'll try," she said as she sat back in her chair, laying her hands in her lap, appearing uncertain. "However, unfortunately I can't remember the exact wording, because I was still groggy when I listened to her message, and inadvertently erased it."

Kierzek frowned. "I know," he said, looking at her statement. "Just tell me what you remember, please."

"Well," she said, furrowing her brow, "there wasn't much to the message. Just that Timmers was up in his room very drunk and she was concerned about her safety because he had acted strangely earlier...something like boisterous and angry. She didn't know how long he'd be passed out, but she was going to stay at the hotel until she reached me. She didn't even want to come over to my house until she knew for sure I was there."

Kierzek glanced up from his notes. "Why didn't you try to call her back?"

"Because the message was over two hours old and I didn't know how to reach her. I certainly wasn't going to call his room," she replied quickly. "And remember, I was still extremely groggy. I fell back down on the couch and slept until your call woke me up."

Kierzek nodded, then sat back in his chair, still appearing puzzled.

"What is it?" she asked.

He looked at her. "I just can't figure why she'd go into the park at that time of night if she was afraid for her safety."

Rebecca nodded. "Yes, that's a good question." She thought a moment. "Although she was used to walking to my place after she'd meet with Timmers. And she was a creature of habit."

"You mean she *always* walked to your place from the hotel?"

"Yes," Rebecca said, "even if it was bad weather. She was so confused after spending the night with him that she needed the time alone to clear her mind. But, of course, that was usually during the daytime. Perhaps she just decided it was safe regardless of the time."

"Perhaps," Kierzek agreed, rubbing his chin with his index finger. He looked down at his notes, thinking, *Many people besides*

Timmers could have known about Laura's frequent "walking through the park" routine.

"You know what?" Rebecca said animatedly, her eyes widening as Kierzek looked up. "Maybe Timmers was with her all the time and she thought he was safe. He was a very persuasive person."

Kierzek shook his head and pursed his lips, answering, "No, I don't think so. The bell captain had seen him in the hotel lobby alone just before dawn. He was in pretty bad shape. And the bell captain had also seen Laura leave earlier."

"Oh, yes, that's right," she replied calmly, sitting back. "Now I remember reading that in the paper. So, I guess he must've stalked her and..."

They both looked toward the door when a knocking interrupted them. Seeing Cuyler looking through the window, Kierzek motioned him in.

Cuyler opened the door and walked in. "Sorry to bother you, lieutenant," he said, handing Kierzek a memo with a receipt attached to it. "But I know you were waiting for this information."

"Thanks," Kierzek said, looking over the memo.

"I'm heading across the street to grab a burger," Cuyler said. "I'll be back shortly."

Kierzek only nodded as Cuyler left and closed the door behind him.

Rebecca watched Kierzek curiously as he laid the memo down and looked up at her, saying, "Do you remember if Ms. Bearnes mentioned anything in her phone message about a new diamond pendant Timmers had given her that night?"

Rebecca thought a moment before answering slowly, "Umm, no...Not that I remember anyway. But then Laura was used to having nice jewelry..."

"I'm sure this piece was different," Kierzek interrupted, pointing at the memo and the bankcard receipt. "We checked with the jeweler in Orange County this morning. Timmers bought it on the day he flew up here. It was very expensive. We doubt she would've taken this gift casually."

"Then I assume it's missing," Rebecca said, appearing puzzled.

"Yes," he answered, still looking at her.

"Well, maybe Timmers didn't really give it to her," she said. "Perhaps he wants to make the crime look like a robbery."

"Perhaps," Kierzek said. "We just have to look at all the angles."

"I see," Rebecca said, her eyes turning downward. "But I really don't know anything about it, lieutenant."

Kierzek flipped to a new page in his notes. "Okay, I only have one or two more questions for today, but they're very important."

"Yes, of course," she answered, growing attentive.

"Do you think her husband ever knew about her affair with Timmers," he asked, "regardless of what he's saying?"

Rebecca hesitated, looking upward to gather her thoughts. "Umm, no," she answered. "No," she repeated, sounding more certain.

Kierzek sat silent, prodding her for more information with a riveting stare.

"Well, at least I don't think so," she added. "When I told him about it yesterday, he seemed more devastated when he realized Laura was murdered because she had jilted her lover."

"Was that during the phone call that took place at your apartment yesterday?"

She nodded. "Yes. He called me right after the Eugene police contacted him at the university. He demanded to know everything." She paused, sighing, then continued, "I had to tell him, though it was very difficult. He sounded as though he was in shambles, like he was falling apart."

"I see," Kierzek said, slowly flipping to another note page while she dabbed her eyes. "Okay, one more. Do you think Mr. Bearnes was a jealous man?"

She paused, digesting his question. "I really don't know," she answered. "I never saw him that way. But then again, I never saw Laura openly give him any reason to be."

"Okay," Kierzek said as he sat upright in his chair and closed his notebook. "I guess that's it for now, Ms. Newell." He reached over, shutting off the recorder.

She stood, appearing relieved as she grabbed her purse hanging from the chair arm. She then paused. "Incidentally, did Monte make it in to see you today?"

"Yes, he did," Kierzek answered, appearing puzzled. "I take it you didn't see him this morning."

"No, lieutenant, I talked to him only briefly last night at his hotel," she answered quickly. "Like I said, he was in terrible shape."

"Oh, I see," Kierzek said. "Well, he came in this morning to clear up some routine matters. Then he picked up his wife's belongings and left just before you got here."

"By any chance do you know what he decided to do with Laura's body?" she asked curiously. "I know that he was considering cremation so he could keep her ashes close to him and Tamra."

Kierzek leaned back in his chair. "Yeah, as a matter of fact, he did mention that he's making arrangements with a local funeral home for the ceremony. I don't know which one, but I understand he wants to hold the church service in Portland because her roots were here."

She nodded, then asked, "Can you tell me when her body will be released? I know her mother is coming in from Olympia, Washington. And I want to assist her and Monte in planning things out."

"Well, I can't pinpoint exactly because that's not my call," Kierzek answered as he stood. "However, I don't think it should take more than a few days. I talked with Dr. Richardson this morning, and he said no major autopsy would be necessary. He also told me all the forms are completed and they just have to be routed through the proper authoritative channels."

"Good," she responded, waiting for Kierzek to walk around his desk.

He politely took her by the forearm, saying, "I'll have Cuyler bring the new statement to you for your signature as soon as we transcribe the additional information from the tape."

"Sure," she said.

He continued, "I want you to know again that I appreciate your cooperation during this difficult period, Ms. Newell. However, I hope you understand I might have to call on you again."

"Of course, lieutenant," she replied agreeably as he escorted her out of the office, walking her to the elevator. "Like I said earlier, I'll do whatever I can to help bring a conclusion to this awful crime."

Kierzek bid her goodbye as the elevator doors closed behind her. He turned and shook his head as he made his way back to his office. He was unsure if all the answers she gave were really consistent with the facts surrounding the case, and those surrounding a sister-close friendship, as she had aptly put it. It also bothered him that Rebecca had made Timmers out to be just short of a night stalker until Laura had given in to his advances. Yet he hadn't gotten that impression of Timmers or the situation when he'd interrogated him.

Walking back into his office, he sat down, deep in thought. He couldn't pinpoint anything suspicious that stood out about her statement, yet something didn't seem right; he just felt it. He realized she had an axe to grind, but she was showing absolutely no mercy. And then he thought about her account of her and Laura at her apartment that afternoon. How Rebecca had indicated that Laura was frightened of Timmers. *Then why would she go and meet him? Why not just call him from the safety of Rebecca's apartment and be done with it?* He shook his head, thinking what he always thought after questioning witnesses concerning their relationship with the murder victim. *You always get only one side of the story. And unfortunately it's a side that can't ever be countered.* He pulled the cassette tape from the recorder and leaned back in his chair, hoisting his feet to the desktop.

Rebecca Newell laid her head back against the headrest as she made her way through Portland's downtown traffic. She mulled over the long, tedious interview she'd just finished with Lieutenant Kierzek.

She felt little remorse over telling him that Laura had seemed afraid of Jonathan when she'd left the message on her answering machine the morning she was murdered. For all she knew, Laura *was* worried about Jonathan's reaction to her leaving him. *So had I really lied to Kierzek?* Rebecca wondered. *Maybe only stretched the truth a bit.* Her eyes narrowed. *And was it really wrong to put the final nail in Jonathan's coffin?*

As she tensely gripped the steering wheel, she knew that Kierzek was nobody's fool. And she hoped she hadn't been one either, as she suddenly made an unexpected turn onto the interstate, heading for Eugene. She had to see Monte. He'd be waiting for her. She was sure.

CHAPTER FOURTEEN

Mid-afternoon, Lieutenant Kierzek's office

Sergeant Cuyler knocked lightly on the office door, hesitant about entering Kierzek's office when he saw his boss deeply submerged in concerned thought, tapping a cassette on the palm of his hand.

Kierzek looked up at him standing in the doorway. "C'mon in, Ed," he said, waving off the interruption by offering him the chair in front of his desk.

Cuyler walked in and sat down, holding a folded up piece of paper. "I saw Newell leaving when I was coming back from lunch," he said. "How did the questioning go? Did she give you anything to go on?"

Kierzek shrugged, appearing unsettled. "A little, I guess," he answered, looking upward for thoughts. "She's a very shrewd woman. I'm sure she never misses a beat. And her answers seem consistent with her original statement."

"Are you questioning her evidence? You sound unsure."

"Well, Ed, I just have to be careful, that's all," Kierzek answered. "If she inflates her statement and the defense nails it, everything could end up in the can—inadmissible. I mean, she's really bent on putting Timmers away."

"For sure," Cuyler agreed. "I picked up on that yesterday when I was with her at the morgue. But isn't that natural? The Bearnes woman was her best friend."

"Yes, her best friend," Kierzek said pointedly. "That's also what bothers me." He paused as he turned around to face Cuyler squarely. "Newell seems to have known what the Bearnes woman was up against that night, but wasn't available when she called. She claims she was asleep." He shook his head and put the cassette on the desk, labeling it "Rebecca Newell, Bearnes Case" with a marker.

Cuyler pointed at the tape Kierzek was holding. "I see you taped her."

"Yeah, I wanted to see her reaction to the recorder. And I wanted to keep an eye on her when she answered the questions."

Cuyler shot him an inquisitive look. "And…?"

"Nah," Kierzek said with a dismissive wave. "I didn't see anything in her reactions to indicate she was lying." He frowned. "But, hell, every time it seemed like anything critical came up, she'd start crying, wiping her eyes with tissue. Maybe it was staged, maybe not. Like I said, she's a shrewd woman."

Cuyler sat back, appearing curious. "What about the husband, Monte?"

Kierzek squinted, focusing his thoughts before answering. "He sure seems crushed over his wife's death all right. It was a helluva scene at the morgue last night. But we got through it."

"I knew it would be rough," Cuyler replied. "He was pretty much a mess when I drove him over there. How'd he come across to you today?"

"Exactly what I expected from a grieving husband, to a T," Kierzek answered, opening his notebook.

"So he didn't have any problem with you questioning him?"

"No, he knows it's standard procedure to immediately question the spouse of a homicide victim," Kierzek replied, checking over his notes. "He claims everything is a total shock to him and he didn't know anything about the affair she was having with Timmers until Newell told him after the murder."

Cuyler sat back, growing interested. "Did he explain where he was at the time of the murder?"

"Somewhat," Kierzek answered. "He says he was in Eugene at the university all night long preparing for his fall classes, taking advantage of his wife's being in Portland."

"Did he leave the young daughter at home alone?" asked Cuyler, surprised. "Isn't she only nine or ten?"

"Just turned nine," Kierzek said with a skeptical tone, paging through his notes. "He said he'd left her with neighbor friends…Bill and Amy Rickerson. They watched her overnight and all the next day and…"

Cuyler interrupted, "You sound unsure of his story, too—like Newell's."

"No, not really. But just like with Newell, I have to be certain," Kierzek replied, facing Cuyler as they locked stares. "And his story is just damn convenient, that's all...maybe a bit flimsy. But, then again, not necessarily untrue."

"Didn't anyone see him while he was at the university?"

"Yes, absolutely, the night before," Kierzek replied. "Although Bearnes isn't sure about all night, or at the approximate time of the murder."

Cuyler sat silent as Kierzek again looked down at his notes.

Kierzek continued, "Bearnes took a break and had dinner with one of the other professors that night, then returned to the university around eleven-thirty. He claims he passed the third-shift security guard when he parked his car in front of the lab where his office is located."

"The guard must have seen him that late at night," Cuyler interjected. "That's the whole point of the guards being there."

"Right," Kierzek agreed. "Bearnes knows he was seen by the guard, because afterward they acknowledged each other a couple of times through the window of his office door when the guard was making his rounds."

"Wouldn't that corroborate his alibi?" Cuyler asked, intensifying his attention.

"Perhaps," Kierzek answered. "But Bearnes doesn't know for sure if the security guard can substantiate that he was there *all* night." He flipped to a new page of his notes. "Bearnes said that sometime around 2 a.m. he took a break and fell asleep on his office couch watching an old movie on TV..."

"Did you ask him which movie it was?"

"Sure," Kierzek answered, smiling at his partner's detective savvy. "A Humphrey Bogart yarn. I haven't checked yet, but I'll guarantee you he's correct."

Cuyler nodded with a smile.

Kierzek continued, "Bearnes says he didn't wake up until about 7:30 and can't say for certain if the guard had seen him sleeping on the couch."

"I see," Cuyler replied, slowly furrowing his brow. "So it's possible Bearnes can't positively verify his whereabouts at the time of the murder. Correct?"

"Correct," Kierzek confirmed, looking up.

Cuyler moved forward in his chair, saying, "And if Bearnes did know about his wife's affair, he'd have a motive for the murd...."

"Right again," Kierzek interrupted. "He'd have both motive and opportunity."

"Key ingredients for a suspect," Cuyler chimed in.

"Uh-huh, exactly," Kierzek said, shrugging. "But I didn't push it."

"By the way, what does he teach?"

"Hang on, that's not an easy answer," Kierzek replied with a chuckle, flipping through his notebook again. Finding the page, he traced through the words with his index finger, reading directly, "Graduate-level psychology...specializes in behavior therapy rather than psychoanalysis."

Cuyler looked at him questioningly. "Behavior therapy? Doesn't everything in psychology center around behaviorism?"

Kierzek wrinkled his face. "Um, yeah, I guess," he said, looking back down at his notes. "Bearnes described his role as viewing human behavior through manipulating the environment, rather than blaming anti-social behavior on problems originating in their past." He looked up. "Whatever the hell that means. You know how confusing all that shit gets."

Cuyler held up his hands, signaling puzzlement. "Right, whatever," he replied sarcastically.

Kierzek laughed. "But I do need to understand it better. I've got a call into our criminal psychiatrist at the Salem pen for a layman explanation. He hasn't called back yet."

Cuyler noticed that Kierzek still appeared uneasy. "Anything else come up?"

"Bearnes said there was a substantial life insurance policy on his wife, half a million or so," Kierzek answered. "But it was a joint policy. And the policies were taken out a couple of years ago. And I suppose that's not unusual for someone of their wealthy status. So I'm not too concerned about that angle, I guess."

"So how'd the conversation end up?"

"Ah, nothing unusual," Kierzek said. "After we finished the interview session he took her possessions with him and..." He hesitated, looking up at Cuyler curiously. "Where's the umbrella we found in Timmers' hotel room?"

"Still locked up in the evidence cage, as far as I know," Cuyler answered.

"Had you mentioned it to Bearnes at all?"

"No, I never thought about it, why?"

"It's just strange he didn't ask about it," Kierzek answered. "It was a nice one. And Timmers told me it had been a present Bearnes had given to his wife."

"Maybe he found out somehow that we had to keep it for the trial," Cuyler suggested.

Kierzek shrugged and closed his notebook. "Yeah, probably something like that. Perhaps I'm just grasping at straws." He shook his head, again frustrated over the mounting loose ends hanging about this once seemingly airtight case against Timmers.

Cuyler said nothing, letting his mentor think.

Kierzek reached over and picked up the memo with the pendant receipt attached to it. "Which reminds me. I'm considering the diamond pendant that Timmers gave Laura Bearnes that night as missing, and now a piece of evidence. Check out the area pawnshops and the local fences. Anywhere someone might try to dump it."

"Okay," Cuyler agreed. "Anything else you want me to do?"

"Yes," Kierzek said. "Check with the security guard at the university to see if he can verify Bearnes' alibi. Bearnes told me he thinks the guard's first name is Albert. He didn't know the last name—he's new."

"Okay, I'll check it out, and I'll get Kelting on the pendant search while I'm doing that," he said. "Oh, incidentally, does Monte Bearnes know about the pendant?"

Kierzek hesitated, recollecting. "He didn't mention it," he replied. "But Rebecca Newell does. So maybe she'll tell him. Anyway, let's just keep it low-key for right now. I'll update Captain Ruskin at our meeting today."

Cuyler nodded, then said, "Brian, I haven't asked you. Off the record, what do you really think about Timmers? I mean, what's your hunch about him killing the woman?"

Kierzek reached for his thoughts, answering slowly, "I dunno, that's a tough one. I don't have any firm hunches yet." He paused, recollecting Timmers' interrogation session. "I watched him pretty closely when I questioned him. I can usually tell if the suspect is lying outright. He didn't seem to be."

"So you're not sure if he killed her?" Cuyler pressed carefully, but persistently.

Kierzek sat back in his chair. "You know what, Ed? I really believe Timmers himself doesn't know if he killed her." He sighed and looked upward, adding, "So how could I know? But I do know I want to get the right person. And I want to be very careful right now."

Surprised, Cuyler gradually digested Kierzek's statement of his uncertainty concerning Timmers' guilt. *This is unusual,* he thought. By this late in the investigation, Kierzek's keen instincts had always told him of his main suspect's guilt or innocence.

"What about a polygraph test?" Cuyler asked, breaking the silence. "I know they're unreliable, but could it help in this situation?"

"I doubt it," Kierzek answered quickly. "I'm sure Timmers would readily agree to it. But you know how those damn lie detectors can be a double-edged sword—even when they're accurate." He shook his head. "Which isn't very often."

"Yeah, I know," Cuyler agreed. "If Timmers doesn't really know if he did it, the machine may indicate he's truthful about his innocence when he's not."

"Correct," Kierzek confirmed. "Or the results might indicate he's guilty because of his current flustered mental state, when he might be innocent."

"So it sounds as though you've firmly decided against it."

"Yeah, for right now," Kierzek replied. "One mistake, and his defense would jump all over it. And if it were found out we were trying to disregard insufficient results…well, you know what I'm saying. It could open a real can of worms."

"I agree, Brian," Cuyler said, a light suddenly dawning as he remembered the note in his hand. "Oh, I almost forgot." He opened the note. "I actually came here to tell you that the botanist who checked out the trees at the death scene called back. And you were right."

Kierzek moved forward, giving Cuyler his full attention with a surprised look. "Really?"

Cuyler handed Kierzek the note, answering, "Yup. She confirmed that the tree branches in the thick foliage behind where the body was found had been broken off recently. Very possibly at the time of death. And the damage could definitely have been from humans struggling."

Kierzek glimpsed at the note. "I thought so!" he exclaimed enthusiastically, looking up. "It has to be the spot where she was killed. Why would park vagrants break off the branches, for God's sake? That's their roof." He sat back in his chair. "I'm convinced she was killed in that foliage and carried to the riverwalk edge."

"Okay, but why would someone move her out into the open?"

"I dunno yet," Kierzek said, glancing down at his desk calendar, remembering he had to meet with Captain Ruskin at 4:30 to give him a progress report. "Probably so the body would be found quicker and easier," he added, checking his watch to see if he still had adequate time.

"But moving the body out in plain sight wouldn't make sense in Timmers' situation," Cuyler commented.

"It doesn't seem like it," Kierzek agreed as he stood up. Grabbing his hat and blazer from the coat rack, he said crisply, "But then again, if he killed her when he was drunk and incoherent, who knows what he'd do with the body. C'mon, let's go. I have to be back here by four-thirty to meet with Ruskin."

"Where we going?" Cuyler responded surprised, rising quickly.

"The riverpark," Kierzek answered. "I want to look over the scene again in the daylight. And I want that shrubbery area around the trees combed clean. Maybe we can radio in a couple of the state boys to help us look things over again. We need to find something more substantial in the foliage area, or I know Ruskin won't let us pursue that issue any further."

"Okay, sure," Cuyler agreed, pulling out his car keys as they headed out the door. "I know it won't be easy getting a techie again. But I'll try."

They turned for the elevator, then saw Officer Phillip Bressler heading their way, saying loudly, "Lieutenant Kierzek, Sergeant Cuyler. We found the vagrant, the witness who found the woman strangled in the riverpark."

Kierzek's eyes opened wide. "Who is he?"

"His name is Marty Spahn, a homeless washed-out war veteran who hangs out in the park," Bressler answered. "He heard we were looking for him, so he came in voluntarily."

"What did you find out about what he saw?" Cuyler asked impatiently.

"He said he was just walking off his hangover that morning and spotted the dead woman," Bressler answered. "So he went to the hotel and told the bell captain. He left because he didn't want to get involved any further, and he says he's seen enough bodies. We're sure he's harmless; murder isn't his M.O."

"Where's he now?" Kierzek asked.

"We let him go after we got his statement. We can always find him through the downtown mission if we need him. Do you want us to bring him in for you to question?"

"Not right now," Kierzek replied, pausing in thought. "Just keep a close eye on him," he added as he and Cuyler turned to head for the elevator.

When they reached the main floor and headed for the back entrance, Kierzek said, "After we're finished at the riverpark, find Spahn again and question him about the missing pendant. Like I said, keep it low key, though."

Cuyler nodded. "Sure."

As they exited the back door into the gloomy daylight, Kierzek followed his street partner to his cruiser. Sliding into the passenger side, he sat back and rubbed his tired eyes while Cuyler radioed the dispatcher to contact the state crime lab for assistance. Hanging up the microphone, Cuyler put on his cap, started the car and quickly backed out of the parking space.

As the cruiser left the lot for the short drive to the riverpark, Kierzek stared straight ahead, again deep in thought. Although he was keyed up over the findings of the botanist and today's questioning of the witnesses, he knew he was mired in a difficult situation. Even if Timmers was innocent, everything was stacked against him. Captain Ruskin and the police chief wanted him put away promptly, regardless of knowing only the surface issues of the crime. And Kierzek was sure the prosecution would be only too happy to comply with their wishes.

And now that the vagrant had likely been cleared of the killing, all the evidence, even though circumstantial, was again pointing to his main suspect. Moreover, Rebecca Newell's statement today clearly showed that Timmers had a formidable witness out to nail him. The victim's best friend...the shrewd one who had him unconditionally marked as a cold-blooded murderer—and openly said so—would undoubtedly show no mercy.

His thoughts turned to Monte Bearnes, the apparent casualty of the sordid affair between his wife and Timmers—and her murder. The unknowing husband, although having no substantiated alibi as yet, was still seemingly innocent.

So then, perhaps Timmers is guilty, he thought, as light rain began to ricochet off the windshield. *And why not move justice along swiftly? But if they were wrong and he was innocent...* Closing his eyes, he grimaced as he laid his head back. And then there was the haunting fact that also didn't help the matter: *Timmers probably didn't even know himself whether he had done it.*

By the time they reached the murder scene to investigate the new evidence of the broken tree branches, and further probability that the body had been planted, Kierzek's intuition told him one thing: His clear-cut conviction package of Jonathan Timmers, all wrapped up with a neat little bow, was unraveling by the hour. He was also beginning to believe that Rebecca Newell might not be the only shrewd one wrapped up in all of this. But Kierzek's intuition convinced him of one thing: he *had* interviewed the killer. *Or at least the people who knew who the killer was.*

Daylight was fading in Eugene as Rebecca slid away from Monte's limp grasp and gently laid his arm on the bed. He uttered a sluggish snort and turned over onto his back, falling into deeper slumber. *She'd let him sleep,* she thought, watching him from the edge of the bed. The Rickersons would surely keep Tamra another night and let Monte have more time alone to deal with his tragic loss. She'd take a shower and then call Amy before she headed back to Portland, she decided. *Yes*, she could call there. They wouldn't suspect anything was unusual because she was with Monte. After all, the Rickersons knew she was sister-close to Laura and Monte. They just didn't know *how* intimate. *Yes,* she decided, *she'd call and let him sleep.*

She pulled the sheet up over her naked body and reached over, softly fondling a lock of hair on the back of his head. She recalled this afternoon and how he'd stood in the doorway with open arms when she arrived unexpectedly. No words were spoken. None were necessary. Everything was *said* when they fell into each other's arms, holding each other tightly. They only needed to be together again after being so near in Portland last night, yet unable to meet because of the heavy police and media activity surrounding them.

She drew her hand back and turned onto her side. Positioning her head comfortably on the pillow, she stared at his exhausted, motionless body. She thought back to early summer, when she'd finally gathered the strength to tell him about Laura and Jonathan. And how her admission to him had started out innocently once she was confident she was doing the right thing for Laura, who Rebecca felt was destroying her storybook life. Breaching Laura's trust had hurt Rebecca, but her disclosure was inconsequential. Monte had been growing suspicious of Laura's ongoing odd behavior and frequent absences anyway. He was about to confront her, and surely he would have broken Laura down into confessing her infidelity.

Rebecca grimaced as she remembered how Monte had suffered so at first, now knowing his once-faithful wife had strayed. How he had blamed his own neglect as the reason for Laura's loneliness, triggering her vulnerability. But after discussing the options with Rebecca, he agreed not to challenge Laura because Rebecca was sure she would come to her senses and leave Jonathan—returning to Monte full of remorse and love. And this way would be better for all concerned.

She remembered how he had absorbed himself in his work, but anguished miserably on those lonely nights when Laura would have to make another unexpected trip to California to meet with the Laguna Art Museum Guild. Yet he knew all along that Laura was there to be with her lover, lying in his arms, surrendering her complete love and intimacies. And how he'd call Rebecca, asking her to come and comfort him and assure him that Laura truly loved him and would be back in his arms soon. As always, she would successfully convince him to be patient with his wife's clandestine rendezvous, allowing Laura to break up with Jonathan in her own way.

Rebecca took a deep breath, looking up and down the manly contour of Monte's lean body lying supinely under the taut sheet as she recalled that steamy mid-July evening. The night he'd driven to Portland during one of his dejected spells to seek her consolation because Laura had made another unplanned trip to Laguna Beach.

How on that evening in the quaint romantic restaurant he had suddenly looked at her across the dinner table with a longing stare. She remembered how she had sat frozen in her chair, swallowing nervously when she realized what was happening. And how the wine, along with their rising passion, was smothering the loneliness that had festered inside her desolate existence of widowhood. And how magical the moment afterward when he humbly confessed that his friendship for her had grown to love during their long intimate meetings that had begun after Laura's infidelity surfaced. And how she had quickly admitted that she adored him and had always had to conceal her strong attraction to him, because he belonged to Laura.

I couldn't deny him, she remembered, stirring restlessly under the sheet. She recalled how secretly delighted she was at surrendering to his unassuming masculine seduction, allowing them both to succumb to their fiery desires. How magnificent and overpowering he was with the skillful lovemaking he'd developed over the years through his personal experiences with women, and his acquired expertise as a counseling behavioral therapist working with sexually troubled couples. How all her inhibitions and the guilt of betraying her best friend had always vanished during the throes of their fierce lovemaking. And how starved she was for his sensitive physical stroking, which brought her to wild orgasms like she'd never experienced in her life.

But their newly found bond had caused her many sleepless nights over the late summer months as she realized what a tangled mess they were all immersed in—first Laura and Jonathan, and now she and Monte. And she also knew that Monte loved Laura the most and always would, so all she could do was try to make herself and Monte happy until Laura decided to return. Rebecca was braced for the fall she'd be taking when Laura would finally escape her life of duplicity and come home—shutting her out of Monte's life forever.

But things had turned out differently, she thought. *Drastically different. Laura wouldn't ever be coming home again.* She put her finger to her lip, impressing it with a kiss, then reached over and lightly brushed it across Monte's lips. She looked at the clock as she swung her feet to the floor and hopped off the bed.

Walking into the bathroom, she crouched and reached into the tub, turning on both faucets to regulate the water temperature. Leaning back on her calves, she paused, seeing Laura's shower cap hanging off the washcloth rack. A pang of guilt shot through her as she looked over her naked body. But she quickly dismissed it. *After all, hadn't Laura been the one who'd strayed from her marriage?* she thought. So why was it wrong for her best friend to be comforting Monte? And wasn't Monte lucky to have someone like her to love him for the rest of his life?

She yanked up the shower diverter knob on the spout and stood, putting her hand inside the warmth of the spray. She slowly reached over and took Laura's shower cap from the rack. Turning to the mirror, she put it on, pausing to find the new Laura that she would soon be in Monte's and Tamra's eyes. And the *new* Laura would love and take care of them both. *Just like Laura had.* And soon they'd love her just as much. *Just like they'd loved Laura.* She turned with a smile and stepped into the tub, immersing herself under the blast of the steaming flow. *Maybe I'll seriously take up painting like Laura*, she thought, plucking the soap from the dish. She gently pressed it to her nose to inhale the flowery scent. *Then she'd be a painter in their eyes. Just like Laura was once.*

Rebecca reached over, turned on the small bedstand light, and gently shook Monte. He groaned sleepily and moved around on the bed, slowly opening his eyes. Seeing that she was fully dressed and had her purse in her hands, he frowned and reached up, tenderly drawing her face down next to his, kissing her.

She gently pulled away, seeing that he was becoming aroused. "No, sweetheart, we don't have time," she said, smiling. "I have to go, but I'll be back soon."

He nodded lazily and turned toward the window, seeing the darkness creeping through. "Where's Tamra?" he asked groggily.

"Still at the Rickersons. I called Amy and she said they'd keep her all night."

"Okay, thanks," he said again, stretching.

"When are you going to talk to Tamra about things?" she asked.

He slid upward, leaning his back against the headboard as he opened his eyes wide. "I decided on the way home today that I'll take her to Mount Hood this weekend," he said quietly, looking downward. "I'll rent one of the old forestry department cabins." He shook his head, exhaling. "I need to prepare her for the funeral next week. And I don't want anyone disturbing us."

"Sounds like a good idea," she agreed. "Then we can start letting everyone know about us. I know they'll all understand as time goes by." She walked to the bedroom doorway, looking back.

"After all, we were all very close. It's not that unusual for a good friend to unite with the family after a tragedy."

He remained silent, still looking down as she blew him a kiss, saying, "Bye."

"Oh, hey," he said, stopping her. "How'd it go with Lieutenant Kierzek today?"

"Just like we discussed," she answered. "I didn't mind stretching things a bit to help seal Jonathan's fate."

"Yes, good," he said, nodding. "Right, baby."

"Well, I'll see you later, sweetheart," she said as she left the room and headed for the front door. "I'll call you tomorrow."

"Right, baby," he muttered sarcastically with a frown after hearing the front door close. "Whatever."

Chapter Fifteen

The assignment, mid-afternoon, Beaverton

Lacey Rosetto dashed into her office and pushed the door shut behind her. She felt good. The George Cooper court matter was completed successfully, and she had finally made it known that she was leaving the firm to go back to California. Even if she still faced the difficult task of telling Mr. Hansen, maybe Jack would change his mind and alert him beforehand. Regardless, she'd meet with Hansen on Monday when she returned from San Jose and her relocation plans were firmer.

Sitting down, she set her purse and briefcase on the floor next to her chair and pulled out her day-planner, setting it on her desk. She flipped it open and smiled, seeing that her agenda was clear the rest of the day. She ran her palm over her newly trimmed hair and began arranging her long weekend. She was sure Mr. Hansen knew she was going and had approved the time off. She'd come in tomorrow, clean up any loose ends and take all of Friday off, flying out of Portland in the early morning. She reached into her drawer and pulled out the phone book. As she thumbed through the pages looking for "Airline" she heard a soft knock on her door.

Looking up, she wondered who it might be, "Come in," she said.

When the door opened, an elderly man stood there. He was fashionably dressed and well groomed; his full head of silvery hair was trimmed neatly just above the ears. With a beaming fatherly smile, William Nicholas Hansen, the founding and senior partner of the firm, entered the room.

"Mr. Hansen," Lacey said, surprised that he would appear unexpectedly. He always gave notice whenever he wanted to see her. And she was always called into his office for the appointment. She instinctively glanced down at her day-planner, thinking she might have overlooked a scheduled meeting or something. As before, she saw that her afternoon was free.

Thoughts raced through her mind as he shut the door and slowly walked toward her desk. Why was he here to see her? He didn't want her to go this weekend. No, Jack must have told him she was planning to leave the firm.

He sat down in the chair alongside her desk. "How are you, Lacey?"

"Fine, Mr. Hansen." She closed the phone book, asking impulsively, "Did I miss a meeting or something, sir?"

"Oh no," he answered, shaking his head. "I just saw you come in and I was wondering if you had a few minutes to chat."

"Of course," she answered, regaining her composure, now knowing that his visit was unplanned and realizing that he was in a congenial mood.

"How did the Cooper case go today?"

"Fine," she answered with a smile. "The matter was completed smoothly, like we all assumed. No jail time, a moderate fine, and Cooper surrendered his license for life. That's what everyone really wanted—to get the old man off the road."

"Another good job," he said. "I'm always proud to have you representing us, Lacey."

"Thank you, Mr. Hansen. I appreciate the words of confidence."

His look gradually turned serious as he said, "Audrey mentioned this morning that you've requested a long weekend off to go home."

"Yes," she replied. "I tried to touch base with you this morning, but you were tied up. I was hoping to leave Friday morning. However, I haven't finalized anything yet, if my absence will be a problem."

He shrugged off her concern. "Of course it's okay. I've even asked Audrey to make the flight arrangements for you. And the flight cost is on me."

"Oh, that's really not necessary," she said, moved by his gracious gesture. "Just the extra day off would be nice."

"I won't hear of anything else," he insisted. "Consider it a small bonus for the way you handled the Shawn Griffith case last week. Proving him innocent was a brilliant maneuver on your part. The firm really looked good."

"Well, I knew his cousin was the one who committed the robbery," she responded modestly. "I could read his guilt the minute I put him on the stand."

"Still, it was greatly appreciated," he persisted. "I know how hard you worked on it. And during the holiday yet. Please accept my token of gratitude."

She now knew that he'd be offended if she refused his offer any further. "Yes, thank you," she said.

"Good, then it's settled," he said. "Give Audrey the details and she'll set things up for you. In fact, why don't you plan on staying in California an extra couple of days? I'm sure the rest of us can handle things until you get back."

"Oh, Mr. Hansen, thank you again," she said, flushing from the growing emotion. She was proud to be thought of as this valuable. Yet she felt saddened that she was going to have to tell him she was leaving for good. *Maybe I should do it now*, she thought, watching him reach into his pocket. *Yes, I should tell him now*. However, her thoughts quickly turned to puzzlement when he pulled out the front section of The Oregonian, Portland's daily newspaper.

She remained silent, but her brow furrowed as he unfolded the paper and set it in front of her. "Lacey," he said, pointing to the front-page article, "have you heard about the murder that happened along the Portland riverfront yesterday?"

She looked down, seeing the headline, **"SOCIALITE MURDERED IN RIVERPARK."** Next to the article was a long-shot photograph of the wooded crime scene that the news helicopter had captured soon after the grim discovery. "Um, I think so," she replied, spreading the newspaper out in front of her. She winced as she focused on the bulging body tarp in the corner of the picture. "I haven't had a chance to learn the details, but I caught some of it on the news last night when I was herding the kids through their baths." She began perusing the story, asking, "Isn't she the prominent artist who got strangled?"

"That's right," he answered, "She was pretty well established in the cultural circles."

Lacey gradually inched down through the story. "Oh, interesting...I see they have a suspect in custody already," she commented as he remained silent. "So it's her lover." She frowned. "She was married," Lacey mumbled as the negative feelings welled up inside her, recalling how her husband had cheated on her before they divorced. "According to this, it's pretty straightforward. A jilted lover out for revenge goes berserk and murders her in the park," she said curtly as she looked up from the paper.

"Perhaps," he replied slowly as he looked down at the newspaper.

Perplexed by his comment, she now realized that he wasn't here to discuss the startling headlines. "What does that mean, Mr. Hansen?"

He glanced up at her, saying, "I've been asked to look into representing the suspect, Jonathan Timmers."

She appeared astonished. "Really!" she exclaimed, frozen in her chair. "May I ask how this came about?"

"Well, to make a long story short," he answered. "Timmers is an author from California. I represented his publisher once in a copyright-infringement matter when I was practicing in Denver. Anyway, Timmers' agent, David Lowell from New York, found out I was in the area and asked for my help."

"Doesn't Timmers have an attorney?" she asked, now pinning Hansen's busy morning to the long-distance phone calls.

"Not really. Lowell is also an attorney, but he isn't licensed to practice out here. Regardless, he doesn't feel he'd be qualified to handle it even if he were licensed in Oregon. He only practices law in literary matters. And I understand Timmers has never before had the need for any criminal representation."

She nodded, then said respectfully, "Sir, if I may ask again, are you really going to get involved? I thought the firm's strict posture was to avoid matters like this."

"Yes, it's definitely our policy to avoid high-profile cases, especially when it involves murder," he answered, wavering. "And this one has the earmarks of being a capital offense."

She sat still, riveted to his words.

"Nevertheless," he continued, "This Lowell is quite persuasive. And I agreed to get involved in the preliminaries to help them find a suitable law firm out here to adequately defend Timmers."

She pointed at the article replying, "I see, but it seems as though the police have firmly linked him to the crime—red-handed."

"Unfortunately, yes, it appears that way," he agreed. "I understand the police have a lot of circumstantial evidence stacked against him, and Lowell told me that the victim's girlfriend is ready to provide everything but the chamber and gas pellets to put this guy away."

Now realizing that he was soliciting her input, Lacey sat back, asking, "Couldn't this thing backfire on the firm with all the negative publicity, even if you did want to handle only the preliminaries?"

"What do you mean, exactly?" he asked, cocking his head.

"Well," she answered. "It seems that with the victim's upscale background, and the apparent motive for the killing, it has heavy potential of being scandalously sensitive in the community. Moreover, Timmers is an outsider from California."

He wrinkled his face with concern as he digested her statement. "Yes, correct, it could be highly sensitive," he replied. "And being associated with him could very well be damaging to our profile." He paused. "I'm almost certain we don't want to get too deeply involved, and will probably move to get out quickly after Timmers assumes new representation."

She saw that Hansen was now in a rare frame of mind. Even though he was a quick decision-maker, he was having difficulty with this one. She remained silent as he looked up to gather his thoughts. She knew he wanted to walk away from this, yet his curiosity and his attorney's creed of maintaining unbiased notions before exploration of the accused were getting the best of him.

Still looking indecisive, he continued, justifying his apparent decision, "Like I said, his agent was very persuasive, and is thoroughly convinced Timmers couldn't have done something like this."

Lacey cocked her head questioningly.

Noticing her inquisitive response, he said, "There are some factors that come into play here that the newspaper didn't report. A major one is that Timmers has no criminal background, or any reported evidence of violence or spousal abuse. He was married once…"

Lacey shrugged impetuously, asking, "Do you think those facts would make any difference in this case, sir? This one seems to have 'sudden crime of passion' labeled all over it."

"Hard to say…maybe, maybe not," he demurred. He paused, then sighed. "Regardless, like I said earlier, I committed to quietly look into things to give Lowell a chance to get himself organized while we give Timmers some help." He paused again, then asked, "Lacey, what do you think about it?"

She smiled, lending him the support she assumed he was seeking. "Well, I can see the uncomfortable position you're in. But I'm confident that you and your partners will take the right direction on this one."

"I hope so," he mumbled half-heartedly as he glanced over at her small crystal desk clock, seeing that time was getting short. He knew she had to leave on time to pick up her children at the day care center. He looked back at her. "Lacey," he said abruptly. "I'd like you to conduct the initial research on this matter."

Her mouth dropped open in surprise. "What?" she exclaimed. "Me?"

"Yes," he said. "You."

Flabbergasted, she stammered, "But...but...I would think you or one of your partners would conduct inquiries on something at this level. I mean, I'm proud you asked..."

Hansen interrupted, "I've already mentioned this to Mr. Jacob this morning. He's in complete agreement with me. And I'll catch Jack when I leave here. He should be back from his Rotary luncheon by now."

She remained transfixed in her chair, asking, "May I ask why you've chosen me for something this important? I mean, something that could critically affect your organization if it's not handled appropriately."

"Simple," he answered. "We feel you can handle it. And quite frankly, we'd also like to take advantage of your woman's intuition when you investigate." He looked down, adding, "I hope that's not being too sexist."

She chuckled. "No, not at all," she said, sitting back in her chair and letting this assignment sink in. She couldn't help wondering if Jack had told him she was leaving the firm for more growth opportunity in high-profile cases. Maybe this was some kind of ploy to keep her—the proverbial carrot. No, Hansen wouldn't beat around the bush in this manner. He'd openly discuss the issue with her, *wouldn't he?*

"Look, Lacey," he said, breaking her train of thought. "As I said, I don't think we'll want to go much further with this thing. It's looking quite bleak for this guy. I'm sure Corey and Jack will agree we don't need this headache to go on for very long."

She nodded. "I understand, sir."

Hansen continued, "We'll probably move very quickly in recommending another law firm to take over his defense." He hesitated, sitting back in his chair. "I'm sure Timmers will probably confess to the crime anyway—if he hasn't already."

She glanced down at the paper, again curious. "That's right. According to this he hasn't admitted he did it."

"No. However, he hasn't totally denied it, either."

She looked up. "I don't understand."

"Well, according to Lowell, Timmers claims he was blacked out from too much alcohol at the time of the murder. Therefore he won't or can't deny guilt."

"I see…interesting," she said slowly while she thought. "Of course, even if he does assume guilt, he must know he can't use voluntary intoxication as a defense for acquittal."

"That's correct," Hansen agreed, "but Oregon does allow voluntary intoxication as a possible defense to remove the premeditation and deliberation required of a murder charge." He paused, pointing to the newspaper. "However, an intoxication defense for leniency in this situation might not hold up."

She looked back down at the newspaper as he explained, "The woman appears to have been stalked and killed somewhere around dawn. So if it was dragged out in trial, the prosecution could argue…"

"That Timmers had sobered and the stalking made it a premeditated act," she interrupted, inspired.

"Exactly," Hansen said, smiling as he thought how perceptive she was.

"That could pretty much kill a chance to plea-bargain for a lesser charge—like voluntary manslaughter while under the influence," she suggested. "He's probably at least looking at second-degree murder."

"Maybe," he replied, nodding. "But let's not get ahead of ourselves. We haven't even talked to anyone yet who's directly involved with the case."

"Right," she said, slowing down her pace as she picked up her pencil. "How far would you like me to take the initial exploration?"

"Why don't you just plan on talking to the Portland police for now," he answered. "Then we'll decide where to go from there."

"You'd rather not have me meet with Timmers at all?" she asked while jotting his instructions in her day-planner.

"I'd prefer you didn't until we discuss your initial findings," Hansen replied. "Timmers is stuffed away for awhile anyway. They're not taking any chances on his skipping out of state. Judge Fredrica Buehler has already ruled no bail."

She looked up. "You mean 'Old Iron Jaw' Buehler is on the case already?"

"Yes," he answered. "They want everything covered from the beginning."

"Wow," she commented. "He is in for a rough ride with her."

He chuckled. "Who else would they assign to this one? It's big."

"I can see that," she said. "Okay, I'll limit my discussion to the police, then I'll report my findings to you and your partners."

"Good," Hansen said, then gave her a solemn look. "Oh, by the way, I did give Lowell my assurance we'd all approach this preliminary step with an open mind."

"Absolutely, Mr. Hansen," she confirmed. "I'll do my best to disregard the newspaper and TV reports. And if for some reason I'm not able to, I'll tell you."

"Excellent," he replied, patting her arm. "Anyway, I talked briefly with the senior detective, Lieutenant Brian Kierzek from Portland homicide. He's in charge of the case."

"Kierzek's the one I should talk to?" she asked.

"Yes, he said he'd make himself available right away," Hansen replied. "He has a feeling this thing will probably be turned over to the grand jury almost immediately if the circumstances don't change on Timmers behalf."

"They are moving quickly," she commented, looking at her calendar.

"Yes, very quickly," Hansen said. "Kierzek told me he'd be available early tomorrow morning at his office in the Justice Center. Somewhere around nine."

She glanced over at her day-planner, noting Kierzek's name. "Yes, I can easily make that. I was just cleaning up some loose ends tomorrow anyway. I'll let him know I'm coming."

"Okay, good," he replied as he stood and made his way for the door. "Oh, on your way out don't forget to have Audrey make your weekend flight arrangements."

"I won't, sir," she answered. "Thank you."

He opened the door, then turned and said with a smile, "Tell you what. I'll set up a meeting for tomorrow about two-thirty with the rest of the team to decide on our next step, and then you can be out of here and on your way to San Jose."

They laughed as he left her office. Rising, she stuffed the newspaper section and her day-planner into her briefcase. Snapping the case shut, she realized she had to hurry to stop by and see Audrey about her weekend flight arrangements before she picked up the twins. She'd also have Audrey call Kierzek and tell him she would be in to see him tomorrow morning.

Buttoning up her blue suit jacket, she took one more glance out the window, noting that the sunshine was rapidly dimming through the heavy clouds that were swiftly moving into the area. She was getting excited about her weekend trip to California. She needed the time off, and looked forward to basking in the sun. She'd ask Audrey to set up her flight out for early Friday morning rather than later. She was sure she could get the twins ready on time. And she *would* take advantage of the extra days off Mr. Hansen had kindly given her. She'd report back to work on Wednesday or maybe even Thursday. *Yeah, Thursday*, she decided.

Opening her purse, she pulled out her small pocket mirror and applied a light coat of lipstick to freshen her face. She paused, looking at herself, noticing a little sparkle returning to her eyes. *Who knows*, she thought, maybe she *would* find that careless conversation along with some quick heated romance this weekend. *If so, she could be careful with protection and remain anonymous to the lucky guy. What the hell,* the pure physical pleasure would be okay for right now. She could find the affection and tenderness some other time. She smiled devilishly and winked at herself before slipping the mirror back into her purse. *Yeah, right!*

As she hurried out of her office she saw Hansen leaving Jack Malcolm's office for his own. She walked over and paused in Malcolm's doorway when she saw his smile targeting her. "Good luck with your new assignment," he said. "I just heard."

She cocked her head and squinted her eyes. "I wanna know, Jack," she said in a barely audible voice. "Did you tell William that I was leaving the firm?"

He quickly threw his hands up in defense and sat back in his chair. "Not a word," he said with widening eyes. "I swear, not a word."

"Okay," she said with a laugh as she turned and quickly paced over to Audrey's desk, where the secretary was waiting with a pad and pencil in hand.

CHAPTER SIXTEEN

Late afternoon, Justice Center, Portland

Captain Joseph Arthur Ruskin, head of operations for the Portland police, sat attentively behind his large wooden desk, watching his ace detective pacing in frustration. Lieutenant Kierzek stopped and pivoted to face the short, plump man, who was dressed in full blue captain's regalia, the golden insignia glinting from his starched collar flaps.

Kierzek's face hardened as he said firmly, "I'm just not sure about things, captain. This murder may not be as straightforward as it appears. I don't feel right about our ramrod tactics. I know there's a lot of pressure on us, but I think we have to slow down some."

Ruskin was growing perturbed over Kierzek's stubbornness, but remained steady. "Brian," he said patiently, "We've been through this over and over. We're not ramrodding anything. The facts are facts. Yes, this is an important case. And yes, there is pressure on us from the top, but the incriminating evidence is there…"

"All of it is circumstantial at this point," Kierzek interrupted.

Ruskin remained firm, saying bluntly, "But you told me you've found the vagrant witness and basically cleared him of the murder. And we have to rule out robbery, regardless of the missing pendant. We don't even know if she had it with her when she left the hotel." He paused. "And there was apparently no sexual assault. So what motive is left, except for Timmers' revenge?"

"Something just doesn't seem right," Kierzek insisted, shaking his head.

"What about the scratches on Timmers' upper back?" Ruskin asked. "And there was skin found under her fingernails. I'm sure the DNA tests will prove…"

"Timmers admits the scratches were from her," Kierzek responded. "He says it happened while they were having sex. We can't disprove that. And there were none on his face, the logical place for her to claw…"

"But Timmers doesn't deny killing her," Ruskin shot back.

"But he doesn't admit to it either," Kierzek volleyed tensely. He hesitated, took a deep breath and sat down at the small conference table next to the desk, rubbing his temples. "Sir," he said slowly, resettling himself, "I'm not judging whether Timmers is innocent or guilty. I just need a little more time to investigate further. To sort through some things that aren't quite adding up."

"Like what?" Ruskin challenged.

"Well, for one, I just know the woman wasn't killed where she was found," Kierzek replied. "So why would the killer plant her out in the open…telegraphing it? Especially if was a revenge killing."

"There's nothing substantial to support your doubts about the death scene," Ruskin argued. "You didn't find anything at the site this afternoon to convince you it's not where she was killed? Kids could have broken those branches off of the firs in the back foliage."

"I know," Kierzek agreed quietly. "But you saw the woman's clothes yourself. They were muddy, and there were fir needles stuck on her pants and jacket. Yet there was no mud or fir needles, or signs of a struggle, where we found her."

"That's right," Ruskin said. "But even if they did fight back there in the foliage, she could've broken free and he caught her at the riverwalk."

"But someone like the vagrant or a jogger might have seen them struggling," Kierzek persisted, looking up with a final appeal. "Or most likely she would have been screaming."

"That's more speculation," Ruskin argued, shaking his head. "She could've been very weak at that point and unable to put up any more of a fight…maybe scared speechless. The point is, Brian, who knows?"

Kierzek slowly hung his head, conceding faintly, "Right."

Ruskin realized that his ace detective was nearly spent. "Look," he said, easing up, "I always respect your findings. And I know you've proven me wrong in other cases before. But this one is pretty much cast in concrete."

Kierzek looked away, feeling somewhat defeated. "Maybe so."

"Incidentally, have you released the death scene yet?" Ruskin asked.

"No," Kierzek answered as he turned toward the window, knowing what was coming.

Ruskin chuckled, attempting to relieve the tension. "C'mon, Brian, you've had the best lab boys swarming all over the scene since yesterday morning. You know we usually only get one or two of those guys for a day or so." Ruskin paused. "Let's clear the scene. There's no more leads gonna come of it. You know we can't really justify prolonging the expense and manpower any longer."

Kierzek nodded as he stood. "Okay, I'll send Cuyler over there to release it."

"Thanks," Ruskin said. "I appreciate your cooperation. Let's just get this damn thing wrapped up."

Kierzek frowned, then turned toward him. "There's another issue I'd like to point out," he said, still refusing to concede. "There's some things about Rebecca Newell's statement that are odd."

Ruskin furrowed his brow. "From what I understand, her story sounds very logical," he replied. "And you can't blame her for turning on the man who is suspected of killing her best friend…and 'laying it on' a bit while she's at it."

"But you didn't talk to her," Kierzek challenged.

"Did you catch her lying?"

"No, it's just the way she said things," Kierzek said. "And her answers just seemed to be calculated and planned out."

"Calculated and planned out?" Ruskin repeated questioningly.

"Yes," Kierzek replied, adding sarcastically, "Shit, she even knows how much booze to take with her Dalmane to put her out just this side of lethal."

"Dalmane? Sleeping pills?"

"Yes," Kierzek confirmed.

Ruskin nodded. "Okay, so she simply went to sleep waiting for the Bearnes woman to sort out her personal problems."

"But her being drugged to sleep is critical," Kierzek hammered. "We can't verify the phone message she said she received from the Bearnes woman telling her that she was afraid of Timmers. Newell said she was groggy and erased it."

"Well, then," Ruskin said, shrugging, "the defense will probably have the tape message thrown out as not provable, or hearsay...whatever."

"In court, yes," Kierzek agreed. "But right now she's making sure the press, and anybody else that'll listen, aware of it. Which obviously sways a lot of people's prior opinion."

"Brian, I'm afraid your suspicions are not strong enough to discredit her," Ruskin answered quickly. "We know she's carrying a grudge, but that's not enough of a reason to disbelieve her."

"I'm not accusing her of lying," Kierzek said. "It's just another thing that's not cleared up in my mind."

Ruskin sat motionless, allowing Kierzek to have his say.

"And what about the husband?" Kierzek continued. "Suppose he did know about the affair. Then he would've had a motive for the killing. And he still hasn't substantiated his whereabouts at the time of the murder."

"Aren't we trying to firm up his alibi with the security guard at the university?" Ruskin asked, showing little concern about the husband's possible guilt. "And didn't I agree to do a background check on him to find out if he had any signs of pathological jealousy or anything along those lines?" He paused. "I mean, I'm interested in sewing up those loose ends just as you are. However, let's move forward. There's simply not enough here to hold us up."

Kierzek abruptly stood, saying, "Okay, captain, I guess your mind's made up."

"Brian," Ruskin responded sternly, standing with him. "I'm fully aware an effective investigator doesn't jump to conclusions based on assumptions and first appearances. But this one is open and shut. We can't delay due process on gut feelings."

Kierzek remained silent, not wanting to say something he might regret.

Ruskin added, "But of course, if you discover something new and otherwise incriminating to Newell or Monte Bearnes, we can take another look at things."

"Okay, so what's next?" Kierzek asked, exasperated.

Ruskin walked around to the front of his desk. "We're just waiting for you to transcribe Newell's statement from your notes and the interview tape to complete your arrest report."

"I'll have it to you by early tomorrow morning, 8:15 or so," Kierzek said.

Ruskin instinctively glanced at his desk calendar. "Excellent. I'll get it to the prosecution right after I look it over."

"What's the expected time frame for an arraignment?" Kierzek asked.

"Well," Ruskin answered, still looking at his calendar, "if nothing changes, the grand jury will probably have Timmers' indictment in front of Judge Buehler tomorrow afternoon, or Monday morning at the latest. 'Old Iron Jaw' won't waste any time after that, you know. She'll move for the arraignment quickly."

"I have no doubt about that," Kierzek cracked sarcastically as he shook his head and turned toward the door. "I need to go home. I'm tired. I'll see you first thing in the morning."

"Okay, see you then," Ruskin said, following him to the door, patting his shoulder. "Get some rest. You deserve it."

Kierzek remained silent as he opened the door.

"Oh, Brian," Ruskin said, stopping him. "Try and leave all of this at the station. I know you're stressed. But I think you bring a lot of it on yourself."

"Right," Kierzek said as he turned and swiftly closed the door behind him. Squinting his eyes in frustration, he struggled to manage his disappointment while gradually digesting the wrenching discussion he'd just had with his headstrong boss. He was exhausted and drawn out from the extreme range of emotions he'd experienced in the last two days. But maybe Ruskin was right—*all the pressure might be self-inflicted,* he thought. Regardless, he'd get through this day just like he always did when things piled up around him. He'd go home and drink a few beers, have a relaxing dinner with his family, and confide in his best friend, his wife, he decided as he turned the corner of the long hallway, making his way toward his office.

Sallie Kierzek looked over at her weary looking husband as he walked away from the refrigerator twisting off the cap of his beer. "You look beat, love," she said, stirring the steaming ingredients of ground beef and tomato sauce. She laid down her ladle and covered the crockpot. "Another rough day?"

"Yeah," he answered before taking a long swig of beer. He looked over at her. "This one is really getting to me, I guess."

"I can tell," she said gently. "You didn't even say hello before you grabbed a beer." She smiled. "That usually means you need to talk."

He managed to match her smile. "Hello," he replied softly. "Sorry, but I'm just not sure what I want to say yet." Beginning to relax, he looked over at the noodles draining in the colander, then over at the crockpot. "Hmm...goulash."

"I'm making it your favorite way, with some Polish sausage added," she replied. "And I bought some key lime pie for dessert. We're not going to worry about your cholesterol tonight."

"Sounds great," he said, reaching over to give her a quick kiss as they embraced.

He slowly pulled away, leaving her hands on his shoulder. "I also made it over to Powell's bookstore today," she said. "Like you asked me to."

He looked at her with anticipation.

"Yes, I found Timmers' latest novel."

"Good!" he exclaimed, looking around the room.

"Over there by the breadbox," she said, looking toward the small bag resting on the counter.

He quickly walked over, set his beer down and pulled the small hardcover book from the bag. He began reading the plot blurb on the back, placed directly under a picture of Jonathan, who was sporting a wide smile.

Sallie began adding the noodles to the crockpot, commenting, "Looks like an okay novel, but probably not enough gore in it for me."

He chuckled, keeping his eyes on the text. "I know, dear, I know," he muttered. "Don't worry, Stephen King will have another one of your specialties out soon."

She laughed at his crack, then turned serious. "The man in the store said they stock Timmers' books, but there isn't a big call for them," she said, stirring the noodles into the steaming meaty blend. "But they figure he's up-and-coming—headed for the big time. They think this one will be a movie."

He nodded as he picked up his beer and walked into the living room, carrying the book. "I'm going to read a little bit before we eat," he said.

"Hey, by the way," Sallie said, hesitating while waiting for him to turn around, "Timmers doesn't look like a killer."

"You never know," he replied, turning for the living room as he fingered through the book, adding, "That's why I want to read his novel—to see how he might think."

The Kierzek family of three finished their small talk surrounding the beginning of Rob's new school year as a freshman at the University of Portland, while they finished their dessert of key lime pie.

Sallie got up from the dining table and began carrying the dirty dishes to the kitchen as Rob also got ready to leave.

Brian poured himself a cup of coffee and looked over at his muscular son. "Rob, before you go I just want you to know I'm proud of you and how you've handled yourself in high school all those years. I know it's not easy staying out of trouble, with the free-flowing drugs and all."

Rob rolled his eyes. "Dad, I hate to break this to you, but I am normal. I've had nights where I drank a few beers, smoked a joint and chased the girls around and sure didn't worry about safe sex." He shot him a wide smile.

His father broke out in a hearty laugh. "Okay, okay, sorry," he said. "But the safe sex thing bothers me a little."

"Oh, don't worry," Rob consoled, laughing with him. "Valerie has cured me of that stuff lately. We're careful."

"Good," Brian said. "I like her. She's very mature for her age. I'm glad you met her."

Sallie walked into the room and sat down, asking, "What's so funny in here?"

Brian looked over at her. "I just made our son out to be...umm, a geek. I think that's what they call 'em nowadays."

"Oh, heaven forbid," she said mockingly, raising her eyes upward. "Heaven forbid."

Rob smiled, then interjected in a serious tone, "But as far as drugs and alcohol goes, that stuff just doesn't appeal to me. I'm too busy working out and tending to school."

"Say," his father replied with a smile, "aren't you a little young to be so politically correct about the vices of life?"

"Maybe so, but it's also not easy getting away with anything illegal when your father is the chief of Portland's homicide division. And as for smoking, well, it's foul and expensive...among other things." He pointed toward his father's chest and gave him a solemn look.

"I suppose," Brian said, nodding.

"Well," Rob said, getting up from the table, "I'm heading for the library. I'm meeting Valerie there. See ya later."

Brian and Sallie said goodbye as he darted out the door.

Sallie looked over at Brian. "Wanna talk now, love?" she asked, pouring him and herself a fresh cup of coffee.

"Okay," he said, "why not?"

"So, what's really wrong?" she asked, settling back in her chair as she sipped on her coffee. "Why is this case bothering you so much? I know the murder victims sometimes get to you, but not usually the suspect. And I have a feeling that's what it is this time."

"It's just that everybody's in such a damn hurry to convict this guy," he answered. "Hell, I'm sure Wolcott is already licking his chops."

"Senior DA Matt Wolcott?" she asked. "The one who's going to run for attorney general?"

"Yeah," he answered. "Wolcott knows this one is big and will get his name in all the papers on the West Coast."

She shrugged, fingering her coffee-cup handle. "Regardless," she said, putting the cup down, "he'll still have to be fair and follow the law according to the charges."

"I know, but he'll recommend the worst to the grand jury and Judge Buehler," he said, grimacing. "He's always sucking up to 'Old Iron Jaw' anyway."

"But isn't this where Timmers' attorney will be able to help?" she asked. "What are they saying?"

"Not much," he answered. "He only has a rookie public defender taking him through the preliminaries right now. His agent is trying to get him some heavy-duty counsel from this area to take over." He paused, taking a drink of his coffee. "But who knows how effective he'll be in doing that from New York."

"Love, do you think Timmers is innocent?" she asked.

He shrugged. "Not necessarily. But I'm not certain he's guilty either."

"But everything points to him," she said. "What makes you so uncertain that he's not?"

"I dunno," he answered quickly. "I guess it's just that Timmers doesn't seem like he'd lose it and strangle someone, even if he was drunk and had been dumped by the love of his life—as he put it." He hesitated, thinking. "And even if he did do it, he doesn't deserve to be lynched. Christ, it's obviously a crime of passion, not a cold-blooded serial killing."

"What are you going to do?"

"I won't let him get railroaded, that's for damn sure," he answered angrily.

Seeing that he was becoming stressed, she reached over and placed her hand on his. "Love, you're very important to Rob and me," she said. "I'm worried about you. Especially your blood pressure and the toll it's taking on you. Will you please try to reduce your stress and make your doctor's appointment for us?"

He smiled, looking up at her. "I'll do better than that," he said, calming. "I'll make my doctor's appointment, and I'm finally going to ask Ruskin for that transfer to the burglary division. I made my decision this afternoon."

Her eyes widened. "Honestly?" she said, beaming. "You're really going to do it this time?"

"Yes," he said, "and they can't really turn me down. Actually, they should have switched my duty right after my heart attack. But because it was regarded as minor, we all swept it under the rug. But not any more. I'll try to make this my last homicide."

She got up from her chair and reached down, putting her arms around him.

He laid his hand on hers, saying, "I'll break it to Ruskin tomorrow morning."

She stood up and began cleaning off the remaining dishes, saying, "Rob will also be very happy to hear about your decision."

"I know," he said as he got up from the table. "Well, I have to go in about daybreak to complete the arrest report for Ruskin." He walked into the living room and picked up Timmers' novel, "I'm going upstairs and read myself to sleep."

"Why did you want his book?" she asked.

"Only curious, I guess," he replied. "I wanted to see his style of writing. And I wondered if it might tell me something more about him."

"And does it?"

"Not yet."

"Is it a good story?" she asked as she stood and walked into the kitchen.

He paused at the steps, glanced at the novel, then at her. "Not bad—a typical detective yarn, I guess." He chuckled. "But I am picking up a few pointers from his hero, Jason Thornhill, the insurance investigator." He turned and headed upstairs. "Goodnight."

"Goodnight, love," she said with a wide smile. "I'll be up soon to join you."

CHAPTER SEVENTEEN

Early Thursday morning, Justice Center

Lacey Rosetto pulled into the parking lot behind the tall concrete-block building and carefully angled her car between two white parking stripes of the "visitor" section. Shutting off the ignition, she sat back and glanced at her watch: 8:25. *Early*, she thought. She hesitated, trying to remember if the few times she had been here she might have worked with Lieutenant Kierzek. *Nah, not a chance.* The senior homicide detective would never have been associated with the petty cases she'd been assigned, although she was sure she'd seen or heard his name somewhere before now. *Probably in the newspaper*, she assumed while grabbing her briefcase and small umbrella from the passenger seat. Getting out of the car, she quickly closed the door, and chose to keep her umbrella folded. She ducked her head and dashed across the lot through the morning gray, attempting to dodge the light sprinkles.

Reaching the main doors, she entered and followed a small passageway leading into the austere reception area that bordered the large room full of scattered paneled open-office cubicles. A few clerks moved about briskly, tending to their business. The burly duty-sergeant sat silently on a stool behind a long counter, watching her closely as she approached.

She handed him her business card. "I'm Lacey Rosetto, from a Beaverton law firm. I'm here to see Lieutenant Kierzek."

He looked at the card, then glanced over at the message clipboard, seeing that her name had been jotted down. "Oh, right, Ms. Rosetto," he said, "I remember getting a call from your office telling me you were coming. But I haven't been able to catch the lieutenant to tell him. I don't know if he saw the message or not. He came in early this morning and went right into a meeting."

She looked disappointed, sensing a probable delay. "Can I wait for him? I'm sure he was aware I was coming in today."

"Sure, his office is on the second floor," he answered, pointing past her shoulder. She turned, seeing the elevators through a wire-screened window in the center of a large door. "Please sign in and I'll give you a visitor key card." He pushed the visitor's log toward her.

"Thank you," she said with a polite smile as she signed the log and accepted the card key he handed her. She walked to the door, inserting the card into the security slot molded into the wall alongside the doorframe. After hearing the unlocking door buzz and click, she entered the small vestibule and approached the bank of elevators.

Stepping from the elevator on the second floor, she obtained the location of Kierzek's office from a passing officer. Following his direction, she saw a row of plate-glass offices and spotted the name "Lt. Brian Kierzek" on the closed door of the end office. The lights were on and the window blinds were open, allowing her to see that it was empty. She noticed a blazer and a hat hanging on a coat rack behind the desk, confirming that he was probably in the building.

Turning, she walked through the bustling room to the visitor chair outside his doorway.

She set her briefcase on the floor and sat down, looking around at the other offices. Some were occupied with casually dressed detectives talking to visitors; the others were dark and empty. She turned, spotting a small group of street officers gathered by the coffee nook at the perimeter of the corridor, engaged in animated conversation about their upcoming shift.

As she began to relax, she was growing excited about the experience she would gain with this interview. She felt proud about being trusted to explore something as important as the "riverpark murder case"—the most visible crime in Portland. Even if the firm probably wouldn't take it any farther than her investigation, it would provide her with valuable résumé background when she searched for new employment in California.

Realizing that she had more time to prepare for the conference with Kierzek, she reached down and pulled out a yellow highlighter and yesterday's newspaper she'd kept after her meeting with Hansen.

She unfolded it and began to carefully reread the story describing the murder. She highlighted the paragraph about how Timmers had been seen in the hotel lobby just before the estimated time of the crime. She slowly moved down the column, noting the part where the victim's woman friend had told the police about the phone call she'd received from the frightened woman shortly before she was killed. And how the police suspect that the motive for the brutal killing was passion and vicious vengeance, because earlier that night the woman had broken off the affair she was having with the suspect. Leaning back, she set the newspaper in her lap and closed her eyes, passing on retrieving today's newspaper. Although she'd heard on the radio this morning that the DA would ask for a murder indictment, she'd let Kierzek update her on whatever was current.

She wondered why Timmers wouldn't just plea-bargain to a lesser charge such as voluntary manslaughter committed in the heat of passion while intoxicated. *Just throw himself on the mercy of Judge Buehler's court*, she thought. *He's already cooked.* She suddenly felt a pang of disappointment shoot through her. She had enough experience to know she should disregard the media reports, and avoid making any prejudicial decisions off the cuff. However, she couldn't help wondering if it really was the news accounts that made it seem obvious to her that Timmers was guilty. Or was it that the negative aspect of the illicit affair between him and the victim had hit too close to home?

Regardless, she needed to stay open-minded and ignore everything except the accurate facts she would gather from her meeting with Kierzek. She was sure she could remain non-biased and keep the situation in perspective while she talked to him, even though it might be difficult because of her personal discomfort.

She'd have to constantly remember that Mr. Hansen was counting on her to present the precise account of the crime as the police knew it. She could easily do that, knowing that Mr. Hansen and his partners would probably unload the case anyway. Even if Timmers decided to plea-bargain for a lesser charge, she doubted that Hansen would touch this one. Defending Timmers in any manner could just be too politically damning—even if by some slim chance he was found innocent.

She glanced at her watch: 9:10. She was glad she had cleared her agenda for the whole day. Now she wouldn't have to deal with any anxious moments of worrying about other appointments, regardless of what time she finally got to meet with Kierzek. She could take her time during the interview and probably have plenty of time to prepare for the late-afternoon progress meeting with Mr. Hansen and his partners.

She was suddenly drawn to the noisy conversation coming from a few officers who were still loitering at the entrance of the break area, sipping on their coffee. Hearing "riverpark murder," she stood and casually headed their way while tuning in to their careless exchange.

Lieutenant Kierzek left Captain Ruskin's office and gradually made his way down the hallway, deep in thought. Stepping into the break room, he poured himself a cup of the aging, strong black coffee. He turned and slowly headed back for the doorway when Officer Cuyler entered, approaching him.

"Morning, Ed," Kierzek said in a wearied tone.

"Good morning, Brian. I'm glad I caught up with you," Cuyler said, appearing anxious. "I have a 10:30 traffic court appearance, and…" He paused. "Jesus, you look tired."

"I didn't get much sleep," he answered. "And I had to come in early to finish Timmers' arrest report for Ruskin. I just left his office."

"How'd it go?"

"Okay, I guess," Kierzek replied. "He's sending the report to the DA's office today. Wolcott's waiting with bated breath."

"I'm sure he is," Cuyler said, frowning, "Anyway…"

"Ed, I think there's something you should know," Kierzek interrupted. "But you'll have to keep it quiet for now."

Cuyler stood silent, waiting for Kierzek's next statement.

"I've formally requested a transfer to burglary," Kierzek said. "I worked out the preliminaries with Ruskin after we finished with Timmers' report. It looks like I'll be going next month."

Cuyler let it sink in, then extended his hand, saying, "I'm glad for you. I know you were thinking about it. I'll miss working with you, but I'd rather see you go out this way and still be around."

"Thanks, Ed," Kierzek replied, shaking his hand firmly. "And you're right, I'm not really going anywhere. I just need some lighter duty for Sallie's sake as well as mine. However, we still have work to do now, so what's up?"

"Just thought I'd tell you that I caught up with the vagrant, Marty Spahn, this morning at the Mission," Cuyler answered. "I'm sure he's clean all the way around. He wouldn't lie to me about the pendant." He paused, chuckling. "Hell, I'm sure he wouldn't even have gotten close enough to the body to see the diamond, much less steal it."

"I figured as much, but we had to follow through," Kierzek replied. "In fact, why don't you bring him in tomorrow morning. I'd feel better talking to him."

"Will do," Cuyler agreed.

"And have Kelting keep on searching the pawn shops and fences like we discussed yesterday," Kierzek requested. "That pendant has to be somewhere."

"Right, I already sent him out looking."

"Good," Kierzek said. "And did you release the death scene last night?"

"Yes, and I took one more look around this morning like you asked." He shook his head. "Nothing."

"Okay, let's forget it, we've done our best there," Kierzek said with a frown of disappointment. "What about the security guard, Albert, from the university?"

"I plan to talk to him today," Cuyler answered. "I'll try to reach him late this afternoon or early evening. His boss says he sleeps during the day."

"Okay, make sure you ask if he got a good look at Bearnes that night," Kierzek said. "Because he might be asked to testify to that in court. Recognizing just his car or something like that won't cut it."

"Right," Cuyler said, glancing at his watch. "Damn, I gotta get going." He began to head for the doorway, then turned and said, "I'll get back to you tomorrow."

"Sounds good," Kierzek said as he left the break room to head for his office and make the doctor's appointment for his annual checkup like he'd promised Sallie this morning. Raising his eyes, he saw the young woman sitting in the chair next to the doorway, jotting some notes in her day-planner. *Aw, shit, must be another reporter,* he thought. *Worse, maybe she's some bloodhound from the chief's office checking up on how Timmers' lynching is progressing.*

Lacey looked up, seeing the man coming toward her. Anticipating that it was Kierzek, she closed the day-planner, picked up her briefcase and stood as he approached his office door. "Lieutenant Kierzek?"

"That's correct," he answered blankly as he looked down to unlock his door, clearly demonstrating that he was uninterested in her visit.

She was unfazed by his unpleasant welcome, realizing that he was fatigued and probably consumed by the Timmers case. Holding out one of her business cards, she introduced herself. "I'm Lacey Rosetto, from Hansen, Jacob & Malcolm. I was told you'd be expecting me to discuss the Jonathan Timmers case."

He turned and paused in his open doorway, facing her while recalling the conversation he'd had yesterday morning with William Hansen from her Beaverton law firm, and how he might be sending up an attorney for Timmers.

"Oh, yes, hello, Ms. Rosetto," he replied apologetically, accepting her card. "I had forgotten about my discussion with your office. Please come in." He walked over to his desk to set his coffee down as she followed him inside. He turned and offered his hand, saying, "I thought you might be another reporter."

"No, I'm not a reporter," she replied sensitively, now understanding his curt welcome. She immediately sensed he'd probably be the type to be honest and forthright with her—exactly what she wanted. "You must have had a busy morning already," she said, shaking his hand. "Have I caught you at a bad time?"

"No, please have a seat," he answered, gesturing toward the visitor chair as he sat down behind his desk. "Sorry about the delay," he apologized. "My meeting took longer than expected. And I admit I didn't pick up my messages telling me you were coming." He took a drink of his coffee. "Oh, sorry—want a cup?" he asked, holding it out.

"No, thanks," she said, sitting down across from him. She set her briefcase on the floor, adding, "I'm fine." She opened her notebook and looked up at him. "I'll try not to take much of your time, lieutenant. I just need a few basic questions answered concerning your suspect."

"Sure," he replied, finishing his coffee. He pitched the empty coffee cup into the wastebasket. "I'll answer them as best I can."

She nodded. "I know the victim was a very prominent woman here in Portland. I would assume things are moving along very quickly in this case."

"Right. I understand the grand jury will be meeting tomorrow sometime," he said. "I'm sure there'll be an indictment coming out of it. And an arraignment will probably be set for early next week."

"Really?" she said, sitting back. "I know the Constitution guarantees a speedy judicial process, but this one is stacking up to be a showcase example."

"Yeah, I know," he answered with a smile. "They want to make sure Timmers stays in jail. You know he's from California."

"Yes," she replied, pulling out her pencil. "I understand why they don't want anything or anyone to slip through the cracks. I'm sure there won't be any bail awarded."

"Not a chance."

"Does he currently have any legal counsel?" she asked.

"Um, yes," he answered, lifting his head to recall the name. "A young man from the public defender's office, Leonard Bronck. He's only advising Timmers through the preliminaries until a private law firm takes over."

"I see," she said, substituting her day-planner for her notepad to jot the name down.

As he listened and watched her methodical manner, he realized that here was a capable woman. Yet he wondered about her youth and presumable inexperience in handling a major felony case like this one—especially a case so visible. He couldn't help asking, "So, are you going to be the one to represent Timmers?"

"I don't know yet," she answered, not wanting to reveal her doubts about the firm's even taking on the case. "I'm going to present the facts from our conference to Mr. Hansen and his partners this afternoon. Then they'll decide their next step. I can assure you their decision will be prompt. I know they're aware that things will move swiftly in this case."

He looked at his watch, seeing that the morning was growing short. "Aren't you even going to talk to Timmers before you meet with your colleagues?" he asked, appearing puzzled.

She hesitated, not having anticipated that question. "Umm, I don't think so," she answered slowly, feeling guilty over his implication that she might be neglecting her client. "Mr. Hansen didn't want me to become that involved yet if for some reason we didn't take the case."

"Not take the case? I don't understand," he said, more perplexed.

She was disgusted with herself for letting that slip out, but knew she had to answer truthfully, knowing he wasn't a man to be trifled with. "Lieutenant, you must realize that this crime carries a great deal of volatility. Our firm isn't in a position to suffer a severe public backlash. Mr. Hansen and his partners need to weigh all the issues before they commit."

"Okay, whatever," he replied, feeling disappointed that there were even going to be loose ends in this aspect of the case.

She noticed his letdown, and was inwardly surprised that a detective might be this concerned about a suspect's representation. "Lieutenant," she said, "I find your behavior unusual for a detective. You seem very concerned about Timmers."

"Ms. Rosetto, I represent the state," he said pointedly. "I'm definitely entrusted to help convict the guilty, but all suspects deserve a fair shake along the way."

"I see," she replied cautiously. "I hope I haven't upset you. May we continue with the interview?"

"Of course," he said, "You haven't upset me."

"Good. I certainly didn't mean to," she said, reaching down. "I'd like to use the newspaper as the basis for my questions." She pulled the paper from her briefcase. "I've written down a few things from the article and I'd like to have you elaborate on them, or please discard the items as inaccurate. Okay?"

He shrugged. "Okay," he agreed, sitting back in his chair with a smile.

She matched his slight smile, now knowing he was the type of man she was going to like and respect. As she glanced down at her notes, she hoped they wouldn't end up at professional odds for any reason. She then quickly looked up, saying, "Oh, before we get started, I assume Timmers hasn't confessed to the crime yet."

Kierzek shook his head. "Nope," he answered. "I talked to Bronck at the jail this afternoon. Timmers isn't saying anything either way. I'm sure they'll call me if he wants to talk."

"So, then I take it he hasn't denied the murder either."

"Correct, he hasn't denied it either," Kierzek confirmed stiffly. "He claims he was drunk at the time of the murder and doesn't remember anything at all."

She nodded. "Yes, Mr. Hansen told me about the alcohol factor surrounding this case," she replied. "Do you know if Timmers has a problem with alcohol or drugs?"

"Doesn't look like it," Kierzek answered, shaking his head. "There's no police record indicating he does, and he's not going through any withdrawal symptoms in jail." He paused. "The witnesses from the hotel know him and say it just got away from him that night. They said they'd never seen him in that condition before."

"So, you say he doesn't have a criminal record?" she asked. "No spousal abuse or anything like that?"

"The only thing we could find on him at all was a couple of traffic tickets he racked up in California. And from what we know, he was happily married until his wife died of leukemia. I understand he stayed by her side until the end."

"I see, interesting, no criminal record," she commented as she looked back down at her notes. *And apparently a model husband too,* she thought. "Okay, I just have some more questions about the relationship between Timmers and the victim."

Kierzek sat back, hoisted his feet up to the top of his desk and dutifully answered her questions. She would occasionally glance up to further clarify his response, depending on the importance of the question. He would willingly comply. Finishing up, she paused and flipped back and forth through the pages, doing a final check. She was momentarily satisfied and sat back, saying, "Well, lieutenant, thank you for a very thorough session. Is there anything you can think of that I should add to this?"

He pursed his lips, looked up and thought a moment. "Yes, there is one other thing. There seems to be an expensive diamond pendant missing. But we don't know if she had it with her or not. She may have lost it."

"But you still don't suspect robbery?"

He shook his head. "No, nothing else points to that. But we are checking the local pawn shops and other places the pendant might've been dumped."

"I see," she said, adding to her notes. "Is there anything else?"

"No," he answered slowly. "That's about everything I know. Of course, I will fax my complete arrest report to your office if you want it. Just call in and let me know."

"Thank you. I'll do that if we expect to pursue this matter further," she said as she bent down to stuff her notebook and newspaper into her briefcase, indicating that she was finished. Yet she wasn't finished, or even satisfied with the results of this conference. She was growing more interested in this case, and the suspect Timmers, than she had originally anticipated. She had a new perspective of him because of Lieutenant Kierzek's concern over his getting a fair shake. And how Timmers was seemingly a happily married man until his wife died—not some scheming womanizer.

Now she wanted more than the formal reporting, she decided while continuing to rearrange her briefcase, stalling for time. She wanted to catch Kierzek off guard and snag his personal thoughts. She wanted something more from him than was required by law. She knew he wasn't lying or concealing any important evidence; just not revealing his helpful intuitive thoughts. Obviously something was gnawing at him about this murder—a crime that might not be as elementary as the initial facts seem to show. She had noticed the concern escape Kierzek's tough façade as he answered the questions concerning the circumstantial evidence implicating Timmers, especially when they discussed the witness statement that the victim's friend, Rebecca Newell, had given. *And his less than positive demeanor when he told her that Timmers was their only suspect at this time, although the husband didn't have a credible alibi as yet.* She had noted that very carefully.

As she snapped her briefcase shut and sat upright, she remembered the bits of the officer's conversation that she'd overheard in the break area about the questionable death scene of the "riverpark murder." That cinched it. She needed to know what that was all about. Unable to stifle herself, she looked directly at him and went for the brass ring. "What do you think?" she blurted. "Tell me, please—in your estimation is Timmers guilty of murder-one?"

Taken aback over her brash leading question, his eyes widened. "Damn, lady," he responded quickly. "You don't mess around, do you?"

She sat unwavering, smiling slightly. "I'm just trying to create headings for my notes, that's all, lieutenant."

Chuckling, he said, "But I was always taught that a suspect is innocent until proven guilty. You certainly should know that." He paused as she kept looking at him silently, wanting more. He softened, continuing in a serious tone, "Like I told you before, I am here to assist in convicting the guilty, but I also have a duty to clear the innocent."

"So, do you think he's guilty?" she pressed.

"Ms. Rosetto, it's quite obvious he's not a cold-blooded killer. However, the circumstantial evidence does point right at him. So right now I'm just doing my job." He threw up his hands, signaling that was all he had to say.

She sighed. "Okay, thank you, lieutenant," she replied, obviously disappointed, as she bent down to pick up her briefcase. She was gambling that he wouldn't let it go, but she didn't want to push too hard, knowing his nerves were frayed.

But she *had* pushed too hard. Her impetuous manner, on top of the recent frustrations of this case, had gotten to him. "Ms. Rosetto," he said angrily, "does your attitude suggest that I'm not giving you all the facts?"

She looked back up at him. "No, sir, I don't think you're hiding anything substantial or official," she answered in a respectful tone.

"Good, because I've told you everything that's factual and relevant to the crime," he insisted, calming. "I really have nothing more to add."

"Lieutenant Kierzek, I meant no disrespect. And I'm certainly not insinuating that you're violating any rules of discovery," she said, taking a further chance with his patience. "But your behavior tells me there's more…and…and…"

"And?" he repeated, sitting up straight, secretly admiring her tenacity, knowing she was also only doing her job.

"Well, your peers think a lot of you," she answered cautiously. "I heard them talking while I was waiting for you. They all know you're not totally satisfied with how things are perceived in this case. I now feel the same as they do."

He slowly turned away and shrugged. "You shouldn't conduct your business by eavesdropping," he answered curtly, adding, "Anyway, it doesn't matter who thinks what; the facts are facts. And if I find anything more I will let everyone know."

Seeing that his guard was diminishing, she pointed toward her briefcase. "Sir, my notebook is put away," she pushed further. "Please tell me about the issue surrounding the death scene."

He sat dumbfounded over her candid and persistent manner. Still, he remained calm, remembering that she might end up helping Timmers. "But don't you have enough to take back with you?" he said. "You might not even take the case, remember?"

"I'm becoming more interested by the minute," she replied. "That's the truth. I'll admit I was biased when I came in here. However, after listening to you I'm not so sure this case is as simple as it appears. And now I have a much different view of Timmers."

Her answer impressed him. He was beginning to feel that maybe she should know what he thought unofficially. He liked and respected her. Yet they were on opposite sides of the fence right now. He couldn't risk being questioned later over careless off-the-record dialogue if the case were tried for murder-one. He'd made that big mistake before when he wasn't sure of one suspect's guilt and made it known. The sting of that major courtroom drama, with the defense lawyer's ruthless cross-examination over Kierzek's doubts about his client's guilt, had left many scars. But then again, what did it matter what he thought right now? This case would really only be processed on the facts. And only the facts would prove Timmers innocent or guilty, not his thoughts. "What else do you want to know?" he finally asked, conceding.

"What about the murder scene?" she asked enthusiastically, charging ahead. "I heard some talk that you don't think she was killed where she was found."

"That's right, I don't mind telling you that," he answered. "I just feel that maybe she was killed back in the foliage and then moved…"

Her eyes widened as she interrupted, "And Timmers wouldn't move her in a murderous fit of passion."

Kierzek continued without confirming her blunt reasoning. "So, anyway, I went back out to the scene and found some scant evidence of the possibility that she was killed in the foliage. However, because we found nothing substantial we're not going to press the issue right now."

She read some frustration in his voice. "But if you're correct, the facts as they appear toward Timmers' guilt wouldn't really add up. Like I mentioned, it wouldn't make sense that he'd move her."

"Maybe, maybe not," he answered, then shrugged. "But she could have escaped from the struggle in the foliage and been caught by him at the sidewalk and killed there."

"That would be quite a noisy scene, wouldn't it?" she asked rhetorically. "I mean, if it was me, I'd be screaming to high heaven to attract some attention. Someone surely would have heard or seen something."

"Perhaps, but who knows for sure," he answered, echoing his boss's thinking. "It doesn't matter. We've done all we can at the riverpark. We released the scene last night."

She sat back, asking, "You're really concerned about Timmers getting a fair shake, aren't you, lieutenant?"

"Well, everyone deserves that, don't they," he admitted.

She nodded, deciding not to question the issue of his being driven by his superiors to wrap this case up, although she knew well that that was the situation.

"What's Timmers' mood?" she asked gently.

"Exhausted, confused and strung out."

"Can I see him today?"

"Now?" he responded, surprised. "I thought you weren't going to take it that far right now."

"I've changed my mind," she answered, abruptly standing. "Can you grant me immediate access to him? I'll go see him now."

"Yeah, sure," he agreed. "He's right here in the center, in the county lockup."

"Thank you," she replied, stooping to pick up her briefcase.

He shook his head in surprise as he reached for the phone.

By the time Lacey left Kierzek's office, heading for the detention center, she was sure that meeting with Timmers was the right decision. Even though Mr. Hansen had requested her not to go that far, she was sure she could somehow justify her actions when she met with him and his partners this afternoon. Besides, this would give her a better perspective of what they were up against should they decide to pursue the suspect's defense. But more important, she now felt that she was doing a thorough job of exploring the murder case of Laura Bearnes, even though she wasn't sure that the law firm of Hansen, Jacob & Malcolm would take it any farther than her investigation. Regardless, at least she would leave on her mini vacation to San Jose feeling better about herself. *And the experience will also add more expertise to my résumé,* she thought.

Chapter Eighteen

Early afternoon, Multnomah County Jail

Jonathan's eyes flinched as he heard the clanking of the keys being jostled into the cell-door lock. He looked over as the guard opened the door, saying, "Timmers, your lawyer's here." Rubbing his tired eyes, he slowly stood, wondering what Bronck wanted now. *He told me there wouldn't be anything more until after the grand jury met and decided about the indictment. It couldn't be over already, could it?*

Exiting the cell, he obediently followed the jailer down the empty hallway toward the heavy barred door that separated the cellblock from the administration area. Pausing while the jailer opened the door, Jonathan still couldn't believe he was here—an accused prisoner suspected of murder. Feeling the tug on his arm, he followed the jailer to the windowed visitor's room just beyond the reception area.

The guard stood aside as Jonathan entered and walked to a table where a youthful, professional-looking woman was sitting, scanning her notes. The guard left, closing the door behind him, and positioned himself in front of one of the windows where he could see in.

Wearing a pleasant smile, the woman stood and held out her hand. "Mr. Timmers, my name is Lacey Rosetto," she greeted, seeing that the handsome man was drained and withdrawn. "I'm an associate criminal attorney from Hansen, Jacob & Malcolm in Beaverton. Our firm represented your publisher on a couple of literary matters some years back."

Jonathan shook her hand. "I remember my agent mentioning your firm the other day, Ms. Rosetto," he replied wearily. "But he wasn't sure if anyone was coming to see me."

"It was just decided this morning," she replied, his polite manner removing her initial image of his being a vengeful murderer. "Do you have a problem meeting with me without any notice?"

"No, not at all. I'm really glad you're here." He sat down with her at the table. "Are you going to represent me, Ms. Rosetto?"

"I'm not sure yet," she answered, removing her dark blue suit jacket. She took a pencil from her briefcase. "Although if I'm not the one, I'll likely consult with whoever it is. So this session will be worthwhile. And please call me Lacey."

"And please call me Jonathan," he said while she maneuvered to get herself organized for the interview. For the first time since he'd been arrested, he was feeling relieved, because he could see he was getting some high-caliber help—even if she wouldn't be the one who would represent him.

She looked at him, asking sensitively, "Jonathan, how are you holding up?"

"All right, I guess," he answered, managing a slight smile. "Considering."

"I understand," she replied, sitting back in her chair. "I know things are looking bad from your standpoint."

"Disastrous," he said, looking down. He slowly looked up, shaking his head with a look of hopelessness. "I couldn't have done it, Lacey. I couldn't have."

"Your agent doesn't think so either," she said, passing him a caring look. She was surprised at how she felt immediate empathy for him, totally eradicating the resentment she had harbored when she had read about him in the paper. "There's always hope, Jonathan."

His face still contorted in anxiety he asked, "How bad is it?"

"Unfortunately, they have a lot of incriminating evidence against you," she answered honestly.

"Is it really that bad?" he asked in a halting voice.

"Well, it's all circumstantial," she answered, realizing that they had to move swiftly and methodically. "So we'll have to talk about things before I can thoroughly assess the situation. You'll need to be totally truthful with me."

"Of course," he said, nodding. "Whatever you need to know."

She hesitated, then looked into his eyes. "I understand you said you were drunk and don't remember whether you committed the crime. In other words, you *could* be guilty. Is that correct and truthful?"

"Yes," he answered quickly, "That's the truth. I do *not* know."

"All right," she said, picking up her pencil. "Let's start from the beginning. Please tell me everything you remember about that night. It's imperative that you don't leave out anything."

He lifted his head in thought. "Okay, I flew in from California on Monday afternoon," he began slowly, attempting to recount everything he could remember from the time he'd arrived in Portland...

Jonathan sat back and faced the attentive attorney. "That's about it, Lacey," he said. "The next thing I remember was waking up in the hotel room, soaking wet. And just before I was leaving to go home, I was arrested," he finished nervously, appearing to concede his grave situation after reciting it all out loud.

Lacey had sat quietly while he spoke, comparing, validating and adding to the information she'd gathered from Kierzek's meeting. The silence was brittle as she glanced back over her notes.

"So," she confirmed, finally looking up at him. "You were blacked out from the time you and Laura left the hotel lobby bar until you woke up the next morning about nine?"

"That's basically correct," he answered. "I have a fuzzy recollection of our going up to my room from the lobby bar, but that's all. I had brought a bottle of bourbon with me." He shrugged and grimaced.

"And the next day you had arranged for a late-afternoon flight out of Portland, when you had had the opportunity for an earlier one?"

"Yes," he said, feeling strained, dropping his head in his hands out of anxiety. "I was hoping she might come back..."

Watching him struggle with his anguish, she had now caught up with Kierzek's evaluation of Jonathan. She believed he definitely was not a premeditated killer. And she truly believed he didn't know whether he had done the crime or not.

He slowly looked up as she said, "That's almost exactly how you told it to Detective Kierzek, which is a very positive sign."

"Lacey, I'm telling you I'm not capable of something like murder! Not even when I was totally blacked-out drunk!" His voice rose in an anxious tempo. "I don't want to be punished for something I didn't do! It's bad enough that I've lost her."

"Try to be strong and patient," she replied gently, reaching out to put her hand on his. "There has to be some leeway here."

He slowly composed himself. "Haven't they found anything at the crime scene that might help me?"

She furrowed her brow. "Not according to Lieutenant Kierzek," she answered. "Not even telling footprints. It was grassy and full of ground shrubbery where they found her."

"So I'm the only suspect?"

"Yes," she said. "Although they're still trying to verify the husband's whereabouts. They may have to interrogate him if he can't substantiate his alibi."

He flashed a look of hope.

"But I won't lead you on," she said quickly. "That's standard procedure, and they don't have any outward reason to suspect him."

He nodded understandingly. "What about the vagrant who found her?"

She flipped through her notes. "Kierzek said they've pretty much cleared him," she answered. "He's a harmless park loiterer named Marty Spahn." She looked up. "However, Kierzek told me he's going to question him once more tomorrow to reaffirm their findings on him."

"But maybe Spahn saw more than he reported," he said, pushing for something more. "Maybe he even saw the killer." He turned away, adding, "Even if the killer was me, dammit. Anything to get at the truth." He looked back up at her. "Even if it was me," he repeated. "Maybe he saw something more."

She looked back at her pad. "No," she replied gently, shaking her head. "Kierzek said Spahn simply reported that he'd seen her lying next to the park sidewalk. He doubts anything more will come of it."

"There has to be more to it than that," Jonathan pressed, frustrated.

"That's all he's telling the police," she said. "Though like I said, Kierzek's going to question him again tomorrow."

Jonathan thought a moment. "It's just kinda strange that nobody saw anything else. I mean, a woman strangled next to the sidewalk...out in the open."

"I know," she agreed. "You're right it seems odd, but then again, maybe not at that time of the morning." She paused.

"Regardless, Kierzek thinks she might have been killed back in the foliage."

"What?" Jonathan shot back. "Kierzek thinks she was killed and then moved?"

She nodded, watching his stunned reaction, then said, "There was damage in the foliage behind her, and she had fir needles and mud on her clothes."

He continued to look surprised, recalling that morning when he came to in the hotel room. "I didn't have any needles or mud on my clothes! They were only wet." He paused. "I know the police would probably claim I wiped them off, but it's just something else that seems too calculating for a drunk person to do."

Gathering interest, Lacey said, "But this is all speculation on Kierzek's part. They can't prove where she was killed, and Kierzek has had to let the issue go for now. Although I know he hasn't dismissed it."

Jonathan turned away, looking more confused and disappointed. "By the way," he said, "did the autopsy report come back yet?"

"Just the preliminary findings," she answered. "The toxicological results won't be known until next week. Kierzek says they do have to conduct some additional testing to make sure she wasn't poisoned."

"Poisoned?"

"Oh, they don't expect that she was," she answered. "But it's standard in most criminal homicides when the intent is questionable. Because poisoning constitutes premeditated murder—an automatic first-degree offense."

"Right," he agreed, remembering his writing research for the degree structure of homicides. He changed the subject. "Was she raped or anything?"

"No, no apparent evidence of a sex crime," Lacey said. She glanced at her notes, adding, "But they did find semen…"

"I know, it was probably mine," he muttered, looking down. "I told them that. And the scratches on my upper back and neck were from her while we were having sex." He paused. "Did you get that information from Kierzek?"

"Yes," she replied. "Unfortunately, a prosecutor might try and use them as murder-scene wounds."

He shrugged. "There's not much I can do about that right now except tell the truth and face it."

She sat back, nodding. "Oh, also, there's an expensive diamond pendant that's missing, and it seems to be an issue," she said. "What can you tell me about it?"

Jonathan thought a moment. "It was one I had given her that night. I'm sure she must have taken it with her. It wasn't in the hotel room. They still can't find it, huh?"

"No, but they're looking for it," she said, appearing puzzled. "However, they still aren't considering robbery as a motive, because her wallet was intact."

Jonathan sat silent as she continued reading her notes.

She looked up. "What's your relationship with Laura's friend, Rebecca Newell? The one who told the police you were with Laura that night."

His face wrinkled. "She was Laura's closest friend," he answered curtly. "And she would always provide a cover for Laura if it was needed when we'd meet in Portland."

"I see," she answered, noticing his mild hostility toward this woman. "Did you have a lot of contact with her?"

"No, not really," he said. "I usually avoided her, because Laura had told me from the beginning that Rebecca was always against the affair. I talked to her a few times on the phone when I was trying to locate Laura."

Lacey glanced down at her pad, saying, "I understand Newell told the police Laura had left a message on her machine just before she was killed."

"Yeah, I know, Kierzek told me at my interrogation," Jonathan said, throwing his hands up with a look of surprise. "And I still don't believe it."

Lacey continued, disregarding his surprise. "I understand Newell couldn't remember the details of the message because she was half asleep and unintentionally erased the message. But she's adamant about the message implying that Laura was very fearful over your reaction to her leaving you."

Jonathan turned steely-eyed. "Like I said, I don't believe it!" he exclaimed. "But I don't look for any support from Rebecca. Like I told you, she'd never had much use for me and never made any effort to hide it."

"I understand," Lacey said.

Jonathan gave her a quizzical look. "How did the police know how to contact Rebecca so soon after Laura's death?"

"I guess they found her name and number in Laura's wallet day-timer."

"Oh," Jonathan answered.

"One more thing," she said, breaking his train of thought. "Had you ever had any conversation or any written contact with Laura's husband, Monte Bearnes?"

"Oh, no, absolutely not," he answered. "I never even made a phone call to her house. Never. Laura was extremely sensitive about that kind of thing."

She nodded. "Do you have any reason to think that somehow he'd found out about the affair?"

Jonathan thought carefully. "No," he answered, "I don't think so. Laura often told me he was probably always too busy at the university to notice that anything was different about their marriage. And she was always very cautious about our communication."

She put her pencil down. "I never did ask Kierzek much about him. I assume you know something about his background."

"Some," he replied. "Laura was very protective of both him and their daughter, Tamra. What do you want to know?"

"What does he teach?"

"Psychology," Jonathan answered. "He's a behavioral therapist."

"Aren't those the psychiatrists who work with a person's environmental factors to treat their fears, like phobias?"

"Yes, among other things," he replied. "Laura told me he's one of the best. He had a private practice once. I understand he strongly believes there's *always* an environmental factor that accounts for one's actions. His clinical findings have been published in some of the leading medical journals."

"Interesting," she said. "Where's he originally from?"

"Somewhere up around Mount Hood…The Dalles, I think."

"Timber and snow country," she commented.

"Yeah," he said. "I understand he loves the wilds. Laura would tell me about their winter trips up to Timberline Lodge. He's a tremendous skier."

She glanced at her watch. "Jeez, I need to get going," she said. "I have to meet with my colleagues and I'm already late."

"Okay, what's next?" he asked, watching her close her notepad and slip it into her briefcase.

"I'm not exactly sure at the moment," she answered, looking up at him. "But you have to start thinking about something."

"What?"

"You'll need to decide what your defense will be if this goes to trial," she said, preparing him for her coming suggestions.

"What do you mean?"

"Jonathan, we have to face this honestly," she said. "There's a chance the grand jury could hand down something less than a murder indictment—like a manslaughter charge." She hesitated, letting him grasp what she was saying. "But if they don't, for whatever reason, you may want to consider plea-bargaining for a lesser charge—like voluntary manslaughter. They might accept it to save them the time and expense of a trial."

"Do you mean to basically admit to the crime and go to jail?" he asked with a stunned look coming over his face.

She nodded slowly. "If nothing else comes up to help your case, plea-bargaining might be your best option," she said. "You could chance a murder conviction if you drag it out in court. You just need to consider it, that's all."

He took a deep breath. "Christ, what's voluntary manslaughter mean in terms of prison time?" he asked as the realism of what she was saying sank in.

She carefully considered his question. "If you continue to demonstrate the same remorse that you have...maybe a sentence of ten to fifteen years, with excellent parole opportunities after about eight served, based on good behavior." She added, "I believe Kierzek would do his best to ask for leniency."

Feeling beleaguered, he shook his head. "Damn, I just don't know...I...I..."

"Jonathan," she said. "I didn't say that was your only choice. It's only something for you to think about. We have time."

He nodded, looking at her. "But you said there's a chance they won't hand down a murder charge, but maybe only manslaughter—something we could fight?" he asked, his face full of fear.

"Possibly," she said, to relieve his tension. "We just don't know."

"Are you going to represent me, no matter what?"

"Do you want me to?"

"Yes," he said without hesitation. "I mean, I don't know your fee, or if you're available, but...I..."

"Don't worry about anything like that yet," she interrupted, not revealing Hansen's concern about even taking on his case. "Because I can't really confirm my representation at the moment." She stood and slipped on her suit jacket. "I have to meet with my colleagues and discuss the preliminaries."

"When will you know?"

"Tonight," she said. "I'll get word to you. But, Jonathan, don't worry. No matter what happens, I'll see to it that you are well represented."

"Thank you," he said, and stood, rubbing his aching temples. "Do you think I have *anything* going for me?"

"Yes, you have a lot going for you," she said reassuringly. "I think you're innocent." He stood still, looking at her as she added softly, "And I have a feeling Lieutenant Kierzek also thinks so. But we have a tough road ahead of us. And like I said, we have to face that honestly."

They shook hands as they headed toward the door.

Lacey thanked Audrey for advising the team that she was on her way to the office, and hung up the public pay phone. As she made her way for the main door of the jail, she felt sure that Mr. Hansen and his partners would understand her delay when she had a chance to explain why she had visited Jonathan. She would surely find a way to tell them during the meeting. But how would she convince them that she wanted to take the case regardless of their apparent bias against it?

As she approached her car, she was amazed at how she had made a complete turnaround in her thinking about Jonathan. How she now wanted to defend him even if he was guilty of the murder, when at first she hadn't wanted anything to do with him, and even believed he was getting the punishment he deserved.

Starting her car, she pulled into the mid-afternoon traffic and headed for Beaverton, knowing she'd be postponing her weekend. She'd ask Audrey to disregard the flight reservations she was contemplating when she got to the office. And she'd also ask Audrey to call the pre-school to say she'd be late picking up the twins tonight. She didn't want any distractions while she pursued her options during the most important afternoon of her career. She knew she was in for a long and heavy session with her associates.

She was also sure of something else: She had a suspected killer whom she needed to prepare a defense plan for—and more than likely it would be a first-degree murder charge she'd have to defend. And that murder defense plan would be set with the support of the Hansen, Jacob & Malcolm law firm, or without it. As she gripped the wheel tightly, she knew she'd made that decision when she was meeting with Kierzek—and talking with Jonathan had only confirmed that it was the right decision.

CHAPTER NINETEEN

Late afternoon, Beaverton: The meeting

William Hansen glanced at his watch and looked up from his desk as Lacey entered his executive office wearing an awkward smile. She realized they had been waiting for her to arrive. She quickly glanced over at the boat-shaped teakwood conference table, seeing the profiles of Jack Malcolm and Corey Jacob as she paused in front of Hansen's desk.

"Good afternoon, Mr. Hansen," she said timidly, facing him.

"Good afternoon, Lacey," Hansen replied quietly, reaching for his phone. "Please have a seat while I call Audrey in."

The room remained quiet as she walked to the table and set her briefcase on the floor. Pulling out a chair, she sat next to Jacob.

Jacob slowly lifted his eyes from the newspaper business section he was reading. "Nice of you to make it," he said, returning his concentration to the paper.

Noticing a faint odor from his lingering martini lunch, she turned and nodded slightly. "Corey…"

"Hi, Lacey," she heard from across the table.

She looked over at Jack Malcolm, who was smiling over the edge of the newspaper sports section from which he'd been jotting down statistics on a pad of paper.

"Hi, Jack," she said, returning a smile to her impassive colleague.

Hansen hung up the phone and rose from his desk with paper and pencil, taking a seat at the head of the table.

Lacey waited for Hansen to settle himself and then looked around at the men. "I'm sorry I'm late, gentlemen," she apologized. "My exploration took much longer than I expected."

Jacob turned the page of his newspaper. "It's all right, Lacey," he said, not looking up. "It's a lazy afternoon anyway." Still focused on an article, he added, "But I have a dinner appointment with a client tonight. I'm hoping this won't take long."

Before she could respond, Malcolm quickly echoed Jacob's pardon. "Yeah, I agree, Lacey. It's okay." He looked back down at the sports section, muttering, "And I have a poker game tonight."

Lacey frowned with annoyance as she turned away and reached down to retrieve her notebook from her briefcase. She clearly saw that Malcolm's and Jacob's minds were already made up. They weren't the least bit interested in representing Timmers. For them this meeting was merely a goodwill gesture—the final motion to dispose of the subject at hand. She knew she'd have to reopen the issue with persistence if she were to get anywhere. And she would have to target Hansen's sincerity to gain any ultimate support.

Hansen watched Lacey straighten up and anxiously resettle herself at the table. He realized something was going on with his assertive young attorney that neither he nor his partners were anticipating. And that she was probably going to spring some new information on them. He also knew that she was about to reach for another level in her professional career, and that he had better be ready for it.

"Well, Lacey," Hansen said smoothly, signaling the meeting to order. "I'm glad you were able to make it in today with your report after all. Now we can get the Timmers matter cleared up before the weekend."

"Yes, I have my report. However, I've learned there's a lot more to this matter than we first thought," she said, preparing them for her intended pursuit. "The case is rather complicated, and I'm not sure things will move along very fast."

Malcolm and Jacob, who had been gradually organizing themselves, caught on quickly. They looked over at Lacey with puzzled expressions.

Hansen furrowed his brow, deciding to strengthen the firm's reluctance to proceed any farther than they had originally planned. "Lacey, you know I always admire your enthusiasm," he said. "But like we discussed yesterday, we've pretty much decided we didn't want to take this beyond your meeting with Detective Kierzek. This was more or less just a courtesy to Timmers' agent, David Lowell, until he could gather suitable legal support."

"Yes, Mr. Hansen, I remember our discussion," she replied pensively, determined about her goals. "Yet…umm…"

"And you're inclined to take the matter farther?" Hansen interrupted calmly, helping her remove her discomfort so they could move more effectively through the meeting. He knew that whatever surprises she had in store for them were going to come out anyway. "Is this what you're trying to tell us?"

"Yes, Mr. Hansen," she said with a hopeful glance. "With all due respect, this is the direction I'd like to propose for our dialogue today."

Malcolm and Jacob sat back, remaining silent. They realized that the decision regarding how far they took things was really in Hansen's experienced hands, as always.

Hansen pursed his lips, pausing before he addressed her appeal. "But Lacey, I thought the precedent we'd set in your office yesterday was almost certainly *not* to take on this case," he argued patiently. "Rather than the other way around."

Optimistic at getting her foot in the door, she continued her intense appeal. "I know, sir. But as I mentioned, some very important issues have come up since our initial discussion that I would like to present to the group."

"All right, Lacey, " he said, conceding to her insistence. "I guess I also agreed yesterday to approach this with an open mind." He looked around at Malcolm and Jacob, who displayed no opposition. "However," he said, turning back to Lacey, "I don't want to proceed on the premise that we're in agreement about taking this farther."

"Yes, I understand, sir, thank you," she said, nodding with excitement as she quickly opened her notebook.

Hearing a soft knock on the door, they looked over to see that it was Audrey, carrying a pencil, a pad of paper and a tape recorder, equipped to take the minutes of the meeting. She had been waiting for the proper time to enter so as not to disrupt their conversation.

"Come in, Audrey," Hansen said, pointing toward his desk. "Why don't you sit there where you have more room."

She nodded, closed the door behind her, walked to the large wooden desk at the far side of the room and settled into his high-backed leather chair. She laid her notepad on the desktop and began setting up the tape recorder.

Meanwhile, Malcolm had looked down at his newspaper and picked up his pencil to take advantage of the break in the action. And Jacob was reaching for his section.

Lacey looked over at Malcolm. "Jack," she said sharply, impatient with his apparent lack of interest after her labored effort to get this far with her mission. "What are you doing?"

Malcolm looked up in surprise. "Umm," he stammered, "figuring out this week's lineup for my fantasy football league team, why?" He quickly put his pencil down, not really needing her reply.

She glanced over at Jacob, who had been alerted by her mild harangue and was quickly folding up his paper, but was also unable to escape her scolding. "Mr. Jacob," she said firmly, "I'm sure you'll make your dinner on time if you, too, will please take this meeting seriously."

Hansen looked away with a smile, apparently pleased with his tenacious young attorney's shifting the team into gear. He knew she had meant no disrespect but was simply now carrying the ball for Timmers.

She glanced around at them. "Please, gentlemen, I apologize for my abrupt behavior," she said gently but pointedly, attempting to dissolve the tension hanging in the air. "But a man's life or freedom may be at stake here. Whether we decide to represent him is not relevant at this point. But I need your full support and definitely your knowledgeable input in helping us make that decision."

Hansen remained silent as Jacob and Malcolm slid their newspapers aside and straightened up in their chairs.

"No, we're the ones who should apologize, Lacey," Malcolm said with a serious look. "You're correct. You were assigned to this matter for the team and deserve our support. You have mine."

"I agree with Jack," Jacob said, apologetically. "You also have my support, for whatever that's worth."

"Thank you, Corey. I assure you it's worth a great deal," she said with a smile, seeing that now they were all positioned in a professional forum to discuss the defense issues of Jonathan Timmers. A man locked away in the county jail, desperately needing legal help. *Adequate legal help*, she thought. *The kind of legal help she knew the four of them could offer him.*

"Excellent," Hansen said, looking over at Audrey and seeing that she was ready. "Lacey, why don't you begin by telling us what you found out today."

Audrey switched on the recorder as Lacey looked down at her notebook, opened it and began to recount everything she'd learned from her meeting with Lieutenant Kierzek, while the others listened attentively.

Lacey was pacing calmly as she finished. She sat back down in her chair, saying eagerly, "And from what Kierzek told me, I believe he's not at all convinced Timmers is guilty. He's neutral on the whole thing."

Hansen shrugged. "But, Lacey, you know the state always has to reveal information that might be helpful to the accused. I don't feel it's unusual for Kierzek to tell you the things he did. He's not out to convict the innocent."

"But Kierzek's not leading the prosecution team," she said carefully, as the room fell silent.

Hansen thought her statement through. "If you're addressing the political aggression of Matt Wolcott, Lacey, I would think that even he doesn't want to chance convicting the innocent for conviction's sake. That would be a serious miscarriage of justice." He paused and sat back. "I firmly believe Wolcott is convinced of Timmers' guilt because all the evidence points to him."

"Yes, I agree," she said, conceding to Hansen's logic, yet undaunted. "But Kierzek really opened up to me. He doesn't seem to be the type to do that easily, and that tells me something. If nothing else, he knows Timmers is not a cold-blooded murderer and that he deserves a better shake than he's getting."

Hansen threw up his hands, appearing confused. "Okay, Lacey, fine," he said. "I understand and respect your zealous attitude on Timmers' behalf, yet there's nothing substantial in your report that we hadn't already known. So I guess, I'm not sure where you're coming from."

"But there's strong potential for new evidence to turn up in Timmers' favor."

"Regardless," Hansen countered, "We have to rely on facts right now. Besides, we had never condemned him." He glanced around at the others. Seeing their looks of agreement, he continued,

"The issue was simply whether or not we wanted to represent him because of the community backlash, regardless of his guilt or innocence. I feel strongly that is still the issue."

"But, Mr. Hansen," she questioned firmly. "Wasn't that issue based on the preliminary accounts of his being guilty originating from the media reports?"

"Well, yes, I suppose that's accurate," he replied, rubbing his chin in thought. He shrugged, looking at her. "However, to repeat my earlier point, all the circumstantial evidence remains solid, and still points to Timmers being guilty of killing Laura Bearnes in a drunken passionate rage."

"Perhaps," she replied, sighing. "But it appears that Timmers is getting only a quick pass-through of justice." She looked up at him. "And I could sense that Kierzek feels the prosecution is really rushing to get this thing wrapped up, because of public sentiment."

Hansen shot her a concerned look. "Oh, be careful with that one," he said reprovingly. "Statements like that can get you into big trouble with those people. Especially statements like that coming from the defense."

"Yes, sir," she said, accepting the reprimand. "I know that, and I would never reveal that thought outside of this office. But I feel I have an obligation to the firm to express how I feel about this case."

He smiled. "Okay, I understand very well that Lieutenant Kierzek is unconvinced about some minor circumstantial evidence," he said. "But it *still* doesn't seem to change the overall scenario for our purpose here."

Frustrated over Hansen's balking, she frowned and blurted, "I just think Timmers deserves more. I talked to him and…" She stopped short, looking around the room at the stunned faces. *Damn,* she thought. This is *not* how she wanted to break it to them that she had gone to the jail and met with Jonathan without Hansen's approval.

Hansen remained silent while the atmosphere settled. "Lacey," he said calmly, "I didn't know you went to see Mr. Timmers."

"You weren't supposed to do that," Jacob interjected firmly.

"I don't understand, Lacey," said Malcolm.

"I'm sorry again, gentlemen." She breathed deeply. "I just felt it was the right thing to do at the time. After interviewing Kierzek

I wanted to at least talk to Timmers before we had our meeting today. If you'll just let me explain..." She nervously looked over at Audrey, who smiled, offering her an obvious show of support.

Hansen held up his hand, motioning for everyone to settle down. "Of course, Lacey," he said understandingly, realizing that she was feeling they were ganging up on her. He knew that wouldn't solve anything, and that she deserved a chance. "I can see why you did it, and it's okay. However, I trust you did not commit the firm to representing him."

"No," she answered quickly, knowing that she honestly hadn't. She had only committed *herself* if Jonathan chose her. "But I told him we'd know what our position was very soon."

"Sure, all right," Hansen responded with a sigh of relief. "Then I don't think there was any real harm done, and I'm curious as to what you learned from him, I guess." He turned to Jacob. "Corey, this is probably going to take a while. If you have to leave, go ahead. I'm sure I'm aware of your views and can speak for you if you'd like me to."

Jacob glanced at his watch and hesitated, realizing that he was an established member of the firm and had a responsibility in its decisions. He turned to Lacey. "Can this possibly wait until tomorrow morning?"

She thought the question through. "I don't think so, Corey," she answered. "The grand jury is getting ready to meet as we speak. Mr. Timmers needs some adequate legal support as soon as possible."

Jacob nodded and turned to Hansen. "Thank you for your courtesy, William, but I'll stay," he said. "However, can we break for a few minutes so I can call my client and tell her I'll be late?"

"Of course, Corey," Hansen said. "I could use some coffee anyway." He turned to Malcolm. "What about you, Jack?"

"Oh, I wouldn't miss this," he answered, concealing the stimulation brought on by Lacey's argument. He definitely wanted to see the next part through. "The poker game can start without me."

Jacob stood and headed for the phone.

Audrey walked from around Hansen's desk, saying, "I'll get the coffee."

"I'll help," Lacey said, seeking some deserved relief from the tense strain that still enveloped the room. She stood, then paused, seeing that Malcolm was reaching for his newspaper. "Go ahead, Jack," she said with a wide smile. "You can work on your soccer lineup, or whatever. I'm sorry I interrupted you earlier."

Malcolm let out a hearty laugh. "That's football, not soccer!" he exclaimed. "No, the lineup can wait," he said, curtailing his laughter. "I noticed there's an article on the Timmers case in the front section. Let me look it over while you get the coffee. Maybe it'll shed some light on our meeting."

"Thanks," she said with a wink, realizing it was his way of letting her know he was now on her side. She turned toward Audrey, who was waiting for her by the doorway.

Hansen, who had remained seated, had noticed Malcolm's gesture, and looked away, raising his eyebrows. He knew the forces were now mounting on the side of their insistent young associate attorney. He smiled.

Lacey and Audrey left the office and walked side by side down the hallway.

"Oh, Audrey, did you reach the pre-school center?" asked Lacey.

"Yes," she answered as they reached the utility nook and paused at the coffee maker. "They know you'll be late, and if need be I'll pick up the twins. In fact, I'm available all this weekend for whatever you need."

"I really appreciate that," Lacey said, rinsing the rancid remains out of the carafe before replacing it on the hot plate. "I might need some help this time. I don't want to break my concentration now."

"Stick with it, lady," Audrey said, filling the pot's water reservoir with fresh cool water from a large plastic pitcher. "I just know you're going to end up representing Timmers."

"Do you really think so?" Lacey said elatedly, glancing at her with a grateful smile as she scooped coffee beans from the container into the filtered basket.

"You betcha!" Audrey exclaimed, switching on the unit as Lacey moved away. "They're buckling. I even think Malcolm is getting excited about taking on this case. And that man doesn't get excited very often about anything."

They both laughed as Lacey's eyes slowly grew wide. "Do you honestly think so, Audrey?"

"For sure," she said as the rich black brew slowly oozed into the carafe. "I know that man!"

"I hope you're right," Lacey said with a smile.

"Oh, incidentally," Audrey said, "I didn't call the airline back to confirm your weekend reservations like you asked. They're as good as canceled."

"Great," Lacey said as she reached for the carafe of the steaming brew. "I'm not going anywhere for a while."

Audrey gathered up some empty cups and a large jar of sugar cookies and followed Lacey down the hallway, inwardly hoping that Lacey wouldn't *ever* go anywhere. *The firm needs her*, she thought. But she also knew that Lacey needed more than they could offer her. And it was only a matter of time before she was gone.

As the women walked back into Hansen's office in silence, Lacey was delighted to see that the three men were sitting attentively at the table. She was relaxed and confident, knowing they were waiting for her. She set the carafe down and looked at them with a gracious smile. "Coffee's ready."

CHAPTER TWENTY

Early evening, Beaverton: The agreement

Dusk was seeping through Hansen's office window, and all eyes were fixed on Lacey as she finished describing the interview with Jonathan that she had conducted at the jail. She had pointed out the important facts surrounding the scattered inconsistencies about whether Jonathan was the murderer, and how those inconsistencies coincided with Kierzek's uncertainties concerning some key evidence. Her associates had abandoned their hardened reluctance, and had eagerly joined in on the discussion with questions while jotting down notes.

"I believe that's about everything, gentlemen," Lacey concluded, flipping through her notebook a couple of times as she sat back.

"Thank you, Lacey, that was very enlightening," Hansen said, glancing around the table for his partners' reactions. "I think we're probably all together on the main facts at hand, right?" When no one disagreed, he continued, "How about if we address the major issues, beginning with the vagrant witness?"

"Sounds good," Jacob eagerly interjected. "So far it's pretty certain that Marty Spahn is cleared of any wrongdoing. I know Lieutenant Kierzek's going to question him again tomorrow, but for our purposes at the moment I suggest we assume he's only an eyewitness who didn't see anything except the body."

"Including Timmers *not* killing her," Lacey interjected.

"Right," Malcolm confirmed. "Spahn hadn't seen the killing—or Timmers at all, anywhere."

"And there doesn't seem to be any robbery motive," Hansen added.

"Except there's a missing diamond pendant," Jacob quickly pointed out, checking his notes. "So there's a chance that robbery could have been a motive."

"But we don't even know if she had the pendant with her," Hansen countered. "Her wallet was intact and her diamond ring was still on her finger, so I think we have to assume it wasn't robbery. However, I agree, we should keep the pendant in the pile."

"Maybe somewhere near the top," Lacey suggested lightly.

Hansen gave her a quick nod, then looked down at his notes. "You know what?" he said, putting his finger to his chin, squinting his eyes in thought as the room fell silent, waiting for him to comment. "I guess what bothers me most is the phone call that Laura Bearnes made to her friend, Rebecca Newell," he said. "The call where she implied that she was afraid of Timmers, just before she was killed."

"We don't know how accurate that is," Lacey said. "Newell claims she accidentally erased the message. So that evidence is inadmissible, of course. And even if it was admissible, we could argue that maybe the nature of the message is only what Newell inferred, not what Bearnes implied."

"Yes," Hansen replied, "but rest assured, whether the message is admissible or not, or the fear element was implied by Bearnes or only inferred by Newell, the jury will get wind of the whole thing somehow. I know Newell is making sure it's well known in all the media reports."

"That's for sure, William," Malcolm commented as he looked down at his notes. "How about the issue of the bell captain seeing Timmers in the lobby and then seeing him leave through the front doors about dawn?" he asked.

"And Timmers woke up in the hotel with wet clothes on," Jacob added, looking at Lacey.

Lacey nodded. "That's right, Corey. But if Kierzek is correct and she was killed back in the thick foliage, Timmers would have had fir needles and mud on his clothes from the struggle. He claims there wasn't any. And I'm sure Kierzek would confirm that fact. They kept the clothes as evidence."

"But Timmers could've cleaned them off in the shower or whatever—even unknowingly," Malcolm said. "And anyway, you told us the police aren't pursuing the premise that she was killed back in the trees, because they couldn't find any substantial signs."

She sighed. "You're right, Jack. Kierzek is only going on logic and gut instinct..."

"There's another thing here," Hansen interrupted, looking at his notes. "I'm very interested in what you said about the husband's alibi. What's his name again...Monte?"

"Yes, it's Monte," Lacey confirmed, turning toward him. "He says he was at the university at the time of the murder. Kierzek said they're trying to verify his story. He hopes it'll be done in the next day or so."

Malcolm sat back. "What happens if he can't confirm his alibi? Did Kierzek say, or give any indication?"

"Oh, then I'm sure Kierzek will question him again," she answered. "That'll be standard procedure, of course. And things could change in Timmers' favor if Bearnes doesn't have a sound alibi. Especially with the doubts Kierzek has about this case."

The silence that gradually enveloped the room suggested all the main points had been addressed and that a consensus-taking of their next move was in order. "Okay, let's try to get a more detailed picture of where we're at," Hansen said, turning to Malcolm. "How about if we start with you, Jack?"

Malcolm picked up his notes and sat back to face the group. "Well, besides the open issues we've just discussed, I think we also have to wait to see what indictment is handed down," he said, pointing at the newspaper. "I don't know if you're all aware of it, but Wolcott's going for the throat—murder-one."

"Why?" Jacob asked, surprised. "I know Wolcott's on a political tear, but why not voluntary manslaughter? I mean, what's his basis for murder-one?"

"According to this," Malcolm replied, sliding the paper across the table toward Hansen's outstretched hand, "Wolcott says the crime doesn't pass the test for voluntary manslaughter."

All eyes turned to the veteran criminal attorney, who was quickly scanning the story. "It looks like Wolcott's going to present to the grand jury that the crime doesn't fully pass the two-pronged voluntary-manslaughter test—adequate provocation, and cooling-off period."

"What's that mean?" Jacob asked.

"Well, first of all, Wolcott is convinced he has the right man," Hansen explained. "And he's operating on the premise that Timmers killed her because she had unexpectedly jilted him as *adequate provocation*, thus passing the first test for manslaughter..."

"So Wolcott basically acknowledges that her murder wasn't premeditated," Lacey said. "That Timmers is not a cold-blooded killer."

"That's correct," Hansen confirmed, looking upward for clear words while all eyes remained riveted on him. "But Wolcott will argue that a reasonable cooling-off period had gone by between their last known physical contact and the killing. Therefore it doesn't pass the second test, so it's now categorized as murder."

"Oh, I see," Jacob said, squinting his eyes in thought. "The provocation of her breaking up with Timmers would hold up for voluntary manslaughter, but if Bearnes left Timmers about two in the morning and she was killed at dawn, it would have given him time to settle down before he killed her."

"Correct, Corey," Hansen said. "And Wolcott will probably add that she was stalked, because of where they found her...away from the hotel. In the park."

Malcolm interjected, "So now the prosecution can charge that the killing was deliberate and calculated."

"Precisely," Hansen replied. "And I'm sure Wolcott will pad his presentation even further by somehow showing that Timmers is a rational man and had plenty of time to attempt another type of revenge, or reconciliation—anything short of murder."

"How do you think Wolcott will handle the issue that she was killed with her own scarf?" Lacey asked. "It's hardly a weapon that would indicate premeditated murder."

"He'll probably claim that the scarf was handy, Lacey," Hansen replied. "I don't think the scarf alone will hold much weight for a manslaughter argument in this case. I mean, weighed against all the other factors we just discussed."

"What about the intoxication factor?" Jacob asked. "Timmers is claiming he was blacked out. Won't that make any difference?"

Hansen thought for a moment. "Wolcott will undoubtedly argue that Timmers' mental state at the time is non-provable, especially with all the time that had passed before the actual murder."

"Oh, I understand," Malcolm said. "No one can prove whether he was really blacked out or not. So initially, intoxication will probably be a non-factor to a grand jury."

"That's right, Jack," Hansen agreed. "I'm sure that element will be swiftly discarded." He paused. "However, the intoxication factor could be significant in the case of a plea bargain."

The room grew silent.

"Who knows, perhaps Wolcott will be more lenient than we think," Jacob said, breaking the lull. "Maybe he'll only end up asking for voluntary manslaughter. After all, Timmers is being cooperative, and he has no criminal record."

Malcolm slowly turned to him, giving him a "get real" look. "Yeah, right, Corey," he said, bringing on some quiet laughter.

"No, I don't think so either," Hansen said seriously, turning to Lacey, with all eyes following. "I'm afraid Wolcott will certainly get his murder-one charge."

Lacey nodded, frowning. "I advised Timmers that this might come up," she said. "I think the reality of it has set in and he's beginning to accept it."

"Okay, well," Hansen said, scanning the faces. "I'd say we're in a bit of a flux at this point. I suggest there are three open issues that have to be resolved before anything can really be decided here: Kierzek clearing the vagrant, verification of the husband's alibi, and waiting for the action of the grand jury."

"All those results should be known in a day or so," Lacey said.

"Good," he said, smiling at her. "Now, what about your weekend trip home to California?"

"I've already canceled my weekend plans," she said, preparing him for her next bombshell. "I need to stay here and remain on top of things."

"Is that really necessary?" Hansen replied, surprised. "We haven't really decided anything yet as far as representation. I mean, it's probably now more feasible that we will, but..."

Lacey looked concerned as she faced him. "May I ask if you've discussed the Timmers matter with another firm?"

"Yes," he replied nonchalantly. "I've been chatting with Charles Burnett from the Burnett & Newton firm downtown. But we haven't decided anything."

"Does that mean they might take over the case?" she asked.

"Possibly, or share in it," Hansen answered, shrugging. "Why? Does it really bother you that much?"

"Mr. Hansen, I may as well be straightforward with you and the firm," she responded respectfully. "I intend to represent Mr. Timmers if he chooses. He needs help *now*. And I feel I can give him that help."

"I see," he replied calmly. "Do you mean you'd represent him with or without our support?"

"Yes, sir," she said softly. "I suppose I should also inform you that I'd planned on leaving the firm anyway. I told Jack yesterday, before all of this came up. I'm just sorry to have to tell you all in this manner." She sighed. "Oh, please understand, Mr. Hansen. I'm somewhat confused."

Hansen nodded slowly, signaling that he understood. "It's okay, Lacey," he said. "I had a feeling you'd be leaving soon for more challenges."

"I was going to talk to all of you after I came back from my weekend trip," she said, glancing around at the silent faces. "I just needed to get some things straightened out in San Jose first."

"It's all right, we understand, Lacey," Hansen said with a smile. "However, now the Timmers matter changes your overall plans, doesn't it?"

"Yes," she replied.

"So," Hansen said, "you're saying that if Malcolm, Jacob and I don't want to take on the Timmers case, you'd leave the firm and stay here to represent him. Is that accurate?"

"Yes, if he wants me to represent him," she said. "But I would rather do it with your help," she added quickly. She turned to Malcolm and Jacob. "And yours."

Hansen reached over and put his hand on her arm. "I think we're all in line with your objectives, Lacey," he said with a warm smile, while his partners continued to remain silent. "And you haven't alienated us."

She smiled with a look of humbleness. "Thank you, sir," she said. "I hope not."

Hansen looked over at Malcolm and Jacob, who had neutral looks on their faces, then back at her, asking, "If we officially take the case on with you specifically representing Timmers, would that mean you'd stay on with the firm long-term?"

"I honestly don't know," she answered. "Like I said, I'm confused about those things right now."

"I see," Hansen said, turning back to Malcolm and Jacob. "May I please have your views?"

Malcolm shrugged. "I don't think taking on this case would be as much of a negative in the community as we first thought. But is it the type of case we want to handle? I believe that's the major question."

They turned to Jacob, who picked up on his cue. "I agree with Jack," he said. "I don't think it would give the firm a black eye." He paused. "I also think the issues are pretty clear-cut. If nothing substantial pops up in Timmers' favor, he should probably plea-bargain for a lesser charge. That defense should be easy to represent. And I don't feel it would wrinkle the firm's posture."

Hansen turned to Lacey. "Do you agree with Corey?" he asked. "I mean, if nothing substantial turns up to bolster Timmers' defense, would you be inclined to recommend that he plea-bargain for a lesser charge?"

She thought the question over for a moment. "Well, at this juncture that seems like a feasible thing to do," she answered. "But I would want to first discuss all the options with the DA's office, depending on what indictment is handed down."

"Of course," Hansen said, hearing exactly what he had hoped he would. "Okay...well, I guess it's time for a vote."

They all agreed with a nod.

Hansen posed his first question to Malcolm and Jacob. "Do we think the firm, and Ms. Rosetto in particular, should represent Jonathan Timmers, who is probably going to be indicted on a murder charge?"

Without hesitation they both nodded again.

Hansen turned toward Lacey. "Me too," he said, also without any hesitation. "So if he so chooses, Mr. Timmers is now formally represented by Hansen, Jacob & Malcolm—with Lacey Rosetto as the lead attorney in this matter."

Lacey sat stunned, her mouth agape in surprise.

Hansen glanced at his watch. "Okay, it's getting late. And I know we all have things to do tonight. I vote we adjourn the meeting," he said, as Jacob and Malcolm rose to leave. "However, Lacey, will you please stay a few minutes and advise me of what your next move is?"

Lacey looked over at Audrey, who quickly said, "I'll pick up the twins and take them home. You can come over later and pick them up. In fact, I will be available any night you need me while all this is going on."

"Thank you, Audrey," Lacey said with moist eyes. "Thank you all," she repeated, scanning the room as Malcolm, Jacob, Hansen and Audrey returned her beaming smile.

"It was easy, partner Rosetto," Malcolm said as he filed out of the office behind Audrey and Jacob. "It was all very easy."

CHAPTER TWENTY-ONE

Early Friday morning, Justice Center

"No sir, lieutenant! Like I told your people before, I don't know anything about any diamond pendant. No sirree...nothin'!" Martin Spahn nervously pushed the frayed sleeve of his worn sweatshirt up past his bony elbow and raised his arms in defense. "All I did was go by and see the woman lyin' dead by the sidewalk. That's all I saw. Then I went straight to the hotel and told the bellman. That's all!"

Kierzek looked up at the drawn, pockmarked face of the gangly man and closed his notebook. "Okay, Marty," he said, sitting back in his chair. "You can go, but I might want to talk to you again."

"Yes, sir, lieutenant," Spahn said, quickly rising from the chair in front of Kierzek's desk. "I'll be around. I'll be at the Mission. Just let me know. I'll be there." He headed for the door and glanced back. "Just let me know if you want to talk to me, lieutenant. For sure, I'll be there."

"Right," Kierzek replied with raised eyebrows and a slight smile. "Go ahead, Marty, take off."

Spahn turned and scurried out of the office, making his way toward the elevators as Kierzek lethargically reached for the telephone and dialed. "Morning, captain," he said into the receiver. "I thought I'd let you know I just finished questioning Spahn...Nope, nothing new to report. I'm sure he's clean." He picked up a scribbled note from his desk. "And I found a message this morning from Cuyler. He said Bearnes' alibi checks out...Yeah, Cuyler is filling me in on the details when he gets in from an accident he's investigating...Right, captain, I don't see anything else new on the horizon. I'll be in my office if Wolcott wants to see me before he meets with the grand jury...Right. Okay, bye."

Kierzek hung up the phone and headed for the break room. Making his way down the hallway, he doubted that the prosecution would really want to meet with him before they presented the evidence to the grand jury. With Marty Spahn's clearing, and Monte Bearnes having a credible alibi, Wolcott now had enough circumstantial evidence to show probable cause against Jonathan Timmers. By the time Kierzek entered the break room and reached into the refrigerator for a container of orange juice, he was certain the DA would do his best to avoid any involved discussions with him. Wolcott knew there were some critical uncertainties surrounding this case, and he wouldn't want to chance delaying any of the procedures with annoying questions from the senior detective. Wolcott was convinced Timmers was guilty and wanted a murder-one indictment—*period*.

Kierzek was jotting down a number on his scratch pad from his opened phone directory when Cuyler approached his office, carrying a Styrofoam cup of steaming black coffee. "Hey, Ed," Kierzek said, glancing up as he set his pencil down. "Just getting my doctor's number. How are ya?"

"Good," he answered, quickly setting his coffee on the edge of Kierzek's desk. "Damn, that's hot!" Rubbing the burning sting from his hand, Cuyler sat down in the chair across from Kierzek, saying, "Making your doctor's appointment, huh?"

"Yeah," Kierzek answered, sitting back. "I'll call and set it up when we're through here." He scowled. "Sallie tells me I'm supposed to have a damn treadmill test this time. So I'll have to find a way to squeeze it in. Especially with the Timmers case taking all my time."

Cuyler nodded. "What's the latest?"

"Well, the wolves have backed away from *my* door for the time being. Matt Wolcott is meeting with the grand jury to present the evidence against Timmers." He looked at his watch, adding, "Probably right now."

"Damn, he's moving fast on this!" Cuyler remarked with surprise. "You only just finished questioning Spahn this morning."

"Right, he sure as hell *is* moving fast," Kierzek answered. "And he's pushing for murder-one."

"Didn't he or anyone from his staff even meet with you to go over your report first?" Cuyler asked. "That's standard procedure, isn't it?"

"Oh, Wolcott made the gesture, I guess," Kierzek answered, rolling his eyes upward. "About twenty minutes after I updated Ruskin about the Marty Spahn clearing and your note about Monte Bearnes' alibi checking out, he called and quickly went over everything with me on the phone. That was it. Shit, the whole conversation only took about five minutes. I didn't get a word in edgewise."

"And going for a murder-one charge yet," Cuyler said. "Wolcott must really have it in for Timmers."

"Nah, I don't really think so," Kierzek replied. "He's just bucking for state attorney general in November, and closing this case will get him a lot of notice, that's all."

Cuyler nodded and picked up his coffee, blowing on it before taking a slight swallow. "Sorry I couldn't be here this morning," he said, "but I had to rush outta here first thing and help investigate a major truck accident on the interstate."

"Right, I heard about it," Kierzek said. "How'd it go?"

"The driver was killed and the trailer was loaded with heroin and contraband," Cuyler answered. "So it got a bit complicated, but everything's under control."

"Good," Kierzek said. "Anyway, it's okay that you weren't here; everything went as I expected with Spahn."

"I didn't think anything would turn up with him."

"Nah," Kierzek agreed with a dismissive wave. "He's clean. Hell, I don't think he'd even have enough strength to strangle anyone. And he's not shielding the killer—no one would trust him to hold up under any heavy questioning."

"What about the pendant, though...think he knows anything about it?"

Kierzek shook his head. "I doubt it. But have Bressler keep an eye on him. Especially if he suddenly seems to come into money."

"Sure, okay," Cuyler said, taking another drink of his coffee.

Kierzek picked up Cuyler's message about Monte Bearnes. "So Bearnes' alibi is credible, huh?"

"Yes," Cuyler answered, "technically, at least. But the whole thing gets kinda crazy."

"Technically?" Kierzek repeated, appearing surprised. "What do you mean *gets kinda crazy*?"

Cuyler sat back, holding his coffee, answering, "I caught up with the security guard, Albert Schaub, on the phone last night, and...."

"Did you record the conversation?" Kierzek interrupted.

"No, he told me he didn't feel comfortable with that, but would sign a statement if it contained the facts as he reported them. I told him I'd get everything on paper and meet with him on Monday to get his signature. Anyway, he said..."

"Wait, hang on," Kierzek interrupted again, pulling out his notebook with Monte Bearnes' interview questions and answers. "Okay, go on."

Cuyler continued, "Schaub says that on the night of the murder he saw Bearnes drive into the complex about midnight and park in front of his office, just like Bearnes told you."

"Right," Kierzek confirmed, glancing at his notebook. He looked up and moved forward in his chair. "Was his car parked there all night?"

"Yes," Cuyler answered. "I understand Schaub even had to walk around it when he made his rounds, because Bearnes had parked so that the hood overlapped the sidewalk."

Kierzek noted the answer. "Okay, did the guard actually see Bearnes in his office like Bearnes had told me?"

"Yes, at first anyway," Cuyler answered.

Kierzek looked up with a questioning glance, wanting more.

Cuyler continued, "Schaub said he makes his rounds past Bearnes' office every hour. And like Bearnes told you, Schaub saw him through the window of his office door. They even acknowledged each other a couple of times with a wave."

"Okay, that checks," Kierzek said. "So then, did Schaub see Bearnes in there when he was sleeping on his couch?"

"Schaub said he saw him, but not exactly. I guess Bearnes has a small TV in his office, and it faces the couch. And lately when he's in there working all night, he'll take a break and watch it. Schaub said it's not unusual for him to sleep through the rest of the night, probably because Bearnes doesn't want to drive home tired."

"Okay," Kierzek said. "And..."

"When the guard looked in on his 2:45 rounds, he saw Bearnes lying on the couch covered with a comforter. The lights were out, but he could make out Bearnes through the glare from the TV screen."

"Did he see his face at all?"

"Nope, I asked him that," Cuyler said. "He said he just saw Bearnes' profile and the back of his head. Schaub said he remembered his hair color."

Kierzek contorted his face in frustration. "Shit! And of course the guard had no reason to go in and check on him."

"Correct, he had no reason to," Cuyler replied. "Like I said, Schaub told me Bearnes has been falling asleep on his couch a lot lately." He paused. "I'm not sure Schaub would've wanted to check on him anyhow."

Kierzek shot him another puzzled look. "Now, what the hell does that mean?"

"Schaub told me off the record that Bearnes is rumored to be quite the lecher on campus," Cuyler answered.

"Huh?" Kierzek said, furrowing his brow.

"Let me take this slow," Cuyler replied. "Remember, this is not recorded, and I want to tell you straight."

"Take your time."

"Well, I guess many of Bearnes' courses involve sexual-behavior therapy," Cuyler said slowly, thinking through his response. "You know, Brian, to prepare his graduating students for clinical counseling to treat the public's sexual phobias and malfunctions."

Kierzek thought through what Cuyler had said, then chuckled. "You're getting pretty good with this sex and psychology stuff, Ed," he quipped, breaking the tension.

"It's an interesting subject," Cuyler said with a laugh. He paused, gathering his thoughts. "Anyway, I guess Bearnes occasionally conducts sexual behavioral training with female students in his office."

"Do you mean one to one?"

Cuyler raised his eyebrows. "Uh, yeah."

Kierzek thought for a moment. "Well," he said, shrugging. "Bearnes is a psychologist. That's not unusual training or practice for someone in his field. I mean his students are there to learn..." He paused, adding cynically, "However, I guess it's how far the training goes, that matters."

"Right," Cuyler said. "Anyway, Schaub was advised by the previous guard not to be too nosy around Bearnes' office if he was in there because he might just be *doing* one of his students—you know, the ol' late-night psychology experiments and all that stuff."

"The previous guard?" Kierzek asked.

"Yes. Schaub has only been on the job a couple of months," Cuyler answered. "Anyway, here's where it starts getting interesting."

Kierzek sat back with renewed interest. "Go on."

"Okay," Cuyler said. "I guess the former guard seemed to be alerting Schaub about being too observant, based on his experience. He told Schaub he'd seen Bearnes through the cracks of the blinds going at it pretty good a few times. And he told Schaub the doors are thin, allowing him to hear the voices."

"You're right, Ed," Kierzek said, shaking his head in amazement. "This is getting interesting." He looked up in thought, saying, "Damn, the old story of the professor seducing the young girls…"

"I know Schaub believes it," Cuyler commented.

Kierzek sat silent for a moment, letting the startling news sink in. "Jesus," he said abruptly. "If it's true, this *is* a new wrinkle. Bearnes' cheating wife is dutifully coming back to him, probably not knowing that he was also cheating…with his students, yet."

"Uh-huh," Cuyler said, "though Schaub told me he doesn't think anything illegal or unethical has ever been brought out against Bearnes."

Kierzek sat back, tapping his pencil eraser against his lower lip. "Jesus!" he repeated, still surprised. "Did Schaub say that he ever witnessed any of this stuff?"

"He said he hadn't," Cuyler answered. "Although he said he's seen the same student leave Bearnes' office on a couple of different occasions when he's been on duty. And he confirmed it was late—during his graveyard shift."

"Do you mean on different nights?" Kierzek asked.

"Yeah," Cuyler answered.

"How does Schaub know it was a student?"

Cuyler appeared taken aback by the question. "Jeez, I didn't ask him," he replied, puzzled. "I suppose he just assumed it was a student. I remember him saying he never got a real good look at her."

Kierzek made a note of it, then asked, "But you say Bearnes has never been accused or charged with anything immoral?"

"Not according to Schaub," Cuyler answered. "But I didn't formally check it out. I wanted to talk to you first." He paused. "Oh, incidentally, Schaub told me the previous guard was fired for drinking on the job, which, of course, questions his credibility."

"For sure," Kierzek said. "His statement probably wouldn't matter anyway. From what I've seen, I'm sure Bearnes would be smooth enough to get away with stuff like that even if it's true."

Cuyler shrugged. "Yeah, and you know this type of thing isn't unusual. Teachers are always getting caught for propositioning or making it with their students."

"Yes, but *this* teacher could be involved in a capital crime of murder," Kierzek said pointedly, looking at him. He paused, his face wrinkled in thought. "But I guess what only matters now is that Schaub is positive that Bearnes was on his couch that night—alone or otherwise."

Cuyler nodded. "Schaub pretty much said he'd swear to it that it was Bearnes on the couch and that he was alone," he replied before draining his coffee cup. "He finally admitted to me that with the rumors about the student sex and all that, he always takes an extra-long curious look when Bearnes is in there."

"So is Schaub prepared to testify that Bearnes was in there *all* night?"

"Yup," Cuyler answered. "Through his 6:30 rounds, at least. I asked him that question twice."

"What about after 6:30?"

"After that the guards don't travel specific routes," Cuyler answered. "Schaub finishes his shift at 7 a.m., and the day guard only bikes around the campus, mainly patrolling the parking lots."

"Okay, so I guess Bearnes basically has an alibi," Kierzek said. "But, then again, he might not, because no one actually saw his face after 2 a.m."

"Exactly," Cuyler confirmed. "That's what I meant about only technically does he have an alibi."

"Right," Kierzek said. "And it would probably hold up in court against any cross-examination."

"Do you think so?"

Kierzek sat back, nodding. "Sure. Bearnes was following his usual pattern when he works all night at his office. And there's no other evidence that points a finger at him. In fact, public sentiment has him labeled as the 'other victim.' So even if the defense had his alibi thrown out as non-provable, the jury would probably still buy into it."

Cuyler threw him a questioning glance. "If it's true about Bearnes laying his students, do you suppose it comes into play anywhere here?"

"I dunno," Kierzek said. "I suppose only if it was something drastic, like his wife had found out about him being a scoundrel and was going to expose him to the university."

Cuyler interjected, "Or if he had actually fallen in love with another woman and he wanted to quickly get rid of his wife rather than be dragged through a messy divorce."

"And a costly one," Kierzek added. "Anyway, it would have to be something like that, because I don't think he'd get jealous and kill his cheating wife if he was just seducing his students."

"Right," Cuyler agreed. "Jeez, you'd think he'd be somewhat relieved and let her go on cheating."

"Exactly," Kierzek said. "But who the hell knows? Anyway, when you go to Eugene to get Schaub's formal statement on Monday, see if you can find out from Bearnes' superiors if he has any sort of checkered past—cautiously, of course."

"Okay, I'll be careful," Cuyler said.

"Oh, and do a background check on the guard while you're at it," Kierzek said. "I doubt that he's lying for any reason, but let's be sure."

"Okay," Cuyler said. He paused and shook his head. "Wow, this is getting confusing. And on your last homicide before your transfer, yet."

"Yeah, my last case," Kierzek said, scowling, as he dropped his notebook to his desk. "And it has to be a tough one."

"By the way, what's the latest on Timmers' defense?" Cuyler asked. "Is that lawyer from Beaverton who was in to see you yesterday going to represent him?"

"Looks like it. Her name's Lacey Rosetto," Kierzek answered. "She called me first thing this morning and had me fax her my full report. I guess she and Timmers agreed on representation last night after she discussed it with her firm." He paused. "In fact, she's probably at the courthouse right now waiting to see if the grand jury hands down an indictment. I called and updated her after I reported to Ruskin and Wolcott this morning."

"Then she knows about Bearnes' alibi?"

"Only what I knew from your note," Kierzek answered. "I told her it had checked out."

"What are you going to tell her now?"

"The truth as I know it," Kierzek said. "I'll give her the new information about what the guard actually saw."

"You mean about the guard seeing Bearnes on the couch, but not his face?"

"Correct," Kierzek confirmed. "By law she needs to clearly understand that part of it." He smiled. "Besides, I wouldn't keep anything from her. She's a fiery Italian...and I like her."

Cuyler nodded at Kierzek's rare compliment as he threw his empty coffee cup into the wastebasket. "Are you also going to mention anything about Bearnes supposedly chasing his students around?"

Kierzek shook his head. "Not unless we can substantiate that fact. It's only a rumor right now. Although it casts a shadow on him, it doesn't appear to be relevant to the case at this point."

"I see," Cuyler said. "What about Bearnes—are you going to question him again?"

"Oh yeah, sure," Kierzek answered, appearing thoughtful again. "But only as a matter of routine to finish up my report. I have no new legal reason to interrogate him. I'll try to reach him this afternoon and set up a time for next week after your visit to Eugene."

"I'll report to you right after I get back."

"Good," Kierzek said. "I'm sure Bearnes will be here for his wife's funeral next week. Ruskin told me they've released her body. I'll try to catch him then."

"So, what's next?" Cuyler asked, sitting back.

Kierzek glanced at his watch. "Lunch. I'm starved. Let's go."

"Okay," Cuyler agreed, standing. "How about a burger across the street?"

"Sure, and I'll treat," Kierzek said, grabbing his hat and blazer from the rack.

As they stood on the busy corner waiting for the crossing signal to change, Cuyler put his hand on Kierzek's arm when he saw that his boss was again mired in deep thought.

Kierzek turned to his partner.

"Brian," Cuyler said, "tell me off the record. Do you suspect Bearnes had something to do with his wife's murder? Even though he seems to have an alibi?"

Kierzek thought for a moment. "Well, Ed, let's just say I still haven't ruled him completely out." He turned back toward the opposite side of the street. "But your report on his alibi sure makes things more complicated for me."

Intrigued by his straightforward answer, Cuyler asked, "Have you always thought of him as a possible suspect? I mean, from the beginning?"

"Oh, yeah, kinda," Kierzek said evenly as they stepped off the curb, making their way toward the restaurant. "But I'm not exactly sure why I've felt that way, or why he'd do it."

"Jeez, if you're right," Cuyler said, "maybe the friend, Rebecca Newell, is wrapped up in it somehow. Maybe she's protecting Bearnes."

"Possibly," Kierzek answered. "I've thought about that."

"And if Bearnes' alibi really is true, maybe he hired a hit man or something like that," Cuyler said excitedly.

"Perhaps…"

"So, what's next then?" Cuyler asked, trying to keep up with Kierzek's brisk pace as they reached the opposite curb.

"Lunch," Kierzek answered with a wide grin. "Like I told you, I'm starved."

Cuyler matched his grin as they approached the restaurant entrance. Pushing through the front door, Kierzek frowned, thinking, *Dammit, I forgot to make the doctor's appointment.*

Chapter Twenty-two

Late Friday afternoon, Beaverton

Lacey turned and stepped away from the whiteboard that hung on the far wall of Hansen's office. She tensely capped the marker pen and turned to face her partners, who were studying her swiftly drawn list of the crime facts, known evidence and potential defense scenarios for Jonathan Timmers.

"That's the big picture as I know it, gentlemen," she said, as their eyes shifted to her. "Once Kierzek cleared Spahn, and Monte Bearnes' alibi was verified, Wolcott had absolutely no trouble getting his murder-one indictment today."

"Just as we thought yesterday, huh?" Jacob commented.

"Yup!" Lacey confirmed quickly. "It went exactly as William explained it would." Frowning, she added, "And nothing has come up in Timmers' favor."

"So then we can write Spahn off completely?" Malcolm asked.

"Yes," she answered. "Kierzek said Spahn's a motley character, but has nothing criminally to do with this case."

Hansen pointed toward the board. "Lacey, I just noticed, what do you mean by Bearnes' alibi being *technically* credible?"

While everyone listened carefully, Lacey explained how Kierzek had called her late that morning and clarified what the guard, Albert Schaub, had actually seen at the university on the night of the murder. And how Kierzek emphasized that Schaub would formally testify he was sure that it was Bearnes sleeping on his office couch all night, even though he hadn't seen Bearnes' face. She added that Kierzek didn't suspect Schaub of lying or doing anything illegal, but that they were conducting a background check on him just to be sure.

Lacey concluded, "So the way I see it, if nothing further comes up to implicate Bearnes, we probably can't push the alibi issue. It's a dead end."

"I agree," Hansen said. "So do you plan on taking it farther?"

"Yes," she replied. "I'll try to learn more about him when he's in the area for his wife's funeral. I read in the paper that it's scheduled for late Wednesday morning."

"What makes you want to take it any farther?" Jacob asked.

"Well, frankly, Corey," she answered. "I'm curious as to why Kierzek speaks skeptically of Bearnes."

"What do you mean exactly?" Malcolm asked. "Did Kierzek tell you something?"

Lacey smiled. "Only in his voice."

"Bearnes will know immediately that you're not with the police," Malcolm said. "What'll be the basis for your questioning if you decide to approach him?"

"I'm not sure yet," she answered. "But I'll think of something."

Hansen leaned forward, focusing hard on the board. "So with Wolcott getting the murder-one charge, Timmers is damned if he does and damned if he doesn't, just as we discussed yesterday," he said, shaking his head. He swiveled to face the conference table, where Malcolm sat at one end with his feet hoisted up on a chair across from him and Jacob was draped across the chair at the other end.

"It looks like it, William," Malcolm agreed. "He's in a real dilemma. If he does plea-bargain for a lesser charge and even manages to get it, he certainly goes to prison. If he decides to ride out a trial, the jury will no doubt hang him on the murder-one charge…or maybe out of mercy, murder-two."

"Murder-two?" Jacob said unemotionally. "Not a chance! If Timmers rides this out, the jury will have him for breakfast."

"I think you're all correct," Lacey said, regaining their attention. "I caught up with Wolcott at the courthouse after the grand jury forum, and…"

"He talked to you?" Jacob interrupted, sounding surprised.

"Yes, he was in a hurry, but civil," she answered. "Anyway, it appears he's holding all the cards. However, as you all well know, they're always obligated to discuss striking up a deal—even Wolcott."

"That's right, but I'm not sure he'll have to deal," Hansen said, thinking it through. "But he might, if all of the evidence they have against Timmers remains circumstantial."

"You really think so?" Jacob asked.

"Perhaps," Hansen said. "He won't want to drag this thing out if he anticipates any snags. All he wants to do is quickly get his man convicted."

"Yeah, I agree, William," Malcolm interjected. "I think *time* is our trump card if we need to pressure Wolcott. Especially when the November election is so close."

"For sure," Jacob said with a chuckle. "This thing's already putting a crimp in his campaign."

"Regardless," Hansen said, "I doubt that he'll fully cooperate until after the arraignment. He'll want to be on firmer footing."

"I agree," Lacey said, nodding toward Hansen. "Like I said, Wolcott's holding the aces at the moment—and he knows it."

"When is the arraignment?" Malcolm asked.

"Monday afternoon at one-thirty," she answered. "It's on Judge Buehler's calendar. She was ready and waiting for the grand jury results."

"They're sure not wasting any time," Jacob quipped. "And 'Old Iron Jaw' will be presiding. Damn!"

They all chuckled over Jacob's mentioning the nickname the local attorneys had pinned on the judge, breaking the tension.

"Do we have any reason to submit a motion for a quash to gain some time?" Malcolm asked.

"Hmm, no," Hansen interrupted disagreeably. "I don't favor that idea. From what I see here that would only aggravate Judge Buehler. There's no way she'd approve it. I'm sure Wolcott hasn't filed anything that defects the indictment."

"Yes, I'm sure you're right, William," Lacey said, walking to the conference table for her day-planner. "But I thought I'd file some obligatory motions to get Wolcott's attention. That is, if you agree to it."

"Sure," Hansen said as the others nodded. "Let's start with the vanilla motion to dismiss, which will be denied, of course. But it'll be expected."

"And how about a motion for a change of venue, too?" Malcolm said. "You know, because of undue or unfair publicity."

"Yes," Hansen agreed, "that'll work too. But let's stop at those two to give us some breathing room. Again, I don't want to aggravate Buehler."

"Okay," Lacey said, jotting down the last of her notes. "I'll come in tomorrow and start preparing the paperwork."

"If you need any help, call me," Malcolm said. "I'll just be home watching college football."

Lacey looked up and nodded, breaking into a smile.

"Incidentally, Lacey," Jacob asked, "do you know if the grand jury even considered the intoxication factor?"

"They didn't, and I asked Wolcott why they didn't," Lacey answered. "It was just as William explained to us yesterday—too much time had passed between their argument in the lobby bar and her killing."

Hansen added, "So Wolcott successfully presented to the jury that no one could prove Timmers was really blacked out when the crime was committed—especially Timmers himself."

Lacey nodded. "Yes."

"But how about the fact of the bell captain witnessing Timmers in the lobby looking like a drunken mess?" Jacob asked, pointing to the "evidence" column on the whiteboard.

"Oh, Wolcott isn't denying that Timmers was drunk," Lacey answered. "They know he'd been drinking heavily, from the hotel employees' statements, but that doesn't prove he was blacked out."

The room fell silent.

"Well," Hansen said. "I guess we're about where we were yesterday, only Timmers is in a bit deeper. He's now formally charged with murder."

"Incidentally, one other item," Lacey said, gaining their attention. "The media are learning that we're defending Timmers. A couple of reporters stopped me at the courthouse, but I put them off."

Everyone turned their attention to Hansen for direction. "Um, let's generally split our camp here," he said as he glanced around. "Lacey, you and Jack handle the immediate defense issues, and Jacob and I will handle the press from here."

Everyone nodded in agreement.

"All right, that's settled," Hansen said, turning to Lacey. "I'll call a news conference for Monday morning to inform the media that all releases will come from our office. That should take the pressure off you for right now. We'll evaluate the situation as we go along."

"Thanks," she said with a grateful smile. "I appreciate that maneuver."

"Okay, good, Lacey," Hansen said. "What are you going to do next?"

She looked at her watch. "I'm going to try to reach Monte Bearnes at the university. And then grab a bite to eat and visit Timmers at the jail to counsel him," she replied. "Kierzek has arranged carte blanche visiting time for me."

"Give me a call on my beeper if you need anything this weekend," Hansen said as he rose from his chair. "I'll be around."

"Me too," Jacob said.

"Thank you all," she said as she closed her day-planner and grabbed her purse. "I'll update you on anything that comes up before the arraignment," she added as she headed for the doorway. Goodnight, gentlemen."

They said goodbye and sat still as they watched her leave the room. They knew her mind was racing but that her mission was under control.

Lacey sat in the jail's visitor room, anxiously fiddling with her day-planner, thinking about how she'd break today's news to Jonathan, when the door opened and he was escorted into the room by the guard. The guard nodded at Lacey, closed the door behind him as he left and positioned himself at his usual post in front of the windowed partition.

She stood as he approached the table. "Hi, Jonathan," she said with a friendly smile and an outstretched hand. "How are you doing?"

He appeared depressed as he shook her hand. "Not so good," he answered downheartedly, pulling out the chair across from her. "I just finished my first weekend supper." He scowled as they sat down. "Cold and soggy fish and chips. I heard it's the regular Friday night fare around here. Garbage..."

"I know it's not easy," she consoled, seeing how depressed he was. She quickly realized he would have to be handled cautiously in order for the meeting to be productive, which was going to make her task even more difficult. "Just try to hang in there while we figure things out," she added encouragingly.

"What choice do I have?" he responded sarcastically.

"Jonathan, please..." she said directly. "I understand your frustration. But let's not start off like this. We need to stay focused if we're going to get anywhere."

"Okay, I'm sorry," he apologized, shaking his head in distress. "I just don't belong here, that's all."

"We're working on that," she said gently as she looked down to reach for her notepad.

"All right," he said quietly. "Go ahead and give me the news. You must be here this late for a reason."

"Yes, I'm here for a reason," she said. "The grand jury handed down the indictment late this afternoon."

He took a deep breath. "And the charge?"

"First-degree murder."

He exhaled, dropping his head in his hands. "Oh, God!" he exclaimed in a rasp as the realism quickly registered. "First degree!? They couldn't have!" He sat back and pounded a fist into the other hand. "It's not right! It's just not right!"

"Jonathan, hold on," she said, reaching over to put her hand on his arm to calm him. "As far as we're concerned, it's a trumped-up charge by the prosecution to gain the upper hand."

He looked at her. "And..."

"I discussed it with my colleagues," she continued. "We're sure we can get the charge reduced, even if we end up proceeding to trial."

"Even *if*? Why wouldn't it end up at trial?" he asked skeptically. "Are you talking that plea bargain stuff again?"

"Anything's a possibility for discussion at this early stage," she answered.

"No, dammit, I won't admit to something I couldn't have done!" he exclaimed. "Bullshit!"

"Jonathan," she again appealed firmly. "This is hard enough as it is without you reacting so emotionally to everything I say. And please don't raise your voice in profanity to me. We need to remain calm and collected."

He swallowed hard, slowly nodded and caught his breath, resettling himself. "Okay, sorry again, I'll try to keep it together," he said, sitting back. "But how can they charge me with first-degree murder when the killing is being labeled as a crime of passion? Isn't that voluntary manslaughter?"

"Well," she began slowly, finding the words for a straightforward explanation, "the prosecution basically presented to the jury that the murder was committed long after the provocation. In other words, a reasonable cooling-off period had occurred between her killing and the time she'd left your presence. They also factored in that she was killed a significant distance from the hotel—not the spot of actual provocation."

"What's a reasonable cooling-off period?"

"It's a guesstimate on their part," she answered. "But with your background, along with the hotel employees' opinions, the prosecution considered you a reasonable man who should have calmed down. The grand jury agreed."

"So," he said, grimacing, "what you're saying is that the prosecution made it look like I stalked her in the riverpark and murdered her long after I should've calmed down...and that's murder-one."

She nodded, knowing that confirming words weren't necessary.

He shook his head and stood to pace the room, attempting to relieve his tension. He turned to face her. "Do you have any good news for me?"

"Unfortunately, not yet," she told him as he began to pace. "The vagrant, Spahn, has definitely been cleared as a suspect, and Monte Bearnes' alibi has been substantiated—sort of, anyway..."

He quickly halted his pace. "Huh, *sort of?*" he repeated, looking surprised.

She locked onto his stare. "Kierzek told me the security guard at the university is formally stating that he saw Bearnes in his office all that night, even though he didn't see Bearnes' face after two a.m."

"I don't understand."

She explained, "Supposedly the guard saw Bearnes sleeping on his office couch in front of the TV. He's sure it was Bearnes because he saw his profile through the window."

"The guard only saw Bearnes' profile?" Jonathan said. "Would that really hold up in court?"

"Probably, at this point anyway," she said. "I really couldn't challenge the alibi unless I had an incriminating reason against

Bearnes. And right now we don't have anything to go on. But we'll be looking...for anyone or anything."

"Maybe the guard's lying," Jonathan said, hanging onto the issue.

"Kierzek said they're going to do a background check on him," she replied. "But I won't lead you on. The chance of the guard being Bearnes' shill is very unlikely."

Jonathan leaned his hands on the edge of the table. "Shit!" he cursed in a whisper, turning away, feeling deflated. "So there's nothing on Bearnes?"

"I'm afraid not," she answered. "And the media have him portrayed as a professional, hard-working and faithful husband who's been tragically widowed because of his cheating wife and her forsaken lover."

He jerked his head up. "Uh-uh! I didn't do it!" he exclaimed bitterly. "I couldn't have. And I'm not going to stand by and be condemned for it."

She sat back to let him vent, hoping he might shed new light on the issue.

He took a deep breath. "And, dammit," he added angrily, "if I didn't kill her, Bearnes must have something to do with it! He has to be questioned further!"

"Yes, Kierzek is going to talk to him again," she said calmly, attempting to compose his intense behavior. "And so am I."

"You are?" he asked, surprised.

"Sure, I'm planning on it," she answered, reaching for her day-planner. "I tried contacting him this afternoon, but the university administration office told me that he's up at Mount Hood with his daughter, Tamra."

"At Timberline Lodge?"

She glanced at her notes. "Um, no, I don't think so. I guess he rented one of the old forestry department cabins so they could be in seclusion when he broke the news to Tamra."

"When's he coming back?"

"They think Sunday night or Monday," she answered. "Because the funeral is next week—late Wednesday morning." She thought a moment, looking up. "You know what? Maybe I'll even catch him at the funeral if not before—but that's iffy."

"Do you really think he'll talk to you?"

"Oh, sure, eventually," she responded, appearing unconcerned. "He'd be unwise not to. He knows he's not a suspect, so I don't think he'd give us any reason to think he has something to hide by refusing to talk with us."

"But what reason would you have to talk to him?"

"I thought about it on the way over here," she answered. "Maybe I'll center the discussion around trying to find another possible suspect—like maybe a family acquaintance." She hesitated, saying pointedly, "And it's true, we are looking for someone else, aren't we?"

"Yes, we are," he replied firmly. "Absolutely."

"Besides, Kierzek told me Bearnes is being very cooperative," she said. "He's even blaming himself for neglecting his wife as the reason she strayed, and for everything else that's happened. He told the media that he has even forgiven you."

"Hooh, booy," Jonathan said with a sneer. "No way! She had fallen totally in love with me, and there's every chance he found out, and there's also every chance he killed her out of jealousy. And if he *did* kill her, we can't let him sweep this thing away while I rot in jail."

She jotted a note and remained silent, realizing that his anger was running deep today. She had not seen him this way before. She was inwardly pleased, hoping his new outlook might spark some changes in his memory, or at least remove the weak defeatist attitude he had harbored since the murder.

"When's the arraignment?" he asked, sitting back down.

She looked up, answering, "Monday afternoon."

"Do you know the judge who's going to hear it?"

"Yes, Judge Fredrica Buehler from Superior Court."

"Is she tough?"

"I'm afraid so," she answered with a frown.

"Christ, I can't get a break anywhere," he said, throwing up his hands.

"Don't worry at this point," she responded. "Buehler's toughness won't make any difference at the arraignment. It's only a procedure to set up a trial. Any judge would follow the same course. In fact, she'll probably move things along very quickly, which is good for you."

"I'll be pleading not guilty, of course."

"Correct," she answered. "Automatically."

He calmed, asking, "Do you think there's any chance I can get bail?"

"Probably not, but I'll try," she answered. "I'll present the argument that you could have left Portland a lot earlier on the day of the murder if you were a flight risk—or left if you knew you were actually guilty."

He nodded, then got a troubled look on his face. "I've been thinking about what you said yesterday concerning plea bargaining."

"Yes..." she responded, listening carefully, knowing now that he was being rational about the issue.

"It still doesn't set well with me," he said. "I just don't feel good about pleading voluntary manslaughter, or second-degree murder, or anything at all, especially if someone else did the crime."

"I didn't *tell* you to plea-bargain," she replied. "I only meant it's an option we should carefully evaluate if we can't see any way out of the murder-one charge. We have plenty of time to decide that before any jury trial would begin."

He looked away and shook his head, again angry. "Okay, but there has to be someone else involved in this! I didn't do it!" he said in a rasp.

She furrowed her brow. "Jonathan, you seem different today," she said, appearing inquisitive. "Is there something new you remember about that night that could help your defense?"

He shook his head in frustration. "Not really," he said. "But I've had time to think things through. For one thing, how would I even have known how to find her in the park if I was stalking her? I'm not familiar with the area at all."

"You never walked that route with her?"

"Hell, no," he said. "I hadn't even gone outside of the hotel with her before. We didn't dare. Whenever we'd meet, she'd leave by herself the next morning and I'd head straight for the airport."

"Okay," she replied, but she decided to remain the devil's advocate to draw more out of him. "You could have followed her that night."

He shook his head. "Jesus, if I was sloppy drunk and she was afraid of me, like Newell says in her phone-message witness statement, Laura surely would have seen me behind her," he argued strongly. "I wouldn't have been able to be that careful. Furthermore, I probably would've attacked her right away by the hotel."

"Well, that makes sense to you and me," she said, pressing further. "But keep in mind that the prosecution is not buying the blacked-out theory at all. They're dismissing it as a feeble defense ploy."

"To hell with the prosecution," he blurted. "I'm telling you what I know. And I was blacked-out drunk, dammit! So what I just told you means it's not logical that I did it. Especially if Kierzek is right and she was killed somewhere else and then moved out in the open by the sidewalk."

"Yes, all right," she said, jotting notes. "I'm getting all this down for further discussion."

"Okay, whatever," he said quietly. "Do what you think is right. But in the meantime I'm going to prove I'm innocent somehow. Can you please get me some notepads and pencils?"

"Um, yeah, I'm sure I can," she said. "What are you going to do?"

"Start writing the story," he answered firmly.

She smiled. "Oh, I see," she responded, delighted over his aggressive attitude. "Okay, I'll drop them off at the reception center."

"Thanks."

"You're welcome," she said with a chuckle. "Of course, I'll have to add my expense to your bill after you're out of here. Until then you can consider it a donation."

He laughed, then said seriously, "I'll also need a copy of the arrest report."

"Sure." She noted the reminder.

"You know what?" he said. "I've already begun writing the story in my head. I'll have this damn thing figured out before I'm convicted—and who's really guilty!"

"Good," she said as she stood up. "And I'll make a copy of Kierzek's arrest report for you and make sure it also gets to the reception center. I'm sure they'll give it to you."

He rose with her. "I appreciate everything you're doing, Lacey."

"I know. Now try not to worry," she replied, feeling that they were finally traveling on a constructive course. "And stay positive."

"I will," he said. "I have a story to write."

"And I have a defense to prepare," she said, holding out her hand.

They laughed as he shook her hand, both realizing that another level of their relationship was developing—in sync with the professional one. They now felt comfortable together with their cause.

As the door opened and the guard stepped inside to lead him out, she nodded when she heard Jonathan say: "Bye."

Watching him being led down the hallway toward his cell, she picked up her briefcase, pleased about their new personal bond. It was a clear indication that they had the potential to become friends. *And why not?* she thought as she headed out the door. It would only help them to reach their goal—*to free him.*

CHAPTER TWENTY-THREE

The arraignment, Multnomah County Courthouse

Superior Court Judge Fredrica Rose Buehler looked up and leaned back in her black, tall-backed tufted chair. She focused sternly on Jonathan, who was standing next to Lacey at the defendant's counsel table. Tense, he swallowed hard, knowing well what Buehler's next question was going to be.

The few spectators who had gotten wind of the quickly scheduled arraignment sat motionless in the public seating area as the room fell into a brittle silence.

The stenographer sat ready, keeping her eyes fixed on her stenotype machine.

District Attorney Matt Wolcott sat at the prosecutor's table with a smug look, softly tapping his pencil on his notepad.

"Mr. Timmers," Judge Buehler said, her high-boned square jaw twitching with edginess. "Do you fully understand the capital charge that has been brought against you by the state of Oregon? The charge that I've just explained to you?"

"Yes, Your Honor," Jonathan answered, stone-faced.

"Let me say further, Mr. Timmers," Buehler said, "if there's anything you don't understand, I'll be glad to go over it again for you."

"No, Your Honor, I understand everything," he reaffirmed, remaining rigid.

"Then how do you plead, Mr. Timmers?" she asked with a steely look. "Guilty or not guilty."

"Not guilty, Your Honor."

A light buzz enveloped the spectator seating area.

"Did you say not guilty, Mr. Timmers?"

"Yes, Your Honor. Not guilty," he repeated.

Buehler quickly nodded and looked down at her calendar. "Trial is set for thirty days from today, October twenty-sixth, at one-thirty in this courtroom." She looked up at him again. "Bail is denied," she added crisply.

"But, Your Honor," Lacey blurted, trying to keep the issue alive. "He didn't try to flee before and…"

"Ms. Rosetto, I have read and completely understood your petition for bail," Buehler abruptly admonished. "However, due to the gravity of this capital crime and the fact that Mr. Timmers is from out of state, bail is steadfastly denied."

Matt Wolcott looked at his assistant and smiled.

Lacey looked down and made no further objections, knowing it was useless and that she didn't want to risk alienating Buehler at this early stage.

"Court will recess for afternoon break," Buehler said, lightly striking her gavel on the small wooden plate, "and will reconvene at three p.m."

Everyone stood as the judge abruptly rose and hurried down the bench steps, ducking into her chambers.

As the marshal walked over and tugged on Jonathan's arm, Lacey sighed and turned to him. "I'm meeting with the prosecution this afternoon to find out what our options are," she said. "And then I'll be meeting with my associates to determine our next best move."

"Okay," Jonathan said downheartedly as his arms were pulled behind him. "I'll try to remain patient. Please come and see me soon."

"Yes, I will," she replied softly, realizing he was feeling more despondent over his being denied bail. "By the way, did you get the writing pads and your arrest report I dropped off the other day?"

"Yeah, thanks," he answered. "It'll keep me busy for a while."

She smiled. "Just stay strong," she said as the guard clicked the cuffs shut around his wrists and took Jonathan by the upper arm. "I should be able to update you on things by tomorrow afternoon. I'll see you then."

"Please do," Jonathan said and faced the floor as the marshal turned him, leading him out through the prisoner's entrance next to the bailiff's table.

Lacey shook her head in disappointment over not having obtained bail for him. She wasn't sure whether it was the legal setback or not being able to freely see him outside of jail that bothered her more. Turning, she saw Jack Malcolm hurrying through the aisle toward her.

Approaching her, he said sheepishly, "Sorry I didn't make it on time. I'm the Rotary Club secretary this week, and…"

"Hey, slow down," she interrupted with a smile, "I'm just happy you came. I was really surprised when I got your phone call yesterday…and during Sunday afternoon football, yet."

"No problem, Lacey," Malcolm said, chuckling at the football jab. "I only wish I could've been more help here. Was it a tough time?"

"Nah," she said in a dismissive tone while bending to pick up her briefcase. "There weren't any surprises. Buehler had the outcome sewed up."

He nodded. "Yeah, that's the way with arraignments," he commented. "There ain't much to 'em…and no bail, I take it."

She shook her head with a grimace, obviously let down. "Nope," she said. "But I knew there wasn't much of a chance for getting it anyway."

"You really look upset," he said. "I mean, for not expecting to get it."

"Well, it would have been much easier to work with him outside of jail," she answered. But she knew deep down that that wasn't the only reason she wanted Jonathan free. They were becoming closer friends as the days passed.

"Okay, what's next?" he asked.

She nodded toward the prosecution counsel table, where district attorney Matt Wolcott was cheerfully chatting with one of the stenographers while stuffing his notepad into his briefcase. "I have a meeting with him at three-thirty in conference room A, on the second floor," she answered. "Wanna go with me?"

"Of course," he said with a concerned look. "I think we need to communicate with him right away."

"What's that mean?"

"I heard *death penalty* today," he answered with a grimace.

Her eyes widened. "What!?"

He put his hand on hers. "There's been some stuff floating around on the news," he answered. "Laura Bearnes' friend, Rebecca Newell, is really stirring up trouble with the media. She's playing off the riverpark stalking issue."

"Dammit!" Lacey seethed in a bitter whisper, tightly gripping the handle of her briefcase. She inhaled to curb her anger. "Okay, what's happening? I haven't had time to catch the news."

"Newell was interviewed on the *Portland Today* talk show this morning," he answered. "She really wants to see Timmers' ashes and isn't being coy about it. She can't understand why there's been no mention of the ultimate punishment from the prosecution."

"Oh, no," she responded with a frown. "That'll get to Wolcott fast, with his heightened political agenda."

"It probably already has," he said. "Newell mentioned Wolcott's name."

"Damn! She'll continue to put pressure on him," Lacey said through pursed lips. "Can't we legally shut her up somehow?"

"Sure," he answered, "As soon as we can file a change-of-venue motion, we can probably get a gag order. But in the meantime..."

"Yeah, I know," Lacey interrupted, sighing. "In the meantime, that woman can do all the damage she wants."

"Exactly," he confirmed. "But I did tape some of her interview while I was having breakfast. It's at the office."

"Good move!" she exclaimed. "I'll pick it up and go over it for our venue motion."

"I figured on that," he said. "Incidentally, Hansen held a news conference just before lunch. He told the reporters that only he or Jacob would be giving updates."

"Great, that'll help," she said, managing a slight smile. "Okay, let's go. I'd like to get a cup of coffee and talk about our strategy before we enter the lion's den. We need to get to Wolcott before Newell does."

He chuckled. "Sounds good! I haven't sparred with Matt since we were in law school." He winked. "And I've won before."

She chuckled with him as they walked out, making their way for the cafeteria to quickly set up their meeting strategy.

Matthew Clark Wolcott, senior district attorney for the County of Multnomah, hoisted his long legs to the edge of the conference table, removed his wire-rimmed glasses and rubbed his graying temples. He turned to Lacey, who was sitting across from him, eyeing him quizzically. "But, Ms. Rosetto," he said firmly, his tired, squinting eyes fixing on her, "Timmers is cooked. Why would we want to plea-bargain?"

"First of all, Mr. Wolcott," she quickly replied, straining to maintain the frustration that had been building throughout the day, "I didn't say we were here to offer a plea bargain. I simply asked what the prosecution's options are if we suggested the action down the road."

Appearing uninterested, Wolcott shook his head in annoyance as he put his glasses on and picked up his cup of Coke, draining it.

"C'mon, Matt," Malcolm urged, backing up Lacey as he leaned against the wall on the other side of the room. "Give us a break. You know we're not dealing with murder-one here. Even if the guy did do it, it was because he lost it after the woman walked out on him."

"No! Now you people give me a break, dammit," Wolcott snapped, swinging his feet off the table while shooting Malcolm an icy glare. "Timmers waltzes in here from another state, steals another man's wife and ends up viciously wasting her because she wants to go back to her husband." He shook his head in disgust, exhaling before continuing his harangue. "And we're supposed to give him leniency? Bullshit! He stalked her and lay in wait for her. We can probably go for the death penalty on this if we push it."

Lacey remained silent, letting the more experienced Malcolm handle this sudden delicate exchange.

"All right, take it easy, Matt," Malcolm said calmly, holding up his hands. "It's just that we're not convinced Timmers did it. And we don't want him slam-dunked if there's the slightest chance he's innocent."

"Oh, Jack, come on," Wolcott droned, rolling his eyes upward. "We're all too busy for this stuff. We're not slam-dunking the guy. The evidence is sound. Hell, he isn't even denying he committed the crime."

Lacey shook her head, interjecting, "Yes, he is…he's denying it now that he's had a chance to think things through."

Wolcott looked at her and shrugged, unmoved.

"So, what if there's any chance you're wrong?" Lacey appealed respectfully. "The only evidence the state's ever had is circumstantial. That's hardly fool-proof."

"No, it's not fool-proof," Wolcott replied, giving way to her statement. "But all the evidence we have points to him, circumstantial or not. And none of what we have points to anyone else on the planet, for Christ's sake."

"What about the husband's questionable alibi?" Malcolm interjected. "No one positively saw him at the time of the murder."

"Whoa," Wolcott responded, quickly turning toward Malcolm. "The security guard at the university will testify that it was Bearnes he saw during his shift. We have his signed statement coming from Kierzek's office this afternoon."

"But the guard didn't actually see his face," Lacey countered.

"And perhaps the guard's lying," Malcolm added.

Wolcott gave them a dismissive wave. "We don't have any reason to believe he's lying," Wolcott said firmly. "We did a background check on him this morning. He's clean." He paused, adding, "Unless, of course, you two know something about him that we don't."

Malcolm and Lacey remained silent, conceding that they had nothing on the guard.

Wolcott threw his hands up. "C'mon, you two are just reaching," he said. "We have nothing on Bearnes to suspect him. He's the other *victim* in this crime, for God's sake."

Lacey looked at Wolcott questioningly. "But what about the uncertainty of the exact murder location, and…"

"Oh, no, Ms. Rosetto," Wolcott interrupted sharply, appearing frazzled. "With all due respect to your thorough defense issues, I'm not going to sort through each piece of evidence again. We've been through it many times and got nowhere. And even Lieutenant Kierzek finally agrees."

She fell silent, frustrated, realizing that he was correct—she had no solid foundation for arguing this issue any further.

"Look, Lacey," he said calmly, trying to wrap up their session in a positive mode. "All we can see is that an outsider came into Portland and took out one of our finest ladies. We simply feel that swift justice is warranted here. So let's just let it be, and allow *that* justice to run its course."

"But swift justice might be wrong justice," Lacey responded. "Mrs. Bearnes had quite a bit to do with this whole thing that could have motivated people other than Timmers to kill her."

Wolcott sighed. "Look, we're not a lynch mob." He paused, then glanced at each of them as he appealed. "For Christ's sake, you two, give me something new and concrete if you want to talk about plea bargaining. Or let's move forward and let things play out as they may."

Malcolm quickly jumped in, seeing an opening. "How about the issue of Timmers being blacked out during the time of the murder?"

"Jack," Wolcott replied with a frown, "do you know how many of those flimsy excuses this state gets a year—that the accused doesn't remember doing it?"

"Yes, I'm aware," Malcolm said, nodding. "But I also know that Oregon allows intoxication as a defense for voluntary manslaughter."

"Right," Wolcott said, lifting his eyes in thought. "And Timmers is an accomplished mystery author. I'm sure we could show that he was probably well versed on that part of the law."

"Regardless," Lacey interjected, pressing the offensive, "we're still willing to fight for this issue. Because if Timmers did in fact commit the crime, we honestly feel that intoxication was a definite factor—*the* factor that should lead to voluntary manslaughter."

Malcolm promptly added, "And we have hotel witnesses who will testify that he'd been drinking in the lobby bar most of all day and all night. And they also have a record of selling him a bottle of wine and one of bourbon."

"And not only that," Lacey said, continuing the blitz, "I've been in contact with a clinical biochemist who specializes in alcoholism and the effects it has on the brain. He's willing to testify that it's very probable Timmers was acutely intoxicated and more than likely blacked out."

Her statement took Malcolm by surprise, but he concealed it.

"But you can't prove it," Wolcott argued weakly. "You can't prove what his mental condition was. Especially with the length of time that had passed before her murder."

"Matt, all we have to do is provide doubts," Malcolm said commandingly, walking to the table and sitting down next to him. "The prosecution has to do all the proving."

"This is after we motion for a change of venue, of course," Lacey said.

"Huh?" Wolcott responded, shooting her a frown. "Hell, you won't stand a chance of getting that."

"We're sure gonna try," she said, sitting back. "We feel that this community already has Timmers unfairly convicted; especially with the stuff Rebecca Newell is constantly spreading around through the media."

"We can't be held responsible for that kind of thing," Wolcott said. "It happens all the time. We'll find an impartial jury. Besides, you'll never get a change of venue through Judge Buehler."

"Like Lacey told you, Matt, we'll sure try," Malcolm said, playing his trump card. "And keep in mind, even if we don't get the motion passed, we'll also get a chance to interview the prospective jurors. We have time—lots of it."

"I see appeals written all over this one," Lacey said, driving the stake a little deeper into Wolcott.

Wolcott sighed and looked away, then faced them with a puzzled look. "What the hell are you people looking for exactly?" he asked. "Jesus, you just told me you weren't offering to plea-bargain."

"We're mainly looking for proper and fair justice," Lacey answered quickly. "Like Jack said, no slam-dunking."

"Matt, we know you're doing your job," Malcolm said, sitting back in his chair, knowing that he and Lacey were now in control. "And all the evidence appears to point to Timmers, but whatever the situation, he's not a cold-blooded killer."

"So..." Wolcott said, shrugging.

"We might want to discuss a plea bargain for voluntary manslaughter," Malcolm said. "That is, if nothing changes outright in Timmers' favor."

"Are you saying you'd give up any court fight for voluntary manslaughter?" Wolcott asked.

"It's a possibility," Lacey said. "Because even if Timmers *is* guilty, that's all the crime amounts to—a murder that was committed in the heat of passion. With the alcohol inhibiting his ability to reason."

Wolcott shook his head. "Jesus, the public would go crazy if we let him off. I'd really look bad, and..." He stopped himself, knowing he had made a big mistake with that one.

"Sir," Lacey said firmly, jumping on her chance to reprove him. "You know very well we can't administer justice based on public sentiment. We must do what's right."

Wolcott remained silent, accepting the reproach, then said, "What about Buehler? I don't think she'd go along with..."

"Yes, she would, Matt," Malcolm interrupted, "if she believed you were recommending proper justice. Buehler's tough, but she's always fair with the issues."

Wolcott looked up. "Timmers would probably still face ten to fifteen in Salem."

"Let's not worry about that right now," Malcolm said, knowing that Wolcott had weakened and relinquished his initial hardened stance.

Wolcott looked at his watch. "I'll think about the options and discuss it with my colleagues," he said. "I'm sure we'll all be in touch soon."

"Okay, thanks for your cooperation," Malcolm said politely, watching Wolcott pick up his briefcase and push his chair back. "However, please remember, Matt, we haven't decided our position, or even discussed this thoroughly with our client."

"Yeah, sure," Wolcott said as he stood and headed for the door. Opening it, he turned and paused. "Tell me, why in the world would you and your firm want to defend a murderer?" he asked, looking at Malcolm. "I didn't think Hansen wanted to take on stuff like this."

Malcolm turned to Lacey, signaling that she was on the line for this one.

"Mr. Wolcott," she said quickly and calmly, "We're not defending a murderer, and definitely not a murder crime. We're only representing a man who is accused of this crime. And even if he was found guilty, he needs to be dealt with fairly by the state and in the proper manner. That's what Mr. Hansen and the rest of us believe—and stand for."

Wolcott shrugged. "Okay, whatever," he said as he turned and left the room.

Malcolm turned to Lacey. "Nice job," he said, breaking into a wide smile. "I couldn't have put that better myself." They stood as he quipped, "Maybe you should start writing my Rotary speeches."

"Thanks, I really appreciate that," she replied with a smile, picking up her briefcase. "And I thought you were magnificent earlier."

"And thank you," he said as they left the room and walked down the hallway toward the front entrance. He glanced at his watch. "By the way, it's happy hour and I'm heading around the corner to The Sports Grotto for a beer. Wanna go with me?"

"Nope, I have a lot to do," she answered, leading him through the doors and into the chilly sunlight of downtown Portland. "I also have to prepare for a funeral I'm attending on Wednesday. There's some people there I may want to meet."

"Are you going to talk to them for sure?"

"I don't know yet," she replied. "It depends on how it plays out."

"You'd better be careful," he cautioned. "Especially where Rebecca Newell is concerned."

"Don't worry," she replied, turning to head for the parking lot. "I'll handle her okay if the occasion arises."

"I'm sure you will," he said with a smile, watching her walk away. "Oh, hey," he called after her.

She turned back. "Yes?"

"I didn't know you'd been talking with a clinical biochemist who specializes in alcoholism," he said with a puzzled look.

"You didn't?" she responded, mockingly. "I thought for sure I'd told you. Hmm, sorry."

"Yeah, right," he said with a laugh, now realizing that she hadn't been in contact with any biochemist. He shook his head as he watched her scurry into the parking lot. Turning, he walked down the busy sidewalk toward the lounge, thinking that Lacey Anne Rosetto was blossoming into a very resourceful attorney. And she'd be sorely missed if she did decide to leave the firm.

Chapter Twenty-four

The funeral mass, Blessed Sacrament Church, Portland

Lacey felt somewhat apprehensive as she parked her car down the street from the church and slowly got out. She was reluctant to encroach upon the funeral, but felt compelled to talk to Monte before he went back to Eugene. After all, she'd tried to make phone contact with him all week with no success. *Perhaps he's not getting the messages*, she thought. *Or perhaps he's avoiding me.* She was also curious about Rebecca Newell. Maybe she'd also talk to her if the opportunity arose. *And maybe not.*

Making her way up the sunny, tree-lined sidewalk toward the entrance, Lacey saw the lengthy procession of cars, each with a small magnetic funeral flag sitting on its hood. A long black hearse, with the rear door sitting open, sat poised in front of the line. She glanced at her watch, then the perimeter of the church. Seeing no one told her that the funeral mass must be well under way.

Climbing the front steps, she hurried through the high-arched central portal and entered the church, waving off the usher with a slight hand gesture and quietly slipping into the very last pew so as not to be immediately noticed. The usher nodded stiffly and returned his solemn stare toward the activity in the front. She moved forward onto the padded kneeling rail and crossed herself, inwardly reciting a quick prayer for the deceased before shifting backward onto the seat.

Settling herself, she glanced around at the cluster of vast domed apses and gigantic marble columns that ornamented the architecture of the splendid structure. She gradually lowered her gaze to the majestic scene at the rear of the chancel that had captured her attention. An immense cross of Christ, bathed in diffused sunlight falling through the brightly colored stained-glass windows of ruby red and blue, loomed gloriously above the high altar.

She focused on the large gathering of mourners, filling the front pews on both sides of the center aisle as a somber funeral hymn rising from the organ chamber resonated in the sedate background. Their grieving eyes were fixed on the altar landing, where a portable silver catafalque supported the casket containing the woman resting in eternal peace.

An uncomfortable feeling began to well up inside Lacey as she began to question her tactics. Was she intruding—desecrating the mourners' dignity and the final respects they were paying to their departed friend and loved one?

Lacey's attention was drawn to the priest, who was carefully descending the altar steps with a downward stare. Clad in ceremonial vestments, he recited a Latin prayer through a reverent pitch while sprinkling holy water on the casket. Lacey knew enough about Catholicism—her ex-husband's faith—to realize that this was Laura's final blessing and that the funeral eulogy in her memory had already been given. And only the closing rituals of the Mass were yet to be performed.

Completing the blessing of Laura's soul, the priest turned and slowly climbed the altar steps, making his way to the rear of the chancel. Pausing in front of the altar, he raised his hands in prayer before reaching into the tabernacle to retrieve the Holy Sacrament of consecrated wine and communion wafers in preparation for Holy Communion. As the altar boy knelt on the bottom step, vigorously wiggling a small altar bell that produced a gentle chime, the priest placed a wafer on his tongue and took a sip of wine from the golden chalice before turning to face the gathering.

Lacey was growing more anxious, knowing that the Holy Sacrament was the final ritual before the gathering would be quickly blessed and would leave the chancel area, with the priest leading the cortege and pallbearers—*in her direction*. She'd have to make her decision quickly as to whether she should stay and talk to Monte.

She spotted a suave, well-dressed man in the front pew standing and tenderly taking the hand of the little girl sitting next to him. As the church hushed and only the haunting hymn continued to echo softly in the background, they stepped into the center aisle and walked to the chancel rail. Standing rigid, hand in hand, they stared longingly at the casket. *Monte Bearnes and his daughter, Tamra*, Lacey thought. She looked to the immediate right of where they'd been sitting and saw a woman with long black hair, sadly wiping her eyes with a wad of tissue. Lacey instantly recognized her from the newsreel tape that Malcolm had recorded at home on Monday. *Rebecca Newell!*

Rising, Rebecca pocketed the tissue and left the pew. Stepping to the rail, she stood next to Tamra and bowed her head. Following suit, the majority of the gathering rose and slowly filed out of their pews, making their way to the rail; but not all. Many remained seated. Lacey thought they probably weren't Catholic and most likely felt uncomfortable about the ceremony. But then she also remembered that the Catholic religion forbade communion if one was bearing mortal sin on his or her soul—*like murder. So if Monte and Rebecca are having communion, maybe they are innocent of any serious wrongdoing in Laura's death*, she thought. *Or maybe they are guilty and are simply disregarding their sacrilege, receiving communion for show.*

Regardless, she again wondered what she hoped to gain here. Even if Monte or Rebecca, or both of them, *were* criminally involved, they surely wouldn't feel pressed to talk in this environment. *Am I this obsessed with proving Jonathan's innocence?* she wondered. Maybe he wasn't innocent at all but Monte and Rebecca were. Then how crude she'd been for callously nosing around the funeral service like a cynical detective. Was she risking a terrible judgment call, at best? *And what if the media got wind of it? Blowing it totally out of proportion...causing her and the firm to look ridiculous.* She decided she could catch Monte at another time and that she needed to leave before she was seen.

As the priest walked to the tabernacle to replace the remainder of the holy elements, the last of the people who had received communion filed back into their pews and settled themselves, facing the front. Lacey knew this was her last chance to leave unnoticed. She stood and slipped from the pew, quickly brushing past the surprised usher as she made her way toward the entrance. But she stopped, stunned, at seeing Lieutenant Kierzek standing in the portal with his hat in his hand, looking at her.

"Hi, Lacey," he whispered nonchalantly with a smile. "How are you?"

"Oh, hi, lieutenant," she whispered back, appearing shocked. "What are you doing here?"

"I'll explain later," he answered, motioning her outside. "C'mon. I was just leaving, too."

She nodded and swiftly followed him down the steps, where they paused at the sidewalk.

"It's a bit stuffy in there," he said, knowing she was pent up and preoccupied. "Wanna join me for lunch?"

Now composed after their startling encounter in the portal, she cocked her head skeptically. "I'm not sure," she answered. "Isn't it a bit odd for the senior detective and the lead defense attorney that are assigned to the biggest criminal case in town to be going to lunch together?"

Kierzek shrugged. "We still get to eat, don't we?"

She smiled at his casual and assured manner. "Oh, why not," she said, deciding that talking with him might help clear up some of her confusion. *Besides, neither of us has anything to hide,* she thought.

"Good, let's go," he replied. "How about that new Mexican place downtown by the courthouse?"

"Fitting," she cracked as they headed down the street for their cars.

Looking in her rear view mirror while starting her car, Lacey saw a few people emerging from the church. She exhaled and shook her head, realizing that she'd barely avoided being seen. *What a dumb idea that had been!* she thought while pulling away from the curb.

Lacey reached to the middle of the table, spooning salsa on the remains of her chicken burrito while Kierzek swallowed the last of his taco, washing it down with a drink of cola. He had joined her in small talk about each other's families to relieve their awkwardness, but decided that now he'd break things open so she could vent. He had decided days ago that even though they were on different sides, they were after the same results—fair justice. Therefore he would help her at times when it was appropriate. *This is one of those times*, he thought. And he'd also decided that this was an appropriate time to tell her about his new status.

He sat back in his chair, asking, "So tell me, Lacey, why did you go to Bearnes' funeral today?"

She shrugged as she pushed the salsa tray back. "Curious, I guess," she lied, still feeling guilty over her initial motive to go to the funeral to question Monte and Rebecca about the murder.

He remained silent as she glanced up at him, continuing, "I suppose I went because I'm involved in one of the most important crimes in Portland and I should at least know what the victim looks like."

"And did you accomplish your mission?" he asked, momentarily allowing her to carry on for comfort's sake, although he knew she was evading the truth.

"No, I only caught a glimpse of the casket," she answered, looking down to pick up her fork. "And I didn't know it would be closed. Besides, after I arrived there I felt like I was intruding."

"Lacey, I know better," he said pointedly, knowing it was time to challenge her. "You went there to question the husband and the girlfriend, didn't you?"

"Yeah," she admitted, nervously toying with her burrito remnants. "I did."

"That's a job for the police outside of court, you know," he said reprovingly.

"I know," she conceded sheepishly, pushing her plate away. "I just…"

"Lacey," he interrupted, knowing that she was really caught up in this. "You're doing everything you can to represent your client. Why are you getting so involved in matters that you can't control?"

She shot him a stern look. "Dammit, Brian, Jonathan might be innocent," she said evenly. "I believe he's been dealt a bad hand. I've had that feeling since the day I met him at the jail." She sighed. "I know you also think so. Will you admit it? Please take my word for it, we're off the record here."

He looked thoughtful. "It doesn't matter what we *think*." He paused, allowing her to focus on his conversation. "Yes, our intuition can take us on a trail to places other than the obvious, but there has to be hard evidence at the end of that trail. In this case, there's none. I'm afraid everything still points to Timmers."

"I'm so tired of hearing that crap," she said as she abruptly sat back, taking a quick drink of her iced tea. "The whole damn thing smells of deception. It has from the beginning."

He shook his head. "That's mostly speculation talking again, and…"

"Wait," she interrupted anxiously. "No one can logically explain why Laura's body was carefully moved from where she was killed to out in the open."

He continued to shake his head. "We couldn't prove that she was killed somewhere other than where we found her."

She ignored his argument, saying, "She was planted by the sidewalk so that she could be easily discovered on that morning. And I know that's what you think."

He nodded. "Sure, I won't deny that, it's all on the investigative record," he said. "That's what I theorized might have happened at first. But even if we knew that's what really occurred, what would it prove? Timmers could have moved her there for some reason. I mean, what would it do for his defense?"

"A lot," she argued. "A murderer in an alcoholic blackout wouldn't normally move a body so carefully, especially if he was in an uncontrollable frenzy. I'm sure I could get a medical professional of some kind to verify that."

"All right," he agreed, "perhaps you're accurate about intoxicated behavior. Still, what would that theory show in this case? The prosecution isn't even formally considering that Timmers was blacked out at the time of the murder."

"Of course not!" she countered. "Wolcott was out for Timmers' blood from the start. He's not going to voluntarily give Timmers any leeway. It might taint his almighty election status."

Kierzek thought it best to refrain from commenting on that remark.

She refused to relent. "What about the missing pendant!?" she hammered, leaning forward. "Why couldn't you people find it!?"

He held up his hands, knowing now that he had to calm her down before there was any regrettable dialogue exchanged. "Hey," he said, "take it easy. I think I'm on your side. I'm after impartial justice also, and I want the one who's responsible for the murder just as badly as you do."

She eased back in her chair and took a deep breath, nodding apologetically. "I believe that, Brian. I'm sorry. I guess I'm just feeling the pressure."

He gave her a forgiving smile. "Okay, I agree the missing pendant is disturbing." He pondered for a moment. "We know it existed and it's valuable. The jeweler in California confirmed that Jonathan had the setting made up specially and picked it up on the morning he flew into Portland."

Lacey's eyes widened, looking for even a grain of optimism from him. "Did you check with the local jewelers to see if anyone has seen it?" she asked.

"Yes, of course, and all the pawn shops, too," he answered. "No one has seen it, or anything that even resembles it. I understand the piece was really unusual."

"Then the motive for her murder could still be robbery?" she asked, reaching.

"Sure, there's always that possibility," he replied. "But once the vagrant was cleared, well…" He paused and shrugged, indicating that a robbery motive for the killing was most likely a lame course to pursue.

"But the issue still has to be followed, doesn't it?" she pushed.

"Lacey, we don't even know for sure that she had it with her. Or if she ever had the pendant at all," he said slowly, letting his last statement sink in.

She looked perplexed. "What do you mean?"

"No one ever saw her with the pendant," he answered. "Or saw Timmers even give it to her in the first place."

"But Jonathan told me she was really excited when he surprised her with it," Lacey said. "I believe him. So someone must have seen him give it to her."

He shook his head. "Maybe, but we checked with everyone in the hotel," he replied. "They all said they hadn't seen anything that had to do with a pendant."

"What about the bartender in the lobby bar?" she asked with a curious stare. "He must have seen them."

"Oh, yes, the bartender clearly remembers them being in the bar," he answered. "But he closed early, leaving Timmers and the woman alone with a bottle of champagne in front of the fireplace."

She grimaced in frustration over this latest dead end.

"Anyway," he added, "the missing-pendant issue could backfire on you."

She thought that over, gradually frowning as she caught on. "Oh, sure, I see," she said. "The prosecution could suggest that Jonathan set the whole thing up to ditch the pendant and make the killing look like robbery."

"Uh-huh," he answered. "I suppose they would if they were pressed on the issue. But right now the missing pendant doesn't constitute any hard evidence for either side. It's really non-existent to Wolcott."

She felt exasperated, but pressed on, grasping for anything. "The husband could have killed her for reasons of passion," she suggested. "Or the girlfriend could have something to do with it—or both of them. I understand they're pretty close. Did you see them sitting next to each other at the church?"

He nodded. "Yes, I…"

"Hey," she interrupted. "You never really explained why you were at the funeral."

"Like you first said," he answered quickly. "Curious, I guess."

"Oh, no, Mr. Brian Kierzek," she shot back. "You were there for professional reasons…to learn something. C'mon, you'll have to tell me anyway if it turns out to be evidence."

He smiled. "No, it's not what you think, Lacey," he replied soberly. "I was close by, and I was really curious. I have no secret agenda."

She cocked her head, still implying his insincerity with a disbelieving look.

"Lacey, I'm not even on the case any more," he said, knowing that this was the right time to inform her.

"What?" she responded, her mouth opening wide in surprise.

"Yes, it's true," he said. "I'm officially in burglary as of yesterday."

"I don't understand," she replied, sitting back stunned. "Why?"

"Well, I was going to transfer out of homicide next month anyway," he answered. "But since this case was pretty well wrapped up, my superiors just moved things along a little faster by a week or so."

"Bull!" she blurted angrily, her eyes narrowing. "They just want you out of there because you're causing too much friction with your suspicions about the case."

He held up his hands in defense of his superiors. "No, the case has dried up," he said. "There aren't any more leads to investigate."

She looked disappointed. "Maybe, but now I'm sure nobody's pushing anything at all."

He thought for a moment. "That doesn't matter. If anything did come up to shed new light on the case, the evidence would probably be so obvious that anyone could handle it. And I could always help if they needed me."

"But they surely can't just completely disregard this thing," she argued. "Who's handling the case now?"

"My former street partner, Ed Cuyler, and a new detective by the name of Jameson," he answered. "But like I said, I'm still around to assist them if they ask for my help."

"Is there any chance you'll transfer back?"

"Nah," he answered, deciding to completely open up. "I also have a health problem."

She shot him another stunned look.

"I was hit with a heart attack last year," he explained. "It was a mild one, but still an attack. I really should've transferred out of homicide then. But everyone turned the other way." He paused. "In fact, if my physical next week shows any major problems, I'll probably have to pension out."

"I see," she said with a sigh, finally softening her stance. She knew there was no grounds for disputing this policy in the police force. "I'm sorry, I didn't know."

"It's okay," he said. "I know you didn't."

"Can I still talk to you about the case if I want?" she asked hopefully. "I mean, if I need clarification on some of our past discussions."

"Maybe, *but*," he responded, wavering his hand. "Well, you know…it should pretty much go through the channels to keep things official. I'm sure you understand how that stuff works."

"Yeah, I understand," she said. "Can I ask you again if you think Timmers is innocent—of course, off the record."

He shook his head and laughed. "I wondered when you'd get to that again," he said. "Lacey, I really don't know. I've never been so unsure over a case in my life. I just don't know. We have to go with the evidence."

"You mean there's nothing else the police have to go on?" she asked. "That's it? Over? Finished?"

"That's the way it looks now," he answered. "We have nothing on anyone else—the vagrant…the husband…the girlfr…"

"Oh, incidentally," she interrupted. "Did you people complete a background check on Monte Bearnes?"

"Sure—found nothing," he replied quickly. "We conducted a thorough one, because I admit that at first I kinda suspected he might've had something to do with it. But now…" He shrugged.

"What about the girlfriend?" she asked. "Did you check her out?"

"Yes, and she appears clean, too," he answered. "We determined it was just how it looked. She was Laura Bearnes' best friend, and…"

Lacey sat back, interrupting again, "And Newell's carrying a grudge against Timmers, who she's convinced killed Laura."

Kierzek nodded. "Yup, that's the way we see it."

She moved forward again. "Then you're saying that you firmly believe Bearnes is innocent of anything to do with his wife's murder."

"No, I didn't say that. C'mon, Lacey," he answered, somewhat irritated at her attempt to corner him. "I'm saying he appears to be clean…that he has no criminal record; not even speeding tickets. And Cuyler interviewed his superiors at the university on Monday—nothing there either. And remember, he has an alibi."

She sat back. "A feeble one," she said, sighing. "But I understand."

Kierzek added, "Hell, Bearnes even called my office and asked if he could help in our investigation on him. He said he completely understood our position and would assist in any way he could."

"Damn!" she said in a whisper. "That's strange."

"You're right on that count," he said. "I do think he's a neurotic man. And probably capable of doing anything he sets his mind to. But that doesn't label him a killer."

"So you never questioned him after your initial session?" she asked.

"Nope," he answered. "Although he offered to come in. Lacey, to beat a dead horse, I'll say it again—we have nothing on him, or Rebecca Newell."

Still disappointed, she shook her head. "Okay, I guess that's a dead end too." She glanced at her watch. "I'd better get going. I told Jonathan I'd come over and update him after the funeral."

"Yeah, I gotta get going, too," he said. "By the way, are you still planning on talking to Monte Bearnes or Rebecca Newell?"

"I'm not sure," she answered, shaking her head. "I felt awkward when I saw them at the funeral. And now that you're telling me you're basically finished with them...I just don't know."

"Incidentally," he said. "I heard you and your associate met with Wolcott after the arraignment on Monday."

"Yes, we wanted to keep all our options open and current," she answered, reaching for her purse. "We have to be realistic about this. The jury would probably give Timmers the death penalty if things remain the way they are and we take it to trial."

"Well, I'm sure you'll get Wolcott to go along with you on whatever you choose," he said, fishing his wallet from his blazer. "I know that he just wants the whole thing finished as soon as possible."

"We're also aware of that," she said. "But we still haven't given up on finding Timmers innocent."

"You just don't want to get too close to the trial day before you make a decision on plea bargaining," he said as he left cash on the table to pay for the lunch. "Especially if they begin jury selection."

"Right," she agreed. "We feel we have a couple of weeks left."

He paused and looked at her. "Well, I know one thing."

"What?" she asked as they rose from the table.

"If I ever need an excellent attorney," he said with a wink. "I'll know where to find one."

"Thanks," she replied, smiling appreciatively as they exited the restaurant and headed for their cars. "And thanks for lunch."

"It's okay, you owe me," he quipped as he got in his car.

"For a lot more than just lunch," she called back with a wide grin as she opened the car door. "I owe you plenty," she added, sliding in behind the wheel.

Lacey followed Kierzek as they both exited the lot but headed in different directions. Weaving through the downtown traffic toward the jail, Lacey was disappointed that she had no positive update for Jonathan—only the same dead ends, which had become more solidified. And now her trusted ally on the police force,

Lieutenant Kierzek, was off the case. She'd have to tell Jonathan that also.

By the time she reached the jail and was getting out of her car, it had dawned on her that Kierzek had slyly given her direction today. He might even have assumed she'd be at the funeral and set up the "chance" meeting so he could help her—off the record. *Sure,* she thought. *He wants fair justice just as badly as I do.*

She reached into the back seat for her briefcase, but hesitated with her next thought. *Perhaps Kierzek was telling her that proper justice is already being applied. Was he telling me that possibly the right man was already in jail?* Shutting the car door, she walked across the lot remembering what she'd told him when they were leaving the restaurant, *she owed him plenty.*

She pushed open the front doors of the jail and entered the foyer of the reception center, unsure of her next step. Now she questioned whether she should try to talk to Monte Bearnes and Rebecca Newell. What would be her reason for approaching them? Regardless, she'd have to decide soon. As she had told Kierzek at the restaurant, there were only a couple of weeks left before they'd have to make a plea bargain decision. *But I'll think about all of this later*, she decided.

At the moment she had to see and update Jonathan. And she still had to find out what her exact feelings were for him—especially if his chances of freedom were fading. Approaching the reception counter, she began filling in the sign-in sheet as the guard walked over to her. She felt uneasy, realizing that the coming month of October was going to be a pivotal time in her life.

CHAPTER TWENTY-FIVE

Mid-October, Beaverton: The decisions

William Hansen rose from his chair and walked around the desk to the conference table, breaking the gloomy stillness that hung in the air. He sat down across from Lacey, who felt dispirited and anxious. She'd been right on that day of the funeral last month after meeting with Kierzek for lunch. The weeks since then were turning out to be a pivotal time in her life. She knew this was going to be a trying meeting before everything she had to tell him was out in the open. She'd have to take it in stages and let Hansen lead the way. She'd know what and when to tell him.

"So," he said, "what you're saying is that everything is pretty much firmed up with the plea-bargain arrangement for voluntary manslaughter?"

"Yes," she answered quietly. "Jack and I completed the details with Wolcott last night after we met and discussed all the options with Jonathan. Everybody knew the decision had to be made before they began the jury selection."

"So, nothing ever came up to give Timmers any hope?"

"Not a glimmer," she answered quickly.

"Not even anything with Monte Bearnes and the girlfriend, Rebecca Newell?"

"No," she answered, shaking her head. "After that morning at the funeral and talking afterward with Kierzek, I just couldn't find any good reason to pursue it."

"Okay, what's Wolcott going to recommend for the plea?" asked Hansen.

"He informed us he's going for the max," she answered. "Fifteen to twenty-five with no parole, because of the way she was killed."

"I'm not surprised," Hansen replied with a scowl. "Wolcott needs to put on a show for the people who are convinced Timmers should be put to death."

"Correct, but I'll be filing a motion to argue for leniency," she replied.

"I'm sure Buehler will allow the argument," Hansen said. "Especially with a voluntary-manslaughter plea."

"Yes," she agreed. "And if I can somehow get Timmers a minimum sentence, he should only have to spend about eight in Salem, with good behavior."

"Probably," Hansen replied. "But, regardless of the sentence imposed, the good news is that Timmers won't be put in with the hard core—probably medium security."

"I hope so," she said. "That's what Wolcott conceded anyway."

"And Wolcott's confident that 'Old Iron Jaw' will buy into the whole idea of the plea?"

"Yes," she answered. "Wolcott told us that he and Buehler have no axe to grind. They're only looking for swift justice."

"Perhaps," Hansen said. "But I know he was concerned about the change-of-venue motions you were going to file, not to mention our plans to appeal if it went to court and they disregarded the alcohol factor."

She nodded. "Oh, I'm sure you're right," she said. "And also because he finally admitted that Timmers is no cold-blooded murder-one candidate."

"I figured he would sooner or later," Hansen said. "Wolcott's okay. He's just convinced Timmers did the killing, and like you said, he wants swift justice."

Lacey turned away again with a look of disappointment, trying to maintain her professionalism.

"How's Jonathan taking the decision?" asked Hansen.

"Not easily," she answered. "He's in denial. But he also knows he can't take a chance on the eventual results of a jury trial."

Hansen interjected, "Or risk any chance of the death penalty if the jury has their say. It may have been a slim risk, but it still existed nonetheless."

"That's for sure," she agreed half-heartedly.

"Lacey, I know you're upset about our having to plea-bargain," Hansen said, responding to her obvious frustration. "But we did everything we could. You told me yourself that Timmers never had a chance from the beginning."

"I know," she said quietly. "I apologize for my behavior. But I just can't help feeling that I failed Jonathan, and it hasn't worn off yet."

He shook his head. "That's ridiculous," he said firmly. "You did a tremendous job. The best job that could have been done under the circumstances."

"Thank you," she said. "I do appreciate that."

He added, "You're taking this too personal, and you damn well shouldn't. Timmers would have been put away for first-degree murder without you."

"Do you really think so?" she asked.

"Of course," he replied, reaching over to put his hand on her arm. "And don't forget, we still don't know for sure that Timmers isn't actually guilty."

"Yes, sir, you're right," she responded more positively, shaking her head. "Like you said, maybe I've just become too personally involved."

"Would you like to talk more about that part of it?" Hansen asked gently, withdrawing his hand. "I know how wrapped up in this thing you are. I'd hate to think you're carrying it around inside you."

"It might help," she answered. "I'll try anyway."

"Okay, good," he said. "First, tell me, is it simply the bitter legal pill you had to swallow that's eating at you, or is it that you lost Jonathan for good? I know you've been spending a lot of time with him the last few weeks."

"Well," she muttered. "We've gotten to know each other quite well and we're quite fond of each other too. I mean...you know, sir, like in the movies."

"You haven't fallen in love with him, have you?" Hansen asked, interrupting her rambling. "I know things like that happen, but this is surprising."

She pondered his question. "Um, fallen in love? No, I don't think so," she answered slowly. "I realize I'm lonely and vulnerable right now, but I wouldn't let myself fall in love with him."

"What do you mean, wouldn't let yourself?"

"There's no future in anything like that now, with anyone," she answered, reaching for the words. "And especially Jonathan. He's going to be in Salem for a long time. And I have a life to live."

"Do you know how he feels?"

"I think so," she answered. "Confused and alone. He really doesn't have anyone but me and his agent, David Lowell, who's also his best friend."

"Not even any relation?" asked Hansen.

"No, he was an only child," she explained. "His father was killed in the Vietnam war right after he was born. And shortly afterward his mother overdosed on drugs. I understand she was into the Sixties thing, and losing Jonathan's father put her over the edge."

Hansen shook his head. "Who raised him?"

"His grandmother. And she died last year of Alzheimer's disease."

"Wow," Hansen said with a frown. "And his first wife dies. This guy's had a rough time of it! Not to mention his situation now."

"I agree," she said. "He told me his life hasn't been pretty. His writing is his only lasting reward."

"It's no wonder he took it so hard when Laura Bearnes left him," Hansen suggested.

Lacey answered with a distant nod.

"What about his personal dealings in California?" he asked, breaking the dismal train of discussion. "I mean, how is he going to straighten out his personal business back there, now that he's definitely not being released?"

"Lowell is flying in from New York to meet with us before the sentencing," she answered. "I'll assist with any legal stuff Lowell needs to wrap things up in California. Jonathan was only renting a condo there. It should all go pretty easily."

"That's good," Hansen commented.

"Yes, Lowell will be the trustee of Jonathan's financial holdings until he's released from prison." She paused. "Incidentally, Lowell will be taking care of our fees when he gets here."

"No problem with that," he said, shrugging. "Anyway, what's the court schedule for Jonathan?"

"It's still scheduled for the twenty-sixth," she answered. "Jonathan will go through the obligatory pleading of guilty to involuntary manslaughter. And then Wolcott and I will present our arguments."

"I see," Hansen replied. "Well, I guess there isn't much else to do in this case except wait for the sentencing day and hope for the best."

"Right," she agreed. "That's about it."

"Okay," he said. "By the way, I'm pulling Jack from the day-to-day issues, if you don't mind."

"No, that's fine," she replied. "All I have to do is update Jonathan this afternoon, then finish up the standard legal paperwork." She hesitated, deciding on how to prepare him for what she was going to tell him next. "It should only take a few days."

"Good," said Hansen. "Well, I guess that's it." He rose, signaling the end of their discussion.

She let him walk to his desk and sit down before saying, "Umm, Mr. Hansen…"

"Yes," he answered, seeing her edgy look. He sat back in his chair. "What is it, Lacey?"

"I know Jacob's on vacation for another week," she replied, slowly setting him up for her next blow. "But I'd like to take that long weekend I never got a chance to take last month."

He glanced at his calendar. "Of course. I should have offered it to you before. Jack and I can handle things around here while you and Jacob are gone."

"I'd like to leave tomorrow afternoon and be back next Wednesday," she said quickly. "That'll give me plenty of time to finish up with the Timmers matter when I get back."

"Yes, sure," Hansen said, then furrowed his brow when he noticed her lingering nervousness. "Lacey, what's the matter?" he asked, but grew a knowing look before she had a chance to answer. "Oh, I know. We're gonna lose you, aren't we?"

She nodded, looking away. "I need to leave Oregon, Mr. Hansen," she said emotionally. "Not only am I seeking more of a professional challenge, but there's so much heartache here. I mean, with my divorce and all the other stuff surrounding the Timmers case."

He thought over her statement, then said softly, "But you know, this is really bad timing on your part."

"What do you mean?" she asked, looking up with a puzzled glance.

"You were just getting my partners in shape," he answered, winking to break the tension. "I haven't even heard Malcolm mention his fantasy football team in a long time."

She remained silent and smiled, realizing the ice had been broken. The real challenge of the meeting was now over.

"What's your timetable?" he asked.

"I'd like to be settled back there by Thanksgiving. I'll be staying with my parents until I get a place of my own."

"Tell me," he said thoughtfully, "do you have any job leads there yet?"

"Yes, I do," she said, with a guilty look. "I hope you're not offended that I had moved this decisively before talking with you."

"Not at all," he answered with a dismissive wave. "You've been candid with us about this issue. Do you feel comfortable telling me about the lead?"

"Sure," she replied. "It's an emerging criminal law firm in Sunnyvale that my mother told me about—Jerold & Jerold. They're brothers—Thomas and Michael."

"Well, you moved swiftly," he said, a bit surprised, but smiling. "I guess your mind is really made up, isn't it?"

"Yes, sir, it is," she answered honestly. "I approached them late last week after I knew the Timmers matter was decided. I sent them a local newspaper story about the case that somewhat flattered me. Again, I hope you don't mind that I did that."

"Nope, not offended on that count either," he answered quickly. "How'd they respond?"

"They're very interested. They want me to come in and talk with them on Monday."

"I see," he replied. "Umm, please sit tight." He picked up the phone and called in Audrey, the secretary.

Lacey sat in silence, wondering what he was up to.

Audrey walked in and immediately sensed there was something unusual in the air—especially when she saw Lacey's questioning look. "Yes, William?"

"Please sit down," he said, offering her the chair next to Lacey. "Lacey is taking a long weekend and going home to San Jose," he continued slowly. "Please work with her on the schedule and make all the arrangements, at the firm's expense, of course, and…"

"But, Mr. Hansen," Lacey interrupted. "I…"

"Ms. Rosetto, please," Hansen firmly responded, putting an index finger to his lips, signaling silence.

Lacey's eyes widened and sat back.

Hansen turned back to Audrey. "And we have to prepare a terrific letter of recommendation for her that she'll be taking along. Let's put together a great one."

"Yes, of course, sir," Audrey answered crisply, shooting a wide smile at Lacey, who was sitting there with a stunned look.

Audrey turned back to Hansen. "I'll get one started for your review. I'm sure we can finish it up this afternoon, William."

"Thank you," he said as Audrey stood and walked out of his office. "I'm sure we can." He turned to Lacey, who was wiping her moist eyes with a coffee napkin. "Now," he said, "you'd better go work with Audrey on your weekend arrangements and then go and see your client, Timmers. I have things to do."

She pushed her chair back and stood up. "Mr. Hansen," she said softly, "I don't have the words to thank you."

He smiled. "Don't worry about it. You deserve it all."

She reached down, slowly picked up her briefcase from the floor and headed for the door, but stopped and turned back toward him when she heard him say, "Lacey."

"Yes?" she replied.

"Will you really be able to detach yourself from this case and from Timmers?"

She thought a moment and nodded. "Yes," she answered. "I'm beginning that task today. I just don't have any sensible alternative."

"Okay, good," he said with a wave. "Bye."

"Bye," she replied as she hurried out the door, her parting look giving him all the thanks she could offer.

Lacey pulled into the afternoon traffic, feeling relieved as she made her way for the jail. Audrey was firming up her long weekend arrangements, Hansen was aware of her relocating plans, and Jonathan's plea bargain was firmly in place. It would now be only a matter of time before things were finished up here and she'd be back in California for good. And she would stick with her decision. Especially now that Hansen would promote her job search by providing her with a glowing letter of recommendation.

Everything is falling into place, she thought as she turned the corner, seeing the Justice Center looming in the distance. *But is everything really okay?* she wondered, glancing at herself in the rearview mirror. What about Jonathan? Had she failed him like she thought? Even if plea-bargaining was the right decision, was she still taking the setback of the case too personally like Hansen had suggested? Did her disappointment truly involve anything more than not proving Jonathan innocent? *Or is it because I'm losing him?*

Pulling into the jail parking ramp, she gripped the wheel more tensely as she searched for a space, wondering how close she and Jonathan had become over the last few weeks. *Have I fallen in love with him, even though I've told myself I wouldn't let something like that happen?* Like in the movies when the attorney falls for the jailed client? *No!* She simply felt sorry for him because he was alone and locked up, that's all. *And that isn't my fault*, she thought. She'd done everything she could to free him. Anyway, she'd tell him today that she was leaving Oregon. She'd tell him right away, she decided as she pulled into an empty space and shut off the engine. *Yes, right away.*

While walking across the lot toward the building it dawned on her that she hadn't told Jonathan about Kierzek's retirement yesterday. *Oh, damn!* she thought. They'd all been so wrapped up in the plea-bargain discussion, and Jonathan was so despondent, that she'd forgotten to tell him! He'd take this news hard, too. It was bad enough for Jonathan when he'd found out last month that Kierzek was transferring to burglary. The one man on the police force whom Jonathan had counted on to find out the truth about Laura's killing. Now Kierzek wouldn't be around at all. Yes, she'd have to inform Jonathan of this today too. She wondered which bombshell she should drop first.

As she entered the main door of the reception center, the feeling that she really hated doing this grew stronger. *Damn! When am I going to be done with all of this so that I can just move and get on with my new life in California with the kids?* As she walked up to the guard at the desk, she decided that she'd never get this personally involved with any case again. *Not ever!*

Jonathan sat at the table, facing Lacey with a blank stare as she sat silently across from him, worrying about how she'd give him the next bit of news.

"God, what a shock," he said, shaking his head. "The one I thought could help me out of this mess. But now…"

Lacey shrugged. "He doesn't have any choice," she said. "He can't stay on the police force unless he accepts a job in records—and that's not going to happen. Kierzek's a street cop."

"When did he find out?"

"After he flunked his treadmill test a couple of weeks ago," she answered. "The doctors took a closer look and discovered some scar tissue and also that a couple of his arteries were blocked."

"How old is he?"

"Nearing fifty, I guess," she answered. "He'll get a nice pension."

"How long before he's gone?" asked Jonathan with a sigh of disappointment.

"Early next month, after his bypass surgery," she answered, recalling the details she'd gotten from Kierzek earlier this week. "But basically he's all done now. He's just cleaning up some stuff at the office."

"What then?" asked Jonathan, finally managing a smile. "He'll drive his wife nuts. He's no stay-at-home gardener."

She smiled with him. "He told me that he's taking about six months off after the surgery, then going into private investigative work," she answered. "I also understand he's got it worked out to consult on some unsolved cases for the Portland force."

"I see," Jonathan said. "And what about you? Does Hansen have any big cases lined up for you now that you're finished here?"

She was ready for this, and faked a look of excitement while she broke this news. "Oh, that was the next thing I was going to tell you," she said exuberantly. "I'm relocating to California and a new law firm close to my home town. And the twins will be close to their grandparents."

Her façade failed to rally him. As her words sank in, his face dimmed. "Christ," he muttered, his voice cracking. "I guess this isn't going to be my year."

"What's that mean?" she asked, appearing surprised.

"Everybody's leaving me when the going gets tough," he replied, realizing too late that that surly remark was a big mistake.

"And what the hell does that mean!?" she snapped, her pent-up anxiety from the day's stress breaking free. She had known that she would have to deal with an attitude sooner or later, but it still unnerved her. "What are you insinuating, Jonathan? That we're all abandoning you?"

He flinched, knowing that he'd hit a raw nerve. "Oh, never mind, sorry."

"No, not never mind, dammit!" she said with glaring eyes. "What is your problem?"

"I said I was sorry and I meant it," he said. "I'm trying to hang in there in spite of all that's happened to me, but sometimes I just lose it."

"We've done all we could for you," she said calmly, realizing that his frustrations were from all the news she'd given him. "Kierzek and I both. Now please give us a break. It's finished. All the angles of this case were picked clean."

"Okay," he said, overwrought, throwing up his hands. "I told you I was sorry."

She frowned, knowing that the issue wasn't over inside him. "Jonathan, what you're doing isn't fair," she said. "You know how sensitive I am about the plea-bargain decision we had to make. But you know it was the correct one under the circumstances."

"I know," he said, nodding despondently, looking away. "Maybe I'm getting what I deserve. We sure aren't able to prove I'm innocent."

"That's right," she said. "And we've both said it over and over many times. The jury would've surely convicted you if you'd have taken it to trial—major-league style."

"All right, I agree," he said, looking at her. "But there's one thing you haven't told me."

"What?" she replied, sighing, knowing it was going to be a tough question. She also knew his attitude hadn't passed.

"Do you think I could actually be guilty?"

"That's not fair either," she answered with thoughtful eyes. "We've become too close for a question like that."

"It's important to me, Lacey," he pressed. "Now please tell me."

"Yes, I believe you could have done it," she answered truthfully. "Because of your mental state at the time. I think you've lost so much in your lifetime that it's possible you couldn't bear up to her leaving you that night. And maybe you snapped." She paused. "Is that what you wanted to hear?"

"Uh-huh, and believe it or not, it helps," he said with a shrug.

"Why?" she asked, puzzled over his nonchalant answer.

"It'll make my jail term a bit more acceptable," he said with a smile.

She shook her head with a laugh. "You're going to make me crazy!" she exclaimed, sitting back in her chair.

"When are you moving to California?" he asked, appearing serious.

"Next month," she answered quietly. "I'd like to be settled in by the holidays."

"Are you going to keep in touch?" he asked, looking away to conceal his growing distress.

"Of course. I'll write you," she said, seeing his hurt, but refusing to surrender to their vulnerability. It would only make things more difficult.

"Good," he said. "I'll like that."

"By the way," she said, trying to alter the air of sadness, "did David tell you exactly when he's coming in?"

"Yeah, next Friday," he answered. "We want to clear everything up before the court sentencing. He'll be heading for my place in Newport Beach on that next Monday."

"He's not staying for the sentencing?"

"Nah," he answered, shaking his head. "He's a busy man, and I told him not to feel obligated."

"Okay," she said. "Anyway, I'll plan on helping in any way I can while he's here."

"Good, thanks," he replied. "Oh, please don't forget, I'll need a laptop."

"Yes," she replied, making a note in her day-planner. "I remember you mentioning it. I'll see to it that you get one after you're settled in Salem."

"Lacey," he said with a determined look, "I'm going to figure out how Laura was murdered. And who's responsible."

She picked up her briefcase. "Well, I'm sure of one thing," she said. "If you run into anything substantial in your favor, I know Kierzek will help you."

"What about you?" he asked. "Will you be interested at all?"

"Yes, sure, of course," she answered as they stood. "You'll have my address." She paused, then said quietly, "Um, I don't know if I'll see you much before the sentencing day. I'm going to California next week for a few days, so I can…"

"I understand," he interrupted. "Let's just let it go for right now, Lacey. We'll keep our friendship alive. I'll be fine."

She lowered her head, nodded and remained silent.

He turned and motioned for the guard.

As the guard opened the door, Jonathan turned to her. "I'll see you soon," he said with a smile, then quickly left the room.

"Bye," she said with a twinge of sadness as she slowly walked out the door.

Leaving the jail parking lot, Lacey knew that she'd have to remain strong while she made it through the next few weeks. And she would follow through with her plans and go home to California, where she could start a new life. *I owe it to myself and the kids,* she thought. And she also knew that Jonathan didn't love her, he loved the dead Laura Bearnes. He was just lonely. And she knew he had simply become attached to her through her constant companionship and protection. But he'd have to bear up to her leaving the state. There was just no way she'd stay here and risk falling in love with him—if she wasn't already. Just like she had told Hansen, *There's no future in it. And that's all there is to it.*

Chapter Twenty-six

Multnomah County Courthouse, Portland:
The arguments

The afternoon rain was cold and persistent, a typical finish to a dreary Oregon day in late October. Small groups of reporters with cameras and miniature camcorders in hand buzzed noisily in the hallway outside the courtroom entrance. They were eagerly waiting to scoop the final chapter of the saga they had dubbed "The Riverpark Murder." Mingling by the bench, the court secretary and stenographer readied their electronic tools while still immersed in their lunch-break chatter. Sitting patiently at his post, the bailiff waited to call the disorderly courtroom to order on cue from the judge, who would soon be emerging from her chamber.

The public seating area was crammed. The spectators had filed in early to view at first hand the reckoning of the California mystery novelist who couldn't magically create a new twist to free himself from this shocking plot of illicit love and malicious betrayal. Many of them held one of his books that they had picked up at a local bookstore. They dreamed of somehow sneaking an autograph from him before he was led away to prison.

Lacey Rosetto, the attorney, sat alone in the middle chair of the defendant's table, with a yellow notepad in front of her. Her briefcase rested at her feet. With her back to the crowd, she knew she was being closely watched, since it was now well known she wasn't a public defender or a court-appointed attorney. Everyone knew she was a member of a private law firm from Beaverton who had the audacity to represent an obvious killer. Many thought how appalling it was that she'd defend an outsider who dared invade their peaceful town and take the life of one of Portland's finest citizens—and the wife of a respected university professor.

But their whispered sniping mattered little to her, because she believed that what she was doing was right—regardless of whether Jonathan was truly guilty. From her first day in law school she knew she'd have to face and ponder that obvious moral question every criminal attorney has to answer sooner or later. *Should she defend a guilty client?* But she had easily answered it early in her career—it would simply depend on the situation. And in this case, just because Jonathan hadn't denied the murder, and was forced to plea-bargain, it didn't prove he was guilty. And despite the nagging moral issues she had to weigh in this case, she felt she had an obligation to stop the prosecution from ramrodding Jonathan through the judicial system with a good chance of charging and punishing him inappropriately. *Yes*, she was right in continuing, she had decided, because Jonathan should get what he deserves. *No more and no less.*

Besides, she could handle these difficult circumstances right now, because it would all be over soon. This would be her last case in Portland before she'd be off to her new position in California with the Jerold & Jerold firm. She was excited that she'd aced the interview so smoothly last week in Sunnyvale. And the stunning letter of recommendation Mr. Hansen had kindly sent along with her had been the Jerolds' decision-maker, icing her employment.

And what was even more gratifying, she'd be off on her new venture with everyone's blessing—including Jonathan's. It was good that they'd openly discussed their feelings for each other after she'd returned from her interview. Although they had revealed that they felt a deep affection for each other, they agreed that they couldn't deal with anything more than that right now. They both had much bigger personal issues to deal with, such as his looming punishment and her major relocation. He was going to prison for a long time to come, and she was picking up and moving out of state. That was enough upheaval to cope with now, they had decided.

However, they had also agreed that they wouldn't just abruptly breach their relationship, either. After he was incarcerated in Salem and she was settled in California, they would keep in faithful contact. And if they nurtured a deeper relationship that evolved over time, so be it. *Yes, so be it,* she thought.

Lacey's thoughts were interrupted when Jack Malcolm ambled up and sat down on her right. She looked over and greeted him quietly, smiling at his red, tired eyes, remnants from last night's bowling-league antics. Yet she was always glad when he joined her at the counsel table for support, or offered her *any* type of assistance, for that matter. She regarded him as a brilliant attorney, regardless of his less than forceful stance. She would miss him the most when she left the firm.

"How do you feel?" asked Malcolm blandly, looking at her. "Are you ready?"

"I think so, although I'm a bit nervous," she answered pensively. "But I'm sure I'll rally after I see Wolcott up there spewing his venom."

"Well put," Malcolm said, chuckling. He slightly nodded his head backward, adding, "And you'll get your chance. Here he comes."

She turned to see a tall man wearing glasses striding up the aisle with mixed emotions showing on his tired face. Matt Wolcott, a top contender in next month's election for state attorney general, sat down at the prosecutor's table and anxiously opened his briefcase. He knew that if he was effective today the Timmers issue would be over quickly and maybe rid him of the stigma of having had to back down to the defense, like the newspapers were reporting. Then perhaps the voters would forget by election day and remember only that he was responsible for the swift justice that was administered. *Yes, perhaps they'll only remember that he was responsible for putting Timmers away,* he thought.

Wolcott leaned back, removed his glasses and rubbed the lenses clean with his white handkerchief while holding them up to the bank of bright fluorescent lights that hung from the ceiling. He grimaced as he put them back on, knowing that people were outraged, thinking they'd been cheated out of ultimate justice when the prosecution dropped the murder charges and allowed Timmers to plead guilty to manslaughter. Nearly all were bitterly disturbed that the sentence was now automatically reduced for a man responsible for the vicious strangulation of his married lover simply because she had jilted him. Timmers has "gotten off lightly," the editorials blatantly stated. But Wolcott knew the people didn't really understand the intricacies of the long court battle this case was targeted for, mired in motions and appeals that might cause long delays and even a chance of mistrial. And they also didn't realize that the veteran criminal attorney, William Hansen, along with the rest of his firm, especially the gifted and tenacious attorney, Lacey Rosetto, were dug in for a long battle and hardly likely to concede.

Anyway, Wolcott knew he'd get his chance for public exoneration when he stood in front of the court and argued for the toughest prison term Judge Buehler could hand out under the circumstances. He'd definitely look good in that light. Buehler would go his way. *She always does*, he thought.

The room suddenly fell silent as the steel door next to the bailiff's table opened and a stone-faced marshal quickly escorted Jonathan inside. After seating him next to Lacey, the marshal reached down and unlocked his handcuffs. Taking the cuffs with him, the marshal sat directly behind them in a wooden chair, keeping a vigilant eye on the defendant's table.

Jonathan, obviously despondent, turned and mouthed "hello" to Lacey and Malcolm, who were looking at him, offering a friendly greeting. In no mood to talk, Jonathan turned back to the front and sat motionless in his orange jumpsuit as he vigorously rubbed the red rings around his wrists. He was oblivious to the chatter the crowd had revved up on his account as he stared at the large mahogany-red bench looming ominously in front of him. The thick-cushioned judge's seat was empty, but it would soon be occupied by the person who would decide his darkened future for a long time to come. He slowly diverted his attention to the U.S. flag. The symbol of freedom seemed to mock him as the torment welled up in his eyes. He turned to the empty jury box, knowing that if he hadn't plea-bargained, the people who would have filled those seats would have found him guilty—surely dealing him much more of a severe punishment than what was forthcoming. *But he was still going to prison.* Overcome, he rubbed his forehead, struggling desperately with the dreaded thought of languishing behind bars for something he knew he definitely couldn't have done. *They're mistaken,* he thought. *They're all very much mistaken.*

Lacey, realizing that Jonathan was agonizing over his fate as she watched him staring at the flag, made a quick note for her argument. She then looked up to him with caring eyes and tenderly put a hand on his wrist. She wanted to comfort him more; to embrace him tightly. But that wouldn't be appropriate in this environment.

As he continued to stare straight ahead, she remembered their discussions about their feelings for each other. And how they'd agreed to dismiss anything other than a friendship. And she couldn't change her mind. *There was no alternative.*

Jonathan finally turned, responding to her caring gesture with a grateful nod.

The bailiff and marshal kept a keen eye on their movements.

Matt Wolcott looked on indifferently from the prosecutor's table.

The clamor in the courtroom faded as the bailiff stood and walked to the center of the room. He stopped in front of the bench and bellowed the court to order. Everyone stood as the door to the judge's chamber opened and the stern-faced older woman, dressed in her flowing black robes, solemnly entered the courtroom. Superior Court Judge Frederica Buehler stepped up the stairs to the bench landing and slid into her chair.

Everyone sat down on the bailiff's cue, but remained attentive as the judge began to slowly scan the room. She halted her gaze on Matt Wolcott, sitting at the prosecutor's table. The middle-aged attorney peered over his reading glasses, tensely fingering his pencil. He gave off a slight look of satisfaction, clearly pleased over today's anticipated proceedings and what would be quick justice in finally closing off this crime. She shifted her glance toward the defendant's table, focusing on Jonathan, who sat frozen in his chair next to Lacey and Malcolm.

Judge Buehler then centered her focus to better address the audience. Her voice was strong and clear. "Today the court will complete the final phase of the state versus Mr. Jonathan Timmers, who has been charged with voluntary manslaughter in the killing of Mrs. Laura Bearnes." She paused and looked down at her notes, then continued explaining the details of the charge as they had been worked out by Lacey, Malcolm and Wolcott—and approved by Jonathan.

She looked up and turned to Jonathan. "Mr. Timmers, would you please rise?"

Jonathan stood up and faced the bench without emotion, knowing this part would be easy.

"Mr. Timmers, have you heard and understood the charge?" Buehler asked.

"Yes," he answered, making solid eye contact with her.

"And how do you plead?"

"Guilty," he answered, without hesitation.

Buehler nodded. "Thank you, Mr. Timmers. Please sit down."

As the courtroom remained quiet, Jonathan sat down, closing his eyes, yet maintaining his composure.

"Mr. Timmers has pleaded guilty to the charge, and the sentence for his crime will be determined and directly handed down. However, before that final sentence is decided, the court will hear leniency arguments requested through motions submitted by both counsels. The court will regard the state's argument first, then finish up with that of the defense. Let's begin. Mr. Wolcott, if you please."

Matt Wolcott took a deep breath and quickly stood to begin his argument for the harshest sentence that Buehler could impose under the law. "Thank you, Your Honor." With narrowing eyes, he walked to the center of the courtroom and pointed at Jonathan, who sat wide-eyed at the defendant's table. "This man, this killer who sits before you..." Wolcott began fiercely in a vigorous tone.

Wolcott's aggressive rhetoric soon faded for one man who sat reticent in the back corner of the spectator area. Lieutenant Brian Kierzek stared at the prisoner sitting stiffly at the defendant's table next to his composed attorney, who was busily taking notes and conferring with her partner.

Kierzek felt mostly responsible for what was happening in the courtroom today. He'd been at the heart of the investigation. But he still couldn't help wondering about Timmers' guilt. Yet, regardless of his gnawing uncertainty about the outcome of the case, the result was a situation he had to accept. He had no choice. The evidence at the crime scene had not proved anything different, and the witnesses to Jonathan's actions that night proved totally damning. With that, Matt Wolcott had successfully convinced the grand jury that the gruesome crime had Jonathan's "signature" written all over it. And Kierzek was sure he would have successfully painted the same picture for a trial jury. *With Wolcott's handling, the guilty scenario for Timmers would have been cast solid.*

Kierzek glanced around at the front spectator row, spotting a man and a woman sitting quietly, apparently at ease. *Vindication day had arrived for Monte Bearnes and the victim's friend, Rebecca Newell,* he thought. Leaning his head back against the wall, Kierzek shifted his attention back to Wolcott, who was now loudly voicing his hardened argument toward the attentive spectators with animated hand gestures.

Rebecca Newell was looking at Jonathan, content with how things had turned out for him, although she *was* disappointed that he wouldn't be receiving the ultimate penalty. How appropriate it would have been if he had ended up with the same fate as Laura—death. Regardless, she was pleased to see him finally being punished. And the severity of his sentence didn't really matter to her any longer, because she knew that any term of imprisonment, plus losing Laura forever, would be enough pain for him to have to endure for a lifetime.

She glanced back over her shoulder, seeing that Kierzek was lost in thought, still sitting where she'd seen him when she walked in. Returning her gaze to the front, she felt a bit remorseful over having exaggerated her witness statement by telling him that Laura's phone message on the night she was murdered had indicated she was afraid of Jonathan. But for all she really knew, Laura might have indeed been worried about Jonathan's potential backlash to her leaving him, but just didn't say that in her message. *So did I really lie to Kierzek? Or maybe only stretched the truth a bit.*

No, she had lied outright only when she and Monte had agreed to tell Kierzek that Monte hadn't known about Laura's affair before the murder. But if Kierzek had known the truth, it would only have complicated things more. Kierzek then would have questioned them both until he and everyone else knew about the affair that she and Monte were having themselves. And that shameful revelation would have been unnecessary, since it had no direct bearing on the crime. *So what real harm was there in that lie?* she asked herself.

She thought about the chat she'd had with Laura on her porch just before Laura rushed off to meet with Jonathan at the hotel. And how she'd fabricated some of their conversation while telling it to Kierzek, so he'd think that Laura was apprehensive about going to see Jonathan because his occasional dark side might erupt. *Okay, maybe that was another truth-stretcher,* she thought. *But was it really wrong for me to have driven another nail in Jonathan's coffin?*

Rebecca sat back, recalling that eventful afternoon on her porch before Laura hurried off. How Laura had told her she'd come back and meet for dinner. But Rebecca had known better. She knew Laura wasn't going to make it back early, if at all. Laura was still deeply in love with Jonathan, and only a mere shell of what she had been before the affair began. She knew Laura would face a torturous evening with Jonathan before she'd find the courage to tell him. *If she was even able to...*

Rebecca's thoughts were suddenly shattered when she heard Judge Buehler's distinct words: "Thank you, Mr. Wolcott." There was a brittle pause in the courtroom before Buehler added. "Ms. Rosetto, please proceed."

Rebecca watched Matt Wolcott take his seat at the prosecutor's table and Lacey Rosetto slowly stand up. Passing the bailiff's table, Lacey hesitated and said something to him, then approached Judge Buehler at the bench. Concerned, Wolcott watched Lacey murmur something to Buehler, but he relaxed when the judge simply nodded toward the bailiff. The bailiff rose from his post and walked over to help Lacey move the portable flagpole from behind the bench and into the presentation area, just in front of the counsel tables. As a curious buzz rose from the spectator area, Lacey positioned herself next to the pole while the bailiff returned to his table.

When the silence returned, Lacey began her argument in a deliberate tone. "Your Honor...ladies and gentlemen..." She pointed at the flag fluttering faintly in the damp breeze that seeped through the slightly opened window. "We all know this symbol represents the United States of America, the land of fairness and liberty..." She paused and walked over to stand in front of the prosecutor's table. She aimed her stare at Matt Wolcott, saying, "While the guilty should never go unpunished in this land of freedom, today in this room we may have before us a highly probable miscarriage of justice..."

Rebecca was as impressed with Lacey's opening as everyone else was in the room, but gradually tuned her out. Her own thoughts about the night Laura was murdered were much too strong. She recalled how she'd phoned Monte at home soon after Laura had bounded off her porch to meet Jonathan at the hotel. And how she and Monte agreed that Laura probably wouldn't be back until the next day. She remembered explaining to him how upset Laura seemed, and asking to please let her talk to Laura first if she did happen to return. She had pleaded with Monte to at least let her tell Laura about their own affair. *At least that much...*

But Monte had steadfastly refused, continually insisting on handling everything himself when Laura would arrive back home in Eugene the next day. And he had nearly demanded that Rebecca not become involved with her best friend's distress that night, because interfering might only confuse her. And he had finally persuaded her by easing up his stance, reminding her that they both loved Laura very much. He promised he'd be gentle and understanding with Laura when he revealed that he'd known about her affair all along and that he knew she'd been in Portland to break it off. And then some time after that, he'd allow Rebecca to tell Laura about their own affair—but only at the proper time. So then they could all start anew, healing their lives. *That finally convinced her to let it go,* she recalled. *Monte could have his way.*

Rebecca closed her eyes, lamenting on how differently things might have turned out if she hadn't yielded to Monte's afternoon pressure and if she had answered Laura's appealing call from the hotel. How frustrating it had been when Rebecca wasn't able to reach Monte at home afterward to see if he would change his mind. And how much more frustrating it was knowing that if he was at the university working all night, he would have the phone turned off so as not to be disturbed, as usual. *If only I could have reached him,* she thought. *Surely I could have convinced him to let me go to Laura's side to console her. And Laura might still be alive.*

Rebecca felt sad as she eyed Monte peripherally, thinking of how they had both lost Laura without any final communication with her. But she felt sorrier for him. Not only was he now without Laura, but he'd have to live with the agonizing memory of knowing she'd been unfaithful till the end without any reconciliation with him. He had never had a chance to tell her that he understood why she did what she did, but that he had forgiven her. And worse, he was now blaming himself for not granting Rebecca the freedom to console Laura if she felt the need while Laura was in Portland. *But what's done is done*, she thought with a sigh.

She suddenly brightened, unable to stop herself from feeling pleased at how things had turned out. At least now she could be with Monte openly and freely. There would be nothing wrong with her being next to her best friend's husband, whom she dearly loved, helping him through his grief. They could let things go on as they were for a while before they'd announce their marriage plans. Then they could slowly emerge as a family—she, Monte and Tamra. Maybe they could go east if he took that position at the university in New York he'd told her about last month. *Sure, no one would even know us there*. But it really mattered little whether they moved or not. Who could really blame them for whatever they did now, or, wherever they settled? After all, Monte was the one who had been victimized in all of this. Yes, they'd all make it together somehow. *Maybe I could even have Monte's baby soon...maybe...*

She reached over and discreetly patted Monte's thigh. He glanced at her and smiled, then quickly refocused on the front of the courtroom. Sitting transfixed, Monte stared at Lacey Rosetto with longing eyes while she mesmerized everyone in the courtroom with a smooth and commanding delivery that centered around leniency for Jonathan.

CHAPTER TWENTY-SEVEN

The Sentence

Lacey looked up at the judge and then scanned the courtroom before settling her eyes on Matt Wolcott. "So what we're asking, Your Honor...members of the prosecution, is to understand that there may be a dreadful miscarriage of justice if this man..." She paused and pointed to Jonathan. "If this man spends one more day than the least allowed for his obligatory mercy plea of manslaughter. Because nothing has ever been proven beyond a shadow of a doubt that this man is truly guilty. And that shadowing lack of proof is especially haunting in his own mind." She slowly directed her point to the flag positioned next to her. "And this icon of freedom still represents the United States of America." She turned back to Judge Buehler. "Thank you, Your Honor."

The room was enveloped in respectful silence as Buehler gradually shifted forward in her chair while Lacey solemnly took her seat.

The judge looked up to face the courtroom. "Thank you, Ms. Rosetto. Court will recess for an afternoon break and reconvene at three forty-five, at which time the court will recognize any of the victim's loved ones who wish to be addressed before the sentence is handed down." She stood and descended the steps, deep in thought. As she reached her chamber door she hesitated and turned, looking back at Jonathan before ducking inside.

Jack Malcolm and Laccy, who had closely watched Buehler's gradual exit, turned to each other in surprise while Jonathan looked on.

Malcolm shook his head, saying excitedly to Lacey, "You've really got her thinking! You were fantastic! That flagpole maneuver was outstanding."

"Thanks," Lacey said, turning to Jonathan with a beaming smile. "You may not know it, Jonathan, but you're responsible for the flagpole tactic. I saw you looking at it, and it gave me the idea."

"Really," Jonathan said, breaking his first smile of the day. "Great!"

Malcolm put his hand on Lacey's arm, regaining her attention. "Yup, you've really got 'Old Iron Jaw' thinking!" he said, looking around the subdued courtroom as people began to mingle, talking in a light buzz. "You've got 'em all thinking."

"You might be right, Jack," Lacey said with widening eyes as she followed his gaze. "You just might be right."

"Look at Wolcott," he whispered with a grin.

She looked over at the district attorney who was sitting back, rubbing his aching forehead, knowing that nothing was cast in concrete any longer. He knew well that an upstart criminal attorney from Beaverton had solidly showed him up today. *She now has them rooting for the underdog,* he thought.

Lacey chuckled over Wolcott's obvious feelings of frustration while she turned to Jonathan. "How are you doing?"

"Pretty good," he said. "I guess from your actions you think that I have a pretty good chance for a lighter sentence."

"It's very possible," she said, patting his arm. "We'll have to wait and see."

They all looked up as the marshal walked over to Jonathan, asking, "Do you need a break?"

Jonathan stood. "Yeah, thanks. I could probably use one." He instinctively put his arms around to the front for the handcuffs.

"C'mon," the marshal said, taking him by the arm and leading him to the prisoner's entrance. "We'll skip the cuffs this time."

Malcolm stood. "Lacey, I'm gonna check my messages. I'll be right back."

"Okay," she said. "I think I'll just sit here and relax." She sat back and watched the bailiff hauling the flagpole back to behind the bench. She felt the most comfortable she had ever felt in a courtroom—she knew she'd done the best she could for Jonathan. *I've been all over it from the beginning,* she thought.

"Ms. Rosetto?"

Hearing her name, Lacey turned to face a leisurely but well-dressed, handsome man standing against the spectator railing, looking at her in a self-assured manner. She immediately recognized him as Monte Bearnes, and instinctively looked around for Rebecca Newell. She spotted her chatting lightly with Brian Kierzek by the courtroom entrance.

Lacey looked back at Bearnes, momentarily stunned because of his penetrating emerald green stare. She felt he was undressing her on the spot. Swallowing, she answered, "Yes?"

"I'm Monte Bearnes," he answered quietly. "The victim's husb...."

"I know who you are, Mr. Bearnes," she interrupted, still surprised that he'd approached her for any reason. "I'm sorry about your situation."

"It's all right," he replied, looking down, then back up. "My misfortune has pretty much sunk in."

An awkward silence hung in the air; she was still at a loss for words. His direct gaze was unnerving her. *God, what magnetism this guy has*, she thought.

"I know this may sound unusual," he said smoothly, holding out his hand. "But I want to congratulate you on your speech today. It was really very good—riveting."

"Thank you," she said, standing to politely take his hand. A chill went up her spine as her female instincts immediately kicked in at his skillful touch. *He is interested in more than just congratulating me*, she thought, slipping her hand from his grasp. She added, "I must admit, your gracious compliment is a bit unusual under the circumstances."

"Perhaps," he said with a shrug. "But I'm a psychologist, and it's my job to understand people's behavior. I simply understand and can justify why Mr. Timmers did what he did. And I agree with what you so aptly pointed out to all of us today—there's no way he's a cold-blooded murderer."

She stood still, not sure how to react to this strange reasoning, considering that it was his wife who was the victim.

He continued, "Ms. Rosetto, I can see you're surprised at my attitude. But I know you're only doing your job. And I've made it quite clear publicly that I feel none of this would've happened if I had been more attentive to my wife."

"I see," she responded, staying cool to his display of self-guilt.

"I also thought you might want to know," he said, "I've formally notified the prosecution that there won't be any statement on behalf of the victim today. I'm going to let the chips fall where they may. And Laura's mother decided not to come in from Washington for the sentencing. So I guess you'll have clear sailing in that respect."

"Okay," she said, noticing that Jonathan was being escorted back inside. This was her chance to escape this uncomfortable situation. "Well, I really need to get back to my client. It was nice meeting you, Mr. Bearnes. And I do appreciate your courtesy."

"Make that Monte, please," he said, breaking into a captivating smile. "By the way, do you have a business card? I may need some legal help sometime."

"Um, no, I'm not practicing in the state any longer," she said quickly while Malcolm walked past them, giving them a curious look as he and sat down at the defendant's table. "I'm leaving for a position in California. But thank you anyway."

His smile evaporated. "Oh," he said disappointingly. "Well, ah, good luck…"

"Thanks again for your kind words," she replied pleasantly, turning and joining Jonathan and Malcolm at the table.

Malcolm leaned over and whispered in her ear, "That appeared to be an interesting exchange. What did Bearnes want?"

She whispered back, "Me."

"Huh?"

She looked at him and frowned.

"Are you serious?" asked Malcolm. "Do you mean he wants you to represent him for some reason?"

"Yeah," she answered, rolling her eyes upward. "That, too."

"You mean he came on to you sexually?" Malcolm asked, looking dumbfounded as he finally caught on to her implications. "Outright?"

"Oh, no," she answered, "not directly. But a woman can usually tell when a man's interested in that way. You know, we have our womanly instincts." She smiled.

He turned and faced the front. "Really…always?"

"Uh-huh," she answered playfully. "You men always tell us with your eyes and your mollifying manner."

He remained silent, appearing nervous.

"Don't worry!" she said, chuckling. "Whenever *you* do it I know it's only your bachelor genes taking over. I never give it a second thought."

He turned toward her. "Lacey, stop this," he whispered.

"Jack, it's all really okay," she said, laughing quietly. "You're never offensive. And who knows? You might just look at me with those thoughts at the right time." She winked.

"Christ!" he exclaimed in an embarrassed whisper as he faced the front. "Will you please stop this?"

She laughed again, but then turned serious. "Hey," she said, placing a hand on his arm to get his attention.

He turned, knowing her mood had quickly changed.

"It's not the same with Bearnes," she said. "He's scary."

He saw an uneasy look in her eyes. "Okay, if anything at all comes up, I'll remember that he approached you," he said. "And that you never reciprocated."

"No!" she confirmed adamantly, shaking her head as the people began to file in to the courtroom to witness the finish of Jonathan's saga. "Never…"

The incessant rain continued to pound against the windows as Jonathan sat rigidly at the defendant's table, hushed and wide-eyed in anticipation of his fate while he faced the judge, who was carefully organizing her notes.

Lacey Rosetto sat next to him, knowing she was now helplessly within the boundaries of the court's mercy. She had presented her facts in Jonathan's favor as well as she could. It was now out of her hands.

Jack Malcolm stared straight ahead.

Prosecutor Matt Wolcott sat anxiously, realizing that his long, virulent argument fighting for the full term of Jonathan's possible imprisonment had been overshadowed by Lacey's appeal for leniency because of so many uncertainties that surrounded the case. But he remained confident that he would look good in the eyes of the voters—regardless of the outcome of today's proceedings.

The spectators sat quietly, divided over what punishment Jonathan should receive because of what they'd heard today from his daring attorney.

Detective Kierzek looked on attentively from his seat in the back, fidgeting with his car keys. Although this was the final chapter for him as a member of the Portland police force, he felt that for some reason this wasn't the final chapter in the river-park murder.

Monte Bearnes and Rebecca Newell sat tranquilly, showing no emotion.

Judge Buehler looked squarely at Jonathan. "Mr. Timmers, both counsels have given their arguments, and the relatives of the victim have elected not to give comment. Do you now wish to be heard before your sentence is handed down?"

"Yes, Your Honor," he answered calmly.

"Please stand and proceed, Mr. Timmers," Buehler replied, sitting back.

He stood and faced her. "Your Honor," he began, "I pleaded guilty to manslaughter even though I know in my heart I couldn't have brutally murdered her. I loved her. But I also know I can't account for my actions that night." He paused, mustering all his courage, and turned to face the muted crowd, directing his stare at Monte Bearnes and Rebecca Newell. "I'm sorry. I know what her loss means to you." He looked past them and into the faces of the spectators. "And I know what she meant to many of you. But I've also lost her. And I want everyone to know I will suffer greatly for the rest of my life, whether it be locked away in Salem or on a sunny beach in California. So please try to find peace in your hearts for my self-imposed suffering, as well as what the court will administer." He turned and faced the judge with sorrow in his eyes. "Thank you."

"Very well, Mr. Timmers," Buehler said, sitting forward. She paused to let the tenseness in the air settle, and for Jonathan to compose himself as he sat down.

Jonathan looked up, signaling that he was ready for what was coming next.

"Would you please stand and face the court," Buehler instructed.

Jonathan took a deep breath, stood, and leaned with his hands on the table to support himself. He began to feel nauseated and weak in the knees.

Lacey sensed his physical duress and put her hand on his. "Hang on," she whispered to him. "Just hang on."

The judge looked at him, preparing to hurl her judicial harangue. "Mr. Timmers, your actions are such that you've pleaded guilty to snuffing out the life of a good and defenseless woman. It was a shocking violation against our peaceful community, as well as the people who loved her. But we have also learned from your able counsel and your display of apparent sorrow that this horrible act was committed at a time when you weren't in your right faculties—and while you were in the heat of passion." She paused to gather her thoughts before continuing. "However, regardless of the reasons, this crime will not be tolerated or go unpunished. Now, the state has asked that you be punished to the fullest extent. Yet, considering the circumstances of your motive and your outward remorse, and furthermore taking your law-abiding background into consideration, the court has decided that a term of not less than ten years and not more than twelve years in prison is sufficient punishment. In summation, Mr. Timmers, you will be incarcerated forthright in the Oregon State Penitentiary in Salem to serve out your term, hopefully repenting over your unfortunate but dastardly actions that night in the riverpark. Sentence is final, and court is adjourned." She struck the gavel against its wooden plate and quickly rose, marching down the stairs to enter her chambers.

The courtroom was enveloped in noise as the bustling crowd stood and began to leave.

Jonathan slowly sat down, still dizzy with confusion because everything had happened so quickly. His fate had not fully registered.

Lacey looked at Malcolm, saying elatedly, "Jack, confirm for me that Buehler didn't say *without parole.*"

He smiled. "Nope, I listened for it. Congratulations!"

Lacey turned to Jonathan, embracing him as the marshal and bailiff softened their vigilance to allow them their brief exchange of comfort.

"You could be out in six or seven years with good behavior," she whispered eagerly as they gradually separated.

"Thank you!" Jonathan said, as he now fully realized that she had gained him leniency. "God, what else can I say?" he said, breathless with shock. He reached over to shake Malcolm's hand. "What can I say?" he repeated.

"Don't worry about saying anything," Malcolm said. "Just try to relax and enjoy the moment as best you can."

"I'll be in touch with you before I leave," Lacey said to Jonathan as the marshal lightly tapped him on the shoulder.

"Thank you," he replied, feeling relieved as he stood up.

She watched the marshal click the handcuffs shut before leading him through the prisoner's entrance and off to jail.

Matt Wolcott, apparently incensed, sitting at the prosecutor's table, angrily stuffed his paperwork into his briefcase.

Jack Malcolm held out his hand to Lacey. "You should be very proud," he said. "You won him the best possible sentence. The best! No one could have done any better."

"I really appreciate the compliment coming from you, Jack," she said, her eyes moist from emotion. "I feel…" She hesitated, catching Matt Wolcott walking toward their table.

"I want to congratulate you, Ms. Rosetto," Wolcott said, forcing the words in a professional tone. He turned to Malcolm. "You too, Jack."

"Thank you, Mr. Wolcott," Lacey responded in a respectful manner.

"Yes, thanks, Matt," echoed Malcolm.

While they watched him walk away, he turned and shook his head. "Ms. Rosetto, I understand you're relocating to California next month."

"That's correct," she confirmed.

"If I make attorney general next month," he said, "would you consider applying for a position on my staff?"

She smiled graciously. "I'd be honored to, Mr. Wolcott. But I don't think I'll want to leave California again."

He nodded. "I understand," he replied, then turned to leave the courtroom, adding, "Just please keep it in mind."

Lacey looked past Wolcott, seeing Monte Bearnes and Rebecca Newell outside the courtroom entrance being swarmed by the media.

"Well, I gotta get back to the office," Malcolm said. "I need to finish up some stuff."

"And I guess I should get ready to face the press," she said, looking up at him. "I'm a bit nervous."

"Don't worry, you're gonna have help," Malcolm said.

"What do you mean?" Lacey replied, glancing back toward the aisle and seeing William Hansen approaching them.

"Mr. Hansen!" she exclaimed. "I thought you were out of town."

"Oh," he said pleasantly. "Let's just say I had a change of plans."

"I have to get going," Malcolm interrupted. "I'll see you both at the office tomorrow."

Hansen and Lacey bid him goodbye as he made his way through the front entrance and past the dwindling crowd.

Hansen turned toward Lacey with a fatherly smile. "That was a dandy presentation you put on today."

"You saw it, sir?" asked Lacey.

"Most of it. From the hallway," he replied. "I'm really proud of you."

"It's your professional guidance coming through," she said. "And I remembered you said to always maintain my patience."

He nodded. "You're gonna do fine."

"Thank you, sir," she said as she stooped to pick up her briefcase, now realizing that he had never intended to be out of town. She knew now that he had just wanted to see how she'd do without him.

"By the way, I hope you don't mind," Hansen said. "I scheduled a news conference for you at five in the court's press-briefing center."

"No, not at all," she answered, glancing at her watch. "That'll give me some time to freshen up. Will you be there?"

"If you want me to be," he replied.

"Yes, please," she said as they began walking toward the door. "I might need your help."

As they approached the courtroom entrance she saw Kierzek still sitting alone in the spectator seating area, looking at her. She looked up at Hansen. "Mr. Hansen, can I meet you in the press room?"

He looked over, seeing Kierzek. "Of course," he said while gesturing "hello" to Kierzek. On his way out the door he added, "I'll see you at five, Lacey."

Lacey slid into the row and sat down next to Kierzek. "Hi, Brian."

"You did a helluva job today, Lacey," he said. "I never believed Timmers would even get away with a manslaughter plea, much less a lenient sentence."

"Thank you," she said as she put her briefcase down.

He continued, "The way you sneaked in that questionable evidence about the crime scene was incredible. Wolcott was cringing when Buehler let you continue with that train of thought."

She broke into a wide grin. "But you're the one who taught me about all that crime-scene stuff," she said exuberantly, then slowly grew serious. "But forget me. I want to know how you're feeling."

"Ah, I'm doing okay," he answered. "I'm glad to be away from the homicide pressures. And my bypass surgery is scheduled next month."

A concerned look came over her face. "I probably won't be here to visit you," she said sympathetically. "I'm leaving for San Jose next week." She looked up, her face brightening. "But I'll write you, and of course be thinking of you."

"Thanks," he said appreciatively, but decided to change the glum subject. "I saw you talking to Monte Bearnes. Was he upset?"

She looked up. "No, he wasn't, Brian. He was very cordial. But the man leaves me ice cold."

"Really?" said Kierzek. "Why?"

"Oh, I dunno," she answered, deciding to pass on explaining to him about Bearnes' indirect sexual allusions. "There's just something about him that doesn't sit right with me."

"Interesting," he remarked, furrowing his brow, wanting to know more.

"Yeah, I know, interesting," she said. "I sure wish we could've firmed up his alibi more. I'd have felt a lot better."

"Lacey," Kierzek said, looking for her complete attention, "you still don't believe Timmers killed the Bearnes woman, do you?"

She sighed. "Oh, Brian, I don't know." She paused for the right words. "There's now some strong personal feelings between Jonathan and me. So anything I think now has to take those feelings into account."

"I see," he replied understandingly.

She gave him a questioning look. "How about you? Can I ask you your latest opinion of Jonathan's guilt or innocence?"

He gave her his usual shrug. "No change from the last time you asked me," he answered. "I just don't know. And that's all I thought about today." He shook his head. "I just don't know."

She shot him another questioning look. "Before I forget," she said. "Jonathan's going to write the story while he's in prison to try to get at the truth. Can I tell him you'll help him if he comes up with anything significant?"

"Sure, why not," Kierzek answered without hesitation, pulling a card from his blazer pocket. "He can reach me through the precinct. I'll be keeping in contact with Ed Cuyler there. He's been transferred to the homicide department."

"Wonderful, thanks. I'll pass it along to Jonathan," she said, feeling pleased as she accepted the card. She glanced at her watch. "I have to get going. Are you coming?"

"No, I'm going to sit for a few minutes," he answered. "You go ahead."

She reached over and embraced him. "I'll be in touch."

"Good," he said as they separated. "I'll want to know how you're doing in your new position in California."

She scooted out to the aisle. "Okay, I'll talk to you soon. Bye, Brian," she said, hurrying out the door.

He sat motionless as he watched her leave, knowing she'd never give up on Jonathan's freedom no matter where she was located.

"Hey, Brian," Kierzek heard. "You gonna sleep here tonight, or what?"

He turned, seeing the bailiff standing by the main light switch at the front of the courtroom. "Oh, hi, Duane," Kierzek said with a chuckle. "No, I'm leaving."

"Okay," the bailiff answered as he shut off the main lights and headed for the prisoners' entrance. "Have a great retirement," he said as the door shut behind him.

"Thanks," Kierzek murmured as he loosened his tie and stood up. Putting on his hat, he made his way for the entrance. Reaching the doors, he hesitated and looked back toward the bench and the American flag, hanging limply in the shadows. *The icon of freedom, as Lacey put it*, he thought. *But there'll be no freedom for Timmers for a long time to come.* That is, unless they could figure out who had killed the Bearnes woman, *if Timmers really isn't the one.* He turned and walked out of the darkened courtroom, the door swinging closed behind him, as he repeated that thought—*If he really isn't the one.*

CHAPTER TWENTY-EIGHT

Christmas Day, Oregon State Penitentiary, Salem

Jonathan sat on his bunk, staring at the Christmas card Lacey had sent him last week, along with his present—a new electronic day-planner and note log. He realized that she'd sent the powerful palm-sized unit with the hope that he'd always carry it with him if he needed to capture anything important that might suddenly pop up concerning the crime. If nothing else, it would come in handy to help him facilitate his effort in writing his book.

He set the items down and reached into the envelope to take out the picture of her and the twins posing in front of the Christmas tree the night they had decorated it. Shifting back against the concrete-block wall, he read the note she'd added, saying that some Christmas soon he'd be able to visit them in San Jose and they would all enjoy the holiday together. He looked up in thought, wondering what it would be like to celebrate Christmas with them, or for that matter, a family of his own. Unfortunately, he'd never experienced anything like that, as his wife had died before they'd had a chance to have children.

Feeling dispirited and alone while trying to forget the holidays, he put the card and picture back in the envelope and placed it under his bunk, as he had done all week. But he couldn't help wondering how many more Christmases he'd have to spend in this walled desolation before he could make that visit to see Lacey and her kids. After all, this was only the first one. And how long would it be before he might experience some of that sunny California weather again? *He missed that dearly*, he thought with a grimace.

Even though he was granted a liberal exercise schedule, it seemed like every time he went outside to the prison yard it was either raining or snowing, *or damn well threatening to.*

He lay back, staring at the empty bunk above him. Maybe he'd be fortunate like his ex-cellmate, Bernie, who had just been released on parole early because of the holidays. *But then Bernie had been put in here for embezzling, not manslaughter,* he thought. *And he had spent his time earning his freedom.*

Anyway, it was no use expending his energy lamenting over a possible parole. *That dream was a long way off.* So Jonathan hoped his new cellmate would be as companionable as Bernie was. They had become good friends in such a short time. And if Jonathan was even more fortunate, his new cellmate would be just as intelligent and as good a listener as Bernie had turned out to be. It had been so uplifting when Bernie would sit patiently for hours, letting Jonathan talk about his affair with Laura and the situation surrounding her ghastly murder. Bernie had taken such an interest, always trying to delve into Jonathan's mind at different intervals of the story to possibly break something free that might be locked inside. But their probing was to no avail. They, like everyone else since the day he was arrested for the crime, just couldn't ever get past the obvious. *Anyway, I'll miss Bernie,* he thought as he swung his feet around to the floor.

Sitting up, he managed to dismiss his distress by focusing his thoughts on the only faith and hope he had at his disposal—his sanity. Bending forward to the foot of his bunk, he picked up the planner Lacey had sent him and selected the calendar function, inserting the twenty-fifth. As the hour-grid appeared on the small green screen, he chuckled to himself as he began to enter the false events, as he did every day since he'd received the gift: 10 a.m.—soak up sun on a Willamette River beach *(Sun, yeah, right!)*...12 noon—shrimp-salad lunch at the Blue Crab café; 2:30 p.m.—exercise at Rocky's gym. He'd then pause before he'd put in the same entry for every night at seven: meet Laura for dinner at a beachside restaurant—afterward, make passionate love. Even though his eyes would burn with longing when he'd finished his little game, he would continue. *He had to if he was to maintain his sanity*, he decided.

Turning serious, he selected the "note log" function and set the planner next to him, at the ready. Reaching down, he picked up the thick manila folder sitting on top of his laptop computer, labeled:

"Guilty as Assumed, The Riverpark Murder"
Property of Jonathan Timmers—cell 231

He was pleased that Judge Buehler had allowed him the freedom to write the book, even though he'd been under a court order to turn over all potential profits to the state of Oregon to pay back his legal and prosecution costs. *That is, if there were would be any profits from a book without a decent ending*, he thought soberly.

Opening the folder, he pulled the papers out and began to lay out the sections he'd carefully dissected from Kierzek's arrest report and Lacey's detailed court documents: characters; clues; events and timing. He was now ready to put the book's outline together, preparing to create another milestone.

With the sections spread out on his small wooden table, he picked up his laptop. And as always, his excitement grew as he switched it on, knowing it was only a matter of time before he would find the answers to the horrific puzzle. Only a matter of time before he would discover something incriminating that the killer had left behind—even if that evidence implicated himself. And it would only be a matter of time before he could contact the one man he knew would help him—Brian Kierzek. *And even if I should strike out in my endeavor, I'd still end up with one hell of a book,* he thought, smiling, as he began to key, labeling the new virtual page "OUTLINE."

Lacey Rosetto sat on the living-room floor, bathed in the chilly northern California sunshine streaming through her large picture window. She lifted her ear, listening for her parents' car to start and leave her driveway. Still dressed in only her pajamas and robe, she was buried in Christmas-present wrappings that the twins had managed to strew from one end of the room to the other. She was exhausted, but contented that she'd been able to handle the stressful relocation from Oregon over the last six weeks and still manage to pull off a decent Christmas celebration with the children. And it felt good when her parents came over to join them for a late breakfast and happily suggested that they take the kids with them back to their house for an overnighter. She smiled as she thought, how fitting an end to the fine Christmas vacation by having the kids spoiled by their grandparents while she had a couple of days at home alone to rest up.

She stood up and lazily made her way to the kitchen to make herself a cup of tea, thinking how glad she'd be when the holidays were over and she'd officially start her new position with the Jerold & Jerold firm in January. While filling the teakettle with fresh cool water, she thought about how beginning anew would be challenging, but nothing would be as traumatic and demanding as the last year she'd spent in Oregon. *And if I made it through that unscathed,* she thought, *I'll sail through this.*

She set the kettle on the burner and turned the control knob to "high." As she watched the bluish gas flame erupt from the grate, she wondered how Jonathan was doing today. She knew he must be lonely, spending his first Christmas locked away in prison. But as always when she felt sorry for him, she told herself there was nothing she could do about his situation. *It wasn't her fault.* And like she'd promised, she was keeping in touch with him. And like they'd agreed, if anything deeper came of the relationship after he was free, so be it. *But right now she and the kids had a new life to begin.*

She lifted the kettle and poured the boiling water into the teacup, immersing the teabag. Watching the spicy brown tea bleed from the bag, she picked up the cup and strolled into the living room.

She set the cup of steeping hot tea on the coffee table, loosened her robe and lay down on the couch. As the sun paled through the high December clouds, she pulled the down-filled comforter up and over her. Yawning, she reached for the television remote and pushed on the "power" button. After sifting through the channels, she found the obligatory afternoon Christmas movie and set the remote on the floor. Snuggled warmly under the comforter, she emitted a faint peaceful smile and laid her head down on the pillow, quickly falling into a blissful sleep.

Rebecca Newell sat numbed in her living room, staring grimly at the inner hearth of the fireplace, which lay cold and laden with week-old ashes. With the afternoon Oregon storm pelting against the window, she was draped across the pushed-back recliner, balancing a goblet of Chablis on the armrest. She was dressed in baggy gray sweats, the same thing she had had on for the last three days. Her eyes were anguished and bloodshot from weeping and lack of sleep. She'd never before felt this lonely on Christmas day. She'd always had family and friends with her—even after her husband had died. She'd always managed to have a wonderful Christmas.

But this one was not only lonely, but also especially devastating because she had planned on openly sharing the cheerful holidays with Monte and Tamra. But it hadn't turned out that way, filling her with confusion, hurt and anger. Monte wasn't even calling her any more. And it seemed as though Tamra had never known she'd even existed.

It was odd how Monte had seemed to have almost disappeared after the sentencing of Jonathan. They had been together only a couple of times. Rebecca had known something was different when they were all having Thanksgiving dinner at Monte's home and he seemed aloof and Tamra lost somewhere in a mental void. And Monte had alluded to wanting to be alone with Tamra during most of the holidays while she gradually got used to being without her mother. He had told Rebecca that night after Tamra went to bed that he felt guilty around his daughter, having someone so close to him this quickly. *"Even if she is a close friend of the family,"* she remembered him saying.

So Rebecca had no problem with leaving them alone for a couple of weeks after that, thinking he'd call her when he got lonely and after he'd prepared Tamra to expect her to be at their home regularly. But he hadn't called. And she would continually make excuses to herself for his insensitive absence. *But leaving me alone on Christmas day?* she thought, taking a long drink of her wine. *That's inexcusable.*

How shocking it had been to come home from work on Christmas Eve and find the mundane greeting card in her mailbox. He had barely noted under the greeting that he and Tamra had left for Mount Hood to go skiing and he'd see her on New Year's day at the Northwest Bistro, their favorite restaurant in Portland. *And there was no mention of New Year's Eve,* the special night when lovers are supposed to begin their new year together.

She was still reeling from this unexpected blow. *Why wasn't I invited to go on the trip?* she wondered. Not even an apology from him for his abrupt departure in that dispassionate message. *This was unthinkable, and she didn't understand any of it.* It wasn't as though she was a strange new woman suddenly appearing in their lives. And she had been poised to be Monte's and Tamra's main comfort, helping them struggle through their unexpected loneliness during the holidays. *But, instead, she had been totally left out of their lives!*

She took a deep breath and sat forward with a start, realizing that for some reason Monte was pulling away from her rather than drawing her closer. Shaking with a jolting fear of ultimate rejection, she took a long swallow of her wine, realizing that she would have to wait a whole week until she could confront him. *She would have to endure another week-long nightmare.*

She grimaced, but realized that she was all cried out and if she were to continue functioning at all she had to put this heartache aside and try to get some sleep. But first she needed something to calm her down. Slowly rising from the recliner, she started for the kitchen, carrying her wine glass. But she stopped at the partly decorated Christmas tree she'd never managed to finish after she'd found Monte's card. She looked down, seeing the presents intended for Monte and Tamra, sitting unopened.

Turning, she went into the kitchen, realizing she'd been wrong. She *did* have a few more tears inside her; they rolled down her cheeks. Opening the refrigerator, she pulled out the chilled carafe of Chablis and filled the glass. She leaned against the counter and took a large swallow, then refilled the glass. Replacing the nearly empty carafe back into the refrigerator, she reached for the small brown plastic container of Dalmane sleeping capsules sitting on the counter. She took out two and popped them into her mouth, quickly washing them down with repeated swallows of her wine.

It took only a few minutes for the pills and wine to go to work. Becoming drowsy, she decided she'd better quickly get to her bed. Clutching her glass of wine, she sluggishly made her way to the bedroom. She clumsily brushed past the tree and knocked a couple of ornaments to the floor. She dismissed her awkwardness with a passing glance and wobbled upstairs, entered the bedroom, and plunked her wine down on the bedside table. By now the potent muscle-relaxing sleeping aid and the wine were doing their jobs well. She flopped down on the bed and closed her eyes as the powerful drugs blotted out the inner pain of her lonely grief.

Brian Kierzek sat on his living-room couch, anxiously twiddling with the decorative band of his new felt hat while looking out at the icy rain ricocheting off his driveway. Glancing at his watch, he put on his hat, stood up, and pulled the car keys from his coat pocket. He walked to the staircase and called in an impatient tone, "Sallie, are you about ready?"

Sallie Kierzek appeared from the upstairs bedroom and came down the stairs, smiling. "Will you take it easy? We have plenty of time."

"I know, but I'm hungry," he said. "It's not often we get to go out for Christmas dinner."

She looked out the window, seeing the deteriorating weather. "Ugh!" she exclaimed. "Let's not drive today! I'll call a cab."

He looked out the window, and nodded. "Okay, I agree," he said grumpily. "But hurry up, will ya? I'm starved."

"Brian, I can tell you're getting well," she said, bursting into a laugh as she found the number in the address book sitting by the phone. "Now relax," she added firmly as she picked up the receiver. "The restaurant will seat us right away. Most people stay home today."

"Well, I know, but..." he said with an abrupt nod as he sat back down on the couch while she made the phone call.

"A cab will be here shortly," she said, hanging up the phone. "There's one in the neighborhood."

He shrugged as he stood and walked to the dining-room table, dropping the car keys.

"You know what?" she said, breaking out in a smile. "I'm glad you've got your strength back, but I think you're going to have a little problem with retirement. I'll bet you'll even miss the hassles at the precinct."

"You've got that half right, my dear," he replied. "I suppose I am ready to hang out my PI shingle, but I sure won't miss downtown. Cuyler told me it's hell around there now that everyone reports directly to Captain Ruskin."

"Oh, really?" she responded.

"Yeah," he answered. "It was somewhat of a shock to Ruskin when he lost that middle-supervisor level as a buffer."

"Do you think it was a demotion for him?" asked Sallie.

"Oh, I dunno for sure," he answered. "I guess they called it a cost-cutting maneuver to bolster the overall crime-fighting funds...whatever."

"That sounds like a smoke screen to get him more involved with the street beat," she said.

"Probably," he agreed. "He's still got the riverpark-murder doubts on his back. Nothing was ever really proven."

She put her hand on his arm, saying gently, "You just can't let that go, can you?"

"Well," he answered. "I told Lacey Rosetto I'd help Timmers if I ever could."

"I know," she said, withdrawing her hand to reach into the closet for her jacket. "By the way, how's your attorney friend doing in California? San Jose, isn't it?"

"Good, as far as I know," he answered, glancing out the front window for the cab. He looked back at her. "Hey, you saw the Christmas card she sent to us saying she was pretty much all settled in and doing okay."

"I know," she said. "But it's been so darned busy with Christmas and your recovery from your heart surgery that I can't even remember."

Mellowing, an understanding look came over his face as he embraced her. "I love you as much as the day we got married," he said into her ear. "I wouldn't have wanted to even make it through if it weren't for you waiting for me on the other end."

She gently pushed him back. "Thank you," she said softly, gratitude filling her widening eyes. "That makes everything worth it. I love you so much."

He stood silent, letting her take in her well-deserved moment of appreciation.

She lifted her eyes, saying with a smile, "Nice hat."

He reached up and took it off, looking at it as he twirled it around in his hands. "It's the best present you got me."

"Well, maybe up until now," she said as she reached inside her purse. "I have our real Christmas present for us," she added, growing excited. "I was going to tell you at dinner, but I can't wait any longer."

He stood puzzled as she pulled out the travel itinerary. "We're going to Hawaii in February. Just us," she said, her eyes twinkling. "For your fiftieth birthday, and to celebrate your retirement."

He looked down at the itinerary as his mouth dropped open. "What?" he responded, surprised. "I mean, how…"

"Never mind," she interrupted. "Rob and I figured it all out."

"You know I've always wanted to go," he said, breaking into a beaming smile. "I don't care how you arranged it."

"And," she added firmly as he still stood speechless, "when we get to Hawaii, we're not doing anything but lying on the beach for those ten days and being waited on. We both damn well deserve it."

"Right. We'll finally see some sun," he quipped.

"That's for sure," she said, laying the itinerary on the table. "Anyway, we'll talk about it over dinner."

"Okay, sounds good to me," he replied, but then a worried look came over him.

"What?" she said, noticing his concern.

"Do you really think it's okay to leave Rob here alone for all that time?" he asked.

"You've got to be kidding," she said sarcastically, breaking into a hearty laugh. "I think he and Valerie will make it just fine around here without us." She paused, then added jokingly, "In fact, I've only seen that boy and his girlfriend once or twice in the last couple of weeks. Does he still live here?"

"Okay, you're probably right," he said, laughing with her.

She looked out the window, noticing the cab pulling into the driveway. "Brian, the cab…" she said, turning to see her excited husband already at the doorway unfolding the umbrella. She smiled as she put on her jacket, grabbed her purse and met him in the hallway. They stepped onto the porch, shut the door and crouched under the umbrella, scampering through the downpour to reach the cab.

CHAPTER TWENTY-NINE

The breakthrough, Cell 231, Salem

Jonathan sat cross-legged on his bunk, staring at the table full of disarrayed papers sitting next to his computer with the "Clues" page displayed on the screen. He had been sitting motionless most of the afternoon with his arms crossed and resting back against the wall—stymied as usual as he fought off his mental anguish. Distressed, he slowly crawled off his bunk and began to pace the cell, mulling over the same material he had gone over so many times before. But he quickly forgot about his book and the crime. Instead, his mind jumped to the upcoming New Year's holiday and the misery of his incarceration. He'd made it through Christmas all right, but now he had another dreadful spell to endure before he'd be through with all of it. *For this year anyway*, he thought with a grimace.

Unable to block the holidays from his mind, he wondered where he would have celebrated New Year's Eve if he weren't locked away in this abyss. *Would I have been in Mexico like last year?* he thought. Or maybe Las Vegas, like the year before, when his friend, David and some of his New York associates had flown in and met him there. He remembered how he had immediately coupled up with one of the unattached women whom David had invited along. And how the group had celebrated the holiday merriment with good-natured gambling, lavish dining and carefree fun at the magnificent floor shows before they all left for home in different directions—promising each other they'd all do it again.

Jonathan squeezed his eyes and cringed, placing his hand against the wall to steady himself as thoughts of Laura quickly enveloped his mind. *What if she were alive and I were in*

California? he dreamed. *What if she were still alive and had found a way to escape Monte and slip into Newport Beach to spend a few glorious days together with me? What if,* he thought, facing the floor. *What if...*

Realizing that he was plunging into despair thinking about Laura, Jonathan abruptly straightened and looked at himself in the small shaving mirror that hung over the stainless-steel sink. He stared hard at the face, fighting to regain a positive frame of mind like he had trained himself to do whenever he'd fallen into one of these discouraging moods. He knew he had to stay optimistic if his reasoning was to remain effective. *So knock it off,* he told himself firmly, managing a smile. *And if Laura might be coming in to meet me for a New Years celebration, I'd better get the events logged in my day-planner and then get back to my writing.*

He walked to his bunk and sat down, pulling out the planner from his box of personal belongings to play his little game. He moved ahead to December 31 and entered "10 a.m.: Pick up Laura at Orange County airport in limousine; 12 noon: Lunch at Newport Bay." He hesitated and chuckled, looking up while he tried to decide where "he and Laura" would celebrate New Year's Eve.

His eyes wandered aimlessly to Rebecca Newell's witness statement sitting on the table while he thought about it. He then looked back at the planner with a smile to enter a fictitious New Year's Eve dinner date with Laura, but froze. His face stiffened! His eyes began to flash back and forth from the day-planner to Rebecca's statement. He dropped the electronic unit on the bunk, snatched up the statement and skimmed through it, puzzled. He set her statement down and quickly scanned Kierzek's crime-scene details. *Nothing substantial there either*, he thought, sitting back, feeling deflated. Yet his thoughts were growing intense, recalling the first meeting he'd had with Lacey in the jail, and their discussion about Rebecca. He again glanced at Kierzek's report, but looked up, knowing there wasn't anything recorded about the incriminating clue that the murderer had left behind.

But the murderer had left his mistake. And Jonathan had a lock on it. He was sure of it!

His mind was racing as he struggled to remain focused through his excitement. He slowly set the papers down, deep in thought. "Oh, yes!" he exclaimed aloud. *Damn! Where is Bernie when I need to talk this out?*

Convinced of his discovery, he turned and crouched down, reaching into his personal box. He anxiously pawed around the bottom, finally finding his leather business-card holder. He opened it, pulling out the "special" card from the top plastic pocket where he'd tucked it away when Lacey had given it to him—knowing in his mind and his heart that one day he'd be reaching for it.

He stood and rushed to the cell door. "Gordy!" he called excitedly, straining to look between the steel bars he was tensely gripping. "Gordy, are you there?"

"Yeah, what's up, Timmers?" the short, roly-poly guard asked, sauntering up to face him. "What in hell are you so worked up about, man?"

"Gordy, please," Jonathan said, holding out the card. "I need to reach this guy right away. I can't use the phone any more today."

The guard took the card and looked it over. "Lieutenant Brian Kierzek from Portland homicide?" he read aloud. He looked up, asking, "You're in a hurry to talk to him? A cop?"

"Yeah, I'll explain when I get a chance," Timmers said. "You can reach him through that office number. He's not there any more, but ask for Detective Edward Cuyler. Ask Cuyler to tell Kierzek I'm trying to make contact with him as soon as I can. It may be lifesaving...my life."

"Ed Cuyler, yeah, sure, okay," the guard answered, shrugging. "But dammit, don't be tellin' nobody I'm doin' this for ya. And remember, you have to mention me in your next book."

"You got it, Gordy," Jonathan said. "It's a lock—no pun intended!" he added with a hearty laugh, watching the guard walking away. "Oh, Gordy," he called out again.

"Yeah, shit, what now?" the guard asked with a frown, walking back to the cell.

Jonathan asked excitedly, "Can you get me a statewide map of Oregon as soon as possible? A detailed one with mileage charts, if you can. It'll probably have to be a road atlas or something like that."

"Oh, shit," the guard cursed irritably. "I dunno. Christ, I'd have to clear it through the reception center and..."

"Gordy," Jonathan interrupted. "I'll make you one of the key characters in my new book if you get it for me by tomorrow."

The guard's eyes lit up. "Really? No shit?"

"No shit," Jonathan confirmed with a laugh.

"Yeah, okay. I'll see what I can do," he said, quickly walking away. "Nothing else though, man, shit."

Feeling upbeat, Jonathan hurried over to his bunk and picked up the business-card holder, pulling out the piece of paper containing Lacey's new California phone number that she'd sent along with his Christmas present. But he'd written back, promising her that he wouldn't phone unless it was an emergency or something critical came up. And at the moment he didn't really have anything positively critical to tell her about. *I'll have to wait to determine that with Kierzek*, he decided as he slid the paper back into the business-card holder.

He dumped the holder back into the box and sat down. He picked up his laptop and eagerly titled a new page in his word processing application "The Solution." But he gradually sat back, feeling solemn. He cautioned himself not to get too excited over this stunning new lead. Nothing had gone beyond a logical presumption in his mind. *Nothing else!* he warned himself soundly. And he knew he needed to keep things in perspective so as not to be overly disappointed if things didn't work out in his favor, as was usually the case.

Yet he still knew he had something substantial to discuss with Kierzek. And maybe Kierzek could even strongly identify with the "key" that Jonathan might have discovered. But he also knew he'd have to have more than just this lead for Kierzek if the detective decided to meet with him. He slowly sat forward and began to type.

Jonathan looked up and jumped off his bunk as the guard walked up to the cell door, saying, "Okay, Timmers, I got through to Ed Cuyler. He was damn reluctant at first, but he called Kierzek and then called me back." The guard hesitated.

"What happened?" Jonathan asked impatiently.

"Dammit, you'd better put me in your book like you promised," the guard said.

"Yes!" Jonathan exclaimed. "Yes!"

"Okay, here's Kierzek's home phone number," the guard said, handing him back the business card with a number penciled on the front. "He's expecting you to call him on your 9 o'clock exercise break tomorrow."

"Thanks," Jonathan said elatedly, looking over the card. "Oh, what about the Oregon map?"

"Yeah, okay. Shit," the guard said as he began to walk away. "I'll get one on the way home tonight and get it to you tomorrow morning. "You're a lot of trouble, man. Shit!"

"Love ya, Gordy," Jonathan called after him with a laugh. "Love ya!"

"You've been in here too long already" the guard yelled back. "Shit!"

Chapter Thirty

The unfolding, Salem

The prison guard escorted Jonathan into the busy visitors' room before stepping back to join his partner, who was keeping a watchful eye on the scattered tables, occupied with buzzing inmates and their visitors. Jonathan, exhausted but optimistic and carrying a large manila envelope, paused and scanned the room. He spotted Kierzek sitting alone by the wire-meshed corner window. Wearing an unzipped rain parka and twirling his hat in his hand, Kierzek appeared lost in thought as he looked out at the torrential winter storm.

Unable to see his face, Jonathan could only wonder if the detective had brought good news with him. But then Kierzek's nature was one of caution and always void of animation. So he realized that whatever news Kierzek had brought with him—good or bad—would have to come out as they went along, with Kierzek leading the way.

Jonathan took a deep breath and walked to the table. "Hello, Brian."

Kierzek turned and stood, offering his hand and a modest smile to Jonathan as he returned the greeting. "Hello, Jonathan. How are you?"

Jonathan firmly grasped his hand and shook it. "Okay, I guess," he answered, his smile quickly evaporating. "Although I gotta admit it's a bit rough getting through the holidays and all."

Kierzek nodded understandingly as he set his hat on the empty chair seat next to them and took off his coat, hanging it on the back of his chair. "I'm sure it's not easy," he said, sitting down.

"Just do the best you can. You only have a few days left before the new year begins."

"I'll manage," Jonathan said as he sat down across from him and laid the folder on the table. "And how about you? You're looking fit. Lacey sent me a Christmas card telling me you'd had heart surgery recently."

"Oh, I'm fine," Kierzek answered with a chuckle. "Hell, that was six or seven weeks ago...history. I heal fast."

Jonathan chuckled with him, then turned serious. "Brian, I really appreciate your coming down to see me. Especially in this lousy weather."

Kierzek shrugged. "It wasn't any problem," he said. "The morning traffic was light, with the holidays and all. And I told you yesterday I'd be here to see you."

"Yes," Jonathan replied, "but I know you're going out of your way to give me a chance to talk to you. Especially considering our positions in this situation."

"I have nothing against you personally," Kierzek said calmly. "I was just doing my job last fall." He smiled. "Besides, when you told me you might want to hire me to help you, how could I resist?"

Jonathan leaned forward in his chair. "Right," he said eagerly, breaking through his fatigue. "Are you available for hire?"

"Possibly," Kierzek said, nodding. "I planned on hanging out my shingle as a private investigator anyway, and..."

"Great!" Jonathan interrupted, sitting back, looking energized. "You're hired!"

"Now, slow down," Kierzek said, holding up his hands. "Let's talk things out to see if you have any good reason to hire me. Until then it's my nickel."

Jonathan managed to unwind, remembering that he couldn't hurry him. Kierzek was a thorough and cautious man. And like he'd said, it was his nickel and his time. Jonathan slowly pushed the folder toward him, saying, "I've been working pretty hard on this the last couple of days."

"You do look beat," Kierzek remarked as he looked down at the folder.

Jonathan remained silent as Kierzek read aloud the handwritten label on the front: "Guilty as Assumed, The Riverpark Murder."

He looked up. "This must be the data for your book that you were telling me about yesterday morning."

"Correct," Jonathan answered crisply. "It's my outline and synopsis data. I'm confident I've figured out what really happened."

"I see," Kierzek said unemotionally, still unmoved by Jonathan's enthusiasm. "May I have a look?"

"Please do," Jonathan replied earnestly. "That's why I've asked you here."

Kierzek opened the envelope, pulled out the rubber-banded sections of the data and separated them on the table. "Of course, you're hoping that there's something in here that'll prove you're innocent."

"Yes!" Jonathan responded animatedly, still trying to stir Kierzek's interest. "And as we discussed on the phone yesterday, I did find something!"

Kierzek scanned the documents, saying nonchalantly, "I assume you're talking about the miniature day-planner I found in Laura Bearnes' wallet at the death scene."

"Yes, please tell me you have it."

Kierzek nodded as he reached into the hip pocket of his parka and pulled out a small notebook and pencil. "Yes, I have it," he replied. "I had stuck it in my desk drawer during the investigation, and then forgot about it as the case wound down and my health became an issue with me. Anyway, I found it in my box of office stuff I brought home after I retired."

Jonathan sat back and closed his eyes with a deep sigh of relief.

Kierzek remained straight-faced, feeling that he might have disappointing news for him. He didn't want to lead Jonathan on and give him any false hope.

Jonathan looked up. "I can't figure out why the day-planner isn't in any of your reports."

"Like I just said, I'd simply forgotten about it," Kierzek replied. "It didn't seem to amount to anything at the time."

"That's what someone else was hoping," Jonathan said assertively, pointing at the "Crime Scene" stack of paperwork. "Anyway, that's why I've missed it until now. I've only been concentrating on the arrest report and witness statements."

"Then how'd you find out about it?"

"Lacey Rosetto mentioned it to me the first time we talked," Jonathan answered. "But everything was so confusing at the time that it didn't register. Then when I was working with my new organizer a couple of days ago I happened to glance over and see Rebecca Newell's witness statement...and bingo!"

"Well, maybe there's something to it, and maybe not," Kierzek replied, opening up his notebook to the first page. He freed the tiny day-planner from under the paper clip and handed it to Jonathan. "Let's find out."

Jonathan quickly opened it and looked at the handwritten calendar entry, his tired eyes widening. "I knew it! That's not Laura's handwriting!" he exclaimed. "Jesus, Brian!" He sat back, stunned. "I knew it! That's not her handwriting!"

"I know that," Kierzek said evenly. "It appears to be Monte Bearnes' handwriting. After you told me yesterday that it was probably fake, I was curious, so I met with Ed Cuyler at the station. We compared it with the receipt Bearnes had signed when he picked up Laura's personal belongings on the day of the murder."

"I knew it was probably his doing," Jonathan said, surprised at Kierzek's continuing mundane demeanor. "It coincides with everything I've come up with. Doesn't this tell you that something isn't right?"

"At first glance, of course," Kierzek said. "But after you think about it, not officially. He could have written it in there for his wife."

"C'mon, Brian!" Jonathan exclaimed disappointed, barely containing his exuberance as he held the document toward him, shaking intensely. "This was planted in her wallet to lead you to Newell, and then back to me!"

Kierzek maintained his poise. "Okay, I can see that it looks phony. But for your sake, let's not jump to any false conclusions. Let's talk it out."

"Okay, all right," Jonathan agreed, knowing Kierzek was right about being cautious. He lifted his head in thought, settling himself while Kierzek remained patient. Jonathan looked back at him, saying, "First of all, Laura and Rebecca were the closest of friends. They were always in contact with each other. Laura wouldn't need to keep Rebecca's phone number with her."

"Oh, I dunno about that," Kierzek replied nonchalantly. "A lot of people keep their friends' phone numbers with them. I sure keep some with me."

Jonathan shook his head. "No, not Laura," he argued rigidly. "She was a meticulous woman who wouldn't keep anything with her that wasn't necessary. Just like in her work...extremely efficient...orderly." He paused. "I even watched her call Rebecca once from a pay phone in California. She never referred to any paper for the number."

Kierzek mulled this over, then pointed at the document that Jonathan had set on the table. "Perhaps it's a new number," he challenged further. "Maybe Newell had recently moved or something."

"I've already thought of that," Jonathan countered bluntly with a smile as he pulled a piece of paper from his shirt pocket with a number written on it. He set the paper next to the day-planner. "I've always known Rebecca's number, too," he said, pointing at the paper. "See! Same number! They match!"

Kierzek sat back and faced him, rubbing his chin in thought as he conceded this part. "You've thought of everything."

"What the hell else have I got to do," Jonathan said. He picked up the document. "And look, there's a fake 'college class appointment' at Portland State University for that night written here. Why in hell would she do that?"

Kierzek remained motionless, listening intently.

"I'll tell you why," Jonathan said boldly. "To make it all look real to you when you found it. Like I said, this thing was planted to lead you straight to Rebecca Newell, and then back to me." He set the document back on the table and stared at Kierzek.

Kierzek picked up the document to examine it as he pondered Jonathan's persuasive argument. "Okay, so it's Monte Bearnes' handwriting, and to us it appears to be a set-up," he said. "But if we confronted Bearnes with this, he could simply say he wrote it for Laura while she was busy. How could we prove otherwise?"

"Yeah, she was busy being set up to be murdered," Jonathan scoffed, sitting back with frustration over Kierzek's balking.

Kierzek disregarded Jonathan's remark, realizing his stress, but had to continue his challenge. "Maybe Laura had Bearnes put the fake college appointment in there for that night to throw him off because she was coming to see you."

Jonathan shook his head, sighed and looked downward, feeling disgusted and defeated. "Why should we even go any further with this?" he murmured bitterly as he stood up, reaching for his papers to put them back in his folder.

"Look, Jonathan," Kierzek said soundly, putting his hand squarely on the folder. "I just want to examine everything before we run off half-cocked. I'm on your side, but I need to be the devil's advocate while we explore things."

Jonathan sat down, fixing his piercing eyes on Kierzek. "Brian, I respect what you're doing, but you know that fucking day planner entry was planted! It was planted on a body that was lying next to the park's walkway so it would be easily found! Now, will you please give me that before I go crazy?"

"All right, take it easy," Kierzek responded, holding up his hands. "I'm listening. I'm very interested in your discovery or I wouldn't be here." He paused. "Okay, I'll give you that—the timer was planted. But dammit, we need more than that to open things up."

"That's easy," Jonathan said as he sat back again, knowing he'd made it to first base with Kierzek. "I've worked day and night on this, and I have more…plenty more. But please, I can't be totally discouraged at every step of the way. You're the only one I can count on right now."

"All right," Kierzek agreed. "I want to hear everything. But I will have to challenge you if needed. You're in prison for manslaughter. We have to be careful about falsely thinking you might be pardoned over just this day-planner issue."

"Fair enough," Jonathan said, again feeling positive. "Now, this gets somewhat complex, so we'll have to eliminate things as we go. Okay?"

"Okay," Kierzek agreed.

"First, let's assume that I'm innocent and that we're looking for another killer together," Jonathan said. "We're working as partners."

"Sure, why not?" Kierzek agreed. "There's nothing going on here yet that's official. So as far as I'm concerned, you're not the killer."

"Good," Jonathan said, moving forward eagerly. "And let's go along with the medical examiner's report that it was more than likely a man who killed Laura, because of the strength it would've taken to carry out the crime."

"Sure," Kierzek agreed again with a nod. "Dr. Richardson is always very accurate on that type of thing."

"All right, here we go," Jonathan urged. "Since the day-planner you found in Laura's wallet was planted, the killer must be Monte Bearnes, or someone that he or Rebecca had hired. Because only those two were intimate enough with Laura to have that information put in the day-planner."

Jonathan paused patiently while Kierzek gave this meaty deduction more thought.

Finally the detective said, "Okay. Either Bearnes or Newell or both were involved in the killing. And if neither actually killed her, then either or both hired it done."

"Yes, that's accurate," Jonathan said. "But let's go ahead and eliminate Rebecca Newell from being directly involved with the crime."

Kierzek furrowed his brow. "Already?"

"Yes," Jonathan answered, chuckling over Kierzek's childlike surprise.

"Why?"

Jonathan answered swiftly, "Because if Newell was in on the murder single-handed and had hired a killer, there would have been no reason for Monte Bearnes to have planted a fake day-planner in his wife's wallet the day before." He paused, letting Kierzek take that in.

"Okay," Kierzek said, nodding. "But why couldn't she have been in on the murder with Monte?"

Jonathan answered, "Because they wouldn't have needed to chance the incriminating fake day-planner. The next morning, Rebecca would have simply called the Portland police to report Laura missing. I'm sure she would have somehow alarmed them enough so that they would have looked for her. And, of course, she'd have told them that Laura had been with me the night before, and..."

"And we'd have searched and found her body in the park," Kierzek interjected.

"Or wherever the killer had done his nasty deed," Jonathan said. "A neat little discovery package that still pointed directly at me."

"So you believe Newell is clean?" asked Kierzek.

"Oh, I think she might have helped Bearnes unknowingly," Jonathan replied. "But never directly with criminal intent."

"What do you mean unknowingly?"

"I'll explain later when it fits in better," Jonathan answered.

"Okay," Kierzek said. "So if we follow along your trail, Monte Bearnes is responsible for his wife's murder by himself."

Jonathan sat back with a smug look on his face, nodding, *Yes.*

"So he hired a killer, and then…"

Jonathan remained silent, altering his nod to a shaking of his head, *No.*

"No?" Kierzek said in surprise, furrowing his brow. "No?"

"Oh, it's possible he hired a killer," Jonathan said dismissively. "But I don't think a hired killer would have been smooth enough for Bearnes. Especially if his intent was to frame me." He hesitated in thought. "Besides, another killer would've made things more cumbersome for him. He knew this crime was going to create a lot of publicity all over Oregon. He wouldn't want to chance another leak."

"So you're saying Bearnes is the actual killer?"

"Precisely," Jonathan confirmed, steely-eyed, leaning toward Kierzek. "Monte Bearnes is the actual killer. He had the motives—jealousy, gaining his freedom, and getting Laura's sizable life-insurance settlement, which you mentioned in your witness-interview report."

"Okay, so he has the motives," Kierzek said hesitantly. "But he'd also need the opportunity…"

"He had both—motive and opportunity," Jonathan interrupted, undaunted.

"But what about his alibi?" asked Kierzek. "I know the university security guard's statement about seeing Bearnes sleeping in his office is questionable. But nobody felt the guard was lying—or certainly not an accomplice."

"The guard's not lying, nor is he an accomplice," Jonathan agreed crisply. "He did see Bearnes. Or at least in his mind he saw him."

"I don't get it," Kierzek said. "Are you implying that Bearnes had some other accomplice on his office couch posing as him?"

"No. I think it's much simpler than that," Jonathan said. "The guard had been behaviorally trained. He was mentally conditioned to see Bearnes on his couch." Jonathan pointed to the "Character Map" section of his book. "Bearnes is a professional therapist…a master at manipulating people."

As Jonathan paused, Kierzek locked stares with him, saying, "Keep going."

Jonathan nodded, pointing over at the guard's witness statement, and continued, "The guard said Bearnes had been falling asleep in his office a lot during that period. I'm sure Bearnes had slept there many times for real, to set the guard up. Then on the night of the murder he simply propped something on the couch with a wig…whatever. He then slipped out of his office and headed for Portland." Jonathan paused. "You still with me so far?"

"Yes, so far," Kierzek said slowly, looking through the guard's witness report, appearing skeptical.

"What's wrong?" asked Jonathan.

"The couch prop," Kierzek answered. "It seems a bit weak for even the guard not to have noticed."

"It could've been a mannequin or a dummy Bearnes used," Jonathan answered. "I'm sure you'll find out it was covered with a blanket or something."

Kierzek still demurred, lifting his head in thought. "But you don't think Bearnes might have used a human accomplice for his 'couch prop'?"

Jonathan shook his head, answering, "I thought so at first. But again, that would be too messy for Bearnes." He rolled his eyes, adding, "Brian, I have to assume the university guard wasn't much of a challenge to Bearnes' plan."

"Okay," Kierzek said. "Let's move forward. What about the guard seeing Bearnes drive up around midnight and park his car in front of his office all night?" Kierzek asked, sitting back.

"That's simpler yet," Jonathan answered. "Bearnes had another car, probably Laura's, stashed just off campus where no one would see him drive it away."

"Stashed?" Kierzek repeated. "When would he have hidden it?"

"Probably on the afternoon before the murder, after Laura had left for Portland," Jonathan replied with ease. "Laura had told me once that they only lived about a mile from campus."

"Why would he have to stash a car by the campus?" Kierzek asked curiously. "Couldn't he have just have gone home and got it if he lived so close?"

"It's possible he went home for it after he sneaked out of his office, but I doubt it," Jonathan answered. "He had a time constraint to get to Portland." He paused, seeing Kierzek deep in thought. "Well?"

"Very interesting," Kierzek answered. "So what you're saying is that Bearnes planted a dummy or something similar on his couch, slipped out the door after the guard had passed by, and sneaked to another car and drove to Portland."

"Yes. Exactly."

Kierzek finally reached for his pencil and began to take notes, raising Jonathan's spirits. He'd finally gotten through solidly to the hard-boiled detective.

Kierzek looked up. "Let's proceed."

"For sure," Jonathan said with a smile, pulling an Oregon map from his back pocket. He opened it and laid it out on the table. "It's only about 110 miles from Eugene to Portland, so he had plenty of time." He diverted his point to the "Crime Scene" section. "According to the coroner's report of Laura's time of death, Bearnes had about a three- to four-hour window to make it there after the university guard had actually seen him last." Jonathan paused, letting Kierzek digest this as he jotted a few notes.

Kierzek looked up, signaling he was ready for more.

Jonathan nodded and continued, "Then after Bearnes killed Laura, he…"

Kierzek interrupted, "Bearnes then drove back to Eugene, left the second car at home and got back to campus somehow later that morning with his own car still parked at his office."

"Absolutely!" Jonathan confirmed with a wide grin, happy over Kierzek's inspiration. "And Bearnes got back to the campus long after the third shift guard had gone home, and when the campus was busy, so that no one would notice him."

Kierzek looked up. "I could check with the taxi companies to see if they have a record of any fares there that morning."

"That's a thought," Jonathan said. "But I doubt you'd find anything. Bearnes is too clever for that. Like I said, his house isn't far from campus. And I'm sure he's not worried about time at that point. So he probably jogs to his office or something. He probably didn't even care if it was raining."

Kierzek interjected, "So he gets back to his office, straightens it up and waits for the *tragic* phone call telling him that his wife's been murdered."

"Yup!" Jonathan confirmed, sitting back.

Kierzek jotted more notes, then slowly looked up. "Okay,

everything seems possible so far. But I have some tough questions for your theory."

"And the first?" Jonathan replied confidently, moving forward.

"How did Bearnes know Laura would be in the riverpark at that time, and that he'd be able to get at her so conveniently?"

"I don't think he *did* know she'd be there," Jonathan answered quickly.

"I don't follow."

Jonathan answered, "I believe he traveled to Portland knowing only that he should probably start where I was staying…"

"How did he know where you were staying?" Kierzek peppered.

"Any number of ways," Jonathan answered with ease. "He could've called the hotels until he found the one I was staying at. Or he could have followed Laura there on another occasion. Or Rebecca might have told him that's where we always met. This is what I meant when I said she might have helped him unknowingly."

"I see," Kierzek said. "Okay."

Jonathan continued, "And then I'm sure he must have followed Laura into the park from the hotel."

Kierzek kept his eyes on his notes. "How did Bearnes know she was still on the hotel premises when he got there? Especially at that time of the morning? I don't think even Newell would have known that."

"He probably didn't know for sure that she was still there when he got to Portland," Jonathan replied. "Perhaps he'd already found out she wasn't at Newell's place somehow. But it stands to reason he would've had to start at the hotel, based on his time issues."

Jonathan again fell silent, allowing Kierzek to try to shoot more holes in his theory. He was all for it, knowing that Kierzek needed to be completely sold if anything were to go beyond this room.

Kierzek signaled to move forward by looking up.

Jonathan continued, "So Bearnes probably spotted her at the hotel." He pointed to the stack of witness reports. "Remember, the bellman states that he saw Laura go outside and hang around for a long time. So there's a good chance that Bearnes also saw her."

"And then Bearnes simply waited for his opportunity," Kierzek added.

"Yes," Jonathan confirmed. "This man understands behavior, and he certainly knew Laura. I'm sure he figured that she was waiting to walk to Rebecca's place through the park, like she always did from there. Regardless, Bearnes could be flexible at this point. The tough part was over for him, and time was on his side."

"So you think Rebecca had told Bearnes that Laura always walked back to her place?"

"I believe so," Jonathan answered. "But let's talk about Newell's role next. Even though I told you why I don't think she's criminally involved in the murder, she certainly played a role in all of this somewhere along the line."

"Okay, back to the tough questions," Kierzek said. "What if Laura left the hotel before Bearnes got there, or left in a cab and made it to Newell's place safely?"

"Then maybe there wouldn't have been a murder," Jonathan answered. "Keep in mind, Brian, he really didn't have to kill her if things went wrong. He simply could have skipped out of there, or only confronted her as a jealous husband and waited for another chance...but then again..."

"What?" Kierzek said.

"I think Bearnes was probably prepared to kill her at Rebecca's place," Jonathan answered.

"At Newell's place?"

"Sure," Jonathan answered. "I'm sure he was determined. He knew how much Laura loved me and that it was probably over between them. Hence his motives that I mentioned earlier—jealousy, freedom, and money."

"Okay, so if he had killed Laura at Newell's place, she would have had to be in on it," Kierzek said. "Or else she would've been in the way."

"You're correct," Jonathan agreed. "I think it's choice two. She'd have been in the way." He paused. "Okay, let's talk about Rebecca Newell now."

"All right," Kierzek said, sitting back. "First, if you don't think Newell was criminally involved in the murder, do you think she was telling the truth about Laura being afraid of you when she called her from the hotel?"

Jonathan now appeared unsure. "Well, I'm not positive," he answered. "But I have to believe it was only Newell's resentment surfacing. I think she actually believes I killed Laura—her best friend."

"I see," Kierzek said, looking down at his notes. "Okay, if your theory is correct, Bearnes would have had to known about the affair all along. Do you think Rebecca was the one who told him?"

"Yes, I'm sure of it," Jonathan answered. "Oh, he could have found out some other way, but there were just too many intimacies he was aware of. The most glaring is that he knew that was the night Laura was breaking up with me. And that would put more emphasis on my reason for killing her as far as the police were concerned."

Kierzek interjected, "Then you think Rebecca was lying to me during my interview when she told me that Bearnes hadn't known about the affair."

Jonathan frowned. "I knew we'd get to that one sooner or later. I admit I've been drawing a few blanks on this one. I can't understand why she'd lie to you about that if she really believed I was guilty of the murder." He paused, squinting his eyes in thought. "Again, maybe she didn't really know that Bearnes knew about the affair, but that doesn't seem likely."

Kierzek suggested, "Maybe she'd just learned somehow that Bearnes had been the one who killed Laura, and was protecting him for some reason."

Jonathan shrugged. "Well, it's obvious that she didn't want you questioning him about having known about the affair," Jonathan said. "Anyway, I just don't know." He sat back and laughed. "Maybe Rebecca had fallen in love with Monte. Wouldn't that have been a hell of a scenario?" he added, laughing harder. "I won't put that in my book, though. No reader would find that plot twist plausible."

Kierzek wasn't laughing with him. He was too busy taking notes and concentrating on his next question. "So if you don't think Rebecca was in on the murder, do you think Bearnes might have killed them both if he had found Laura at her place?"

"Yes, if he was enraged enough," Jonathan replied seriously. "That's the only sense I can make of it if he was set on killing Laura. He knew they would've still pinned the double murder on me." He paused. "In fact, he might have been planning on that anyway to get rid of Newell."

Kierzek looked up. "I just got a sobering thought," he said. "If you're right about that, she could still be in danger."

Jonathan reached over to put his folder back in order. "It's possible, if he thought she was a threat to his being caught. I'm just not sure about that part of it. But I am convinced that Monte Bearnes killed Laura single-handedly."

"All right, Jonathan, this is a brilliant piece of homework," Kierzek said, sitting back and looking at his notes. "Maybe you should have been a cop instead of a writer."

"Hey, I'm both," Jonathan replied with a laugh. "Remember, I'm also my protagonist Jason Thornhill, the stupendous insurance investigator who always solves the crime." He paused, then said solemnly, "But, you know what?"

"What?" Kierzek said, looking up at him.

"My murder schemes are never this complicated," Jonathan answered. "Bearnes is masterly. And his greatest gift is his patience."

"Yeah, I agree," Kierzek said. "But he went up against a desperate man."

Jonathan nodded. "Okay, where do we go from here?"

"Well, there's a lot here, but it's really strung tightly in Bearnes' favor," Kierzek answered. "We have to find a way to shake things loose."

"You're right," Jonathan agreed. "I think the key in getting to Bearnes is through Rebecca somehow."

"I think so too," Kierzek said, appearing puzzled. "But that's step two. We have to get some basic proof before we can move with any kind of a plan."

"There has to be something incriminating in Bearnes' office," Jonathan suggested. "Do you think you could persuade Judge Buehler to help you get a search warrant?"

"I'm not sure," answered Kierzek, shaking his head. "Like I said, there's a lot here, but it's all speculation—even with the planted day-planner issue. I don't know if Buehler would buy into it." He paused. "I'll run it by Cuyler and Captain Ruskin first. And then if they're sold I'll see if they'll help me approach Buehler to work with the Eugene police on getting a warrant."

"Umm, aren't we forgetting about Matt Wolcott?" Jonathan asked quietly.

"Oh, damn, that's right," Kierzek said, looking up. "I guess he's really a pain in the ass since he lost the election. I understand that now if he had his way he'd throw even the juvenile delinquents in the pen for life."

Jonathan laughed. "And I'm sure my case didn't help him any."

"No," Kierzek answered. "He'd probably love to get another chance at you—and fry you this time around."

"That's the chance I'll have to take," Jonathan responded firmly.

"Okay, I'll talk to Ruskin and Cuyler," Kierzek said, looking back down at his notes. "I'll start with Cuyler as soon as I get back. He knows why I'm here."

"Maybe we should have Lacey back here to approach Buehler," Jonathan said.

"I know that would put the fear of God in Wolcott," Kierzek said with a chuckle, as he scanned his notes.

Jonathan chuckled with him, but then said, "Brian, I'm serious."

Kierzek looked up, surprised. "You mean bring her back here to Oregon?"

"I didn't say bring her back. That would have to be her decision."

"Does she even know anything about all this?" asked Kierzek.

"No, I promised I wouldn't alert her to anything unless it was critical," Jonathan replied. "I guess I'm asking you to make that decision."

Kierzek looked up in thought, realizing that Jonathan was anxious and worn out. Kierzek had seen the need in his eyes to have his friend and attorney, backing him up again—whether she was here in Oregon, or in California. *Whatever, Jonathan at least deserved for her to make that choice*, he decided. "Sure, I'll talk to her," Kierzek said, jotting a note. "But I can't promise you anything except to tell her that maybe we're onto something. I can't predict how she'll respond."

"Brian, all I'm really after right now is that you and she believe in my innocence," Jonathan said, a deepening plea in his eyes.

"Of course, I already do," Kierzek agreed. "And I'm sure she will too." He glanced at his notebook calendar. "She's probably still on her holiday vacation. I'll call her tonight. Do you have her number handy?"

With a big grin, Jonathan opened the palm of his hand, revealing a piece of paper with her name and number on it.

Kierzek laughed and took the paper. "Okay, I'll get right back to you with a plan after I talk to Cuyler," he said as he put the wallet day-planner and notebook back in his pocket. "I'll also see if I can get Ruskin to pull some strings to get me quick access to you through the warden, if it's necessary."

"Great. Thanks!" Jonathan said, feeling relieved over completing his mission.

They both stood up as Kierzek put on his jacket, saying, "You just sit tight while I get things started. You've done enough."

"Where in hell do you think I'm going?" Jonathan said sarcastically.

"Yeah, right," Kierzek said with a laugh as he picked up his hat from the chair.

"By the way, great hat," Jonathan said.

"Thanks," Kierzek said with a proud smile as they both headed for the door.

Chapter Thirty-one

New Year's Day, Northwest Bistro Restaurant, Portland

Rebecca Newell anxiously swirled the icy remnants around in the bottom of her glass, then tipped her head back and swallowed the last of her drink. She plunked her glass down on the bar top, becoming annoyed with the last of the college bowl games echoing from the numerous televisions peppered around the bar overhang. *Enough football!* she thought. *Enough stupid football!*

"Another rum and Coke?" the bartender asked politely from the end of the bar, having realized early on that he should keep his distance.

She turned to face the elderly man, who was dressed smartly in a scarlet dress shirt, black bow tie and freshly starched white restaurant smock. "Nah, just a diet Coke," she answered quickly, deciding that she needed to stay clear-headed for her date with Monte. "Same glass, though," she added, pushing it toward the approaching bartender. "And can you please turn off this damn television that's right over me?" She abruptly pointed directly above her.

"Of course, ma'am," he replied calmly, reaching up and pressing the "power" button, shutting off the television.

"Thanks," she said, scanning the deserted lounge of the grandiose riverbank restaurant.

"No problem," he said as he picked up her glass and began refilling it with a brown beverage oozing from the bar-gun.

"How late will you be open?" she asked, fixing her gaze on the entrance.

He set the drink in front of her and glanced at his watch. "The lounge will probably be open till about ten, but I'm sure the restaurant will close around eight." He looked around. "It's pretty dead tonight."

She turned back toward the bar and nodded, looking down in thought.

"Sure you don't want some peanuts or cashews or something?" he asked pleasantly, trying to crack the frown that had been etched on her face since she'd arrived. "I also have an appetizer menu."

"No, thanks," she responded civilly, but without looking up. "I'm waiting for someone."

Taking this firm cue to leave her alone, he walked away.

She turned to peer out the restaurant window at the barren Willamette River, rippling calmly in the serene twilight. Yet the tranquil setting did nothing for her. Her mood was hardly one of peace or happiness. Although she'd managed a few nights of decent sleep with the help of Chablis and her trusty Dalmane, her nerves were jangled. And she was still lonely and angry. It had been a wrenching two weeks since she'd heard anything from Monte. His unexpected trip to the mountains without her was shocking enough, but jilting her on Christmas and New Year's Eve was inexcusable. That special night you're supposed to be with the one you love. *Intolerable!* she thought. She grimaced as she recalled the rushed and dispassionate message he'd left on her answering machine yesterday, confirming that he'd returned but wouldn't make it up to see her until late today. She was confused, and had to find out what was going on in his mind. But she knew she'd have to stay calm and collected and move cautiously. Monte wasn't the type to be hassled. Besides, he might be here to give her bad news. *And she was already chuck-full of bad news*, she thought. So if she were going to have to hear more, she would have to gradually work into that blow.

Her eyes moistened as her thoughts turned from anger toward Monte to missing Laura, remembering how on every New Year's Day they'd meet somewhere for a late brunch to share their new year's goals and aspirations. They hadn't missed this tradition in their three years of close friendship. How joyful it was when Laura's face would brighten with excitement when she talked about the upcoming spring and summer art shows they'd be doing together.

She squeezed her eyes shut in sudden anguish as she recalled last year's luncheon and how Laura had decided that Rebecca was ready to be fixed up with someone special; a man who'd remove the emptiness that had filled her life after her husband had died. And now how hurtful it was to think she'd found that man—*Laura's man*. And how painful the horrible circumstances in which that union had come about.

Frustration replaced her sadness as she turned back toward the bar and glanced at her watch. *And where is that man?* She took a swallow of her bland watery drink and grimaced. Needing something stronger, she motioned to the bartender, who had been dutifully watching her but still wisely keeping his distance.

"Could I have another rum and Coke?" she asked tersely, then hesitated. "Wait, make that a glass of your house Chardonnay instead."

"Yes, of course," he answered patiently. He reached into the cooler for the bottle of white wine. "Nasty weather brewing," he commented.

She pivoted and looked out the window at the dark swirling clouds swiftly rolling in over the river's horizon, suffocating the earlier tranquil setting. *Fitting*, she thought. *It certainly wouldn't be calm inside either when Monte showed up.*

The bartender uncorked the bottle and filled the wine glass he'd pulled from the rack while watching her stare out the window, knowing that her mind was again adrift with the river's current. Remaining silent, he set the glass down and walked away.

She turned and picked up the glass of wine, taking a swallow while looking at her reflection in the bar mirror. Her face was deeply troubled. She wondered if she would soon have to face the reality of living with her loneliness and her anger. *Is Monte working up to leaving me? I'll know soon,* she thought. *Very soon.* She glanced at her watch again, shaking her head in disgust. *Where is he? Dammit!* she cursed under her breath, setting her glass down. *This whole thing is going to be difficult enough without him strolling in late as though nothing is wrong.* Tense, she took another long drink of her wine.

Her thoughts were shattered by the tap on her shoulder. She spun to face Monte, looking devastatingly handsome, as always. His classy new outfit of a designer blue blazer, dark khaki slacks and a yellow cotton pullover complemented the rugged outdoor tan he'd attained while skiing on the mountainous slopes.

"Hi, sweet," he said softly, breaking into a modest smile.

"Hi, Monte," she returned, her pent-up contempt quickly melting in his mesmerizing presence. Yet she quickly noticed that he was missing some of the natural dazzle that always accompanied his arrival. "You look very nice today."

"So do you," he replied in an obligatory tone, while turning to the approaching bartender. "Scotch and soda," he promptly ordered.

"I've been waiting here for a while," she said—her way of hinting that she deserved a reason for his arriving late. She'd start with the simple stuff first and progress to the more important issue afterward.

"Yeah, sorry I didn't make it on time," he apologized weakly, bending forward to give her a quick kiss. "Tamra threw a tantrum just as I was leaving. I had to stay and calm her down before I took her to the Rickersons." He stepped away from her to accept the drink the bartender was handing him. Taking a hefty swallow, he drained his glass and immediately signaled for another.

"It's all right, I understand," she lied into his ear, feeling that his excuse was insincere for not having seen her in so long. But she still realized she shouldn't confront him at this point. *Don't rush him*, she told herself.

"I'll make it up to you," he said, stepping back in front of her. "We'll have a nice time here and then go and do whatever you want to afterward."

"Okay," she replied with a smile, feeling some relief after his remark. "I'm glad you finally came up to see me. I miss both you and Laura a lot today. Seeing you eases some of my ache."

"I know, baby, I know," he answered quietly, yet appearing preoccupied and unnerved. He picked up the second drink the bartender had set on the bar and took a long swallow.

"Are you staying with me tonight?" she asked gently as she looked up at him.

"Yeah, sure," he said, taking another drink. "That's why I'm having Tamra stay at the Rickersons. I've missed you, too."

"Good," she said, yet still seeing that he was bothered. "Is something wrong?"

"Ah, no, not really," he answered. "I'm just a little confused. I was wondering if you'd heard anything new about Laura's murder case."

"New?" she repeated with a puzzled face. She looked up in thought. "No, I thought that it was all wrapped up with Timmers going to jail."

"Me too, but..."

"Oh, wait a minute," she interrupted, her brows furrowing. "Now that you mention it, I did see a TV news item or read something in the newspaper the other day that Lacey Rosetto, Timmers' attorney, was back in Portland."

His eyes locked on her. "Did the report say why she came back?"

"No," she answered, shaking her head. "I didn't pay that much attention. I assume she's back finishing up some business. You know how the press always followed her around when she was defending Timmers. But why does it matter?"

He took another swallow of his drink. "My friend Professor Filson called me this morning asking if Brian Kierzek had caught up with me," he replied. "I understand he was at the university nosing around and had talked to Filson..."

"When?" she asked, her face wrinkling with curiosity.

"I dunno," he answered uneasily. "A couple of days ago, I guess."

"But I thought he'd retired," she said. "Is he back with the police?"

"Hell, I dunno that either," he responded with an anxious shrug. "Filson just said he was down asking for me at the administration office."

"Well, did you try to reach Kierzek to find out what it was all about?"

"No, not on New Year's Day," he answered, setting his empty glass on the bar. "I thought I'd check with you first to see if you knew anything about it. You know, like if maybe Kierzek had found out about us."

"No," she said, looking up in thought. "Nobody's talked to me about anything. Anyway, so what if it did come out about us? Why would it trouble you so?"

"Oh, I guess it doesn't," he said, glancing around with a shrug. "It just seems odd, that's all."

"I'm sure it's something routine," she said calmly. "Maybe it has to do with Laura's substantial life insurance settlement you're getting. You know how skeptical the insurance companies get. Perhaps Kierzek is working for them."

"Yeah, probably something like that," he agreed with a nod. "I'll try to reach Kierzek in a couple of days."

"Good idea," she said, taking the final swallow of her wine.

"Are you hungry?" asked Monte, changing the subject. "I ate a big lunch with Tamra, but maybe we can order something off the appetizer menu to go along with a bottle of champagne before we have a late dinner. How's that sound?"

"Not just yet," she said. "Maybe another wine. But I'm not hungry, and let's wait on the champagne." She pointed to the far side of the room. "Let's move to a table by the window where we can be more comfortable."

"Okay, sure," he said, as he gestured to the bartender for fresh drinks.

She set the empty wine glass on the bar and rose, deciding it was time to unravel in complete privacy the serious matters concerning their relationship

They walked to the table and sat down facing the river as the rain sprinkles began to splatter against the window, turning the darkening night colder.

Rebecca looked at him, saying, "I'm sure Tamra is having a pretty rough time of this whole thing. But she never seemed to be the type to throw tantrums."

"It's an on-and-off thing," he answered nonchalantly. "She's managing okay, but she's still very confused. She really misses her mother."

"Of course, and I'm very sorry for her," Rebecca sympathized while deciding to begin getting at the heart of the matter. "I thought that I could've been a comfort by being with you two during the holidays, but obviously you didn't seem to think that was a good idea."

"It just seemed awkward at the time," he answered blankly, peering out the window. "It was just too soon for anything like that."

She concealed the pang of this thoughtless jolt, asking, "Have you told Tamra that I am more than a special friend, and to expect me around?"

He balked with a slight hand gesture. "Well, not yet. I..." He paused when the bartender walked over and set their drinks in front of them.

Rebecca looked up, finally noticing the man's name tag. "Thanks, Raymond," she said. "Just keep things going on my tab."

"Yes, ma'am," the obliging bartender said respectfully as he walked away.

Rebecca turned back to Monte, who was stirring his drink with a miniature bar straw, appearing distant again.

"I don't understand," she said as the emotional hurt began to overtake her patience. "You told me that you'd tell Tamra about us after Thanksgiving."

"I know," he said, looking at her. "But I said I'd do it when the time is right. That's one of the reasons I took her to the mountains last week. To try to tell her. But it didn't work out."

"What?" she responded with a dejected look, unable to curb her severe disappointment. "You left me all alone for two weeks during the holidays and you didn't even end up telling her about us?"

"No, it just didn't seem right," he said, taking a swallow of his drink. "I decided it might be too strange for her to have the impact of a new mother..."

"What do you mean?" she interrupted with a stunned look, realizing that he felt absolutely no regret for neglecting her during the holidays. "I'm not trying to be a new mother to her yet."

"I know, but..." he responded with a frown, becoming agitated with her intense questioning.

"Monte, does Tamra understand this whole thing?" she asked directly with a rigid look. "Does she really understand everything that's happened?"

"No, not everything," he answered with contempt in his voice and a bold look. "She's not old enough yet to know the really bad part."

She realized he'd grown spiteful and combative, but she continued to press for the answers. She now knew there was never going to be a *good* time to get through this. "What do you mean, she doesn't know the bad part?" she asked, maintaining her unyielding stance. "What are you telling Tamra?"

"Oh, I dunno," he answered belligerently, fidgeting with his glass. "I suppose she knows that her mother was bad and that's why she died."

Her hard look turned to one of shock. "Bad!" she exclaimed abruptly. "Are you telling Tamra that Laura died because she was *bad*!?"

"Not exactly in those words," he snapped angrily. "C'mon, you know what I mean. Don't interrogate me, for Christ's sake. It's not that important!"

"Not important?" she shot back in a seething whisper. "You're coloring Tamra's mother as *bad* in her eyes. And you're telling me it's not important?"

His eyes darted from his glass to her brittle glare. "Well, wasn't she?" he challenged as he picked up his drink and finished it.

"Monte," she fired back. "Laura was not a *bad* woman."

He shoved his glass aside, countering, "No? Well, what do you call a woman who openly fucks around on her husband?"

Rebecca furrowed her brow, astonished at his abnormally callous attitude. "Now look, Laura had made a crucial mistake and was very confused about things," she argued. "But I know she loved you and was trying very hard to resolve the situation for everyone's sake."

He shrugged. "But she didn't resolve anything!" he exclaimed harshly with narrowing eyes. "And when she didn't come back to your place that night, it proves she probably wasn't going to stop seeing Timmers."

She sat back and shook her head in disbelief. "I know she hurt you deeply," she volleyed calmly, realizing that the hostility wasn't helping anything. "But I can't let you smear Laura's memory in that little girl's head. She idolized her mother."

He nervously reached for his glass, seeing that it contained only an icy residue. "Okay, okay, I'll talk to her," he conceded sharply, looking around for the bartender. "Now, quit worrying."

She sighed and looked down, fingering the stem of her wine glass. "Monte, you told me that you'd managed to understand what Laura was going through," she said quietly, easing her stern stance. "And you told me you knew that she was deeply and emotionally troubled." She slowly looked up at him. "But you've never understood, have you?"

He didn't answer her as he scanned the room, seeing only a couple settling themselves at the bar. "Dammit, where'd the bartender go?" He turned back to her, looking irritated. "C'mon, let's just get past this, okay?"

"No, we won't just pass by this!" she shot back insistently, her anger flaring again. "If Laura was bad, what do you call what *we* did?"

"That's different," he responded quickly, not realizing what a big mistake he was making with what he was saying. "I never would've gotten involved in any of it if Laura hadn't left me like she did. You and I were just taking care of each other's needs."

Rebecca sat bewildered, her eyes becoming moist and wide. "I can't believe you just said those things," she said in a trembling voice, looking down.

He took a deep breath. "All right, I'm sorry," he said, looking away. "I'm full of stress lately and don't always know what I'm saying. Let's just forget it."

Her pain was slowly turning to rage. "Don't tell me to forget anything!" she fumed, shooting him a fiery glare. "I now realize you have all kinds of serious psychological problems over this mess. But don't you dare ever imply that our relationship was just a simple tryst."

"Look," he appealed, reaching for her hand. "Everything is just so confusing for me right now. Like I said, let's just forget it."

"I will not!" she responded defiantly, her eyes blazing as she jerked her hand away. "You've basically implied that to you I'm just a warm body, only a fu…"

"Excuse me, but is everything okay over here?" asked an uneasy voice, interrupting Rebecca's fierce tirade.

Rebecca and Monte looked up, seeing a middle-aged muscular man, dressed in slacks, dress shirt and a V-neck sweater, approaching the table.

"Yeah, why?" Monte asked brusquely, looking at the man's chest for a name tag that wasn't there. "Who are you?"

"I'm Geoege, the restaurant manager," he answered. "Raymond has gone home for the rest of the holiday. Anyway, the folks at the bar are a little concerned about you two."

They all looked over at the young couple sitting at the bar, looking back at them with worried looks on their faces.

Embarrassed, Monte calmed down and apologized. "I'm sorry, we're just a bit hassled from the holidays." He managed a smile and waved toward the bar, signaling that everything was all right.

"Yes, I'm sorry, too," Rebecca echoed, feeling the same embarrassment. She looked at the couple and also managed to send them a smile. She said to the bartender, "Please give them a drink and put it on our tab."

"Okay, I sure will," the bar manager agreed, appearing relieved.

"And how about a bottle of your best brut champagne for us?" Monte said, looking up at the manager. He reached over and put his hand on Rebecca's, adding, "Oh, and an appetizer menu, too, please."

"Of course, folks," the manager said as he walked away. "Immediately."

Monte quickly turned, looking into Rebecca's eyes with a disarming gaze and a soothing smile. "Darling, I'm sorry for everything," he said softly with a look of guilt. He squeezed her hand. "I've been neglecting you. I've been wrong about everything lately."

She returned a loving look, happy he'd finally said that he'd missed her in a meaningful way. "I understand, sweetheart," she said in a forgiving tone, her distress dissolving. "I'm strained, too. It's been a very rough year for us."

"Well, then," he said, sitting back. "Let's talk about the new year."

"Do you mean *our* new year?" she responded happily.

"Yes," he replied lovingly. "*Our* new year."

They sat and looked into each other's eyes as George came back and set the silvery chilling urn on the table and handed each a menu. He placed two flutes in front of them and pulled a bottle of French brut from the ice, holding it out for Monte to inspect. At Monte's nod, he turned away from them and twisted off the wire coif. While Monte and Rebecca silently scanned their menus, the manager gently nudged off the cork. He filled the glasses with the bubbly froth and stuffed the moist bottle back into the ice before stepping back to wait for their order.

Monte looked over at her. "How about our favorite? The seafood tasting platter and a side order of smoked albacore?"

She smiled warmly, setting her menu down. "Yes, sounds fantastic."

Monte looked up at him with a confirming look. "That'll do it for now, George. We'll order dinner later if we're still hungry."

"Thank you, folks," he said politely as he took their menus and began to walk away. "I'll put the order in immediately."

"Now, where were we, sweetheart?" Monte asked, matching her smile.

"Talking about our plans for the new year," she answered buoyantly.

"Ah, yes," he said, reaching over to take her hand again. "But first let's talk about Tamra." He paused as she sat attentively, looking into his eyes. He continued in a guilty tone, "I haven't really smeared Laura's name, even though the whole thing gets quite agonizing for me sometimes."

"I know what Laura meant to you," she consoled, squeezing his hand. "But I'm here for both you and Tamra now."

"Yes, and maybe Tamra should stay with you for a while," he suggested softly. "It'll give me some time to adjust. That little girl's well-being is too important."

Her eyes opened wide as she sat back in surprise. "Do you really mean that?" she responded excitedly. "Oh, I'd love that! How soon?"

"Now, slow down," he said with a chuckle.

She fell silent, her beaming smile still fixed lovingly on him.

"Do you remember that professorship at New York University I was offered?" he asked. "I'm going to take it. Now that my life has changed so drastically, there's no reason for me not to accept their proposal."

"Oh, really?" Rebecca replied, the joy in her face dimming.

"I mean for all of us to go," he said, brightening her up again. "Tamra could stay with you while I'm out there setting things up. Then you two could join me."

"Oh, yes," she replied, thrilled. "That would work out perfectly. You could be alone to think clearly during your move. And Tamra and I could get to know each other better; and it would also give me time to clear up all my business here."

"Yes, terrific," he agreed, picking up his glass of champagne. "That's exactly what I was thinking. Let's toast to it."

She picked up her champagne and they reached over to clink their glasses together before taking a swallow.

George walked up and set the appetizer, small plates and silverware in front of them. "I'll check back with you," he said politely, walking away.

"Yes, please do, thank you," Monte said, unfolding his napkin.

Monte reached over with the bottle, filling Rebecca's glass with the remainder of the champagne. "You deserve the rest of this," he said.

She giggled, saying with a slight slur, "I've drunk pretty much the whole bottle."

"I know, I'm trying to get you drunk," he said with a wink and a roguish grin.

She laughed. "It's worked, you sly devil," she prattled, bobbing her head while tipping the glass back for a swallow.

He laid the bottle on the empty appetizer platter. "Lousy service," he murmured in a whisper, seeing the manager busily rearranging the stock in the coolers. "He should have taken the dirty dishes away long ago."

She sat back with a glow on her face. "I know, but who cares," she said, still giggling. She tipped her glass back and emptied it, then set it down on the table as she moved toward him and took his hand.

"Yes?" he said softly, moving toward her.

"I think we've had enough of this restaurant," she said seductively, parting her lips to run her tongue slowly across her bottom lip. "Don't you think?"

A delighted look came over his face as he said in a heated whisper, "You know what?"

"What" she whispered back, her eyes half closed.

"I think you've been a naughty girl, talking back to me today," he answered quietly. "And you'll have to be punished like a naughty girl."

She slightly brushed her finger across his lips. "Really?" she replied teasingly, with a shameless look in her eyes.

"For sure," he whispered, winking. "And I want you to know I've brought the cuffs with me. So you might as well not plan on fighting it."

"Hmm, the handcuffs," she purred softly, moving back. She closed her eyes and sighed, the sexual tension building inside her.

"Sure, I'll take my just punishment, like always." She smiled at him.

"Good, then let's go," he said slowly as they rose from the table. "I'll take care of our tab. And we'll buy another bottle of champagne on the way home."

"Fine, darling," she said with a reckless smile as she walked unsteadily toward the entrance. "I have to make a stop. I'll meet you by the front door."

"Okay," he said, his smile fading as he watched her leave the room.

He turned and walked over to the empty bar, seeing the manager turning off the televisions. "George, I want to settle up the lady's tab with cash," he said.

George walked over to him and handed him Rebecca's credit card that they'd been holding for security. "Um, sure," he said apologetically. "But I've closed this register. Lesley will take care of it at the main register in the restaurant. Just tell her it's the Newell tab."

"Oh, okay," Monte said, taking Rebecca's credit card.

"I hope everything was satisfactory," George said.

"Yeah, everything was great," Monte answered as he pulled out his wallet. He paused when he noticed the manager scanning the room, obviously looking for Rebecca. "She's in the ladies' room," Monte said in a somber tone.

"I hope she's all right," George replied courteously, turning to Monte.

"Oh, absolutely," Monte said. "She's just had a rough time of it during the holidays with being alone," he added. "I'm an old friend, and I let her take her lonely frustration out on me today. I hope we weren't any trouble."

"Nah, I understand," answered George with a dismissive wave. "The holidays always bring out the worst of hurts. By the way, she's not driving, is she?"

"Oh, no," Monte said, shaking his head. "I'm going to drop her off at home, or with one of her friends. Whichever she decides on the way."

"That's a good idea, sir," George commented.

Monte took a fifty-dollar bill out of his wallet and laid it on the bar. "Have a good new year, my friend," he said as he walked away.

"Why, thank you, sir," George said with a wide smile of gratitude. "You have a great year, too," he added as he watched Monte leave the bar.

The manager shook his head, his smile turning to a look of concern as he turned and stuffed the bill into Raymond's tip jar that was sitting on the back bar.

CHAPTER THIRTY-TWO

New Year's Day-evening, Rebecca's apartment, Portland

Monte Bearnes sat on the couch in worried thought as he looked out the living-room window at the icy mist reflected in the wintry glare of the corner streetlights. His mind was riveted on Lieutenant Brian Kierzek and the attorney, Lacey Rosetto. Why had Kierzek been down at the university nosing around? Why had Rosetto come back to Portland? Why were they interested in the case again?...*Or maybe they weren't*. Maybe it was like Rebecca had suggested. Perhaps Kierzek was now working for the insurance company or something just as meaningless. And maybe Rosetto was simply back to clear up some old business. *Perhaps Rebecca is correct,* he thought. *Regardless, he would have to go through with his plans*, he decided.

He stood and made his way to the kitchen and looked around, spotting the container of Rebecca's Dalmane relaxant pills sitting on the counter. *Her main addiction,* he thought. He checked behind him before he quickly picked it up and twisted off the cover, shaking a couple into his hand. He slipped them into his pants pocket before re-closing the container and setting it back where he'd found it. He then reached into the refrigerator for the bottle of champagne, hesitating when he saw her "essential" carafe of Chablis sitting in the back of the top rack. *Her next favorite addiction.* Smiling, he pulled out the bottle of champagne and a clean flute from the cupboard, toting both as he left the kitchen.

Growing anxious, he turned toward the stairs, then glanced at his watch as he made his way into the living room. He wondered what was taking her so long to simply "get comfortable." He hadn't seen her since they'd walked in the door and she opened the champagne, poured herself a glass and scooted upstairs with it. He set the champagne down on the couch table and turned, switching the floor lamp to the low setting. Reaching behind the couch, he pulled the drapes closed. He walked to the small hallway window by the front door and peered out, seeing that the street was deserted. The spattering of cars that were parked along the curb appeared as though they'd been setting there for a while, the same situation as when they'd arrived—no more and no fewer. He assumed that people must have gotten home early from their holiday trips. *Isolation...perfect setting*, he thought.

Beginning to relax, he walked over to the fireplace and crouched, pushing the fire screen back. Using the fire poker, he stoked the fire until it flared to a moderate blaze, producing a warm, cozy glow throughout the room.

He stood and stopped, taken aback by seeing that Rebecca had arrived in radiant form. She was sitting on the couch, gazing at him with a sultry look. She was dressed only in frilly bikini panties and a sheer, pink chemise that reached her thighs. Although her face beamed with happiness, it was only slightly made up, with a fresh coat of lipstick and a couple dabs of rouge. Her black hair was brushed back, looking damp but silky.

"Hi," she said in a sensual whisper as she slowly drew her legs up next to her, positioning herself sideways on a corner of the couch. She held out her empty champagne glass for him to fill. "I'm so relaxed, but I want more."

He could smell the spicy fragrance of bath oil that lingered in the air. "You took a bubble bath," he said softly with a delighted smile as he sat down next to her and picked up the bottle of champagne. "No wonder you took so long upstairs."

"Uh-huh," she answered tenderly, matching his smile. "You aren't complaining, are you?"

He shook his head playfully. "Oh no, baby," he said eagerly, filling her glass with champagne. He reached over and brushed his lips across her cleavage, inhaling to take in the delicate flowery scent she emitted. "Hmm, I missed you."

She winked and leaned back, taking a long swallow of her

champagne. She stroked his thigh with her big toe. "Why don't you get a little more comfortable?" she suggested sexily, her eyes blinking with a weary strain.

"I'd love to," he responded, keeping his eyes on her as he slipped off his blazer and shoes. He put his feet up on the coffee table and poured himself a glass of champagne, biding his time.

She took another drink, trying to maintain the sexual arousal. But her attempt was failing as the weariness sapped her exhausted body. She was falling into a blissful but slumberous mood. Her contentment of the moment was working with the abundant alcohol she'd consumed all day. She lay back against the side cushion, closed her eyes and draped her legs over his.

He watched her closely. "Comfy?" he asked as he took a drink from his glass of champagne and then reached over and kissed her. He withdrew, seeing that she was immersed in a mellow lull. He began to massage her feet, slowly rubbing his hands up and down her legs, nurturing her drowsy condition.

Heavy-eyed, she let out a gentle sigh. "It's so nice you're here with me," she mumbled.

"Yes," he said as he reached over to the side pocket of his blazer. He pulled out a pair of handcuffs and rattled them slightly to test her.

She blinked, then closed her eyes. "Oh, no, honey," she murmured. "I've changed my mind. I don't want to be punished tonight. Please."

His eyes turned downward, darting back and forth in thought. "But, darling," he said in a quiet sinister tone, "don't you think you were a naughty girl today?"

She giggled nimbly. "Uh-huh," she murmured sluggishly. "But no punishment tonight," she droned. "Maybe tomorrow."

He gently turned her over and began to massage her shoulders and upper back, submerging her deeper into soothing ecstasy. He bent down toward her ear. "Sure, baby," he whispered tenderly. "I suppose we could pardon you tonight. How about if we just go to bed and snuggle all night...and only sleep?"

"Oh, darling," she murmured, desperately struggling to stay awake. "What about you? It's been awhile since we've...."

He moved closer to her. "Don't worry about me, sweet," he interrupted softly. "I just want you to relax." He nudged her over onto her back and reached into his pocket for one of the Dalmane pills, putting it in her hand. "Here, take one of these. It'll help you sleep all night."

She barely opened her eyes, recognizing the feel of her trusted pill. "But I don't wanna sleep all night," she mumbled. "What about you?"

"That's why I want you to take one," he replied softly, weaving his web. "If you don't, you'll wake up in a couple of hours and I'll be sleeping. That won't work." He paused. "I know—I'll take one, too. Then we'll both sleep and wake up, make love all morning and drive up to the mountains afterward."

She nodded faintly, too weak to argue.

He lifted her head off the armrest while she swallowed the pill, washing it down with a gulp of champagne.

He took the glass from her hand, then reached over and turned off the lamp, leaving only a small appliance bulb over the kitchen stove and a smoldering fire to give off light.

"C'mon, sweetheart," he said, helping her up. "Let's go upstairs. We'll snuggle in bed as we fall asleep."

She stood, wobbly, while he draped his blazer over his arm and picked up her glass of champagne. They slowly made their way upstairs arm in arm, entering the bedroom. A small glimmer from a lighted candle on the nightstand accented the fresh, blue satin sheets that were pulled back on the big double bed.

He smoothly helped her lie down, then suggested softly, "Here, darling, have another drink before I get undressed." He put the glass to her lips.

Groggy and unsteady, she took another sip as he had urged, while the Dalmane was taking effect, gradually decreasing her oxygen intake. As her head sank back on the pillow, he knew he had to move quickly. He pulled the other Dalmane tablet from his pocket and put it into the remainder of her champagne.

"How are you?" he asked loudly, briskly swirling the glass until it was dissolved.

She muttered something indistinguishable, her words slurring.

"Yes, sweetheart," he said, reaching into his pocket for the handcuffs. But he looked at her limp body and decided he wouldn't need them to finish up. There was no fight left in her. He slipped them back into his pocket.

He raised her head off the pillow. "Whaa..." she muttered. "Need slee...."

He helped her lean forward. "Yes, sweetheart, finish your champagne," he whispered softly. "And I'll let you sleep." He tipped the glass to her lips and she haltingly swallowed the last of the drink.

"Good night, sweetheart," he said as he laid her head back down on the pillow. Her breathing was becoming shallow and labored. *She's out*, he thought.

He quickly hopped off the bed and reached inside his blazer breast pocket, pulling out a pair of latex gloves and an object wrapped in tissue. He slipped on the gloves and removed the shimmering diamond pendant from the wrapping. He wiped it off with the bedspread and crouched down to Rebecca, putting the pendant into her hand. He closed her fist around it and put pressure on her fingers, then hurried into the adjoining master bathroom and set the pendant on the counter. He started to leave, but stopped when he saw a bottle of rubbing alcohol. He picked it up and put it in his pants pocket as he walked into the bedroom.

Reaching back into the breast pocket of his blazer, he pulled out a handwritten letter, opened it and pressed Rebecca's fingerprints on it, then laid it on the bed next to her. He turned and rushed downstairs.

Entering the kitchen, he opened the refrigerator and pulled out the carafe of Chablis—her typical drink. After filling a goblet from the cupboard, he picked up the Dalmane pill container and shook a bunch of them into the sparkling wine, smiling as they began to dissolve. He pulled the rubbing alcohol from his pocket and poured some in the goblet, wincing at the thought of its intended results. Throwing the empty bottle into the trash basket, he opened the small utility drawer and reached in, pulling out the small wine-bottle funnel he'd given her months ago. He slipped it into his blazer side pocket. Picking up the goblet, he dashed from the kitchen.

Rushing through the hallway, he suddenly stopped, his eyes opening wide as he heard a knock on the front door. *Jesus Christ!* he exclaimed inwardly.

He looked around tensely, seeing that all the drapes were shut tightly, realizing that no one could see him at this moment.

But what about before the drapes were shut! he thought. *And my car is out front!* He grimaced and ducked back into the kitchen, putting the funnel and glass of toxic concoction into the back of the refrigerator. He crept to the side hall window and peeked out from behind the drape, seeing the porch, instantly recognizing the woman staring at his car parked in the driveway. *Lacey Rosetto!* he thought, backing away from the window. He couldn't believe what he'd seen. *Lacey Rosetto standing on the porch! What now?* he wondered, lifting his eyes toward the upstairs bedroom. *Jesus Christ!*

Lacey pulled her trench coat more snugly around her to ward off the icy chill, then turned and knocked harder on the front door again. She looked up when it opened.

Monte faced her with a surprised look on his face. "Ms. Rosetto!" he exclaimed.

"Hello, Mr. Bearnes," she said nervously, looking him up and down, seeing that he was fully dressed. "I know this is an odd hour on New Year's Day, but there have been a few things that have come up concerning your wife's case, and I wonder if I could speak with Ms. Newell?"

"Isn't this a bit unusual?" he responded, appearing puzzled. "I mean, can't it wait until tomorrow? She's sleeping."

"I'm sorry, but I don't have much time," she replied. "I'm leaving for Sunnyvale the day after tomorrow and..."

"Come in, please," he interrupted, now appearing calm.

"Thank you," she said, stepping inside.

He held out his hand, saying, "How are you?"

"I'm fine," she replied, looking around the room as she shook his hand.

He noticed her concern, saying, "Rebecca's had a pretty rough time of it during the holidays—with the loneliness and all. I came up to visit her today to help her get through the holidays."

"Oh, I see," she said with a nod and an understanding look.

He glanced toward the stairs. "Like I said, she was sleeping soundly the last time I checked on her." He paused, his brow furrowing. "Maybe there's something I can help you with?"

"Ah, no," she answered. "I'm afraid not. It has to do with the direct witness statement she gave to the Portland police."

"Oh, okay," he replied pleasantly. "Well, would you like me to go up and see if she's awake?"

"No, that's not necessary…"

"It's certainly not a problem," he replied, turning toward the stairs.

"Well," she said, "If you really don't mind. I'm really short on time."

"Of course," he said, walking toward the stairs. He hesitated, turning back to her. "Why don't you just come on up with me? If she's awake, you can chat with her up there. I'm sure she won't mind."

She hesitated in thought, then said, "Um, no, that's okay. I'll just wait here."

"Sure, okay, no problem," he said with a smile. "I'll be right back."

He calmly made his way upstairs and walked into the bedroom. Rebecca was still passed out, but appeared okay. He breathed a sigh of relief and went back out to the landing, seeing Lacey standing at the bottom of the steps. "She's sleeping like a baby," he said with a laugh. "Wanna come up to try and wake her?"

"No, of course not," she said with a dismissive wave. "I'll readjust my schedule somehow and come back tomorrow morning."

He walked back downstairs. "All right," he said politely. "That's fine."

She walked to the door, saying, "I'm really sorry I bothered you tonight, Mr. Bearnes."

"Please call me Monte," he responded. "And there's no problem. I'm on my way out of here shortly to go back to Eugene, anyway."

"Then I probably won't see you again, Monte," she said.

"Probably not," he answered as he followed her to the door. "In fact, I'm taking a new position back east after the holidays." He paused and looked her up and down. "But maybe we'll run into each other again soon somewhere."

"Maybe," she answered politely as she opened the front door. "Maybe so."

"Bye, Ms. Rosetto," he said. "Have a nice trip back to Sunnyvale."

"Thank you, Monte. Goodbye," she replied as she left, hearing the door close behind her.

He leaned back against the door, took a deep breath and reached into his pocket for the latex gloves. "Damn!" he cursed, slipping them on. *That was close!*

Hearing a car start up, he turned and peeked through the hall window, seeing Lacey's profile in the car that was driving away.

He shook his head to clear his thinking while planning his next move. *He had to go through with his plan now,* he decided. He'd take his chances with explanations later, if needed. There'd be nothing to formally incriminate him here afterward.

He rushed back into the kitchen and collected the plastic container of Dalmane, the carafe of Chablis, the funnel and the goblet of deadly poison. He bounded upstairs and into the bedroom. He placed everything on the nightstand. Taking the letter back out of his breast pocket, he laid it on the bed like it had been before he had to snatch it up because of Rosetto's intrusion. He paused, looking at Rebecca's curvaceous body. He frowned. *Too bad*, he thought.

Taking a deep breath, he turned Rebecca over and leaned her up against the bedstead. He unruffled the bed, pushed the letter next to her hand and propped her head back. He grimaced as he wedged the small plastic funnel into her mouth, saying softly, "I'm sorry, baby."

Picking up the wineglass from the table, he watched intently as he carefully lifted it to pour the poison into the funnel, not wanting to spill any.

But he stopped when he heard a low resounding voice. "Freeze. Don't let any of that touch her mouth."

He whirled to face Brian Kierzek, who was standing in the doorway facing him with his service revolver aimed at his head. "I mean it, Bearnes," he said with a hardened stare. "I'll shoot your vicious head off. I'd love to."

"I heard you," Monte said, holding the goblet in mid-air. "I'm not moving."

"Carefully put the glass on the table and stand up," Kierzek ordered sternly. "Keep your hands up where I can see them."

Monte slowly backed off the bed, set the glass on the table and stood against the wall, holding his hands up.

Kierzek kept a keen eye on him as he pulled a small cellular phone from his breast pocket with his free hand and pushed a speed-dial button. He put it to his ear and spoke. "Ed, call the paramedics and get up here to the bedroom fast. Bring Lacey and

Jameson." He pocketed his phone and walked to the bed, gently pulling the funnel from Rebecca's mouth while still keeping his eyes on Monte.

Within minutes the front door opened, followed by the thumping of feet racing up the stairs. Lacey, Cuyler, and Detective Jameson rushed in.

Monte stood frozen, stunned at seeing Detective Jameson was the bar manager "George" from the restaurant.

"Jameson, see to Newell," Kierzek said as the detective quickly went to the aid of the unconscious woman.

"Ed," Kierzek said evenly, still not taking his eyes off Monte, who had hung his head, staring at the floor. "Cuff him, read him his rights, and call for backup to book him. You'll need to stay and supervise the scene."

Cuyler nodded and walked around the bed. Turning Monte, he brought his arms to his back. He handcuffed him and grasped him by the forearm, leading him out the door, reciting, "Mr. Bearnes, you have the right to remain silent. If you decide to give up that right, anything you say..."

Jameson looked up from the bed. "She still alive, but her breathing is labored," he said. "There's not much we can do for her but try and stimulate her physically until the paramedics arrive."

"Okay," Kierzek replied. "Let Lacey work with her. How about keeping an eye on that glass on the nightstand. Don't let it out of your sight until a techie gets here and signs for it. I'm sure it's our key piece of evidence."

"Yes, sir," Jameson said as he backed off the bed.

Lacey sat down on the bed and began to vigorously rub Rebecca's back while she chatted in her face, trying to rouse her to consciousness.

Kierzek put his pistol in his holster. "How about staying with her, Lacey," he said. "See if you can make her presentable."

"Sure," Lacey replied as she reached for Rebecca's robe at the bottom of the bed. She wrapped the robe around Rebecca and looked into her face, seeing that she still had some color. Lacey looked back up at Kierzek with a smile.

Kierzek smiled with her as he picked up the letter from the bed, and walked out.

While walking down the stairs he heard the siren, signaling that the paramedics were here, probably with some reporters right behind. He looked out the doorway where an officer was sealing off the front entrance with yellow police tape. And a police cruiser with two officers was pulling out, escorting Monte off to jail. Cuyler nodded to Kierzek as he entered through the front door and headed upstairs to join Jameson who was closely guarding the goblet of poison.

Kierzek saw two paramedics rush through the doorway as he walked to the fireplace and stoked the embers. He sat on the hearth for warmth and pulled the letter from his pocket, reading it in the light from the fire.

Lacey stepped down the stairs and walked over to him, placing her hand on his shoulder. He looked up from the letter.

"I'm sure she'll be all right," she said. "They're going to pump her stomach. And she was already breathing much better when I left."

He nodded, appearing tired. "Good," he said. He held the letter up toward her as she stood watching him curiously. "Bearnes is a pretty slick character. It's a letter from him telling Newell that he understood what she did to Laura. But that he couldn't be her lover any more. And he was moving back east without her."

Lacey's face brightened with understanding. "Oh, I get it," she said. "A setup to make it look like Rebecca was responsible for Laura's killing because she was in love with Bearnes. And then she killed herself because Monte was leaving her."

"Basically," Kierzek replied. "Something that would justify his innocence, anyway." He paused and frowned. "And he was just here tonight to make sure she did *kill herself.*"

"Ruthless bastard," Lacey said bitterly, with a disgusted look. "I guess our nosing-around plan worked. Bearnes got spooked."

He nodded as he folded up the letter and put it in his pocket.

She sat down next to him on the hearth, smiling. "Nice job tonight."

"Me?" he said with a surprised look. "You're the one who got nervous and left us to drive over and knock on the door." He paused. "What told you to, anyway?"

"Woman's intuition," she answered. "I got concerned when the lights went out in the living room. And Rebecca was alone with that man."

"But what if she had been okay and answered the door?"

"Hey," she answered. "I had some questions ready for her." She hesitated. "In fact, I still do."

He chuckled, but appeared quizzical. "How'd you know she wasn't already upstairs dead after you let me in?"

"I didn't," she answered. "But you'd never have let me go up there alone with Bearnes to check on her."

"That's for sure," he said with a firm nod.

She shrugged. "I knew that," she answered. "So if I'd had gone upstairs and she was all right, you might have given yourself away and we'd have lost our opportunity to catch Bearnes in the act."

"And if she was already dead?" he asked.

"And if she was already dead," she repeated, "you'd have been here to catch Bearnes at the death scene, or probably before he could get too far away with Cuyler and Jameson right outside."

"And if there wasn't going to be any killing at all?" he asked. "What then?"

"Well, then you'd have had to find a way to sneak out of here," she answered with a wide grin. "Or it sure would've been embarrassing for you when they found you hiding in her hall closet. You'd have looked pretty silly."

"I see," he said, breaking into a hearty laugh as he stood.

"By the way," she said, standing with him. "Will Captain Ruskin be upset that you sneaked inside the house with no warrant?"

"Nah," Kierzek answered. "I had cause to feel that Newell was in danger."

"Okay," she said skeptically. "But he'll probably ask what *that* cause was."

"Whatever," he responded with a shrug. "How about a cup of coffee somewhere before you drop me off at home?"

"Sounds good, lieutenant," she replied. "But aren't you still on duty?"

"Nope," he said, chuckling, as they headed for the door. "Ruskin had postponed my retirement to help with this last case. It was my going away present. But I just turned it back over to Cuyler."

They walked out the door, seeing Cuyler was back in the yard confidently voicing a statement to a gathering of reporters.

Kierzek looked at Lacey and said, "See what I mean?"

She put her arm inside his as they walked to her car. "Yes, sir."

Chapter Thirty-three

Days later, Captain Ruskin's office, Justice Center

Captain Ruskin sat back, propped his feet up on the end of his desk and frowned at Kierzek who was sitting across from him. "But what if they'd only been screwing or something when you snuck up the stairs behind Bearnes?" Ruskin said firmly. "They probably would have seen you. Then you'd have been in a hell of a legal mess—not to mention how foolish you would have looked."

"But they weren't screwing, and Newell was about to be murdered," Kierzek countered. "It was a chance I had to take. I trusted Rosetto's instincts."

"And that's another thing," Ruskin said, turning toward Cuyler, who was sitting attentively next to Kierzek. "What the hell was the attorney doing tagging along with you, anyway? You know how dangerous that is. And the liability issue—Jesus!"

"But, captain, she's a very forceful woman," Cuyler answered defensively. "Besides, she had her own car and I couldn't officially keep her away, or from bolting to Newell's house when she did, for that matter."

Ruskin shook his head and looked at Detective Jameson, who was sitting behind Kierzek and Cuyler, appearing nervous. "And you," Ruskin said. "A bar manager, for God's sake! Hooh booy! What if Bearnes had caught on?"

"I did some bartending while I was in college, sir," Jameson answered hesitantly. "I felt I could handle it. And we decided we needed to keep a closer eye on Bearnes when he and Newell began fighting and then…"

Ruskin dismissed the explanation, interrupting, "And their manager, Stan, told me that you messed up the cash register trying to look authentic for some customers at the bar."

Jameson nodded slightly. "I know. Well, Raymond took off on me…"

"Of course he did," Ruskin interrupted again. "You scared the old fart outta his skin when you came in flashing your badge to take over."

Kierzek raised his hands. "Give us a break, captain," he said evenly. "We tried to get warrants and move in on Bearnes with conventional means, but you know Buehler and Wolcott weren't available because of the holidays. We had to go with our gut instincts when we began running out of time."

"Yeah," Ruskin argued. "But when I agreed to postpone your retirement and let you hang in on this one, you told me you'd only go after Bearnes if you had hard physical proof…" Ruskin paused to think things through, shaking his head.

"We just didn't have a lot of choices," Kierzek pressed.

"Okay," Ruskin conceded, lowering his tone. "I guess Bearnes would've been long gone and we would've had another homicide on our hands if you had waited."

They all sat back and faced Ruskin with looks of relief.

"By the way," Cuyler asked, breaking the silence, "has Bearnes confessed to his wife's murder?"

"Yes, this morning," Ruskin answered, looking at his notepad. "After the Eugene police found a wig in his office and learned he had access to a university car-test dummy, Bearnes knew his alibi was crumbling."

"He's a slick one," Kierzek interjected, wrinkling his face.

"And treacherous," Cuyler added. "Did you hear what was in that glass he tried to force down Newell's throat?"

All eyes turned to Cuyler.

"An overdose of sleeping pills, right?" Jameson asked, his brow furrowed.

"Right, along with a dose of rubbing alcohol—Isopropanol," Cuyler answered, grimacing. "Really bad shit. Dr. Richardson said the pills probably would've finished her all right, but that stuff would've torn her insides up and quickly put her in a coma and sealed the job with all the booze she had in her."

"Bearnes should never again see the light of day for that alone," Jameson said disgustedly.

"He probably won't," Ruskin said. "He'll get life without parole just for his wife's murder. He'll be charged for lying in wait—first degree. And Wolcott said he's going to throw in the life insurance policy as a kill-for-profit motive for good measure."

"So then the Newell attempted-murder charge will just be icing on the cake, right?" asked Jameson.

"Exactly," Ruskin said. "Although Bearnes will probably avoid the death penalty because of his complete cooperation with the DA's office."

"How's Newell doing, anyway?" Cuyler asked. "Anybody know?"

"She's recovered fine," Ruskin said. "She gave us her complete statement yesterday." He paused. "A factual one this time."

"Is she in any trouble with the prosecution?" asked Cuyler.

"Nah," Ruskin replied, shaking his head. "Wolcott told me that she was pretty much innocent of any criminal intent—not even any perjury charges."

"Oh," Jameson said. "I understand the missing diamond pendant was found in her bathroom."

"That's right," Ruskin answered. "And Bearnes confessed to planting it there. But I don't think Wolcott's going to use it."

"Why not?" asked Cuyler.

"It's too nebulous of an issue, and they don't feel they need it," Ruskin answered. "So Wolcott's going to give the pendant back to Timmers right away. He figures he deserves it."

Cuyler looked at Kierzek. "Brian, do you think Bearnes kept the diamond pendant from the death scene just to set Newell up?"

"Well, it's obvious he's pretty clever," Kierzek answered. "He was definitely playing this whole thing on Newell's loneliness." He paused, thinking a moment. "But then again, a lot of killers keep mementos of their crimes. And Bearnes was probably just neurotic enough to do it for that reason, too." He shrugged. "But, who really knows?"

"Do you think he set up the affair with Newell just to frame her?" asked Jameson.

"Hell, I think she was convenient for him regardless," Kierzek answered. "I mean, take a look at her…"

"Yeah," Jameson interrupted with a chuckle. "I guess that was a dumb question."

"What about Timmers?" asked Cuyler, turning to Ruskin.

Ruskin answered, "I understand Rosetto has his release motion all filed with the court, and Judge Buehler put it on her docket right after Bearnes confessed."

"How long before he'll be out?" asked Kierzek.

"Pretty quickly," Ruskin replied, glancing at his desk calendar. "Probably within the next couple of days." He scanned the silent faces. "Well, I guess that's it, guys."

"Great," Kierzek said, slowly standing. "I gotta get going. I'm meeting Sallie at the mall. We're going shopping."

"What?" Ruskin said with surprise. "You, shopping? You're going shopping?"

"Yeah, why not," Kierzek responded, looking at Ruskin indignantly. "We're going to Hawaii next month for my fiftieth. We need some new clothes."

Ruskin rolled his eyes. "Oh, I se-ee," he droned, drawing chuckles from the other two detectives.

Kierzek scanned the room with narrowing eyes. "That's it!" he exclaimed in mock anger. "I'm retired! You're all on your own."

They all broke out in heavy laughter, including Kierzek as he walked toward the door putting on his hat, with Cuyler and Jameson following closely behind.

Ruskin stopped them, saying, "Oh, one more thing, men."

They turned back toward the captain.

"Good job," Ruskin said with a widening smile. "I'm proud of you guys."

They all thanked him with nods and looks of appreciation before turning for the door.

"Incidentally, Lieutenant Kierzek," Ruskin said, again stopping him.

Kierzek turned with a furrowed brow.

"I really like your hat," Ruskin said.

"Thanks," Kierzek said, smiling. "It was Sallie's doing."

As Ruskin watched them leave, he sat back, his smile slowly changing to a frown. He secretly admitted to himself that he was sorely going to feel the loss of Brian Kierzek, his ace detective. *It won't be the same around here*, he thought. *The department has lost a pillar.*